Sandhya Menon is the *New York Times* bestselling author of several novels with lots of kissing, girl power, and swoony boys. Her books have been featured in many cool places, including the *Today Show*, *Teen Vogue*, *NPR*, *BuzzFeed*, and *Seventeen*. She makes her home in the foggy mountains of Colorado. Visit her online at sandhyamenon.com.

Sandhya Menon

10 Things I Hate about Pinky

HODDER

First published in the USA by Simon Pulse,
an imprint of Simon & Schuster Children's Publishing

First published in Great Britain in 2020 by Hodder & Stoughton
An Hachette UK company

This paperback edition published in 2020

1

A CIP catalogue record for this title is available from the British Library

B format ISBN 978 1 529 32537 9
eBook ISBN 978 1 529 32538 6

Printed and bound in Great Britain by Clays Ltd, Elcograf S.p.A.

Hodder & Stoughton policy is to use papers that are natural, renewable
and recyclable products and made from wood grown in sustainable forests.
The logging and manufacturing processes are expected to conform to
the environmental regulations of the country of origin.

Hodder & Stoughton Ltd
Carmelite House
50 Victoria Embankment
London EC4Y 0DZ

www.hodder.co.uk

For Sandhya's Sweethearts,
the greatest street team any writer
could ever ask for!

CHAPTER 1

Pinky

The dead body was an especially nice touch.

Pinky Kumar grinned at her friend Ashish's prone figure.

"This is amazing," she said, touching Ash's face. It looked waxy and pale, and his lips were the exact right color of death. Well, what death *probably* looked like, anyway. "You said Sweetie did this?"

"Yeah, she took a stage-makeup class last year," Ash said, cracking open one translucent eyelid. "Does the hair look okay, though? I did that myself."

"The hair's poppin'," Pinky said, lifting up a few strands of the purple wig he wore, the thick locks falling past his shoulders. "You look like you could start shredding on a guitar any minute."

They were in Pinky's living room, where they'd lit a dozen LED candles all over the furniture and floor and drawn the shades for extra ambience. Ashish was lying on the couch, his arms crossed on his chest, barely breathing. Of their friend group, he was the only one who'd been able to help her out on short notice; everyone else had already flitted off to various holiday destinations. Ash himself was leaving for Hawaii later today.

"Okay, do you have what you need now?" Ash said, shifting a bit on the couch. "This wig's pretty itchy."

"Almost." Pinky stepped back and took a couple of pictures with her phone. "Let me get a wider angle. . . ."

"What charity's this for, again?" Ash asked, peeking at her through the fringe of his wig.

"Don't you ever listen when I talk?" Pinky asked, huffing a bit.

Ash laughed. "Seriously? This is, what, like, charity number thirty-two you're helping this week?"

He had a point. "Fine, fine. It's for the GoFundMe page of that nonprofit Super Metal Death," Pinky said, taking another picture. "They used to be just Metal Death, but they really amped up their community-outreach efforts last year."

Ash raised a thick eyebrow but kept his eyes closed. "Right, of course, Super Metal De—"

Pinky peeked out the big bay window. "Oh, crap."

A white Porsche Cayenne had just pulled up, and a moment later, her mother stepped out, eyes hidden by her sunglasses, Hermès pantsuit still perfect after an eleven-hour workday. She speed walked to the house, her thin face wearing that same harried, pinched expression it always did.

For just a moment, Pinky felt a surge of panic. Her mom was, at the best of times, an extremely formidable adversary. But when she'd had a busy day at work and just wanted to unwind with her Sudoku book and was instead confronted by yet another one of Pinky's special projects? Picture that girl from *The Exorcist*, with her head spinning, only instead of green vomit, Pinky's mom wore pantsuits and spewed straight-up acid.

"What?" Ash said, cracking open one eyelid. He itched his scalp, and his fingers moved his wig so it was now half covering his face. "What's wrong?"

But before Pinky could answer, her mom had opened the front door and was clip-clopping her way to the living room. Pinky stood there, frozen in indecision, and then it was too late. Her mom's shadow came first, and then her mom herself emerged into the living room, her sunglasses pushed up on the top of her head.

As she took in the transformation her once-perfect living room had gone through, her face went from pinched to blank to confused to—

"Priyanka! What the hell!" Her mother rushed to the couch, frowning. "Is that a doll?"

Pinky opened her mouth to tell her the truth, but then a tiny pinprick of gleeful defiance bloomed in her chest. Why did her mom insist on calling her "Priyanka" when she was mad, when she knew perfectly well Pinky despised her full name? Also, why was her mom so quick to judge all the time? Why couldn't she approach this situation with a joyful curiosity instead of freaking out? "No, it's not a doll. It's . . . a dead body."

Her mother stopped short, her face going sallow. "No, it's not," she said, but there was a thread of uncertainty in her voice as she took in the candles and the dark room and thought about all the things she likely did not know about her delinquent daughter.

Pinky stared at her mom without smiling—and then grinned. "You totally believed me, didn't you?"

Ash sat up, grinning too, and Pinky's mother shrieked and jumped backward.

"It's just Ashish, Mom," Pinky said, giving him a fist bump. "Pretty sick beat face, right?"

"Pretty what?" her mother said, blinking at the big dude on her couch. "*Ashish?* Is that really you?"

"Hey, Ms. K," Ash said, waving and pulling off his wig.

Her mom looked at the wig for a long moment and then back at Ashish. "Why are you . . . corpsing . . . on my couch?"

"It's for Super Metal Death," Pinky explained. "I'm raising money for them. They're crowdfunding to bring hot meals to band members from defunct bands. Did you know that eighty-two percent of formerly famous band members now live in homeless shelters?" She took a seat beside Ashish, her fishnets digging into her thigh a bit.

Her mother frowned. "There's no way that statistic is right."

Adjusting her position, Pinky swung her black military-style boots onto the couch. "Sure it is. People don't realize how brutal the music industry can be."

But her mother was glaring at her, no longer listening. "Get your shoes off the couch."

"What's the big deal?" Pinky said. "We're going to get them cleaned soon anyway."

There was a tense silence, and then her mother smiled a little at Ashish. "It was very nice seeing you, Ashish," she said. "Please tell your parents I send my regards." Turning to her own flesh-and-blood daughter, she added in a barely controlled voice, "Can I please speak with you . . . alone?"

Ash stood, looking nervous under the cadaverous makeup. "Ah, I better be going. See ya, P. Have a good summer vacay, Ms. Kumar."

"You too, Ashish." Her mother was doing one of those scary,

plasticky smiles that made her look like a mannequin. Actually, *she'd* make a pretty good corpse.

Pinky flipped Ashish the peace sign even though her nerves were jangling at the prospect of the argument she knew was coming. "See you when I get back, Ash. Have fun in Hawaii. And tell Sweetie I said thanks for lending her makeup skills to a great cause."

Once the front door had closed behind him, Pinky leaned back against the couch, her arms crossed. The clock on the wall ticked. The air hummed.

Her mom said, in a super-calm voice, "Where's your father?"

Pinky shrugged. "I guess he's still at that meeting in Menlo Park."

"So you invited a boy here when you're home alone. That's against the rules, as you well know. Four days into summer break and you're already—" Her mom broke off and rubbed a hand over her forehead.

"Already what?" Pinky said, her heart starting to trot. When her mom remained silent, she changed tack. "Anyway, it wasn't a *boy*. It was just Ashish."

Pinky's mother pinched the bridge of her nose for a long moment, then walked to the entertainment unit to get the LED candle remote. She turned off all the candles and grabbed another remote to open the motorized blinds covering the big windows.

Turning back to Pinky in the suddenly bright room, she said, "Have you even started packing for the trip yet?"

"We're not leaving till tomorrow afternoon. I've got plenty of time."

Pinky's mom's stare turned icy. "No, you've *had* plenty of time. Pinky, come on. I just want you to be a bit more responsible. Stop spending your time on these ridiculous ventures that don't mean anything—"

Pinky held her breath for a moment. "They mean something to *me*," she said finally, quietly, bunching her fists up on her fishnet-covered thighs. "Why is that so hard for you to understand?"

"And I just want you to make better decisions," her mom said, looking down at her from her vantage, making Pinky feel even more like a little kid. "Why is that so hard for *you* to understand?"

They stared at each other, at one of their many, many impasses. Finally, her mother exhaled, broke eye contact, and unbuttoned her suit jacket. Taking it off, she hung it carefully over one arm.

"One day, Pinky." She shook her head, beginning to turn away. "One day you'll understand that I'm not your enemy. And one day you'll see why it hurts my heart when you insist on making these weak choices."

Pinky threw her hands up in the air, her ankh pendant swinging with the force of her movement. "I didn't make a weak choice! I'm helping charity! Name *one* weak choice I've made lately!"

"Aside from this one? All right," her mother said, turning slowly to face her again. "Preston."

Pinky felt her face close off. Crap. She'd completely forgotten about freaking Preston, her last boyfriend.

"Yeah?" she said, as if she didn't know where her mom was going with this. As if it wasn't the exact same place she'd gone with it ever since Pinky had brought Preston home (well, not exactly "brought him home" in the traditional sense. She'd sneaked him in her window and her parents had caught them).

Her mom gave her a *you know exactly what I'm talking about* look. "He got mandatory community service for something you still haven't disclosed to us."

Pinky groaned. "What's your point, Mom?"

"My point is that maybe this summer, if you happen to get a new boyfriend, as you usually do every month or so, you could find a *real* boyfriend. Someone who isn't prone to finding themselves on the wrong side of a jail cell."

As her mom walked off to the kitchen, Pinky narrowed her eyes. A "real" boyfriend? What'd her mom think Preston was, a ghoul? Besides, Pinky thought, slipping her phone out of her pocket to post her pictures to the Super Metal Death GoFundMe page, "real" boyfriends didn't exist in her world. Though, thanks to the little conversation they'd just had, that wouldn't stop her mom from micromanaging every cute guy Pinky hung out with this summer at their lake house. It would probably become her summer project or something.

One thing was certain: This summer vacation was going to majorly, definitely, monumentally suck.

Samir

One thing was certain: This summer vacation was going to be the most epic summer vacation in the historical record of summer vacations.

The smell of freedom invigorated every fiber of Samir's being. Here he was vital; he was unstoppable. He paused to admire the skyscrapers towering over him, steel and glass glinting in the bright sunlight, the bright blue cloudless sky, the people in business suits rushing past, typing on their phones, cars honking their impatient horns. A giant truck drove by, belching exhaust right into his face, and Samir launched into a volley of red-faced coughing.

Okay, so maybe that truck wasn't part of the perfect picture. But still, the point stood: Washington, DC, was his fresh start. This was where he could stretch his wings—damp and weak and slightly damaged from all his years at home—and let them grow thick and strong in the sun. Samir was trying really hard not to skip along the sidewalk. First, he didn't think these high-powered DC types would look too kindly on that. And second, this suit was his only business-appropriate suit—staying home day in and day out didn't really require much beyond polo shirts and shorts—and he didn't want to accidentally rip it or something. He adjusted his tie (freshly ironed this morning by laying a damp white cloth over it to protect the fragile silk fibers) and walked on.

Thinking of home made him think about his mom, and Samir felt a familiar shot of guilt. Should he call her? No, come on. It was fine; *she* was fine; *he* was fine. She'd call him tonight and he'd tell her about the first day of his internship.

He grinned, squinting up at the glass and steel building that loomed before him now. This miraculous structure housed the offices of Iyer & Whitman, attorneys-at-law, easily in the top five most prestigious corporate law firms and nearly impossible to get an internship with. Yet he'd done it. It had been a complete fluke, too, Samir thought as he walked up the broad concrete steps to the revolving-doors-and-stone-lions-adorned entrance, his messenger bag bouncing against his hip.

He'd heard about the internship on a prelaw forum he hung out on. He hadn't even told his mom about it; he knew she'd dismiss it outright like she'd dismissed so many other opportunities that took him out of her realm of comfort and care. It was why he went to an online high school. Plus, he hadn't wanted to panic her for nothing. Samir was used to being the levelheaded one in their duo, the one who took care of things, the one who didn't require much.

So he'd applied in secret, writing the essay at his desk at night and sending off the electronic application without any hope that he'd get picked. And instead, he'd gotten the call.

He was one of the top five applicants, and they wanted to do a phone interview. He still didn't tell his mom then, thinking there was *no* way he, a homeschooled boy with no law connections, would ever get picked. He'd done the interview when his mother went out for her weekly visit with his friend Ashish's mom. And then, a couple of days after that, he'd gotten the email. Attorney Leon Stepping, a senior partner, had picked Samir as his summer intern.

Now Samir walked up to the enormous front desk, thinking about the conversation he and his mom had had after that, the feeling of a claustrophobic, heavy net tightening around him with every "no" she verbalized. But he'd looked her straight in the eye, stood up straighter, and told her he'd made his decision. He was going.

He remembered her looking at him, her mouth opening and then closing again. And finally, after five long seconds of heart-pounding silence, she'd said, "Fine. Okay." Samir had felt the thrill of exhilaration: It was the first time he'd ever asserted himself like that. He knew what had changed for him. A couple of months ago, his best friend, Ashish, and his . . . frenemy . . . Pinky had convinced him there had to be a better way to do life than he was currently doing it. At the time he wasn't so sure, but he supposed he'd just wanted the internship so badly that he'd spoken before he had a chance to overthink it. There were other things he still hadn't changed, though. For example, he hadn't yet told his mom he wanted to be mainstream schooled for senior year, and he wasn't sure he would. Wasn't that taking things too far?

"Hello!" he said now to the muscled, blond, female security guard at the front desk, who responded with an apathetic "Mm." Undeterred, Samir continued cheerfully. "My name is Samir Jha. I'm here to see Leon Stepping of Iyer & Whitman."

The security guard looked at a clipboard at her elbow, her eyes running down the list of names. Samir saw hesitation cross her face, and then she looked back up at Samir. "I need to make a call," she said, picking up the phone. "Have a seat." With her free hand, she gestured over to a small collection of aesthetically pleasing potted plants and leather armchairs clustered around a tabletop fountain.

"Oh, um, is there a problem?" Samir asked, feeling his mouth go just the tiniest bit dry. He wanted, *needed*, to be up on the fourteenth floor, being shown where the copier was.

But the security guard only held one authoritative finger up and then gestured to the seating area again. Opening his mouth and then thinking better and closing it again, Samir turned away like some door-to-door salesman who'd been told the dogs would be set on him if he didn't take his leave. *Except I was* invited *to be here*, Samir thought, straightening his shoulders. This was clearly a mistake. Leon Stepping probably just forgot to put his name on the list.

Pinky

Aboard the Boeing Something-or-Other aircraft, Pinky sat in her first-class seat behind her parents. Her dad turned around and winked at her, his face soft and rounded and pale, completely the opposite of her mother's.

Technically he was her stepdad—he and her mom had met when Pinky was a baby and had gotten married when she was four—but she couldn't remember life before him. One of her first memories was of throwing a lump of sweet potato at him and him laughing uproariously. So, naturally, toddler Pinky had done it again.

"You comfy there, kiddo?" her dad asked now.

"Yep." She'd promised her mom she wouldn't wear her ripped shorts and midriff-exposing crop top, so instead she was dressed in an off-the-shoulder top and distressed capris, which was practically formal wear in Pinky's eyes. She glanced at her reflection in the plane window. At least her hair, with its unruly pieces of teal and magenta and green, and her nose and eyebrow piercings still helped her feel like herself.

Her mom turned around. "Pinky, can you please turn down your music? I can hear it up here."

"I have AirPods in!" Pinky said, gesturing to said Pods.

Her mom sighed and turned around, and Pinky saw her dad murmuring to her. Probably talking her off the ledge of abandoning Pinky in one of those safe-shelter places.

"Excuse me." An older man in a suit stood in the aisle, frowning. He looked down at his boarding pass and then back up at the seat numbers. "I think I'm . . . in that seat." He gestured to the empty window seat next to her.

Pinky hopped up and let him slide in. When she sat back down as he adjusted himself, he turned to her and motioned for her (kind of rudely) to take out her AirPods. Pinky did slowly, her eyebrow raised. This better be a medical emergency.

The skin on his face was papery white, nearly as white as his thinning hair. "Are you *supposed* to be in this seat?" he asked, looking at her clothes kind of pointedly.

"Um . . . yeah?" Pinky said, frowning. "It's 2D, right?"

"Right . . ." The man opened his mouth as if to say something else. Finally, he added, "And you're sure *this* is your seat?"

Pinky opened her mouth to respond, to ask the guy precisely what he meant by that comment, but then her mother turned around, looking very much a first-class traveler in her Armani cardigan and silk pants. Glaring at the old dude, she said, "That is her seat as much as the seat you're sitting in is yours. Is there a particular *reason* you think her seat might not be hers? A reason that isn't blatantly based in discrimination, that is?"

Pinky chuckled at the guy's thunderstruck expression. "That's Veena Kumar, my mom. She's a partner at Kumar & Strong. You might've heard of them—the biggest corporate law firm on the West Coast? Oh, and that's my dad, Howard Yeung, next to her. They're *both* lawyers, incidentally." Her dad was also giving the dude the evil eye, which Pinky knew was hard for him to do. He was as much a teddy bear as her mom was a werewolf/Komodo dragon hybrid. (How

12

the heck they'd ended up together was completely beyond Pinky.) She smiled sweetly at the man in the seat next to her. "Just FYI."

The man turned an alarming shade of fuchsia, shook out his copy of the *Wall Street Journal*, and began to read. It was as if he suddenly couldn't understand what they were saying and was definitely not a part of this conversation anyway.

Pinky beamed conspiratorially at her mom, thrilled at this rare moment of solidarity. Her dad winked at her, and her mom said, "Turn down your music. You'll damage your hearing." And then she turned around and went back to the *Times*.

After that, the old man pretty much left her alone. He didn't even ask her to get up so he could go to the bathroom, and Pinky knew for a fact that his bladder had to be hurting after all those Bloody Marys.

They landed what felt like forever later. Grabbing their luggage, they made their way outside, Pinky blinking in the afternoon sunlight.

Ellingsworth Point. It was the same as Pinky remembered it. She looked around at all the women in pastel-colored clothes, like walking Pez candy (her mom was one of them). Luxury cars glinted in the sunlit parking lot as far as the eye could see, most of them driven by chauffeurs.

The summer people had arrived. Pinky had mixed feelings about being a "summer person," but then again, she had mixed feelings about being here at all.

One of the lesser frequented Elizabeth Islands in Massachusetts, Ellingsworth still thought of itself as relatively unspoiled and unmarred by tourists (unlike its cousins, Martha's Vineyard and Nantucket), though that was rapidly changing. Although there were beautiful beaches on Ellingsworth, Pinky's family had a lake house in the more interior part of the island and they spent all their time swimming there. Her dad had a weird aversion to sand for having been born and brought up in coastal California.

"Ready?" her dad said, leading them to the rental car area.

Pinky glanced at her mother, who was dictating a work email into her phone. Two whole months in the lake house with her, with not even school or Pinky's Atherton friends to interrupt.

"As I'll ever be," she muttered.

The drive to the lake house took about an hour, and Pinky and her dad played *Antakshari*, which was an Indian game where people had to sing a song based on the last letter sound of the song the player before them had sung. It was supposed to be played with Hindi songs, but since neither Pinky nor her Chinese-American stepdad spoke Hindi, they played it with English-language songs.

Her dad gave a sonorous rendition of "My Heart Will Go On," and when he was finished, Pinky tapped her finger on her chin. "'On' was the last word, so that leaves me with the letter *N* . . . Hmm . . ." She glanced at her mom's profile, always so serious. "Mom? What's an *N* song I can sing?"

Her mom smiled. Pinky was constantly taken aback how much her face transformed with the simple act of baring her teeth. "*Never gonna give you up, never gonna let you down—*" her mom began, grinning at her father.

"No, no, no." Her dad guffawed. "You know darn well that song begins with, 'We're no strangers to love,' you cheater."

Her mom laughed and looked at Pinky in the rearview mirror. "What do you think, Pinky?"

14

"Well, since that song's from, like, the Mesopotamian age, I'm not really sure, but I can Google it."

"The Mesopotamian age?" her dad said, glancing at her in the rearview mirror with wounded eyes. "How old do you think we are?"

Pinky laughed as their rented BMW turned onto the gravel road that led to the lake house. "I refuse to answer on the grounds that it might incriminate me."

Her dad guffawed. "Well played, kid."

Pinky smirked. "I learned from the best."

She looked out her window at the encroaching house, feeling a frisson of excitement in spite of herself and her utter conviction that this summer was going to suck. The house was enormous—five giant bedrooms, six bathrooms, a wraparound bi-level deck with a hot tub, a gazebo, and a barn in the backyard, and the lake within walking distance. She'd spent nearly every summer of her childhood here. There were so many heat-baked, happy memories—paddleboating on the lake while the sun beat down on the top of her head, visiting the island's butterfly habitat with her parents, she and her cousin Dolly playing in the big barn and making "nests" out of dead leaves for a fictional cat they hoped would give birth to kittens there that summer. Pinky's family and Dolly's family (Dolly's mom and Pinky's mom were sisters) owned the house together.

As if on cue, her cell beeped.

Dolly: Where are you???? We've been here forever!

Grinning, Pinky responded, **We're pulling up! I can't wait to see you!**

Dolly: Me either! This summer is going to be soooo fun. Low key, doing a whole lot of nothing, just you and me hanging.

Pinky typed back, **I KNOW. I can't wait.**

She looked up at her parents. "Dolly's already here."

"Excellent!" her dad said, tapping his fingers on the steering wheel as he waited for the garage door to open. "Prepare for the inevitable Boggle beatdown."

Pinky rolled her eyes and laughed.

"I can't wait to hear what Dolly's been up to all year!" her mom said as they pulled in next to Dolly's family's rented Jetta. Her voice was buoyant, like she was filled with bubbles. "Wasn't she up for some big teen humanitarian award?"

Pinky slumped back in her seat. If there was *one* thing she could change about her perfect cousin, it would be . . . her perfection. And the way her own mom responded to it—moth, flame, et cetera. Couldn't Dolly have at least one tiny flaw? It didn't have to be anything major, just a tendency to spill ink on Pinky's mom's important papers or something.

Pinky unbuckled her seat belt. "Yeah," she said reluctantly, in answer to her mom's question. "And I think she won it."

Samir

Samir was considering throwing a penny in the fountain for good luck on his first day when his phone buzzed in his pocket. He pulled it out and glanced at the screen.

His mother. He swiped and held the phone to his ear. "Ma?"

"Samir!" Her slightly husky voice came floating down the line. "Where are you?"

Samir looked around the busy lobby. "At Iyer & Whitman. The law offices?"

"Good, good. Did you remember to starch your cuffs and collar this morning? I forgot to ask you."

"Of course I did." That would be a rookie mistake, forgetting something as basic as *that*. He'd been starching his clothes since he was in third grade. And before that, his maid used to do it for him. "And I put a laminated copy of my itinerary on the fridge, so it'd be easy for you to find it." He wasn't expecting his mom to be totally rid of her old habits.

He could hear the smile in his voice as she answered. "I found it. Thank you, *beta*."

"You're wel—"

"Mr. Jha?"

Samir turned to see a young bespectacled brown-haired woman in a suit that was just slightly too big for her. "Yes," he said, holding the phone away from his ear. "Just a moment, please." To his mother, he said, "I have to go now. I'll call you later, okay?"

A brief pause, during which he knew she was debating arguing. But then she said, "*Thik hai*. Talk to you soon."

He pressed end, slipped his phone back into his pocket, and smiled precisely and politely at the young woman. Holding out his hand, he said, "Hi. I'm Samir."

The woman took his hand in her own small, pale one and shook, her grip firm and dry. "Margot Peterson. I'm Mr. Stepping's legal assistant."

"Oh, great!" Samir's smile got bigger, then dimmed a little when Margot looked at him with a mixture of pity and unhappiness.

She gestured to the couches right behind them. "Here, let's have a seat and chat for a moment."

"Okay." Samir sat, his pulse speeding up. "Is . . . something wrong?" He was suddenly intensely afraid that she was going to say they'd meant to invite some other Samir Jha. That he was the wrong one. Maybe the real Samir was already up there, learning how Mr. Stepping liked his coffee in the mornings.

Margot sat across from him and leaned forward, her hands clasped between her knees. "Samir, Mr. Stepping had to take an unexpected sabbatical. He's going to be gone for the next three months."

Samir blinked. That was not even in the same zip code as what he'd readied himself to hear.

"What?" Not the most elegant response. *Come on, Sam, you got a 720 on the vocabulary section of the SATs. You can do better than that.* He cleared his throat and tried again. "Ah, I mean . . . What?"

Margot sat back and considered him, her brown eyes bright behind her glasses. "He's gone. Ergo, he's not taking on any interns this summer after all. I'm sorry, but your internship has fallen through."

Samir took a beat to process this. There seemed to be a block of ice in his brain, though, that refused to let any coherent thought pass through. "But . . . I flew all the way from San Francisco to be here."

"I know." Margot pursed her lips. "All of this just happened this morning. I wish we'd had time to tell you before you spent your time and money doing that. I'm so sorry."

"This just happened this morning? He decided to take a sabbatical on a whim?" Samir wasn't a lawyer yet, but that seemed really shady to him. "Sorry, but that makes literally no sense."

Margot shifted, and a faint flush of color rose to her pale cheeks. "Certain things have happened that forced our hand."

Samir continued to stare blankly at her. The universe was making no sense today. "What?" he said again. It was apparently his new favorite word.

Margot sighed. She looked at him for a long moment, opening her mouth and then closing it again. Finally, she said, "This is confidential."

Samir nodded slowly. "Okay."

"I shouldn't be telling you."

He nodded again. "I won't say anything to anyone." What the *heck* was going on?

Margot studied his expression and then seemed to come to a decision about his trustworthiness. "I'm telling you because I know how much it must suck to have something like this happen. And we really liked your application." She took a deep breath, and her voice fell another notch. "Mr. Stepping had to go to rehab. That's where he is. Things sort of . . . came to a head today."

Rehab. Holy crap. The dude wasn't off eating pain au chocolat in Paris or whatever. He was in *rehab*. Which meant, yeah, Samir was SOL. "What about one of the other lawyers?" he said, aware that he sounded about as desperate as a door-to-door salesman now. The muscled security guard glanced over, alert at the first sign of trouble. Samir forced his voice into a more natural speaking tone. Being deloused in preparation for a prison term was not how he wanted this day to end. "Maybe someone else could take me on."

Margot shook her head. "Sorry. Only three lawyers were taking interns this summer, and neither of the remaining two want another one." She stood. "Please let me know if there's anything else I can do for you. Maybe stay in DC a while, take in the sights?" She shrugged, as if to say she was all out of helpful suggestions, and then walked off, swiping her badge to get through the turnstiles.

Samir stood there, staring after her, his DC dream in a pile of ashes at his feet.

He sat at an outdoor café, staring morosely into his latte as streams of people in business suits and sneakers rushed by him. Then, taking a deep breath and straightening his shoulders, Samir pulled out a small, monogrammed planner from his messenger bag, along with a pencil box full of colored markers. Flipping open to the current date, where he'd denoted each task that lay before him—6 a.m.: wake up. 6:15 a.m.: brush teeth. 6:20 a.m.: shower, 6:30 a.m.: iron shirt, tie, and pants, etc.—he crossed out the 8 a.m. entry: begin internship. Then he sat back and sighed.

The rest of the day was blank, because he hadn't been sure what, exactly, his tasks for the day would be. The plan had been to fill that in for the rest of the week based on how today went. Maybe he should just fill in "be a directionless loser" for the rest of the summer.

He knew he could always go back home, maybe get a job at the country club as a tennis coach. Spend time with his mom making smoothies and granola and stuff like they had last summer. The thought almost made him gasp for breath, it was so stifling. And, of course, he felt completely guilty for feeling that way. It wasn't his mom's fault she was how she was.

The thing was, his family . . . His family wasn't like other families.

Samir's dad had died in a car crash when Samir was just a baby. It had always been just him and his mom, the "two musketeers," as she called them. And then, when he was ten, his mom was diagnosed with really advanced breast cancer. That was scary enough, but what made it worse was that her own mom, Samir's nani, had died of the same thing when she was his mom's age.

Against all odds, in spite of what the doctors said, his mom managed to fight it off and live.

Samir didn't know if her doctors had written "kicked cancer's ass" in her medical file, but they should've. And then, after she was cancer-free, his mom became a little overprotective of Samir. It was as if she felt she'd been given a second chance to make sure his life was perfect, that he was set up for success, in case . . .

It really stung that his internship, his jailbreak—okay, that was a mean way to think of it, but there it was—had been snatched out from under him so abruptly. Not that he wasn't happy that Mr. Stepping was off getting the help he needed. But man, did he have to do it the *day* Samir was due to work for him? Couldn't he have had his breakthrough in the fall?

Samir sighed, took a sip of the latte, which was still piping hot, thanks to the relentless summer sun beating down on the concrete patio, and slipped his phone out of his pocket.

Internship canceled, he typed in his text message to Ash, who was on a family trip to Maui. All of Samir's friends were off having their own summer adventures. Which meant that if he went back home, he'd basically have just his mom for company. 24/7. The vise around his chest tightened and he tried to take a deep breath. It only kind of worked.

Ash: What?? Dude, what happened??

Attorney went on sabbatical. Long story. Anyway, sitting at a café now wondering what to do.

Ash: Dude, that freaking blows. Hey, you wanna come out to Hawaii? Gita Kaki brought Crabby. To freaking Maui. He called me a gringo, Sam. I don't think he knows what it means, only that it's an insult, but still. I could use the distraction.

Samir snorted. Gita Kaki was Ashish's eccentric aunt who was convinced messenger parrots were this era's email. And Crabby, a giant parrot who cursed almost nonstop, was her pride and joy. **No thanks man. I'd rather watch all four Twilight movies back to back.**

Ash: Don't lie, you've been on Team Edward forever. Anyway. So what are you gonna do? Go back home?

Sam: Idk thinking about it. How's Sweetie?

Ash: :) good good. She's visiting her cousin but it's gonna be awesome when we reunite. Hey do you think girls like bacon roses or is that a weird present

Sam: um yeah I'd rethink that

Ash: yeah you're probably right. hey you sure you gonna be okay? You know my mom would love to have you

Sam: I appreciate it man but I'm okay. Gonna stay the night and head out in the morning. Maybe I'll get a job at the country club caddying or something, get out of the house a bit

Ash: Good idea. I'll be back in a couple weeks and then we'll have a major bball tournament

Samir smiled. Ashish was trying to make him feel better, and weirdly enough, it sort of worked. **Thanks bro enjoy Hawaii**

Putting his phone down on the metal table, Samir signaled for the check. While he waited, he sat back and watched the cars whizzing by on the street. His hotel was right down the block from here. He was supposed to be subletting an apartment for the summer, but he'd already texted the Georgetown student to tell her his internship had fallen through. She was sympathetic but not heartbroken. Apparently she had a waiting list of twelve people who wanted to be notified in case his plans fell through.

Should he go back home? That would be the smart thing to do. It was still early in the day; there were lots of flights back, he was sure. Except . . . except he didn't want to go home. Not yet.

For now he'd go back to his hotel and watch a really bad movie, he decided. Maybe one of the older Godzillas. Watching a fake disaster unfolding might distract him from his very real one, at least for a couple of hours.

CHAPTER 2

Pinky

"And this is the homeless shelter Dolly helped build," Dolly's mom Meera (Meera Mausi to Pinky) was saying, beaming around at everyone with her phone on display. They were at the kitchen table, Dolly and Pinky sitting together, sharing a big bowl of grapes between them. As usual, conversation had turned to Dolly's many brilliant accomplishments, as it did every time the family came together.

Dolly's dad, Abe, swiped the screen. "Oh, look at the smile on Dolly's mentee's face!" The Montclair family laughed.

Pinky popped another grape into her mouth, her foot hooked around her chair leg. She was trying her best to smile and laud her cousin's every accomplishment, but with every picture, her smile was getting more rictus in nature. Pinky's mom kept smiling at her and her dad, as if she had anything to do with Dolly's accomplishments. Pinky's dad surreptitiously bumped her foot with his under the table and winked, but that just made her feel worse. Like it was just so obvious that Pinky couldn't hope to compete with Dolly's many varied accomplishments.

"Oh, but look at this one!" Dolly said, swiping past a bunch of pictures of her and her friends at the beach. Dolly even had perfect, unblemished skin. Abe was white, and Meera Mausi was dark like Pinky and her mom, and Dolly had gotten this smooth, sun-kissed complexion. She stopped at a picture of a giant golden retriever grinning the doofiest grin Pinky had ever seen. "This is Sigmund," Dolly said, gazing as proudly at the picture as if it were her newborn on the screen. "We got him last August. He just passed the canine good citizenship test and now he's a certified therapy dog! Mom says I can take him to the pediatric ward on the days she works in the hospital."

"Awesome," Pinky forced herself to say, though she really wanted to do a cartwheel right out the window into the lake. "He's really photogenic." *Like your entire family.*

Dolly studied the look on Pinky's face and then set her mom's phone aside. "But that's enough about me." She smiled a perfectly kind, empathetic smile, as if she'd ordered it from the "therapists' progeny" catalog. "What have you been up to, P?"

In spite of her almost-eerie perfection, it was impossible to hate Dolly. She was like a Teletubby. They could be annoyingly upbeat, sure, but you knew they were all about making the world a better place and it was hard to disagree with that. Pinky shrugged. "Not much, really." She didn't think she'd bring up her graffiti wall by the train tracks at this particular moment in time.

"That's not entirely true," Pinky's dad said, putting a pale hand over hers. "Tell them where you've been spending so much of your time this year."

"I volunteer at the soup kitchen in Berkeley," Pinky said, not adding that she started doing that as a punishment, after her mom caught her FaceTiming with Preston when she'd been expressly forbidden to see him on account of his recent juvenile detention situation.

Dolly made a noise very much like a squeal. Her cheeks were actually pink with glee. "Ohmygosh, that is so cool! I do that too! Except mine's a women's shelter, but same difference. Isn't it the most incredible feeling to help all those people?"

"Dolly actually got a commendation from the mayor for her work at the shelter," Abe said, smiling fondly at his self-actualized daughter.

"Oh yeah?" Pinky said. "For what?"

"I sort of founded the shelter," Dolly said, shrugging. Like founding shelters was something people did on the regular, when they got bored on any given Tuesday. "But it wasn't just me," she added, her unironically earnest eyes back on Pinky again. "A teacher at my school helped me get it all going and stuff, and we had the *best* volunteers who helped fund-raise."

"Wow, that's so cool," Pinky said, suddenly feeling extremely tired. "You know, I think I'm going to go hang out on the deck for a bit." She pushed her chair back and stood. "I'm just so exhausted after all that flying."

The adults all looked at her, some of them smiling hesitantly. Not wanting to be rude, but definitely needing to get out of there posthaste, Pinky held up a hand in farewell and tried not to leap for the French doors.

Pinky tucked the bottom of her shirt into the band of her bra and sat on a chaise lounge chair on the deck. The sky was an interminable blue, the sun a blazing ball of heat. Pinky looked out over the enormous backyard, complete with the old barn and the newer gazebo her parents had put in two summers ago, and took a deep breath. There were a few other summer families nearby, and through the wooded lot, she could make out the white siding of the Millers' house to the north. To her right lay the vast expanse of lake, glimmering in the afternoon sunlight. Maybe she'd go for a swim in a bit.

The French doors opened and Pinky turned to see Dolly walking out to her, holding her phone in her hand.

"Hey," Dolly said, looking like a wildflower in a pair of pink shorts and a yellow halter top. Her chocolate-brown hair lay in waves past her shoulders.

Pinky nodded.

"Do you want to be alone?" her cousin asked, and Pinky could tell it really was a question, not just a statement meant to be responded to in the negative.

"Nah," Pinky said, smiling up at her.

Dolly sat on the rocking chair a few feet away from Pinky, setting her phone on the table between them. "Did I annoy you with all those stories? I realized after you left that I probably sounded like a total ass."

"You didn't annoy me," Pinky said honestly. "But it's a little hard not to feel . . . What's the word? Oh yeah, like a total dumpy loser when I compare myself against all the stuff you've done." She kicked off her sandals and put her feet on the warm striped fabric of the chaise.

"You totally shouldn't feel inadequate!" Dolly said, and Pinky did not fail to notice the more elegant phrasing her cousin had chosen.

"You have a lot of stuff going on too. It's just different stuff than mine, that's all."

A vivid image of Ashish lying on the couch in his purple wig, pretending to be a corpse, flashed through Pinky's brain. "Right."

"Hey, do you want a strawberry lemonade? I'm gonna get myself a glass."

Pinky smiled at this peace offering. "Sure. Thanks."

Dolly hopped up and walked into the house.

Pinky lay back on her chaise and closed her eyes. The thing was, Dolly was right. There was absolutely no reason for her to feel inadequate. She and Dolly were fundamentally different, and Pinky was fine with that.

Dolly was a peacemaker, the kind of person who founded clubs and edited the school newspaper. Newspapers to which people like Pinky wrote angry letters to the editor decrying the hazards of peanut M&M's in the school vending machines. People like Dolly built monuments. People like Pinky graffitied them. There were few things Pinky enjoyed more than waging war. Pissing people off, especially people in power, and then getting them to do exactly what she wanted? Totally her thing.

Below, an incomplete list of causes for which she'd gone full-on beast mode (and won) in the past three years alone:

1. Getting Richmond Academy to change the prom king/prom queen graphic on the announcement TV in the main lobby to say prom queen/prom queen when Loretta Smalls and Mariana Jimenez won due to an overabundance of write-in votes

2. Helping YouTube stars crowdfund for ring lights
3. Setting up the first raccoon hospitals in the Bay Area (they were *not* just diseased rodents that deserved to die)
4. Getting vegan makeup options to prisoners in the local county jail

Pinky Kumar knew who she was—a social-justice warrior. She wore that metaphorical badge with pride, laughing at those anonymous Internet trolls who tried to use the phrase as a slur. What was wrong with being passionate and fiery and outraged? What was wrong with wanting the world to change, to expand its collective mind, to dig a little deeper to find the last dregs of empathy it could muster up?

So yes, Pinky knew and loved who she was. The only tiny niggling doubt, the only thing that gave her pause, was how much her mom seemed to enjoy Dolly's brand of helping more. Why was it so easy for her mom to overlook the things she did? What was it about Pinky that her mom just couldn't understand?

Dolly's phone twinkled with an incoming text.

If Pinky's mom could just accept—

Dolly's phone chimed again and again and again. Jeez. Someone was really trying to get ahold of her. Pinky sat up and grabbed it, swinging her legs around to give the phone to Dolly. The phone chimed two more times.

The French doors opened and Dolly stepped out with two glasses.

"Hey, your phone's going off—" Pinky began.

The expression on Dolly's face could only be described as pure panic. She ran to the table, set the glasses down with a clatter, and snatched the phone from Pinky's hand. "Thanks," she said breathlessly, her cheeks a vivid pink as she read her texts.

A slow smile spread across Pinky's face. "Wait," she said, leaning forward and lowering her voice. "Is that a hot guy? Or a hot girl?"

"Um, n-no!" Dolly said, but the squeak in her voice gave her away. She pocketed her phone. "It's no one."

Wow, the girl was the worst liar in the world. And anyway, what was she being so shy about? Historically, Dolly's boyfriends and girlfriends had all been gag-inducing do-gooders. Her latest breakup had been super amicable, with her ex-boyfriend heading off to the Peace Corps. Dolly had even written him a recommendation letter. And before that there had been Gretchen, the girl who'd been a National Merit Scholar and got a full ride to Tufts.

Pinky's mind drifted back over her own many, many boyfriends. All of their faces began to blend and merge in her memory. But had any of them really, truly loved her for who she was? And had she ever loved them for who *they* were?

Something she'd never told anyone: In spite of the slew of boyfriends she'd had, in spite of the fact that she was rarely single, Pinky never felt more alone than when she was dating.

Blinking, Pinky brought herself back to the present. "Oh, come on. What's the big deal?" She grinned at her cousin. "Is it someone your parents wouldn't approve of?" Pinky asked the last question sarcastically, because not only were Dolly's girlfriends and boyfriends perfect, but they also always, always got along with Meera Mausi and Abe.

"No!" Dolly said, her eyes wide. "It's nothing, I told you. Anyway, do you want to go for a swim?"

"Sure," Pinky said slowly, not wanting to push. There was definitely something very, very interesting going on. "Let me grab my suit and I'll meet you downstairs."

They floated on Ellingsworth Lake on inner tubes. (Everything on Ellingsworth Point was named after the founder, James Ellingsworth— Ellingsworth Lighthouse, Ellingsworth Beach, Ellingsworth Luxury Toilets—because of some edict he'd passed back in the late 1700s. Apparently the dude's ego had been as big as the island.) A gigantic blue heron—the technical term for them was "great blue Ellingsworth heron," but Pinky thought "gigantic" fit better—stood near the shore, watching them nonchalantly. To Pinky, a gigantic blue heron sighting at the lake signaled the official beginning of summer vacation, kind of like the opening of the neighborhood outdoor pool did for other people. Flashing it a thumbs-up, Pinky put her hair in a high bun and let her head fall back, her eyes closed against the bright light of the sun. There was virtually no breeze; her feet trailed in the still, lukewarm water. "I could seriously just do this for a living," she said.

Dolly laughed. "What? Float in an inner tube?"

"Yeah?" Pinky squinted at her cousin, who was dressed in a blue-and-white-striped tankini. "Is that not a job?"

Dolly shook her head, still smiling. "Hey, I like your bikini. Is it new?"

Pinky glanced down at her black bikini. The long silver and gold fringe along the edges waved lightly in the breeze, and the rhinestone KALI twinkled in the brilliant sun. "Yeah, I just got it a couple of weeks ago at this hippie store in Berkeley. I could *not* believe they had Kali bikinis!"

"Right." Dolly chuckled. "I forgot about your obsession with Kali."

Pinky threw her hands up in the air. "Dude, how could anyone not love her? She's always shown physically dancing on Shiva—a god—while he lies quietly under her. And in one story, she was the only one who could defeat hordes of demons. Oh, and let's not forget she wore a garland of freaking *skulls* while she did it. And then, when all the demons had been slain, she *danced on their corpses*. I mean, seriously, how metal is that? She's the OG feminist."

Dolly trailed her hands in the water; she'd heard this all before. "Definitely." She looked over her shoulder at a group of people around their age who'd walked out onto the pier. They were all dressed in designer nautical-themed board shorts and bikinis, as if they'd stepped off the pages of a Harvard-students-in-the-summer catalog.

"Hey," Pinky said as the group hopped off the pier and into the water, splashing and laughing. The heron flew off, probably annoyed by all the activity. Pinky waited till Dolly met her eye. "Is everything okay? You seem super distracted."

"I'm fine—" Dolly began, but then the group of people were swimming out toward them, laughing and shouting.

"Hey, girls," one of the guys said, swimming up to them and resting his muscular arms on Dolly's inner tube, splashing them both with water.

Pinky was just about to ask him if he'd ever heard of the concept of personal space when she realized she recognized him. "Cash?" she said, squinting at his floppy brown hair and his extremely even teeth. Whoa. "Cash Miller?"

"Yo." He gave her a finger salute, then went back to leering at Dolly. "Lookin' good, Dolly."

Pinky caught Dolly's eye and made a gagging motion. Dolly's cheeks turned pink, and she turned back to Cash. "Thanks," she said, smiling. "You too."

She wasn't lying about that at least. Cash Miller was one of the other summer people; his family had the lake house to the north of Pinky's and Dolly's. They'd last seen him about two or three summers ago, when he'd been a gangly kid who wore braces and too much cologne. Now, he was shirtless and completely ripped. He looked a bit like Brad Pitt in his younger days. No wonder Dolly was staring at him like that.

"We're getting ready to take my boat out," Cash said, incorrectly. Pinky was pretty sure the boat belonged to his dentist dad, not him. "You girls want to join us?"

"No, thanks," Pinky said. "We've got a Boggle tournament later." She raised an eyebrow when Dolly was silent. Family Boggle tournaments were, like, Dolly's thing. She and Pinky's dad totally dominated the game. Last summer they'd even made a cheesy little trophy out of an old Boggle timer and Boggle letters and called it the Dolly-Howard Cup. What was her problem now?

"Yeah," Dolly said finally, looking away from Pinky and back at Cash. "Sorry, but we promised we'd be there for that."

Cash smirked and rolled his eyes. "Whatever. If you get tired of *Boggle*, though, you let me know. We have beer. B-E-E-R." He laughed at his one witticism and did a lazy breaststroke back to his friends.

Pinky raised her middle finger at his retreating back. "What a jerk. J-E-R-K," she muttered, shaking her head at Dolly.

Her cousin gave her a limp smile in return.

Later that evening, Pinky hopped out of the shower and got into her pajamas. The Kumars, Yeungs (or one Yeung), and Montclairs had played charades and then moved on to the Boggle tournament. It amused her greatly to see her family loosen up and make fools of themselves. Especially her mom. Meera Mausi had made sangria, and her mom had drunk two glasses, which was two glasses more than she usually drank, and then she'd announced to everybody that she might just quit her job and take up painting houses as a career. Everyone had laughed, and her mom had said seriously, "I'd get to be outside during the day. It would be *freeing*."

And the weird thing was, she'd looked at Pinky when she said it. But then the moment was gone because Pinky's dad had made the word "luminosity" and won the game and everyone had begun yelling and cheering and Dolly had ceremoniously awarded him the trophy.

Pinky walked across her room to the window, wet hair dripping down her back, wondering what her mom's whole career crisis had been about. She didn't really want to paint houses. Pinky knew that. Veena Kumar lived, breathed, and ate corporate law. If they ever opened her mom up for surgery, they'd find contracts stamped on her internal organs.

Pinky grabbed the cord to lower the window shade when something way out in the yard caught her eye. Frowning, she opened her window and leaned out into the cool night air. Her bedroom faced the lake, mostly, and just a bit of the yard. To really see it, she had to twist her torso at a pretty painful angle. Was that . . . fire? Some kind of orange light?

"Hello?" she called out the window, her voice carrying in the stillness. "Is anyone down there?"

But no one answered. Weird. They probably just couldn't hear her, and anyway, maybe it was just the adults down there with flashlights or something. They liked to go talk in the backyard sometimes, though usually not at . . . Pinky glanced at the alarm clock on her nightstand. Almost midnight. She considered going down into the yard, but decided against it. It had been kind of a long day, and she was ready for her book.

She crawled under her covers and was grabbing her Kindle when her phone beeped. Grabbing it off her nightstand, she read the incoming text.

Ashish: Dude, I just heard from Samir

Pinky: What's up what'd he say

Ashish: You know that DC internship he was so excited about?

Pinky: Yeah you mean his reason for freedom

Ashish: Exactly. It got canceled

Pinky frowned. **What do you mean canceled? They can't just cancel an internship at the last minute**

Ashish: Well they did so now he has to go back home. He was already in DC when they told him

Pinky: Seriously? I thought he was like 1% of the applicants picked?? Why can't he find a different position at the same place?

Ashish: Idk man but it's rough he's pretty bummed

Pinky: Yeah I can imagine

Ashish: I invited him to HI but he didn't wanna come. Any chance you could invite him there? Maybe he could be like a buffer between you and your mom

Pinky snorted. **What makes you think he'll come to my lake house if he didn't want to go with you to HI? Pretty sure Samir would rather live with the bears in SF Zoo than come hang with me for the summer**

Ashish: Yeah you're probably right idk . . . just feel bad for him I guess

Pinky: Hey how's Sweetie

Ashish: :) Good. Hey what do you think about bacon roses as a romantic present

Pinky: Sophisticated meat treat

Ashish: Right? That's what I thought. Sweetie's gonna love them. Man I can't wait to see her again to take her in my arms and hold her close

Pinky: Okay that's gross bye

Ashish: Lol bye

Fools in love. Shaking her head, Pinky set her phone on her nightstand again and turned back to the thriller she was reading. But way before she'd figured out who the killer was, she was asleep.

"Pinky."

"Pinky, wake up."

She groaned and tried to roll over, but the person had her shoulder in a vise grip. Pinky opened her eyes and squinted as her mom's worried face came into focus.

"What?" Pinky croaked. The room was almost completely dark,

with just a tinge of orange light coming in from outside. "What is it?"

"We have to get outside. Now."

The urgency on her mom's face had her following orders without even realizing she was doing it. "Why?" she asked, stumbling after her mom to the door. "What's going on?"

In the hallway, Dolly, Abe, Meera Mausi, and her dad, all dressed in pajamas and slippers, were talking in urgent, loud voices. The clock on the wall said it was four a.m.

"Let's go!" her dad said, shepherding them all toward the stairs. "We need to get outside, to the bottom of the driveway." He grabbed her around the shoulders and firmly guided her.

"What's going on?" Pinky asked again, her heart racing. "What happened?"

"There's a fire," her mom said, pulling the front door open. The cool night air rushed in and wrapped them all in its arms. "In the backyard."

"The backyard? What kind of fire? Where'd it come from?"

"We don't know, but the fire trucks will be here any moment."

Pinky followed her family to the bottom of the large driveway and turned around, her breath catching in her throat. The huge old barn was ablaze. It looked like a giant torch in the night, spitting embers into the sky. Even at this distance, she could feel a faint heat. Pinky clapped her hand over her mouth. "Oh my God!" In the distance, she heard sirens.

She glanced at Dolly, sandwiched between her parents, looking just as stricken as Pinky felt. They'd played in there every summer when they were little. It was their "reading fort" for a while. Pinky's dad put an arm around her and pulled her close. "I'm sorry, sweetheart. I know it's hard to watch."

Her mom stood on his other side, holding his free hand. She gazed at the flames, her face glowing orange.

"Mom?" Pinky said, leaning around her dad. "How do you think this happened?"

Maybe it was silly that she, a seventeen-year-old rising senior in high school, expected her mom to know that. But that's just how it had always been—in scary situations, Pinky went to her father for comfort and her mother for knowledge.

Her mom glanced at her, a slight crease between her eyebrows. "I don't know," she said slowly, just as two fire trucks came screaming around the corner, their sirens blaring, red lights bathing everything in their strobe. "But I think we'll have some answers soon."

CHAPTER 3

Pinky

"You're lucky you noticed the fire when you did, Ms. Kumar," the cute fireman said, shaking his head. "Windy night like this, if you'd waited even ten minutes to call, the fire would probably have engulfed your entire yard; possibly even your house and your neighbors' properties."

The firefighters had finished putting out the fire in the barn, and except for Mr. Cutie, they were all packing up. Pinky's and Dolly's families had gotten shoes on and were standing in the backyard now, looking at the smoking wreckage and smelling the crispy smell of burned wood.

"I got up to go to the bathroom," her mom said, shaking her head. "I'm just so glad I did."

"Me too," Pinky's dad said, putting one arm around her mom and another around Pinky. "Do you know what caused the fire?"

The fireman nodded. "One of the other guys found what looked like a few kerosene lanterns in there. Someone must've forgotten to turn them off when they left. There was also some debris that looked like bottles of alcohol." His eyes brushed past Dolly and settled for just a moment on Pinky, on her wildly colored hair and her eyebrow piercing. Dolly's mom and dad gasped softly, but Pinky's parents were still. Smoothly, the fireman turned to look back at her dad. "I'd advise against lighting fires in enclosed spaces like that next time. Especially if there's any alcohol around. Alcohol, as you probably know, is highly flammable, as is kerosene."

Her dad opened his mouth, but her mom got there first. "Of course it's flammable! We would never do something as irresponsible as lighting a fire in a wooden barn!" Before the fireman could respond, she rounded on Pinky, her eyes flashing. "What do you know about this?"

Pinky stared at her, her mouth dropping open. "What? *Me?* I don't know anything!"

"Do you think I'm stupid, Priyanka?"

Pinky heard Dolly begin to speak. "But it's not—it's—"

Pinky's mom spoke right over Dolly. "Drinking alcohol, lighting fires, sneaking out at night—do you recognize this song?"

"Now, honey," Pinky's dad said, "let's give Pinky a minute to speak for herself."

"Speak for herself?" her mom said, still glaring at her. Her silk pajama bottoms flapped in the stiff breeze, and her hair blew behind her in a thick black stream. "How can you *possibly* defend yourself from something like this? What were you *thinking*?"

"I didn't do anything!" Pinky said, finally getting over her shock and feeling a wave of hot anger engulf her. "Why am I always at the top of your suspect list?"

Her mom barked a laugh. "Are you joking? How many times have we caught you and your delinquent boyfriends sneaking alcohol or

40

vandalizing something or doing precisely whatever it is we've told you not to do, over and over again?"

Pinky opened her mouth and closed it again. The ghosts of boyfriends past hovered between her and her parents, all of them jostling for space.

"So?" her mom said. "Which one of the summer boys was it? Whose parents do we need to go speak with about this?" She thrust her hand at the charred remains of the barn.

"No one! I'm not—" Studying the hard, angry lines of her mom's face, Pinky felt a monstrous indignation swell within her. This was so ridiculously unfair. Her mom hadn't even *glanced* at anyone else before immediately sentencing Pinky. There were *two* teenagers in this house.

Pinky looked at Dolly, who stood huddled into her dad's side, her big hazel eyes wide and scared, and then turned back to her mother. "I didn't do this, and I definitely wasn't drinking out here with some random summer boy—"

"Sure," her mom said. "And you expect us to believe that."

"I don't care if you believe it because it's true!" Pinky said, her mouth forming the words before her brain had a chance to react. As if from a great distance, she heard herself add, "It *couldn't* have been me out here with a boy because—because I already *have* a boyfriend! And he's . . . he's nothing like any of the boys I've dated before! He'd never do something like this!"

Her dad looked surprised, but her mom's expression didn't change. Finally, shaking her head, her mom turned on her heel and stalked off. Pinky stood staring after her. After a long moment, her dad kissed the side of her head. "I'll go talk to her," he said quietly.

Pinky looked into his eyes. "What's the point?" she said, raising her chin. "She'll just think whatever she wants to think, and what she wants to think is the worst of me."

"I'm going to try," her dad said. "Go back to bed, okay?"

Pinky watched him walk away.

Someone took her hand. "I'm going to fix this," Dolly said, her eyes feverish and bright when Pinky looked over at her. Meera Mausi and Abe were walking out of the backyard, talking to the cute firefighter. "Okay? I'll fix it."

Pinky frowned. "Fix what? What are you talking about?"

Dolly just looked at her, the sparkly straps of her Hello Kitty pajamas glittering in the near dark. "Don't worry about it." Then she strode after her parents, a determined set to her shoulders.

Pinky couldn't sleep. She'd let herself in via the back door, and as she walked down the hallway to her room, she'd heard Dolly and her parents murmuring in Dolly's room. She'd been super tempted to stop and eavesdrop, but she'd made herself walk into her bedroom and close the door instead. What was going *on*? And why had Dolly said she'd fix everything? What did that even mean?

As she lay gazing at the ceiling, the morning sun lightening the sky bit by bit, she couldn't stop thinking of the way her mom had looked at her, eyes blazing, voice full of judgment and anger. Judging her without even giving her a chance. Her mom's voice echoed in her ears. *How many times have we caught you and your delinquent boyfriends sneaking alcohol or vandalizing something or doing precisely whatever it is we've told you not to do, over and over again?*

And Pinky's response: *I already have a boyfriend! He'd never do something like this!*

Okay, maybe the "boyfriend" part wasn't true in the *Webster's Dictionary* sense, but what was she supposed to have said? Her mom was totally haranguing her and trying to make her feel guilty for something she hadn't even done.

And now her mom and dad would ask if she'd really meant what she said about her boyfriend and she'd have to tell them she just made it up. God, she'd feel like such a loser. Who made up a boyfriend? It would just convince her mom that she was a liar and a cheat, someone totally capable of burning down a barn.

Pinky balled her fists in frustration and turned on her side, her eyes falling on the phone on her nightstand. If only there were some kind of a rent-a-boyfriend app she could use, just for this summer. Just imagining her mom's face if she paraded around some stand-up guy in a respectable striped polo shirt who casually talked about how he was applying to Princeton—

Out of nowhere, an image of Samir Jha popped into her head. Pinky blinked.

Near perfect to the point of being a robot, not a single anti-establishment bone in his body, dressed like a J.Crew catalog, wanted to apply to Harvard, handsome in that conventional, square jaw, made-Pinky-yawn way . . . She sat up in bed, her pulse pounding. Sure, all of those things sounded mind-numbingly boring. But what made *Pinky* want to fall into a dreamless stupor was exactly what impressed her mother. Ash had said Samir was knocking around DC, dragging his feet about going back home. He was aimless and internship-less.

And Pinky was in need of a boyfriend. A perfect summer boyfriend.

Before she could think too deeply about it, she grabbed her phone from her nightstand and began to type.

Samir

Using a fork to avoid messy orange fingers, Samir carefully speared another cheese puff, popped it into his mouth, and chewed while a meteorologist on TV nattered on about the weather. Maybe the salt in these things would kill him before he needed to fly back home. He glanced at the alarm clock on the nightstand in his hotel room. Five a.m. In three hours, he'd be on an airplane, flying west, back to Atherton. Samir closed his eyes and let his head sag back against the headboard. There was a weight on his chest, getting heavier and heavier—

His phone beeped with an incoming text. He frowned. It was only two a.m. in Atherton; it couldn't be his mom. All communications from her ceased at nine p.m. her time and didn't resume again until seven a.m. Samir set his fork down on a napkin that lay neatly folded on the nightstand and grabbed the phone.

But the text wasn't from his mom. He read it again.

Wait, what?

Pinky: Hey you still in DC?

Pinky Kumar was texting him? But why? They really only com-

44

municated when Ashish was around. He was like the glue that held them together; when he was gone, they floated off in their own directions.

Um, yeah, he typed, confused. **How'd you know?**

Pinky: Ash told me. Sorry about your internship

Samir: Thanks

He paused, wondering if he should say something else. Ask her what she was up to or something, to be polite. But before he could, another text came in.

Pinky: I have a proposition for you

Samir: Huh?

Pinky: An invitation, a proposal

Samir: Yeah I know what a proposition is but wth are you talking about

Pinky: You don't want to go back home I'm guessing and I need something you could give me

Samir waited, but she didn't say anything else. This was getting weirder and weirder.

Okay . . . , he typed.

Pinky: I need . . .

Samir waited. She needed what? And why contact him? There was a beat of silence. Two, three.

Pinky: A boyfriend

Was she serious? Pinky and *him* in a relationship? The thought made Samir want to move to the wilds of Australia, be adopted by a pack of dingoes, and never come back. Snorting, he typed, **Lmao okay haha**

Pinky: ????

45

Samir: You're joking right? This is some kind of weird burn that I'm not getting yet

Pinky: Omg dude this is not a joke. I'm serious. I need you to be my fake boyfriend this summer.

Samir studied the words, frowning. **Your what?? That's not even a thing**

Pinky: If you pretend to be my bf it'll be a thing

Samir: But . . . why??

Pinky: Because I'm tired of everyone looking at me like I'm a little delinquent

Samir: Yeah but you are

Pinky: Shut up. It'll be for a month or maybe six weeks tops. And it's at my parents' gigantic lake house in Cape Cod so it's not like you'd be slumming it

Samir: Don't you have anyone else to ask?

Pinky: Let's just say my mom has a type and you're it

Samir's frown deepened. He shouldn't even be entertaining this ridiculous idea. He should tell Pinky to sleep off whatever she'd taken. He should put his phone away and get ready to go to the airport.

He found himself typing, **What's in it for me?**

The response came quickly, as if she'd been waiting for him to ask.

Pinky: My mom's looking to take a high school intern over winter break. I heard her talking to my dad about it. You'll be with her at the lake house. Impress her and she'll give it to you

Whoa. Pinky's mom was Veena freaking Kumar, of Kumar & Strong.

Samir: But won't she hate me if we pretend to break up at the end of summer break?

Pinky: I'll tell her *I* broke up with *you*. If anything, it'll just make her feel more sympathetic toward you. She's always saying I make terrible decisions. I just need her to look at me this summer as if I made one good one

Holy crap. She'd thought this through. But . . . It was a ludicrous idea, right? Just plain out-of-this-world stupid. It would never work. He could never pretend to be her boyfriend. To be honest, he barely tolerated her, and the idea of having to be all lovey-dovey for an entire month, maybe more? Holding her hand and smiling while she went off on wild tangents about rebuilding beaver dams or whatever it was she did for fun? He felt bad that things weren't going well for Pinky and her mom; he knew what that felt like. But he could never pull this off. Not without some serious acting lessons.

Samir: Okay fine

He stared at the words he'd sent, confused. He'd totally meant to say no. He'd meant to say he was heading back home in a couple of hours. But apparently his brain had other ideas.

Pinky: Omg. You'll do it? Seriously?

Samir read her message. She . . . she really wasn't joking then. She really wanted him to do this ridiculous, wild, laughable thing. But . . . but the thing was, he really, *really* didn't want to go back home. Especially not stinking of failure. He knew what his mom would say: *See? You should stay close to home. The world just holds disappointment. Stay here, stay with me, stay here.* And he didn't want that. Like, at all.

When do you need me there? he typed, his heart pounding, a small, slightly hysterical smile at his lips.

Right now, Pinky shot back. **Today, if you can.**

Samir hopped out of bed and headed toward the bathroom to get showered and changed. **No problem.**

There was no way this was happening. Samir sat in the terminal, waiting to board. He'd added in *10 a.m.: Fly to Nantucket* to his planner and was waiting to check it off. He kept alternately grinning and sweating, like some back-alley murderer. Either this was going to be the best day of his life or the day that culminated in him getting a prison record and being disbarred before ever becoming a lawyer. And if that wasn't possible, he was sure Veena Kumar would make it possible somehow, just to get her vengeance.

Samir knew lying wasn't a good idea. Especially not if you planned to work for the person you were lying to someday. These kinds of things had a tendency to go south. But seriously, when the choices were between going back home or going to a summer lake house, pretending to be Pinky's boyfriend, and then landing a dream internship—even more so than the DC one—what would anyone who wasn't Gandhi or Abraham Lincoln or the pope do?

He pulled his phone out of his pocket and made the call he'd been putting off.

"Hey, Ma, it's me."

"Samir! How are you? How is the internship?"

There was a beat. The lie just wouldn't come—lying was *so* not part of his DNA—but he forced the word out. "Fine." His voice was just a notch too high, so he cleared his throat. "Um . . . busy. Good. Great." *Stop talking, Sam.*

48

"Okay . . ." His mom sounded like she thought her only child might be having an aneurysm. "Are you . . . all right, *beta*?"

"Mm-hmm. Yep. Totally fine. Just . . . you know. Letting you know that it's going well. And I'm getting busier, so I might not be able to call regularly. But don't worry, okay?"

There was a pause, and Samir could tell she didn't like this at all. But then she sighed. "Okay. I won't worry."

Samir smiled a little. This was hard for her, he knew, but he was proud of her for the progress she was making. "Take care, Ma."

"Bye, Samir."

He hung up just before a message began blaring over the airport intercom. Phew.

Samir sat for a minute, feeling a sense of inevitability. He was really doing this. A thrill ran through him; he'd traded one failed internship for another, better opportunity. If he aced this, he'd be a shoo-in for Harvard. He tapped in a text message.

Samir: You'll never guess where I am

Ashish: On a blimp in Nauru. In Ariana Grande's car. Eating breakfast in bed with Elon Musk's cats

Samir: Why can you never answer that question like a normal person

Ashish: Okay sorry where are you

Samir: Going to Pinky's lake house

Ashish: What? She asked you?

Samir: Dude get this. She asked me to be her FAKE BF for the summer and if I do it she's going to get me an internship with her mom aka VEENA KUMAR

Ashish: I have so many questions

Samir: I know but it's gonna be great. Harvard ducking Law, here I come

Frowning, Samir added, **Stupid autocorrect**

Ashish: Okay man if you're sure. Just don't get on Pinky's mom's bad side. She's kind of scary like her nickname in court is legit The Shark

Samir: No kidding dude I've read articles about her and seen pics on the Internet

Ashish: Yeah well the Internet does not prepare you for the real thing

Samir: I packed my big-boy pants just wish me luck

Ashish: Luck and send me an update soon so I know you're still alive

Samir sent Ashish a *Jaws* GIF and then sat back. The Shark he could take. It was the Shark's daughter he was more concerned about.

It wasn't that Pinky wasn't nice. In fact, she was kind of mysterious and intriguing in the spiky, murdery way the Black Widow was mysterious and intriguing. Anytime you were near her, you got the distinct feeling that she might get the sudden urge to use your face for target practice or rip out your eyeballs to make a necklace or something. She was unpredictable and fairly rude and he didn't get her at all. Also, Pinky had never made a secret of the fact that she thought Samir was an overgrown man-child with fewer nuts than a squirrel on a glacier.

So basically, Samir was about to walk, willfully, into a viper's pit.

CHAPTER 4

Pinky

Pinky hissed.

She'd brushed her teeth with so much vigor (brought on by nervous energy), she'd accidentally poked herself in the gum. Rinsing her mouth out and putting her toothbrush back in the holder, she stared at herself in the mirror, noting the slightly wild-eyed expression on her face.

She was really doing this? She was really doing this.

It was nine thirty a.m. and she was awake and ready for the day; that definitely pointed to some major shenanigans. She could hear her parents downstairs; her stomach roiled with expectation and anxiety and excitement. As of this very moment, Samir was in Dulles International Airport in Washington, DC, buying a ticket to head here, to Ellingsworth Point and Pinky's lake house. She'd offered to buy the ticket for him, but he'd been very insistent that he wouldn't take her money. Probably because he was so old-school and chivalrous that the thought of taking a girl's money made him wilt. She frowned at her reflection at the thought. Whatever. It wasn't like he was her *real* boyfriend. He could be as provincial as he wanted.

"What am I going to tell Mom?" Pinky wondered aloud, pushing some pomade through her hair, separating all the different colored chunks. Slipping out of her pj's and into her tank top and shorts, she decided it didn't matter. She'd always been good at improv; she'd just say whatever came naturally in the moment. Samir, of course, was the exact opposite. He'd probably need to read lines with her for two hours beforehand or something. But she could handle him.

Pinky strode out of her room and glanced at Dolly's door. Closed, which meant Dolly was still asleep, which was definitely weird. She remembered Dolly telling her last night during the chaos of the fire and her mom's accusations that she'd "fix it." What the hell did that mean? Pinky planned on figuring out exactly what was going on.

She headed downstairs to get some breakfast and caught sight of her dad and Dolly's dad watching some game on TV in the den. She didn't say hello on her way to the kitchen. She wanted to talk to her mom first, before she talked to any other adult. She had to tell her about Samir.

As Pinky neared the kitchen, she heard Meera Mausi saying something in soft, urgent tones. Urgent usually meant it had something to do with her. Pinky lingered outside the doorway, out of their line of sight, listening.

"Are you sure?" Pinky's mom said, her voice drenched in disbelief. "It sounds to me like Dolly's taking the fall for Pinky."

"Oh, I'm sure," Meera Mausi said. "Dolly made a very bad decision. She was clear about that."

"So she confessed of her own volition? Without you asking her to?"

"Yes. I think it was too painful for Dolly to see Pinky getting in trouble for something Dolly did. She'll apologize to everybody once she wakes up. I'm so sorry, Veena. I'm not sure what got into her, but needless to say, I'm going to get to the bottom of it."

Wait. Were they talking about the fire? Had *Dolly* burned down the barn?? Holy crap. But why? Pinky leaned in closer, her pulse racing.

"She's such a good kid." What? *What?* Her cousin had freaking set fire to the entire property and her mom was calling her a "good kid"? And let's not forget she'd pretty much burned Pinky at the stake (pun intended) for the same crime. Pinky glared at the wall, as if her mom might feel the heat of her disapproval through the drywall and wood.

"Don't give Pinky the short end of the stick," Meera Mausi said. "I don't know why you're so hard on her. Especially after your own pa—"

"That's *precisely* why I'm hard on her," her mom said, her voice sharp. "Don't you see? She's going to make the same mistakes."

Mistakes? What mistakes? Pinky tried to beam mind-control waves at her mom. *Speak about your mistakes. Be clear and transparent.*

Meera Mausi sighed. "Should we make *kheer* for dessert today?"

Noooo! They were just going to move on? Pinky waited a moment or two, but nope, they were definitely moving on.

Pinky backed up a few steps and then walked casually into the kitchen, whistling. Both Meera Mausi and her mom were sitting at a table. Meera Mausi wore leggings and an athletic tank, but her mom wore neatly pressed khaki pants and a pearl-buttoned cardigan. Khaki pants. *Pearl* buttons. On vacation.

"Good morning, Meera Mausi," Pinky said, going to the cabinet to get a bowl for her cereal. Then, tossing her mom a withering glance: "Mother."

Her mom sighed. "Pinky, there's something we need to talk to you about." Pinky turned around and leaned against the counter, watching the glances her aunt and mom were exchanging. How could two people who looked so alike—same long black hair, same big brown eyes, nearly the exact same skin tone—be so different?

Her mom nodded slightly, and then Meera Mausi said, "Pinky *beta*, I'm so sorry, but Dolly was the one who accidentally set the barn on fire. She feels terrible that you were the one who was accused"—here Pinky darted a sharp glance at her mother, but her mom was looking at Meera Mausi—"and she'll tell you all about it when she wakes up. We were up very late talking about everything, but Dolly was insistent that she got to apologize to you."

"Really?" Pinky said, folding her arms slowly and looking at her mother. "I would be happy to hear Dolly out. But I don't think she's the only one who owes me an apology."

After a pause, Meera Mausi stood. "I'm going to go see what the men are up to." She smiled at Pinky, patted her mom on the shoulder, and walked off.

Pinky's mom folded her hands neatly on the table and looked Pinky right in the eye. "I'm sorry," she said.

Pinky raised an eyebrow and waited.

"For accusing you of something you hadn't done in this instance."

Pinky frowned. "That's not a real apology!"

Her mom continued to study her with an infuriating calmness she probably used in her multimillion-dollar negotiations. "What would you consider a real apology?"

Pinky threw her hands up in the air. "How about 'I'm sorry for defaming your character with absolutely no evidence'? How about 'I should never have even uttered the words I did last night without being completely sure of what I was saying'? How about 'I judged you and condemned you for absolutely no reason'?" Pinky's voice had risen with every question until she was aware she was almost shouting. She took a deep breath.

Her mom remained aggravatingly unruffled, like always. Was she capable of any feeling besides intense disappointment? "I understand that you're upset," she said, a phrase that sounded suspiciously borrowed from Meera Mausi. "But, Pinky, can you blame me?"

"What?"

"Can you blame me?" her mom asked again, lifting her hands. "You know what they say. Past behavior is the best predictor of future behavior. Would you say you've given us a reason to believe it *wasn't* you? Can you honestly say that?"

Pinky opened her mouth to bite out a response, then closed it again. "I . . ."

Her mom pushed her chair back and stood. "I didn't think so. I told you. If you continue to make weak decisions—"

Arrgh! How could she be so casually condescending? So coolly judgmental? She was just so sure Pinky was a giant walking catastrophe, wasn't she? "But I've made a great decision! I have a boyfriend! One even *you'd* approve of," she couldn't help but add.

Her mom looked up and folded her arms neatly across her chest. "You said that yesterday."

The 'but' was hanging in the air, waving in the breeze. "But?"

Her mom took a deep breath. "But . . . I'm not sure I believe that. You've not said a word about this boyfriend, and if he is as good as you say he is, why haven't you? The only boyfriends you ever hide are the ones who have a history of shoplifting hubcaps."

Pinky felt her cheeks flame. "That was one time! And it was, like, two hubcaps!"

Her mom raised her eyebrows.

"A-and anyway," Pinky continued, not willing to be deterred. "He *is* real. In fact, he's coming to stay with us for a bit. So you can all meet him."

Her mom's arms dropped. Ha ha ha. That's right. *Now* she was listening. "What?"

"Hmm?" Pinky examined her glitter-painted nails. "Oh, yeah. I invited him here, so you could all meet him. I mean, since you clearly didn't believe me about setting fire to the place and everything and you were *obviously wrong*. I decided it was time for you guys to meet him. So you can finally believe something I say."

"I see," her mom said, looking completely stunned. "So . . . when's he coming?"

"Later today. He had a really prestigious internship at a DC law firm lined up, but it fell through."

Her mom's eyes widened, as Pinky had known they would do. So *that's* what her mom looked like when she was impressed. "A law firm in DC?"

"Mm-hmm." Pinky smiled innocently. "It's okay that I invited him here, right?"

"Yes, of course," her mom said, looking and sounding completely dazed, like she was one of those cartoon characters with birds flying around their heads in a slow circle. "That . . . that's fine. What's his name?"

"Samir Jha," Pinky said. "Oh, and did I tell you? He's planning to go to Harvard next year." She grabbed her cereal and poured it into her bowl, whistling again.

Pinky walked outside after finishing her breakfast. For the first time in a *long* time, she felt . . . not exactly happy, but smug. Like she finally had the upper hand.

She kicked a pinecone out of the way as she headed out of the backyard, down a small path, and into the forest that bordered their property on the west side. Why couldn't her mom just have believed her about the barn? And okay, she had a point that Pinky hadn't really given them a reason to believe her . . . but at least she could've been more conciliatory! If she had sincerely apologized to Pinky, maybe said something along the lines of, *I don't know how I ever doubted you, my darling girl*, Pinky would've totally forgiven her dramatic outburst the night before.

The sun beat down on her shoulders through gaps in the trees. It was hotter than usual in Ellingsworth this time of year, and Pinky was glad she was dressed in a tank top and shorts. She looked around at the forest, at the spruces and the horse chestnuts and the oak trees that had all sprung up out of the ground, unfettered by human meddling.

Pinky stopped walking for a moment and took a deep breath, inhaling the smell of sun-warmed bark and pine needles and grass. A songbird chirped questioningly at her from a branch above. Pinky smiled; she loved this place. In spite of all the drama of the past two days, this felt like home. When she was here, she knew everything was going to be okay. It was peaceful. Nothing could go wrong.

Someone grabbed her by the shoulder.

Pinky let out a scream that could make mighty mountains cower and swung around, her hands out in a karate pose she saw in a Batgirl movie once.

"Just me," Dolly said, her eyes wide. Her hair was in two braids, which made her look innocent and sweet. Pinky was pretty sure she herself had never looked that innocent and sweet, probably not even on the day she was born. "Sorry."

Pinky let her hands drop. "You're lucky I didn't chop you in half."

"Yeah." Dolly smoothed down her dragonfly-print sundress. "Hey, I came out here to find you and . . . apologize."

"Oh yeah?" Pinky began walking again, and Dolly stepped in beside her. She ran her hand along the trunks of the trees they passed, but every sense was attuned to Dolly.

"I know my mom must've told you, but uh, it was me. I was the reason the barn caught on fire. I'm sorry for that—I know we both loved that barn—and I'm also sorry that your mom blamed you. And I'm sorry for being reckless."

Pinky raised an eyebrow and looked at her cousin. "That's a lot of apologizing."

Dolly shrugged. Her shoulders were already turning pink from the sun. "Well, that was a lot of unthinking irresponsibility. I should never have done that."

"Wait." Pinky stopped, frowning. "So you just went into the barn and set it on fire?" Was her flawless cousin some kind of closet arsonist who'd totally fooled everyone?

"No, of course not." Dolly bent down and picked up a skinny stick. Twirling it in her hands, she said, after a pause, "I didn't tell

58

my parents this part, but I . . . I was in there with a boy. We lit the lanterns and I guess one of them got knocked over when we left. I thought we'd put all of them out, but maybe there was still a small flame or something—"

"Whoa, whoa. Go back to the boy part," Pinky said. What?? Dolly with a boy? Being all out of control and stuff? "Who was it?"

Dolly's cheeks stained a bright red. "Um . . ." She poked the stick into her thigh gently. "Cash Miller." And then she began walking again.

Pinky stood there astounded, watching Dolly walk away, her bright-pink Vans crunching on the stiff pine needles. Then, rushing to catch up, she said, "Are you kidding? You were in the barn hooking up with Cash Miller? That douche canoe from across the lake?"

Dolly winced. "I know. It was awful. He brought beer, which I expressly forbade him to do, and then the entire time we were together, he kept talking about his boat and his car and his Jet Skis. . . . It was like he was trying to get me to say how great he was. Talk about a hollow self-concept. And he wasn't even a good kisser."

"You know, none of that surprises me. Well, I don't really know what a self-concept is, but all that other stuff you said." Pinky glanced at her cousin. "So, um, if he's so awful . . . why did you go to the barn with him?" Dolly had once told her, a long time ago, that therapists stayed away from "why" questions because they could be construed as judgmental. Maybe she should rephrase. "Um, I mean, you don't usually date people like him, so what got into you, dude?" Crap. "What I'm trying to say is, you usually have good taste and even *I* could tell Cash Miller sucks." None of this was coming out right. "Let me try that again—"

Dolly gave her a small smile. "It's okay. I got it. And you're totally right. It was a huge lapse in judgment."

"Right," Pinky said as they passed a fragrant false indigo bush. A line of sweat trickled down the center of her back. She wanted to go inside, but this was just too good. "But, like, *why*?"

Dolly looked at Pinky for a long moment. "What one word would you use to describe me?"

Pinky wanted to get back to Cash, but she played along. "Um . . . perfect?"

Dolly shook her head. "What you mean is 'predictable.' Or 'boring.'"

"That's not true—" Pinky began, but Dolly cut her off.

"It *is* true. Everyone thinks they know me, you know? Like, take my parents, for instance. Their expectation for me is that I'll make As. They never pressure me—don't get me wrong—but if I get a B, they get all therapisty and say things like, 'Test anxiety is very common, Dolly. Let's work together on some coping skills for next time.' They don't even *think* that maybe I just didn't study! Like, maybe I got distracted and watched *Riverdale* all night instead. And you know what Richard said to me when he went off to the Peace Corps and we broke up?"

Pinky shook her head, too flabbergasted by what was being said to speak.

"He said, 'In a couple of years this'll be you.' Can you believe that?"

Pinky stared at her. "How . . . horrible of him to think that about you?" Was implying someone would join the Peace Corps an insult she didn't know about?

"It's not horrible, Pinky. It just delineates how monotonous a person I am! Everyone forecasts what I'm going to do before I even do it! I *had* been thinking about joining the Peace Corps!" Dolly looked more distressed than Pinky had ever seen her. Her hair was sticking to her neck, her skin was splotchy, and she didn't seem to notice that sweat was running down her face.

Pinky stepped closer to her. "But . . . what's wrong with that? All the things people think about you are *good*! My own mother thinks I'm capable of burning down a barn in cold blood."

"At least people think you have a mind of your own. You're out there, living your life, being totally independent. You're an *artist*, Pinky. You make people sit up and take notice. I blend in. I'm like—like boring old burlap and you're a duochrome, ombre, brilliant rainbow." Dolly stopped abruptly and sat down on a tree stump. After a moment, Pinky joined her, sitting cross-legged on the ground.

She bumped Dolly's foot with hers. "You're not boring."

Dolly glanced at her and then away. "Yeah, right."

Pinky laughed a little. "You know what's funny? Every time I'm around you I have, like, this low-level anxiety. Everyone thinks you're so perfect. Everyone's always fawning about your accomplishments and all the amazing things you've ever done and how you're going to save the world one day. And I just sit there like some pierced miscreant bent on destruction."

"That's not at all how I see you," Dolly said vehemently, putting her hand on Pinky's.

"That's what I'm trying to say, though. We're both ogling each other's grass, thinking it looks green and beautiful. It's ridiculous."

Dolly smiled a little. "Yeah, I guess so."

"I'd still rather my mom looked at me like she looks at you," Pinky said. "Since we're being honest and all."

"Your mom loves you," Dolly said, looking right into Pinky's eyes.

"Mm-hmm, sure. Maybe because she has to. But if she had a chance, I bet she'd trade places with Meera Mausi. And say what you want about being boring or predictable, but your mom sure as heck wouldn't trade places with mine." Pinky looked away, the smirk slipping off her face. Saying it all out loud like that *hurt*.

Dolly got off the tree stump and put her arms around Pinky. "I'm sorry," she whispered. "I acted like a total tool because I was trying to prove something. I'm really sad our barn is gone."

"It's okay." Pinky patted her back. "Maybe we can put a new one up this summer."

Dolly sat back on her tree stump, laughing. "You're always looking for a project."

"So, are you going to tell Cash it's over?" Pinky picked up a dried leaf off the ground and crumbled it to dust between her fingers.

Dolly sighed. "I already did. I texted him earlier and he just left me on read. Like you said. A total . . . douche canoe."

"Jerk," Pinky said. Then, straightening her back and taking a breath, "Oh, by the way, I invited someone here, to the lake house. He'll be here later today."

Dolly raised an eyebrow. "He? Who is it?"

"My boyfriend," Pinky said, feeling a little bad about lying to her cousin after the heart-to-heart they'd just had. But Dolly was a notoriously terrible liar. Once, when they were little, Pinky had stolen two ice cream sandwiches from the deep freezer in the garage and told Dolly not to tell. They'd eaten them and gone back inside, and the first thing seven-year-old Dolly blurted out was, "We didn't eat any ice cream sandwiches."

"What?" Dolly said, her eyes lighting up. "Who is it? Why didn't you tell me?"

"Well, we were kind of keeping things quiet, you know, not wanting to say anything until we knew it was going somewhere." Pinky looked over her shoulder at the woods as she spoke, hoping Dolly wouldn't notice her inability to make eye contact. Hmm. Maybe Dolly wasn't the only bad liar in the family. "Um, anyway, his internship in DC fell through and he didn't want to go home yet, so I invited him here. His name's Samir Jha."

"Wait, wait, is this the same Samir you told me about in the spring? The one whose mom is a little overprotective?"

"A lot overprotective, yeah," Pinky said.

"Oh," Dolly said thoughtfully. "I got the impression you found him kind of irritating."

Pinky felt herself begin to sweat even more, as if that were possible. "Oh yeah, no, I did. But, um, things kind of changed. We've only been dating, like, a month, so."

Dolly frowned a little. Pinky's heart thumped. If Dolly, the most trusting and innocent person in the world, wouldn't buy this, she had no hope of making her mom buy it. But then Dolly's face broke into a smile. "I'm happy for you," she said, and Pinky could tell she meant it. "I can't wait to meet your boyfriend."

Yeah, me too, Pinky thought. She stood up, dusted off her shorts, and held out a hand to her cousin. "Let's go home. I sweated out all the salt in my body and now I'm dangerously close to death."

Laughing, Dolly took her hand and let herself be pulled up.

They walked back toward the house, their clothes damp and sticking to them. "Wonder what the parental units are going to be like when we get back," Pinky said. "You think they're going to be walking on eggshells around their strange teenage daughters?"

Dolly sighed. "Either that or my parents are going to want to find me a therapist, stat."

Pinky snorted. "Yeah, that sounds about ri—"

Dolly let out a high-pitched shriek that rang in Pinky's ears.

"What?" she said, half-concerned, half-annoyed.

"I almost stepped on that rat!" Dolly said, pointing to a spot just off the path. "Is it—is it dead?"

Pinky looked and saw that it wasn't a rat at all. It was a small, furry gray opossum, probably still a baby. It lay on its side, very still, its mouth and eyes open. Everything about it was extremely limp. A greenish substance was leaking out of its mouth.

"Oh God," Dolly said, clapping a hand over her mouth. "Do you think it got poisoned or something?"

"No obvious injuries," Pinky said, looking it over quickly. "So maybe."

"Where's its mom?" Dolly looked around jumpily, like the opossum's mom might be hiding behind a bush, waiting to charge them.

Pinky knelt next to the little thing, frowning. "It's probably weaned. Look how big it is. Remember when I helped establish that raccoon hospital back in Cali? Raccoons only nurse for about three months, and I remember reading possums were the same. This one doesn't look older than six months or so. Oh, and look—its little paw is injured." Something struck her as she studied its face. "Wait. What if . . . ? What if it's not dead?"

"Um . . ." There was a pause and then Dolly knelt beside her and rubbed her shoulder. "I know it's hard to accept, but it's dead. I mean, just look at it." She paused. "You always did have such a soft spot for animals." Dolly smiled one of her gentle, Mother Teresa smiles.

Pinky rolled her eyes. "I mean it might not be actually dead because opossums *play* dead. Sometimes for hours. It might have gotten stressed out and then decided to faint or whatever."

"Are you sure?" Dolly asked. "I mean . . . look at that stuff coming out of its mouth." She shuddered audibly. "Maybe we should just leave it. Or we can come back with a shovel and bury it."

"We can't leave it here for predators to find! Or to die from the heat!" Pinky said. Then, making an executive decision: "I'm taking it home." She reached out to pick it up.

Dolly shrieked. "It could have fleas!" she said, aghast, like fleas might be the gateway insect to the Black Plague or something. Oh, right. They actually were. "Or rabies!"

Annoyed because Dolly might actually have a point, Pinky pulled out her phone. Ten seconds later, she said, "Nope, possums don't get rabies." With that, she picked up the possum and cradled it in her hands as she began walking toward the lake house. When she realized she didn't hear any footsteps, she turned to find Dolly rooted to the spot. "Come on," she called. "What're you waiting for?"

That prodded Dolly to action. "Are your parents going to be okay with that?" her cousin asked, eyeing the limp possum as if it might suddenly make like a rattlesnake and strike.

"Who says I'm going to tell them?" Pinky asked. There was a snorting kind of noise from Dolly's general direction. "You can pretend you didn't see this if you want," Pinky added. "That way if I get caught, you can just tell them you had no idea."

"No way!" Dolly said, studying the possum a little dubiously. "We're in this together."

Pinky smiled, and Dolly smiled back. Maybe this was her way of making up for the whole barn fiasco. "Okay. Then we're going to need to make a nest."

Dolly's smile slipped off her face. "Right. A nest. Of course."

CHAPTER 5

Samir

The taxi pulled up to a ginormous Cape Cod–style, beachy-looking house with slate-blue siding, big windows, and two decks. It was immaculately kept, overlooked the water to its right—Ellingsworth Lake, according to Google—and was sheltered by huge horse chestnut trees. Honeysuckle vines tumbled over the backyard fence, and bees darted lazily in and out of the flowers, drunk on the heat and pollen.

"This it?" the taxi driver said, peering out through his windshield. "Fancy."

"I think so . . . ," Samir said, looking for cars parked in the driveway, but there were none. Maybe they parked in the garage. It was weird, but when he'd imagined Pinky's house, he didn't see this tasteful, well-designed structure. He'd kind of been expecting a yurt, to be honest. Or an environmentally friendly geodesic dome with a wildlife refuge out back or something. "Well, I guess I'll find out." He paid and got out, his hand slightly sweaty around the handle of his suitcase.

He heard the taxi's tires crunching over the gravel as the driver turned around and sped away, and stood still for a minute, listening to the birds calling in the trees. Across the water, someone started up a Jet Ski. Samir walked around the corner of the house, pausing by a Japanese maple. In the far distance, he could see a red-and-white striped lighthouse towering over the island. As if he couldn't tell he was near the beach from the way his hair was puffing up in the humid air. There was no denying it: He was really here.

Well, if this was indeed Pinky's summer house, he was really here.

Suddenly, Samir was sure this was a giant mistake. Maybe he should just go home and stay with his mom. What did he know, exactly, about fake dating anyone? He'd never lied about anything major his entire life. Well, except that one time when he told his mom a bird had flown in the window and eaten the entire cake she'd baked and was letting cool on the counter. But that didn't count; he was, like, seven or eight. What made him think he could handle lying to a couple of lawyers? Especially when one of them was the Shark?

Bad idea. Very, very bad idea. Samir turned around, starting to head back down the drive. Where was that taxi dude? Maybe if he walked quickly, he could catch up to him at that little cross street—

"Yo." Something hit him on the head and bounced into a nearby rhododendron bush. He turned to see Pinky on the second-floor deck, squinting in the sun as she looked down at him, her elbows resting on the banister. She wore a blue tank top and bright pink shorts, her long brown legs ending in bare feet. And she'd rubbed lotion on them or something, because there was the slightest shimmer to her bronze skin—

"Getting a good look?"

Samir's eyes snapped up to Pinky's, and he felt a slow, hot flush creep up his neck and envelop his face. "Huh, uh, who?"

She raised an eyebrow. "Mm-hmm. Where are you going anyway?"

Samir felt his head with his free hand. It stung, he realized, somewhat belatedly. "Wait. Did you *throw* something at me?"

"It was just a baby carrot. Relax," Pinky said. "Seriously, where the hell are you going?"

"Yeah, it's nice to see you, too. And you're welcome. You know, for coming all the way from DC to participate in your little deception—"

"Shh!" She put a finger to her lips and glanced behind her. Turning to face him again, she said, sotto voce, "Come around the side and I'll meet you at the backyard gate."

Samir finger combed his hair quickly and walked around the side of the house. The honeysuckle smell got stronger, and he noticed with consternation that there were quite a lot of bees humming busily around the white flowers. "Um . . ." Samir reached out for the gate and then pulled back, not wanting to anger the tiny terrors.

The gate swung open and Pinky stood before him, still barefoot. She was nearly as tall as him, even without shoes on. "Hey." She looked him up and down slowly. "Nice."

He felts his cheeks getting warm again. "Oh, thanks. You look nice too."

Pinky rolled her eyes. Her eyebrow ring—a new addition; he hadn't seen it yet—sparkled in the sun. Her bangs were all wavy on her forehead. "No, I mean you look exactly like the kind of guy my parents keep harping on me to date."

Samir glanced down at his button-down shirt, which was tucked into his dark slacks—the sleeves rolled up—and his black shoes. His tie was slightly askew and he adjusted it. He didn't normally wear ties, let alone expensive, designer silk ties, to visit friends, but he'd wanted to impress Veena Kumar with his maturity. "What kind of guy is that? Levelheaded? Sensible? Going places?"

Pinky turned around and walked into the yard, and he followed. "Prudish. Traditional. Pruditional."

"I am *not* pruditional!"

"Mm-hmm. Nice cuff links."

"My sleeves are rolled up!"

"Did you or did you not have cuff links on at some point this week, though?"

"Okay, but I took them out. Besides, it was just for the first day of my internship! I have other clothes in here. *Weekend* clothes."

Pinky glanced at him as they walked to a small gazebo, tucked into a corner, away from the watchful windows of the house. The sun sizzled on the crown of Samir's head. "Oh yeah? What are those? Wait, let me guess. Polo shirts, khaki pants. Loafers?"

"No," Samir said. After a pause, he added in a half mumble, "They're khaki *shorts*." Annoyed, he added, "What about you? Did you fall into a vat of melted Jolly Ranchers, or is that something you paid someone to do to your hair?"

Pinky scoffed. "Nice comeback. For a third grader." Then she climbed the steps into the gazebo. It smelled of wood and plants and sun, like summer was supposed to smell. Once they were both inside, she turned to face Samir. "Look, like I said, that's totally fine with me. The entire point of this whole thing is for you to impress my parents."

Samir set his suitcase down and then did a double take. Squinting past her at the far corner of the yard, he said, "What the hell?"

She turned to look over her shoulder. "Oh yeah. That."

Samir walked toward the railing around the gazebo and leaned forward. "Did you have a fire?"

"Yeah . . . that was kind of the catalyst for you to be here."

Samir spun around to face her. She wasn't quite meeting his eye. "You didn't say anything about a fire! Did *you* set the fire? What am I, your patsy? Listen, Pinky Kumar, I am *not* going down for arson—not for you, not for anyone."

"Oh my God, will you relax?" Pinky stared at him. "I forgot how uptight you are. And who says 'patsy' in real life anyway?"

Samir narrowed his eyes. "Tell me about the fire."

"All right, all right. My mom thought I'd set the fire and basically called me an arsonist. Well, I'm not. I didn't set it, okay? Turns out D—someone else did it. But naturally, my mom immediately suspected me. Because hello, who else would do something as messed up as that, right?" She laughed, but the laugh was tinged with some real anger. Samir kept silent. "Anyway, then she said something about how I'd never had a boyfriend she approved of or something and I found myself telling her you were my boyfriend. So." She shrugged. "Don't worry." Pinky rolled her eyes. "No one's going to think you're an arsonist, Mr. Khaki Shorts. They already know who did it."

Samir relaxed a bit and leaned back against the gazebo's narrow wooden pillar. "The entire reason I'm here is so you can show them you're capable of dating someone they'd approve of? So they think you're, what, a decent, upstanding citizen incapable of arson?"

71

Pinky glared at him. "I *am* a decent, upstanding citizen incapable of arson."

Samir's shirt was sticking to his back in the sweltering heat in this enclosed space and he was getting kind of annoyed. "Are you always so defensive?"

"Are you always so annoying?"

Samir crossed his arms. "You know, I can just call a cab and head back to the airport. I don't need this."

"Oh yeah? Head back where? To your nonexistent internship?"

They stared at each other. Out on the lake, there was a big splash and some dude *whoop*ed. "Fine," Samir said finally. "I do need this. But so do you. So can we at least try to get along?"

Pinky smirked. A bird warbled in the trees, sweet and sad, in direct contrast to this baby shark he was stuck with in the gazebo. "What do you think this is, kindergarten? We don't need to get along in the sandbox, Samir. Stay out of my way and I'll stay out of yours."

Samir blinked. Whoa. "Wow. Okay."

Sighing, Pinky ran a hand along the back of her neck. "Look," she said, shrugging, "I just want my parents to like you and to see me as something other than a delinquent."

Interesting. And why did that seem to get under her skin so much? But whatever. He wasn't her therapist. Samir held up his hands. "Hey, that works for me. So what are the ground rules for this thing?"

Pinky frowned and leaned against the handrail. It seemed she had only three expressions: smirk like a jerk, frown in disdain, or glare with intent to maim. "What do you mean? You have to pretend to be my boyfriend. Why do we need rules?"

"Well," Samir said, wiping a trickle of sweat off his forehead. He glanced nervously at the house looming behind Pinky, hoping no one in her family would choose this moment to step outside and see what she was up to. "We'll need to get our stories straight. For instance, how long have we been dating? Where did we meet? Who asked who out? What was our first date like? Is it okay for me to hold your hand?" He raised an eyebrow. "Kiss you?"

Taking a step back from him, Pinky looked outraged. "You wish!"

Samir laughed.

"What?" she asked.

"Your self-confidence never ceases to amaze me," he said, still chuckling. "Anyway. Have you thought any of that out?"

Pinky regarded him pensively, drumming her sparkly polish-doused fingers on the railing. Of course she used sparkly polish. Nothing about Pinky was ever plain. Or easy. "No, but it's just like making a Sims character, right? How hard can it be? Okay, so to answer your first question, we've been dating a month. That's why I haven't told anyone. I wanted to make sure it was going somewhere. We met at Ashish's place and you asked me out. I was really skeptical at first, but I said yes because I felt sorry for you."

"Really?"

Her fingers stilling, she made some extremely challenging eye contact. "Really. This is my plan. I get to say what goes."

Samir sighed, shook his head, and sat on the almost painfully warm wooden seat running around the interior of the gazebo. "All right, whatever. Keep going."

Apparently satisfied, Pinky took a seat opposite him and continued. "Our first date was at . . . a restaurant. That fancy seafood place Ashish likes so much. What's it called?"

"Poseidon?"

"Yeah, that one."

Samir scratched his jaw and tapped his foot on the wooden boards beneath him. "Huh."

"Problem?"

Shrugging, Samir said, "It's just that I don't think I'd be that unimaginative. I mean, I'd take you somewhere really memorable on our first date, not to a seafood restaurant my friend likes. Plus, I don't really like shellfish."

"Really." Pinky raised an eyebrow. "And where would *you* take me?"

Samir considered her, his head cocked. "Somewhere that fits your vibe. Like a cool underground art showing by an avant-garde artist no one's heard of yet. Or, like, a guided tour of the city's best graffiti or something." He laughed. "I know those sound kind of pathetic, but that's all I could come up with on the spot."

Pinky was staring at him.

Samir frowned, narrowing his eyes. "Or maybe I'd take you to a circus. What? My ideas not cool enough for you?"

She blinked and looked away, out toward the burned barn. "Nothing. You're right. Those are, um . . . Anyway, this is fiction. It doesn't matter where we'd really go on a first date."

"Sorry, sorry. I thought we wanted this to be believable. Continue."

She turned back to him. "So, as for the holding-hands stuff, let's just play it by ear, okay? If my parents warm up to you, it'd be okay to, like, take my hand on a walk or something. But absolutely no kissing." She paused and leaned forward on her seat, her shirt falling open just a bit, showing a hint of brown skin. "No matter how much you want to. None."

He looked away and leaned back against the railing behind him. "Please. It's not like I'm dying to kiss you. You've probably got a poisonous film on you, anyway. To repel humans."

Pinky rolled her eyes. "Anyway, my cousin Dolly and her parents are here too. So, are you ready to go in and meet everyone?"

"Yeah," Samir said, standing and grabbing his suitcase. "Before I melt would be nice."

"Get used to the heat," Pinky said, flashing him a fake sweet smile. It transformed her face to something cherubic. How disturbing. "There's a record-breaking heat wave on the Cape this summer, and you just signed up to wallow in it for the next six weeks."

Pinky

Pinky kept darting sidelong glances at Samir as they climbed the stairs to the house. He was effortlessly carrying what looked like a very heavy suitcase. It was taking her aback, how . . . grown-up he looked in his business attire. The tie complemented his brown eyes, and that button-down shirt strained just slightly against his biceps and shoulders. "Handsome" was the word some other people might use, but not her. She just thought he looked sort of nice in a super-boring, overly starched way. If she went for that kind of thing, she might think he looked dashing. Thank Kali she had more sense than that.

"Wait," he said, trailing after her. "What do I call your parents? Uncle and Auntie?"

"Yeah, or Mr. Yeung and Ms. Kumar—whatever floats your boat. Definitely don't call them Howard and Veena, though; they reeeally don't like that."

Behind her, Samir made a soft gasping sound. "I would never do that."

Pinky laughed. "You're hilarious."

"I'm glad I could amuse you." But the way he said it, it was clear he wasn't glad at all.

Pinky opened the sliding glass doors on the deck. "After you," she said, sweeping her hand through the air. "And good luck."

He mumbled something like, "Yeah, I'm gonna need it," and then stepped over the threshold into the cool air inside, his fist tight around his suitcase handle.

Pinky pointed him toward the dining room, but then, unable to contain her excitement, elbowed him out of the way and entered first. Her entire body was simmering with energy, effervescent bubbles of anticipation popping in her stomach. Hells to the yes, she was ready for this. *This* would show her mom. Now she'd see she'd been totally wrong to judge Pinky so quickly and harshly and then not even be sorry about it.

"Everyone!" she said, clapping her hands. They were all in the dining room/kitchen area, Abe and her dad getting vegetables together for what was probably going to be a salad and her mom and Meera Mausi sitting at the table with Dolly, all three of them sipping iced tea. A pitcher of the stuff sat sweating on the table. "I have someone I want you all to meet!"

They all looked expectantly at her. Relishing the moment, Pinky smiled and stepped aside, allowing Samir to enter. He walked in, set his suitcase down, and immediately smiled a congenial, I'm-so-polite-I-help-old-ladies-with-groceries-in-my-free-time-and-you-can't-help-but-immediately-like-me smile. Already he was lapping all her other boyfriends.

"Hello, Uncle, Auntie," he said, looking at both sets of adults. "And you must be Dolly. I've heard so much about all of you." He held out a hand, and Dolly shook it, looking a little blindsided by his J.Crew good looks. "I'm Samir Jha. I hope it's not a terrible inconvenience that I'm here, but my internship for the summer fell through and—"

"And his mom's out of town, so I told him it'd be fine for him to come here," Pinky put in, looking around at her parents. "Mom, Dad, Samir is my *boyfriend*." She couldn't help but put a little emphasis on the word "boyfriend." *Be cool, Pinky,* she thought. She could feel her eyes sparkling in her head. This was so great. Look at their faces! They were completely surprised. She could practically hear the thoughts from the adults, clamoring for space:

Meera Mausi: *He's* her boyfriend??

Abe: But how?? And why??

Her mom and dad: Oh my God, she wasn't lying. She really does have a serious boyfriend who doesn't look fresh out of prison. Wait. How did she manage to trap such a good kid?

Her mom was the first to break out of her trance and speak. "Of course you can stay here, Samir," she said, now reaching her hand out to him. "Welcome. I'm Veena, Pinky's mom."

The adults went around, shaking his hand, looking at Samir as if he'd appeared from a glade of unicorns, holding a glowing specter. To his credit, Samir seemed completely unfazed. Cool under pressure. Good.

"So what internship was this?" Pinky's dad asked, gesturing to an empty chair at the table. "The one that fell through?"

"Ah, it was one in DC," Samir said, going over to the sink and washing his hands. "For the law firm Iyer and Whitman. If you don't mind, I'd rather help you with lunch. My mom taught me never to sit idly by while others work."

Ha. Ha ha ha. Pinky saw her dad and Abe exchanging flabbergasted looks. That's right, she thought. Get ready for a *lot* more flabbergasting over the summer.

"Iyer and Whitman?" Her mom set her glass of iced tea down, looking like she might keel over. "You were selected for a summer internship there? And you're a rising senior?"

"He was one of only three people out of hundreds of applicants," Pinky put in, not even caring how boastful she sounded. "He even beat out some first-year Columbia law students." She wasn't sure that was strictly true, and by the withering glare Samir was giving her, she was probably taking things too far. Shutting up, Pinky took the empty seat Samir had relinquished.

"But it fell through?" her mom asked. "What happened?"

"Oh, it was . . ." Samir looked at her frankly from the kitchen. "There was a last-minute change with one of the partners at the firm, but . . . I'm sorry. I can't talk about it. It's another person's story to tell, not mine."

Holy crap. He was good. He was really, really good. Pinky's mom looked like she might just gather him in a hug. "Ethics," she said instead, nodding approvingly. "Tell me, Samir, where do you hope to go to law school?"

"I've had a soft spot for Harvard since I was about nine years old and someone got me a Harvard Law T-shirt," he said, smiling as he put on a striped apron. "I'd love to do my undergrad and grad school there if it works out like that."

"That's my alma mater," Pinky's mom said, looking completely bowled over. "It's the best school you can hope to go to if you want to practice law."

"Hey, now, there's nothing wrong with NYU," Pinky's dad put in, grinning.

Samir laughed easily. "I'm sure not!" Turning to the men, he added, "So. What can I do?"

"Here's a knife," Abe said. "Can you cut those tomatoes?"

"Sure. Diced or julienned?"

Pinky basked in the looks of admiration that Samir earned as if it were all for her.

After lunch—Samir had made mini quiches for everyone; who even *was* that guy?—Pinky's mom smiled at her over her empty plate and the other detritus of a delicious meal. "Why don't you show Samir to his room? He can have the one next to Dad's and mine."

Putting Samir on the other side of them was a strategic decision, so her parents were sandwiched between Samir and her. You know, to cut down on romantic tête-à-têtes. Pinky felt her mouth twitch. The idea of Samir sneaking into her room or vice versa made her want to laugh hysterically. "Okay, Mom," she managed to say with a straight face.

"So you guys haven't said yet," Dolly said, beaming at them. She'd eaten three mini quiches; she was clearly also a Samir fan. "Where did you meet?"

"At Ashish's place," both Samir and Pinky said together, apparently each remembering word for word what they'd agreed to out in the gazebo. They glanced at each other, Pinky feeling a little nervous. Did that sound too rehearsed? No, come on, don't overreact. She just needed to add some little detail that'd make it feel seamless and believable. "At his Memorial Day weekend party in May," she added, right as Samir said, "A couple years ago when I stopped by to drop off a book. Pinky just happened to be there." They stared at each other, frozen.

"What?" Dolly said, smiling, but clearly a little confused.

Pinky heard herself giving off this really shrill, slightly frenzied noise meant to be a laugh. How could they already be messing up? How?? "Well," she said, taking Samir's hand and squeezing, maybe technically harder than she needed to. To his credit, he didn't even flinch. "Um, I guess we actually met when Samir was dropping off a book a couple years ago. But um, we agreed to start dating at the Memorial Day party this past May."

"Oh!" Dolly grinned. "That's so cute! So who asked who out?"

"I did," Pinky said, just as Samir said, "I asked her."

They froze again. The parents glanced at each other. Oh. My. God. Samir was ruining it. Maybe they should've spent a *little* more time practicing.

"We—we kind of asked each other out at the same time." Samir laughed. His palm was sweating in hers. "It was a really cute coincidence, you know, we . . ." He trailed off and took a sip of his water.

Pinky grinned idiotically at everyone, as if this were perfectly normal behavior.

"Well, you can certainly cook, Samir," her dad said, patting his stomach. Pinky wanted to launch herself across the table and hug him for changing the subject like that. "Where'd you learn?"

"Oh, my mom taught me," Samir said. "It's one of our hobbies, cooking together."

Pinky narrowed her eyes as the grown-ups (and Dolly) around her made *ooh*ing and *aah*ing noises. They hadn't caught the slight sadness tinting Samir's words. She wondered if his mom had taught him around the time she'd been diagnosed with cancer.

Her dad tipped his chair back. "Maybe you can teach Pinky a little," he continued, oblivious. "She burns water. At this rate, we're worried she's going to starve when she moves away to college next year!" He guffawed, his cheeks pink with glee.

"I know how to cook stuff!" Pinky said, offended. "I toast Pop-Tarts all the time!"

Samir stared at her, his mouth open.

"What?" Pinky asked, not able to keep the annoyed edge out of her voice. She ripped her hand out of his.

"Pop-Tarts?" Samir said incredulously. He folded his napkin neatly into a square and put it on the table. "That's not cooking. But come on. You know how to make . . . scrambled eggs, for instance, right?"

Dolly snorted and Pinky glared at her. Her cousin raised her hands, laughing. "Sorry. Just the idea of you in the kitchen, trying to scramble eggs . . ." She dissolved into laughter again.

"Okay!" Pinky said, flicking water from her glass at Dolly. "Time for us to go get you settled in. Come on, Samir."

Samir smiled at everyone. "Thanks again for welcoming me into your home on such short notice," he said, also scraping his chair back. "I really appreciate it."

Oh God. He was so wholesome, they should put a little heart-healthy sticker on him.

"Leave the door to your rooms open when you're in there!" her dad said, wagging a finger at them.

Pinky felt her cheeks get warm. "Oh God, Dad," she muttered, tugging on Samir's shirtsleeve and practically pulling him toward the stairs.

CHAPTER 6

Pinky

"So my room is this way," Pinky said, walking down the carpeted second-floor hallway, past the gallery wall of family pictures. The photo frames had been replaced just last year; they were now all made from sustainable, recycled Styrofoam waste. Her mom had been about to buy a set at Target, but Pinky had managed to convince her to invest in these instead. It was one of those rare moments when her mom actually saw her side and agreed with it; if Pinky could've framed *that*, she would've.

Opening the door to her room, she walked in. "Just in case you need anything."

"It's nice," Samir said, a little dubiously. As he set his suitcase down, his eyes took in the rose-hued walls (complete with a glitter border) and the lacy, bow-adorned curtains. "More Jojo Siwa than I expected, but . . ."

Pinky glowered at him. "That's a remnant from when I was ten. I need to repaint it at some point."

"Let me guess," Samir said, walking to her windows and peering out for a moment before turning back around. "You're going to paint it charred-heart black."

"Ha ha," Pinky said, walking over the furry white rug to her walk-in closet. She opened the door and knelt down, pulling out the little nest she and Dolly had made out of a cardboard box for the possum baby. "Hello, little one."

"What the *hell* is that?"

Pinky looked over her shoulder at Samir, who was staring at the possum like he'd never seen a marsupial in his life. "It's . . . a possum?"

Samir chuckled mirthlessly. "Right, of course. A closet opossum. You know, I read in *Architect* magazine that all the fancy houses come with those nowadays. What version do you have because mine's a 2.0." He walked forward and the possum fell over, its legs sticking straight out. "What!" He jumped back, like it had leaped out at him instead.

"Will you relax?" Pinky said, glaring at him. "Your negative energy is really messing with her. She's just playing dead. She has a tendency to do that."

"Right . . . and how long have you had it? Um, her?"

"Only a couple of hours. I found her this morning."

Samir leaped back again. "So it hasn't been tested for rabies."

"Possums can't get rabies!" Pinky said. "Why are you such a scaredy-cat?"

"Oh, I'm sorry I don't want to die at age seventeen from preventable and communicable diseases," Samir said. "What a coward."

Pinky shook her head and pushed the box back into the closet. The possum wasn't waking up anytime soon. "This could take several hours," she said. "I'll come back later with some snacks."

"Seriously, you need to take that thing to a vet. Get it some shots."

"I'm researching vets. We're keeping our options open." Taking an animal to a vet was a serious decision. First she needed to be sure the vet wouldn't just call animal control or something. It wasn't a decision she could rush into. Jeez.

She could tell Samir thought she had problems. But instead of listing out what they might be, he raised his hands in surrender and walked to the door to pick up his suitcase. "All right. Maybe just show me to my room, then."

"Fine," Pinky said, striding past him and back out into the hallway. Vet, vet, vet; could he seriously not say *any*thing else about the fact that she was rescuing a helpless animal? How could someone her age be *that* much of a boring, risk-averse adult? And he'd only been here about two hours. This was the most one-on-one time they'd had, and she was already beginning to rethink her whole summer fake-dating plan.

It was clear Samir was going to get the better end of this deal. The way, way better end.

Samir

Great. It was pretty obvious he was going to come out the loser at the end, when all was said and done. Was an internship with Veena Kumar really worth all *this*?

Samir glanced at Pinky as he followed her back down the family-picture-studded hallway to his room. There seemed to be a few pictures of a very chubby-cheeked Pinky when she was young. He didn't have time to study them, though. She was stomping quickly ahead of him, letting her annoyance at his sensible suggestions drive her. Jeez, did she have to be so caustic all the time? It was like she thought every single thing he said was ridiculous. Anyway, he just needed to keep his eye on the prize. He may be a husk of a man by the time the summer was done, but at least he'd have a totally sick internship with Veena Kumar. It was obvious that as much as Pinky hated him, her parents were just about ready to adopt him as their son, even the Shark. He side-eyed Pinky. He couldn't really blame them.

"Okay, this is your room," Pinky said, flinging open the door.

Samir walked in and looked around. It was a big, bright room, although not as big as Pinky's and much lower on the Jojo Siwa meter. He walked to the closet and peeked in. "Oh." He raised his eyebrows at Pinky. "No complimentary closet rodents?"

She smiled the fakest smile he'd ever seen. "Not right now, but I'll see what I can rustle up for you, sweetie pie."

Scoffing, Samir turned to examine the rest of the room. The walls were a soothing sea blue that matched the sky outside perfectly, with sand-dollar and seashell paintings and sculptures dotting them. The crisp, fresh covers on the bed had a nautical vibe too—navy and white stripes. Someone had left a window open; a balmy, lake-scented breeze blew in, fluttering the gauzy white curtains.

He set his suitcase down at the foot of the bed and took a deep breath. "This is nice. Thank you."

"Yeah, and you have your own bathroom," Pinky said, jabbing her thumb in the direction of a closed door in the far corner.

"So I think all of that went pretty well, don't you?" Samir said, since apparently she had no intention of thanking him in return. "I mean, I really won your parents over right away."

"Seriously?" Pinky put her hands on her hips. "You don't think forgetting when we met or who asked who out first were huge red flags?"

"Those were minor details," Samir said, unlacing his shoes, toeing them off, and then setting them neatly inside his reach-in closet. Turning back to her, he said, "I don't think anyone noticed."

Pinky's nostrils flared and she stepped forward, somehow kind of looming over him as he shrank back. "Are you serious? You don't think anyone *noticed*? Samir, maybe this is just about an internship to you, but this is my whole life we're talking about, okay? It's extremely important to me that we get it right!"

Oh, crap. This was it, wasn't it? She was about to go all Black Widow on him. Samir glanced longingly at the door, but it was too far away to make a break for it.

Pinky

Pinky couldn't *believe* his total cluelessness. "They were all staring at us!"

She walked closer to him so they were just a foot apart. The door was open, per her dad's "rules," and she didn't want to mess with that. They needed to see Samir as someone they could trust, and by association, *Pinky* as someone they could trust. "Why would you make up that convoluted thing about us meeting years ago when you dropped off a book, anyway? Just stick to the basics! We were both at the Memorial Day party in May. Why couldn't you just say that?"

"Because!" Samir said, throwing up his hands.

"Because why?" Pinky insisted. "It makes no sense."

"Yes, it does."

"No, it doesn't!"

Samir glared at her. "Yes, it does, because that *was* the first time I saw you."

"You—" Pinky stopped. A breeze from the open window blew a strand of purple hair in her eyes and she brushed it back. "What?"

"The first time we met was in seventh grade. I had ridden my bike over to drop a comic book off at Ashish's house, and you happened to be there." He rubbed a hand along his jaw, his slight stubble making a scratch-scratch noise.

Pinky felt like a slowly deflating balloon. "I don't remember that."

"Well, I do," Samir said. They looked at each other for a long moment, not speaking.

"Hey, Sam—oh!" Pinky's mom raised her eyebrows and looked between them, a big, fluffy stack of towels in her arms. "Am I interrupting?"

"What? No!" Pinky said, leaping away from Samir. Which, come to think of it, probably wasn't the best idea if the plan was to convince everyone they were madly in love. She tried to move back closer to him, but her feet wouldn't obey.

Samir, apparently thinking the same thing, stepped close to her and easily took one of her hands in his. "Of course not, Ms. Kumar. Please come in."

Pinky could smell his annoyingly preppy, J.Crew-worthy after-shave; he was that close. She forced her shoulders to relax. How was he so good at this, anyway? She knew for a fact that he'd never had a girlfriend, thanks to his Black Hawk helicoptery mom, and yet right then he was the one who was completely at ease and she was all bunched up like an anxiety-ridden accordion.

"I just wanted to make sure Samir had towels," her mom said, handing the stack over.

He untangled his warm hand from hers and took them. "Thank you."

"Mm-hmm. Do you think you'll be comfortable in this room?"

Samir smiled. "Yes, of course. It's beautiful!" He gestured out the window. "The lake is just stunning."

"Thank you. All the bedrooms have at least a partial view of the water." Pinky's mom smiled. "We should go paddleboating soon."

"That sounds great." Samir sounded like he meant it. Weirdo.

"Pinky, can your dad and I speak with you a moment?" Her mom turned to her, and although she was using that fake-casual voice she used when she tried to find out if there'd be drinking at the party Pinky was going to, Pinky could smell the agenda on her breath.

"Um, sure." She turned to Samir. "I'll be back soon."

"Sounds good." He raised his eyebrows, a secret message that probably meant *good luck*, and walked to the bathroom with his towels.

Pinky's mom led the way back to her and Pinky's dad's room. "So, I'm missing a yellow cardigan, and I wondered if you'd taken it by accident?"

Pinky frowned. "What?" A yellow cardigan? As if she'd ever take something like that even by mistake. She followed her mom into the master bedroom and shut the door behind them.

Her dad was sitting at a little table in the corner, reading a newspaper. Her mom went to join him.

"Oh." Pinky crossed her arms. "This is an ambush."

Her dad looked up over the top of his reading glasses. "What?"

"Relax. Dad didn't even know I asked you to come in here." Her mom crossed her legs neatly. "So. Samir."

Pinky shrugged, like, *Yeah? What about him?* But inside she was a ball of ice-cold anxiety. Was this where her mom said she didn't believe the story an iota and did Pinky think she, a Harvard-educated lawyer, was an idiot?

Her mom smiled. "I like him."

Pinky waited for a "but . . ." but there didn't seem to be one coming. She dropped her arms. "Seriously?"

"Oh yes, me too," her dad said, setting his newspaper down. "Much better than that fellow before Preston. What was his name? Cashew?"

"It was *Pistachio*." Pinky sighed.

"Right," her mother said, pinning her with her gaze. "'Pis' for short, as I recall."

"Anyway," Pinky said, eager to get off the subject. She walked farther into the big room and sat at the foot of the canopied bed, which was made up with peony-patterned sheets. "You like him, huh? You actually *like* one of my boyfriends." She savored each word as she said it, sure she would never be able to say them in that order again.

"We do," her mom agreed. "Good choice, Pinky."

Whoa. She actually looked like she meant it. Pinky felt a thrill go through her—this was what approval from her mom felt like?—quickly followed by a hollow thud of guilt. She was no stranger to deceiving her mom (wouldn't you deceive your captor if she forced you to live in a corset and you were more an Empire-waist kind of girl?), but this . . . this was on such a grand scale. Still, it was all for the best in the end. Samir would get his internship and she'd get the modicum of respect that she deserved if her parents finally began appreciating her accomplishments and decisions. "Okay, great. Well, I'm going to go make sure he's getting settled in."

"And tonight I'm making pork belly bao!" her dad put in. "Hope Samir brought his appetite."

Pinky smiled at the both of them and slipped out of the room, shutting the door behind her. Phase 1: infiltration, complete. She heaved a sigh and walked down the hallway to her room.

Samir

An hour and a half after Pinky left his room with her parents, Samir was all finished ironing and putting his clothes away (they were wrinkled from the suitcase, and he found ironing them before putting them away helped cut down the time he spent ironing before he wore them), taking a shower, and calling his mom for a quick check-in (*the internship's going well, I'm on a break, gotta go*). He walked down the hallway with the extra towels that wouldn't fit in the tiny linen closet in the bathroom and knocked on Pinky's door.

There was a scuffling sort of noise. "Who is it?" she called, sounding distracted.

"It's me. Um, Samir."

More scuffling. "Come in!"

He walked in. "Hey, your mom gave me too many towels. These don't fit in the linen closet—" He stopped, looking at the shoebox on the floor. Pinky sat cross-legged beside it. "It still hasn't woken up?"

Pinky smoothed the opossum's fur. "*She* hasn't woken up yet. I checked. Definitely female. Besides, this could take up to four hours."

Samir chuckled nervously. "You're not going to keep that rodent in your bedroom for another two hours." He paused, realizing that was exactly the kind of thing Pinky might do. "Are you?"

"She's not a rodent," Pinky said, tucking the blanket in around the opossum. "She's a marsupial, like the koala or the kangaroo. In fact, the possum is North America's only marsupial, even keeping their babies in their pouches, much like the kangaroo of Australia." She glanced at him. "I read up on them today."

"Uh-huh." Samir ran a hand through his hair, shifting his weight on his feet. "But you do realize this is ridiculous, right? I mean, you can't have an actual wild animal in your *room* for an indefinite period of time. It's dangerous. And unhygienic. Why don't you call some kind of nature preserve or something?"

Pinky leveled a Look at him. "We're hours from the closest big city with resources like that. Where do you imagine this magical nature preserve exists? In a cloud kingdom on the highest treetop?"

"I don't know! Can't you schedule, like, a pickup?"

Pinky laughed. "What, like pizza? Come get your possum take-out!" More seriously, she added, "Look, I'll drop her off at a wildlife refuge on the way out from Ellingsworth. I already Googled it and emailed to tell them I'd be coming. I just need to make it another month without my parents finding out."

Samir set the towels on her dresser. "Mm-hmm. Hey, pretty out-there idea, but try to stay with me: You could just return the wild animal . . . to the wild. Where you found it."

"She's prone to fake dying." Pinky pointed at the weirdly still creature and stared at him. "She'd be a magnet for predators. How heartless are you? This is a *baby*."

"A wild, possibly infectious, *dangerous* baby." Samir paused and then frowned. "That might be the weirdest phrase I've ever said."

"No one's asking you to do anything," Pinky said, standing. "I just need you to keep your mouth shut about this around my parents and Dolly's. Okay? Jeez." She began to stride out of the room.

"Wait," Samir said, tossing a panicked glance at the unconscious, green-goo-exuding rodent. Um, marsupial. "Where are you going?"

"To get her some fruit for when she wakes up. Just keep her com-pany, will ya?" Shaking her head, she walked off in a halo of purple-green-pink-blue hair.

Samir stood staring at the opossum for a minute, shifting his weight from foot to foot. Finally exhaling, he went to sit in the arm-chair across from it. "This is bizarre," he muttered. "This is so freak-ing bizarre, Sam. You could've been in DC right now. You could've been at a kickass internship. But no, you had to hop on a plane so you could come babysit this freaky-looking kangaroo in the butt crack of Cape Cod."

The opossum's nose twitched. Samir watched, frozen, as its nose twitched again, and then slowly, it sat up. Its mouth was still open in that gross grimace that had looked like a death rictus. The creature looked around, its breathing normal now.

"You are such a total weirdo," Samir breathed, watching as it explored the confines of its box as if nothing at all untoward had happened. "Kind of a perfect fit for Pinky, come to think of it."

Pinky walked back in, a plate of cut apples in her hands. "Oh my God," she said softly, her eyes going wide. Her smile shone on her face, and Samir wondered how often the world got to see that. He guessed not very often at all. "She's awake." She approached the opossum's box carefully and placed the apples in. The creature began to eat at a frenzied pace. "Hungry," Pinky crooned. "Are you a hungry girl?"

Samir snorted, a move that earned him a glare.

"What?" Pinky asked.

"Nothing. It's just . . . pretty weird to see you being all maternal."

"I am a *very* maternal, loving person," Pinky countered. "When it comes to animals."

"Ah." Samir bit the inside of his lip. "Good to know."

"Okay, what we need to do now is take her outside for a walk," Pinky said thoughtfully. "But we still need to keep her contained somehow so she doesn't run away and end up eaten by something bigger than her."

Samir tried not to gag at the image of something finding this rat-tailed thing delicious.

"Hold on," Pinky said, oblivious to the workings of his mind, workings that she probably wouldn't be sympathetic to. She walked over to the desk in the corner and rummaged in a drawer. A minute later, she pulled out what looked like a large purple belt. "Aha. I knew I had this somewhere."

"What is that?"

"It's Lucifer's halter."

Samir stared at her blankly. "Are you surprised that I have no idea what you're talking about?"

"My cat, Lucifer," she clarified. "He died when I was ten, but I used to take him out for walks in this halter. It's a little worse for wear, but it should be fine. . . ." Pinky fiddled with the buckles for a moment. "Oh, shoot. The one that goes around her tummy is broken."

"You could just *not* use a leash on the rodent," Samir suggested.

"She's a mar—"

"Marsupial, yeah, I got you." Samir walked over to her. "Let me see it." She handed it over and he looked at it, turning it this way and that. "Hmm. What if we . . . ?" Samir jerry-rigged the straps with complicated-looking knots. "There. That should hold."

"Wow." Pinky took it from him and buckled and unbuckled the halter, looking genuinely impressed. "Thanks." She grinned. "Did you learn that at Boy Scouts or something?"

Samir raised his eyebrows. "Yeah, actually. Is that funny for some reason?"

"Um, nope," Pinky said, but she was biting the inside of her cheek to keep from laughing. "Not at all."

Annoying little renegade freak. What was wrong with the Boy Scouts? "*Any*way." Samir turned to face the opossum. "So you're just going to slip the harness on her and, what? Stroll out the front door?"

"You think so little of me." Pinky walked over to her closet and pulled out a large canvas tote bag. Grinning toothily at Samir, she reached for the opossum.

"Wow, I did *not* think that was going to work," Samir said once they were outside, in the wooded glen past the lake house property line. The sun's heat wasn't nearly as oppressive in the shade of the trees, but he still felt like he was covered in wet, hot towels. They walked through a buzzing cloud of gnats and he closed his eyes and held his breath so he wouldn't accidentally inhale one. Or twelve. Once they were out of the danger zone, he said, "She just held so still in that bag."

"She did," Pinky said, gazing fondly at the opossum, which was now happily sniffing around the grass, wearing its ridiculous purple halter. "I half thought she was playing dead again, but no. I guess she just sensed that I needed her to be quiet."

"Your parents and uncle and aunt were pretty enthralled by Dolly's reenactment of her class-president campaign though, to be honest. That made it easy."

"They're always enthralled with her," Pinky said, kicking a pebble, and Samir thought she was mostly just talking to herself.

"Really? And with you, they're . . ."

"Exasperated."

Samir snorted and brushed away an insistent mosquito. "No kidding."

Pinky gave him a look that could wither mighty oak trees. "What does that mean?"

Somewhere in the distance, Samir could hear splashing on the lake. "I have a feeling you give your parents plenty of reasons to be exasperated." He gestured to her marsupial. "Case in point." He wasn't her parent and even *he* was kind of exasperated, to be honest.

Pinky tugged the opossum away from a pinecone she was trying to eat. "Or maybe they—and you—could be *inspired* by me. Ever think of that?"

"Ha. Inspired by your complete lack of respect for rules?" Samir pushed a branch out of the way as they wound deeper into the woods. "Or by your affinity for dangerous situations?"

"I know you spend all your free time arranging your sock drawer by color, but out here in the real world, independence, bravery, and passion are positive traits," Pinky said, her voice bitingly sarcastic. "Just FYI."

For a fleeting moment, Samir considered shoving her into a small hole in the ground they were passing. "And out in the real world, bragging about your positive traits is considered a very negative trait. Just FYI."

"I'm not bragging," Pinky said, her jaw clenched as tight as the fist that held the opossum's leash. "I'm just aware of my good qualities."

Samir ducked under a tree limb and took a deep breath. "You know what? Let's talk about something else."

"Fine."

They watched the opossum for a minute, the tension still thick and soupy in the air. Finally, to clear it, Samir said, "So? What are you going to name it? Her? Your opossum, I mean."

"You can just say 'possum' like the rest of America, you know."

"But technically, she's an opossum," Samir explained, baffled. "Why wouldn't you want to say it correctly?"

Pinky groaned and ripped a brown leaf off a bush, crumpling it to dust in her frustrated hand. "Because! Everything's not about being accurate and perfect!"

"I know that!" Samir said, losing his cool. Why was she so—so *rude*?

Pinky made a big show of breathing in and out slowly. "So. Back to your question." She gave him a big fake smile, meant to restore the peace, he imagined. Really, she just looked like an alligator about to attack. "I have to name her?"

"Um, yeah. If you're keeping her the rest of the summer, she has to have a name. Saying 'that grotesquely ugly giant rat that sometimes dies' could get strenuous."

Pinky huffed a surprised laugh. "You might have a point there."

As they watched, the opossum scurried over to a Tupelo tree, its tiny nose twitching at ninety miles an hour. A leaf detached from the tree and floated down in a lazy circle right in front of it. The opossum took one look at the leaf, its beady eyes going wide in shock, and suddenly fell over.

Samir and Pinky stared at it.

"Is it . . . ?" Samir began.

"Dead again." Pinky sighed. She walked over and sat cross-legged next to it. "I guess we'll just wait here for her to wake up. Maybe it'll be faster this time."

A laugh burbled up from Samir's throat. "Oh my God. That's all it takes? A freaking *leaf* to twirl down in front of it?"

Pinky looked up at him indignantly, but her expression melted into a smile. "I guess," she said, laughing too. "I don't think that's normal, though."

"Oh, great," Samir said, laughing even harder. "So this thing's weird even for its kind."

"She's just a bit dramatic," Pinky said. Then, her eyes shining, she added, "That's it. That's her name. I'm gonna call her Drama Queen."

His irritation gone for the moment, Samir ran a hand through his hair and went to sit by Pinky. "Drama Queen. Pinky and Drama Queen. I like it. You have to wonder, though."

"What?"

"How these things haven't gone extinct yet."

Pinky sighed again and shook her head.

CHAPTER 7

Pinky

Pinky turned the car off and looked at Samir. "We're here."

He craned his head to look at the giant red-and-white-striped brick lighthouse looming ahead of them; it was the same one he'd seen from Pinky's property. With the bright blue sky surrounding it, it gave off a very New England–themed-calendar vibe. "Wow. This is so cool."

Visiting the lighthouse had been his idea. Once Pinky had managed to sneak Drama Queen back into the house, Pinky's mom had asked what she and Samir were going to be doing the rest of the day. Pinky had shrugged, but Samir had immediately popped out with, "I'd love to see the lighthouse. If Pinky wouldn't mind taking me."

Naturally, her mom and dad had thought that was the best, most wholesome idea ever and had enthusiastically given Pinky the keys to their rented BMW. Something they would *never* have done with Preston or Pistachio, btw.

Now, Pinky shrugged as they unbuckled and got out of the car. Rolling, wet heat wafted off the asphalt of the parking lot and enveloped her. Ocean waves crashed in the distance; the beach lay past some big marshland and a thicket of trees to their right. "Yeah, it's pretty awesome. Come on, I'll show you."

She didn't mind visiting the lighthouse; it was actually one of her favorite things to do on Ellingsworth. But bringing Samir here alone felt . . . weird. Like something you'd do on a real date. She wished Dolly could've come to act as a buffer, but someone had to stay back at the house and take care of Drama Queen while Pinky was away.

Samir looked around the empty lot on their way to the lighthouse trail. His buttercup-yellow polo shirt (the same color as Pinky's mom's cardigan—big surprise, they actually liked the same boring lawyer-y things) was already beginning to stick to his back. "I'm surprised there aren't more people here." Giant white seagulls screeched overhead, as if in agreement.

"I mean, it's really hot right now." Pinky could feel her hair expanding sideways in the humidity, this close to the ocean. "Most everyone comes at dawn or dusk. But I figured you wanted to see the inside, and it's best to do that when you don't have to jostle to share the view." Plus, a lighthouse tour at dusk was just wayyyy more rom-com than she wanted to deal with.

"Good deal." There was an actual pep in Samir's step as he headed up the wooden stairs made of railroad ties, his big flip-flop-clad feet kicking up puffs of sand. His sensible, professional-looking messenger bag bopped against his hip. The guy was like an advertisement for some spine-chilling combination of a Boy Scout and a church choir boy. "Ooh, look at this!" He was standing in front of a sign right outside the lighthouse that described its history. Pinky hadn't realized that people under the age of sixty read those signs. "Wow. Ellingsworth Point Lighthouse was built in 1857 in a different spot. Apparently they had to move it back almost a thousand feet from the ocean in the nineties because of rising sea levels."

Walking past bushes of beach grass that made a grab for her bare legs, Pinky pulled her wayward hair into a multicolored bun and walked up to join him, little prickles of curiosity getting through her stoic exterior. "Really? Weird. Wonder how you move a lighthouse."

Samir glanced at her, his cheeks flushed from the heat. If she didn't get him inside soon, he might just expire of heat exhaustion. And her parents would find a way to blame his demise on her. "I thought you'd been here before."

Pinky gave him a look. "Many times. I just never read the sign."

They stared at each other for a long moment, the silence punctuated only by the sound of ocean waves and a flock of seagulls arguing with each other in the distance. "But . . . but you have to walk *right by the sign* to get to the entrance." Samir gestured to the entrance in front of them as if she couldn't see it.

"I *know* that," Pinky said slowly, feeling her short fuse getting shorter. "So what? Not everyone wants to stand around reading signs, Samir. Some of us want to actually get to the good stuff."

"The sign is *part* of the good stuff!" Samir said, throwing his hands up in the air.

Pinky scowled. "Do you want to see the stupid lighthouse or not?" Before he could respond, she turned and headed past the lighthouse keeper's neat green cottage to the entrance of the lighthouse proper.

Samir

Man, she was . . . flammable. It was like all her emotions were gasoline, and he just happened to have a match. Although, to be completely honest, she was making *Samir* grumpy too. There was just something about her scowly, flippant, irreverent way of being that got to him. Who didn't read the *signs* outside historical monuments?

Huffing a frustrated breath, he clomped after Pinky into the lighthouse. But his annoyance dissipated the moment he was inside.

It was cooler in here; they were sheltered from the sun by thick, protective, ancient brick. Directly in front of them was a narrow, winding wrought-iron staircase painted a dark brown. "Look at the detailing," Samir whispered, running his hand along the scrollwork. "That's gorgeous."

Pinky, who was already four stairs up, glanced down at him. "Um, yup. Super cool. But the view is the best part." And then she kept going.

Sighing and shaking his head, Samir followed her, his footsteps clanging on the metal.

The near-vertical climb almost fifty feet up was kind of tough, and he and Pinky were both winded by the time they got to the top. The upside was, they didn't speak much the entire time they were climbing, and less speaking meant less fighting.

"Ta . . . da!" Pinky flung her arm out at the view before them, panting slightly.

"Whoa." Samir stepped forward, toward the big, curving windows of the observation deck. There wasn't much room to move around—he and Pinky could stand side by side, but adding even two or three more people would've been a squeeze. None of that mattered, though, because the view . . . the view was incredible.

Samir could see for miles and miles; the ocean lay bright and blue as a piece of silk ribbon in the distance, dotted with a couple of fishing boats. He could see the trail he and Pinky had walked up, and swaths of marsh and grass and low, clumpy trees. It looked like a postcard for Cape Cod, almost too perfect to be real.

"Pretty incredible, right?" Pinky stood beside him, her hands on her hips, her face awash in sunlight. "I love that one quote by Thoreau; he actually said it about another Cape Cod lighthouse, but it applies here, too: 'A man may stand there and put all America behind him.' You're looking out toward Nova Scotia right now."

Samir darted a surprised look at her and she cocked her head, brown eyes flashing. "What?" she asked. "You don't think someone like me could quote Thoreau?"

"I didn't say that," Samir said, turning around, though obviously, that's exactly what he'd been thinking. There was a beacon behind him that he'd missed somehow, probably blindsided by the view. As he looked, it flashed a bright blue light for just a moment before going dark again. A placard beside it said it had been flashing the same pattern since the lighthouse had been built in 1857. Samir set one hand on the beacon's clear casing, feeling its heft, its age, its purpose. "It makes you feel like everything's going to be okay, doesn't it? I mean, this place has been here for a hundred and sixty-three years. They saved it from being swallowed by the sea so it could continue to protect people." He turned to look out the windows at the sea again, expecting Pinky to come back with some snarky remark.

"Yeah, actually," she said softly, looking out at the sea too. "That's what I really love about this place. It feels like . . . I don't know, a protector of the island. It's pretty cool."

They stood in silence, breathing in tandem, letting the lighthouse cradle them.

Pinky

Weird. Pinky had never thought for a second that she and Samir could agree on anything, let alone something so . . . deep. She glanced sidelong at him. Maybe, in some tiny, small, minute way, he wasn't *quite* as bad as she thought—

He was unsnapping his messenger bag and pulling out a small notebook and a marker. Setting the notebook against his thigh, he checked something off.

Pinky squinted. "What are you doing?" She couldn't make out the tiny writing, but it looked like a list of some kind.

He put the notebook and marker neatly back into his bag (in their appropriate pockets) and snapped the bag shut before answering. "Checking 'see Ellingsworth Point Lighthouse' off my to-do list for the day."

Pinky stared at him, waiting for more of an explanation that would help all of this make sense, but it didn't seem like there was any coming. "You . . . made a to-do list for today?"

"Uh-huh. I make one for every day."

Pinky chuckled and leaned against the railing of the observation deck. "No, come on. Not *every* single day."

Samir arched an eyebrow. "Yes."

There was no way. No way. "Even . . . your birthday?"

He nodded.

"Diwali." Another nod. "Christmas." A nod again. "The first day of summer break?" Yet another nod. "What do you even put on a day like that?" Pinky couldn't help but ask. "I mean, it's the first day of summer break! The whole point of it is to do nothing! Or anything!"

"'Only through focus can you do world-class things, no matter how capable you are'—Bill Gates." Samir shrugged. "Since you like quotes so much."

Pinky scoffed. "Seriously. Don't you think the whole planner thing is a little on the control-freak side?"

Samir leveled a gaze at her. "Sometimes, being in control is the only thing you have going for you."

Something in his tone had her swallowing back her sarcastic retort. Pinky rested her hip against the handrail, digesting his words. "Oh," she said quietly, feeling a little bad. "Did you learn that when . . . when your mom got sick?"

He looked away, back out at the marsh and the sea in the distance. "Something like that."

Pinky wondered whether she should say what was on her mind and then realized she couldn't *not* say it. She and Ash had already helped Samir with his mom once. Maybe this would help him too. "But she's not sick anymore."

Samir looked at her. "So?"

"So it's not like you're trying to solve the climate crisis or something. What do you need *that* much focus for?"

Samir's gaze turned stony. "You wouldn't understand." He walked around the tiny observation deck, as if to put as much space between them as possible, and pretended to reread the placard about the beacon.

Pinky crossed her arms. "And why not? Because I don't have any worthwhile goals like you do?"

Samir looked at her over the top of the beacon. "Frankly? Yeah. I see you with all these resources and parents who would support you no matter what you want to do, and all you're interested in is"—he waved his hand at her—"getting to the top of the lighthouse. Whatever your latest madcap scheme is. Honestly, it's pretty irresponsible."

"Ha!" Pinky hadn't meant to exclaim so loud; it echoed around the deck. "Okay, number one: Only people as old as this lighthouse say things like 'madcap scheme.' And number two: You don't know anything about me! You see my hair and my eyebrow ring and my willingness to think for myself and suddenly you're an excellent judge of who I am?"

"Are you denying that you're immature and irresponsible?"

"Yes!" Pinky couldn't believe he'd even ask her that.

"Okay, fine." Samir reached a hand over and covered the placard next to him. "How many times have you come to this exact spot?"

Pinky frowned, not sure where this was going. "Um . . . like, twenty or thirty times?"

"Mm-hmm. So tell me what the flash pattern is for this beacon."

"What?"

He smiled, a smug, annoying thing that made Pinky want to throw him off the observation deck. "What's the flash pattern for this beacon? How many seconds on and how many off?"

Pinky tugged at her bun, aggravated, and took a few steps toward him (secretly hoping to catch sight of the placard's writing between the gaps in Samir's fingers). "What the hell does that have to do with anything?"

He narrowed his eyes while adjusting his fingers so she couldn't see anything. Damn. "I'm just trying to prove that, for all your outrage, you're still completely ignorant about the world around you. You can't even tell me something as basic as the flash pattern for this beacon you've visited dozens of times. Does that seem mature or responsible?"

Pinky took another step forward, calculating her next move but keeping her voice casual. "Okay, first, that is a completely stupid thing to test. And second, *you* got to study it, so it's not fair that you're—ha!" She launched herself at Samir, grabbing his hand with both of hers, trying to pry his fingers off the placard.

They wrestled, but his fingers were clamped on there like they were fused to the metal or something. Dammit. She hadn't expected him to be so strong. "What is your *problem*?" he yelled, trying to block her with his body. "Let go of my hand!"

"I will not!" Pinky yelled back, her bun coming loose, her frizzy hair all over Samir's face and her own. "What's *your* problem? Can't you see you're being totally unreasonable?"

"*Me? You're* the one who just *attacked* me for no reason!" He grabbed her by the shoulder with his free hand, not pushing but not letting her get any closer to the placard, and she grabbed his upper arms, intending to pull him away.

Except that she found her fingertips flexing on the hard muscle of his biceps under the skin of her palms and fingers. She gazed into his eyes, only a few inches away from her own, realizing his pupils had little flecks of red mixed in with the deep brown. A vague, distant part of her brain registered that they'd stopped struggling with each other and were just . . . standing there, closer together than was socially acceptable. And still Pinky stood there, touching him and staring at him because she couldn't think of a single thing to say. Not one single thing.

He looked at her with those eyes, those strange, beautiful, weird, nice eyes. And then he cleared his throat and blinked, and the freaky-ass spell was broken.

Releasing his arms, Pinky took a hurried step away from him, banging her heel against the wall of the observation deck, pain flaring in that spot and embarrassment flaring everywhere else.

"Are you okay?" Samir asked, concerned.

"Fine," she said, even though her heel was freaking throbbing like a heartbeat. "Totally fine." She tucked her hair behind her ear and let her eyes slide casually across the placard. "One second on and three seconds off, by the way," she added, in the most dignified tone she could manage. "That's the beacon flash pattern. I knew it all along; I just . . . temporarily forgot."

And with that, she turned and clomped down the stairs.

Samir

Samir watched her go for a long second, her footsteps clanging, fading the farther she got.

What . . . the . . . hell had just happened? One second she'd been quoting Thoreau at him, and the next she'd launched herself at him like some kind of human cannonball, and then . . . then she was in his arms, gazing into his eyes. And he was gazing right back into hers, if he were being totally honest. Her eyes were like midnight, almost black, but not quite, and it must've been the heat or something because he found himself getting really confused and kind of almost *enjoying* the weight of her on him, the way her hands felt on his arms, small and warm . . .

He blew out a breath on the empty observation deck and rubbed the back of his neck, looking out at the sea again. A few seagulls circled the lighthouse, their mouths open like they were laughing at him. Obviously, he'd lost his mind because it was way, way too hot for him. He was a Cali boy, not used to this kind of weird East Coast heat.

"Are you building another observation deck up there or what?" Pinky's voice came floating up to him, crabby and sarcastic.

Narrowing his eyes, Samir scoffed. Yeah, *definitely* just the heat. He could never *ever* find someone like Pinky Kumar even vaguely attractive. "So sorry to make you wait, my liege," he called back down, equally sarcastic, and began the climb down.

Pinky

"Lots of sunscreen," her dad was saying, one morning a couple of days after the lighthouse trip.

Pinky blinked up at him through the steam emanating from her coffee cup. "Say what?" she mumbled. God, why did people insist on talking to her before ten a.m.?

Samir was, of course, bright-eyed and chowing down on his blueberry pancakes. Which he'd probably helped make. Dolly was out on the deck with her parents, all of them drinking chai together on the rocking chairs, smiling like they were in a commercial for a Realtor.

"We're going paddleboating today," her mom said, walking in wearing a linen top, white capris, and pearls. She made a beeline for the coffee maker. Pinky's caffeine addiction was a genetic gift. "Didn't Dad tell you?"

"No," she said, glaring at her dad.

"Actually, he did," Samir said merrily. "But I think you were mostly asleep."

Pinky's dad chuckled. "Story of my life. But what do you think, Samir? You don't get seasick, do you?"

Samir grinned. "Not at all. Actually, I'm on the sailboat team at our country club."

"Of course you are," Pinky mumbled into her coffee cup.

"Excellent!" Her dad was practically glowing. "Then you and Pinky can team up! Every time we take the boats out, she manages to paddle her way into a clump of bushes somewhere. Maybe someone with a sense of direction can help her out." He guffawed like he'd told the best joke.

Pinky's mom took a seat between her dad and Samir. "Well, we used to go fishing, but when Pinky turned about five, she would cry every time we hooked one."

"Aw." Samir turned to her, smiling. "You cried because you were sad for the fish?"

"Fishing is a disgustingly Neanderthal pastime," Pinky retorted.

"So, tell me, Samir," her mom said quickly, because she obviously didn't want her wayward daughter scaring off the one good boyfriend she'd ever brought home. Ha ha. *Joke's on you, Mom. He's not even a real boyfriend. Just a guy with absurdly pretty eyes and biceps like grapefruits.* "What kinds of things do you and your family like doing together?"

Pinky noticed the smile slide off Samir's face and felt a pinch of sympathy for him, remembering the "intervention" she and Ash had staged.

"It's, ah, just me and my mom. My dad died when I was really little. My mom . . . my mom doesn't really like doing too much, so we mostly just hang out at home. And read together." He drank his milk, as if to stop himself from saying too much. He looked so uncomfortable, she didn't even silently make fun of the fact that he was drinking milk in the morning like an eight-year-old.

"Read together?" Her mom frowned. "Well, that's commendable, I suppose, but surely you like to do other things besides—"

Pinky drained the last of her coffee. "Mom. I forgot to tell you. I have a pet possum now."

"You *what*?" her parents said in perfect synchrony, and Samir darted her a grateful look for this kamikaze move. As well he should. He owed her big-time. Pinky wasn't sure what, exactly, had made her pull such a stunt. But there was something about watching her mom poke and prod at an obviously sensitive spot in Samir's psyche that just . . . didn't feel right.

Pinky shrugged and got up for a coffee refill. "She's just a baby. I can't release her into the wild because she's been abandoned by her mom, so on the day we fly out, we're gonna have to make a pit stop at the wildlife refuge."

"And . . . where is this rodent right now?" Her mother's voice was dangerously calm.

"Marsupial, actually," Pinky said, leaning against the counter with her mug in her hand. "She's in my room."

Samir frowned at her and mouthed something she couldn't make out. Her mother rushed out of the kitchen without another word, no doubt headed to Pinky's room, but her dad paused. He shook his head, his brown eyes somber. "Why do you purposely get under her skin, honey?" he asked, and then, without waiting for an answer, he walked out too.

Pinky drank her coffee, the sound of her swallowing thunderous in the silence. "What?"

Samir shrugged. "Nothing. I just . . . I don't know why you told them like that."

"Like what?"

"Like you were purposely trying to antagonize them." He brought his dirty dishes to the sink and, donning an apron, began rinsing them off for the dishwasher.

"What do you care?" she snapped. "You should be thanking me. I saved you from talking about something you obviously don't like talking about."

His cheeks flushed, and Pinky felt immediately bad about calling attention to his family stuff. "I didn't need your help."

Pinky raised an eyebrow. "You could've fooled me."

Samir narrowed his eyes at her. "You know what, stop changing the subject. The point is, you could've told them more gently, but you chose to be a total brat. I'm guessing that's pretty standard for you."

Pinky barked a laugh. "Name calling? Really mature, Samir. Besides, it doesn't even matter, okay? You've been here for, like, two seconds, so you don't know this, but they're going to be mad at me anyway for something."

Samir set his cup into the dishwasher with a rattle. "But that's the thing! You could've told them how long you spent researching the habitats of opossums and what they need in captivity. You could've told them how I said you should abandon Drama Queen, but you couldn't do that. You could've told them a lot of nice things about yourself, but instead you . . . you positioned it like you were just doing this all on a whim. To piss them off. Admit it."

Pinky stared at him. Was he right? Had she somehow *wanted* to piss her parents off? No way. What sense did that even make? She decided to change the subject. "Whatever, dude. So, you ready to get your butt kicked in this paddleboat tournament?"

Samir took off his apron and paused, obviously wondering whether to take the bait and change subjects or not. Luckily (for him), he decided to go with it. "Tournament? I thought your dad said we were just taking them out on the lake for fun."

"Ha. You obviously don't know my family. Everything is a competition. Don't let him fool you; he's gonna be vying for the upper hand the whole time. Just prepare your gracious-loser face. He's pretty unstoppable."

Samir grinned an uncharacteristically evil grin. "Well, then, Pops can bring it on."

"Who can bring what on?" Her father was back in the kitchen.

"Um, n-nothing," Samir said, his eyes going wide and innocent. He hung his apron from the hook on the wall. "Sir."

Pinky smirked at him.

"Pinky," her father said, a pinched expression on his face. "Mom and I would like to talk to you in your room. Please."

"Good luck," Samir muttered sarcastically.

Pinky threw him a peace sign before she sauntered out after her dad, still just a tad uneasy at what he'd said: that she'd been *trying* to piss her parents off. But that was ridiculous, right?

"So they're letting you keep her," Samir said, squinting in the sunshine.

"Oh yeah. I just had to promise I was litter-box training her. They're not completely heartless." They were at the boathouse on the lake, pulling out their paddleboats. Pinky's parents and Dolly's family already each had their three-person boats and had headed into the water. Samir and Pinky were the last to go. "They just like to make it seem that way. My mom, especially. You know they call her the Shark in legal circles?"

They took their seats, and Samir untied their boat. As they began paddling out after Pinky's family, he said, "Yeah, I think I may have heard that somewhere."

"Oh, right," Pinky said, regarding him with a small smile. "I forgot."

"Forgot what?"

"That you're, like, this baby lawyer shark." She pedaled harder, shaking her head. "It's pretty strange, you know."

"Being a lawyer is strange? Don't tell your parents that."

"No, I mean the fact that you already know what you want to do and you're basically like this tiny version of my parents."

Samir raised an eyebrow. "Tiny?" He gestured to his muscular body. "Excuse me?"

"Hmm, maybe not tiny," Pinky said, her gaze sneaking off to trace his broad shoulders without her permission. She forced herself to look away. "But young, I guess."

"I've always known what I wanted," Samir said, the sun glittering off the lake and casting patterns on his face. "I don't know, I guess it's strange. It just feels normal for me, though."

Pinky studied him. She'd brought this up at the lighthouse and it didn't go well, but . . . ah well. She was nothing if not a jump-in-with-both-feet kinda girl. "And it's not because of . . . you know. Your mom and her cancer? How being in control helped you take care of her back then?"

Samir gave her a sharp look. "Your parents are way too far ahead. We should catch up with them."

Hint taken. "Yep."

"I can't believe we're lost. How did you get us lost on a *lake*? It's an open body of water, enclosed on all sides, for crying out loud." Sweat was dripping off Samir's forehead in steady dribbles. He'd taken his shirt off fifteen minutes ago, about the same time Pinky had taken off her T-shirt, leaving her in just her bikini top and shorts. Rivulets of sweat were now running down the center of Samir's bare back. His back that had more muscles than Pinky knew any back could have. Seriously. Sailing boats at the country club and shooting hoops with Ashish gave you that kind of musculature? Maybe she should accompany her parents to the country club more often.

She forced her brain back to the problem at hand. Samir. Irate. Lost. "Right. We're not lost. It's just confusing because it's so big and there are all these little islands and things. You need to go that way around that bend and then stick a right past that gnarly-looking tree and we'll find them. I texted my dad."

He spared her a withering glare. "We're here because, as I recall, you wanted to go look at that 'endangered frog' you saw that turned out to be a pinecone. So forgive me if I stick to my sense of where we are."

"No, we're here because you wanted to paddle right when we were supposed to go left. Probably should've recorded that in your planner."

"No, you were supposed to—ow, crap." Groaning, he reached one hand behind his shoulders.

"What are you doing?"

"I have this spot on my back between my shoulder blades that always gets sunburned."

Pinky leaned back to take a peek. "Holy moly, yeah, that's, like, bright red. I guess that's what you get for being so fair-skinned."

Samir chuckled. "We can't all have perfect, smooth bronze skin." Pinky could tell he'd tried to say it lightly and flippantly, but it had come out like he was hitting on her. His smile slipped off his face and his eyes went wide with mortification. "Ah, I mean, not that, like—"

Pinky felt her cheeks warm and reached into her tote bag to hide it. "Um, I have some sunscreen." She thrust the tube at him. "Here."

He looked down at the tube and then back up at her as they drifted past the same scraggly-looking tree they'd passed a few minutes ago. Her dad was going to send an extraction team if they didn't find their way soon. The water sloshed lazily against the paddleboat, rocking them gently in their seats. "I can't really reach that spot; that's the problem."

"Oh." She glanced down at the tube in her hands and swallowed. "Um," she said, not really meeting his eye. "I could . . . I could smooth it on for you."

There was a weird expression on Samir's face all of a sudden.

"Or not," Pinky said quickly, her cheeks flaming. Thank the goddess for melanin. Disguising, discreet melanin. "It's just, like, you know, a suggestion. I've heard skin cancer is a real—"

"N-no, no, I mean, yeah. That'd be good." Samir licked his lips while focusing on the lake in front of him like he had to memorize every ripple. He looked about as awkward as she felt. The awkwardness was super weird, for her, because she'd had more boyfriends just last fall than most people have during their wild college years. "Thanks."

"Really? I mean, you'd be paddling on your own for a few minutes."

He gave her a look. "I have a feeling I've been pretty much paddling on my own this entire time anyway."

Pinky snorted. "Okay, I didn't know you knew that. I've pretty much just been sitting here, pretending to work."

She scooted over to the center seat, which had previously been empty, her slender dark-brown thighs sliding right next to Samir's much thicker, golden-brown ones. She squeezed a bit of sunblock onto her fingers and twisted her torso so she could more easily reach Samir's back. "Um, I'm just gonna . . . um, touch you. Now."

"Okay." Samir was still staring straight ahead, and he nodded his head vigorously without looking at Pinky. "Yeah, that's . . . yep."

Jeez, it wasn't like she'd never touched a boy before. And this wasn't like the cringesome, weird thing that had happened in the lighthouse where she found herself holding him while gazing into his eyes. She couldn't even see his eyes from here. And anyway, this was a *medical necessity.* So why the heck was she acting like some twelve-year-old kid? Pinky forced her fingers to make contact with his back, rubbing the lotion in circles, pretending not to notice the way Samir's muscles first stiffened at her touch and then relaxed. She realized that her face was really close to his. In fact, if he were to turn his face, they'd be kissing distance apart.

Samir glanced at her sidelong. He had really long eyelashes. Thick, black, silky. "Thanks. That feels good."

Pinky kept on rubbing the lotion in, though she was pretty sure it had all worked its way off her fingers. "Good. I'm glad that feels good." The smell of sunblock and water and something that was very specifically him tangled in her nostrils, filling her senses.

The boat juddered to a stop, the tremors rolling through its body and hers. Pinky shrieked and tried, unsuccessfully, to grab the side. She wasn't sure exactly how, but in the next second, she tripped and began to go down, flat on her back. She saw Samir's face register shock and then alarm, and before she knew it, he'd reached one of his arms behind her to catch her. And then she was gazing up at him like a dancer who'd been dipped by her partner, her hair streaming down to the floor of the boat, Samir's face just inches from hers. They could've kissed.

They didn't, though. Obviously. They just stared at each other, both of them breathing slightly hard. Pinky found herself gazing into those eyes again, which, in the sunlight, had a bit of gold. Her arms were gripped tightly around his bare waist to keep from falling, and she realized how hot his skin was. As if he were a mini sun himself.

And then Samir cleared his throat and helped her up in a very gentlemanly manner. Pinky stood up straight, going completely wordless again, as she tended to do in close physical proximity to Samir. What the hell was that about? She didn't even find him that attractive; he was so not her type!

"You okay?" he asked, as the boat rocked them gently from side to side.

She nodded immediately, her voice still MIA.

"Good." He smiled a little, almost expectantly, as a lake breeze blew around them, raising goose bumps on her skin.

What was the expectation about? Did he want to kiss her? Did she *want* him to want to kiss her? Did he want her to want him to want—

"Pinky. You're, ah . . . you're still . . . you've got your arms around me."

"No I don't," she said immediately, still gazing up at him. But then she realized in the next mortifying moment that she totally did. Her arms were still tight around his waist. She was virtually

120

hugging him. She let her arms drop like they were heavy boulders and stepped aside, tucking a hair behind her ear. "Oh, right. I, um, just needed to make sure I was steady on my feet. That's all."

Samir's lips twitched, like he saw right through her. "Sure," he said easily, and now released from her grasp, turned to survey what had caused the boat to stop. "Oh, hell." They'd hit the bank of the lake, hard. "Great, not only are we lost, but we've wrecked the boat, too." Samir, red in the face, took his seat again and backpedaled to turn them around.

Pinky slid back into her seat quickly, like she was trying to fool them both that she'd never been close to him at all. "Right, yeah," she heard herself saying in this defensive tone of voice, her cheeks hot. "I know I got us lost, but do you have to keep harping on it?"

"What?" Samir asked, looking at her, somewhere between confused and irate. "What are you talking about? I was just saying—"

"Yeah, I heard what you were saying." Pinky wasn't sure *why* she was trying to pick a fight exactly. Only that she felt off-kilter from rubbing that lotion into his shoulders and needed to put some emotional distance between them. Samir was here to be her *fake* boyfriend. He was a control freak, rigid, unimaginative, and boring. He was not at all the type of person she dated. She was trying to prove something to her parents, and she didn't need any complications. "Just paddle the boat."

Samir stared at her. "You're unbelievable, you know that?"

Pinky trailed her hand in the cool water and tossed him a sarcastic smile. "Thank you."

"Doesn't swinging on your pendulum ever exhaust you?" Samir asked, his hand gripping the side of the boat. "Seriously."

Pinky glared at him, saying nothing. He opened his mouth, then closed it again, sighed, and shook his head.

They paddled in relative silence for the next few minutes. Pinky's brain swirled with tumultuous thoughts. Samir was handsome in a classic way, sure. And he seemed nice enough on the surface. But she was *Pinky Kumar*. She dated boys who had juvie records and unhealthy obsessions with eyeball tattooing. She was the hookup queen, the cautionary tale parents told their teenagers about. She was *not* someone who dated a guy who knew he wanted to become a Harvard-educated corporate lawyer. She may as well marry her own dad. Ew.

Besides all that, the last thing Pinky needed was another person in her life against whom her mom could compare her unfavorably. A summer transaction was one thing, but she could just imagine the train wreck her life would become if she and Samir extended this beyond the summer. All of his many accomplishments would supply her mom with an endless round of ammunition against her. No, thank you. Whatever that frisson of . . . whatever . . . was between them, she would kill it with fire.

Samir turned to her. "We're here."

Pinky followed his gaze to see her parents and Dolly's family waving at them enthusiastically from the pier where they'd all congregated, waiting for Pinky and Samir. "Oh, right." She stood and smirked at him, her hands on her hips. "So I guess I didn't get us totally lost, huh?"

Samir studied her steadily, his brown eyes shimmering in the sun. Pinky's heart thudded. "No, you didn't," he said finally, calmly, not rising to the bait. Something in his expression told her he knew exactly what she was trying to do—pick a fight so she didn't have to focus on what the actual issue was, a.k.a. that weird little *thing* between them.

Feeling slightly off-balance, Pinky hopped off the boat and sauntered to her family, feeling his lingering gaze on her skin.

Samir

Pinky's and Dolly's parents had laid out a picnic on the grassy bank of the lake. The food was delicious too, chicken and masala potatoes and chickpea salad. Too bad it all tasted like cardboard to Samir.

He couldn't stop sneaking glances at Pinky. What exactly had just happened between them? Thirty minutes ago, there'd been some definite vibeage going on. And then she began arguing with him for no apparent reason. He glanced at her again. She had her shirt back on, a strappy-back tank top of some kind, and was spearing each chickpea very studiously with her fork, refusing to even look his way. Normally he'd admire such precision, but the ferocity with which she was stabbing those poor beans freaked him out a tad.

Samir shook his head and went back to his lunch. What had he been thinking anyway? Pinky had the right idea—pretend the strange tension between them had never happened and move on. He was here on a business trip of sorts. He couldn't even imagine what it'd be like to be in his first relationship (there was that kiss with the nineteen-year-old tennis instructor at the country club last year, but that was nowhere close to a relationship) with someone like Pinky. Actually, he could. It would be disastrous. A colossal mistake. They could barely complete a conversation without arguing, for flip's sake, and there was a reason for that: She was a hotheaded, unpredictable, irresponsible mess. Samir was always on a mission to organize and simplify and streamline his life—not toss it into complete chaos.

"So, Samir!" Mr. Yeung said, looking pleased. There was a bit of mayonnaise at the corner of his mouth that he didn't seem to know was there. Samir fought against every impulse that told him to pass Mr. Yeung a napkin. "Are you ready to admit defeat?"

Pinky tossed Samir a brief look at that, a kind of *See? I told you.* Then, apparently remembering she was ignoring him, she went back to her meal.

"Defeat?" Samir said, turning back to Mr. Yeung. He focused his gaze on Mr. Yeung's forehead, though the mayo taunted him in his peripheral vision.

"We beat you by at least ten minutes!" he said, gesturing to the paddleboats at the pier behind them, gently rocking on the water. He rubbed his hands together, a mad glint in his eye. "Or do you want to see how you do heading back? Aim for a tie, maybe?"

Pinky's mom reached over and dabbed the corner of his mouth with a napkin, and Samir sagged with relief. "Howard, please. Try not to scare the boy."

Dolly laughed. "I doubt Samir scares easily. He's dating Pinky, after all."

Pinky threw a grape at her. "Samir's not the competitive type," Pinky said at the exact same moment Samir said, "I love a little healthy competition."

They stared at each other, frozen, for a moment.

Mr. Montclair, Dolly's dad, laughed. "I sense a little incongruence! Which is it?"

"As the psychologists Luft and Ingham would say, perhaps Samir's blind spot is warring with his arena." Mrs. Montclair chuckled.

Samir had no idea what they were talking about. What he did know was that both of Pinky's parents and Dolly were frowning at him and Pinky. He cleared his throat. "No, ah, Pinky's right. I . . . I don't usually like competition. But in this case, I think it'll be fun."

"You don't have to pretend to be someone you're not just to impress my parents," Pinky said, raising an eyebrow, her eyebrow ring glinting in the summer sun.

What? Was she seriously just throwing him to the wolves like that? She hadn't even attempted to salvage the situation and she was going to criticize *him*? "I wasn't," he bit out, smiling rigidly at her. "But not all of us feel the need to fight with the adults around us all the time, *sweetie*."

Pinky eyed the tines of her fork before slowly setting it down. "What's that supposed to mean?"

"I think it's pretty obvious what it means," Samir said. They glared at each other.

Mr. Yeung coughed a little. Oh crap. He'd kind of forgotten the end goal. Now all of them looked halfway between awkward and confused.

Samir forced himself to walk across the picnic blanket and sit next to Pinky. He slung an arm around her narrow shoulders and kissed the soft side of her temple (maybe that was technically breaking a rule—she'd expressly said no kissing—but this was a dire situation). He couldn't help but inhale (a boy had to breathe, after all); she smelled like lake and sun and flowers. Samir blinked, trying to remind himself that even poison could smell nice, when he realized that Pinky was just sitting there, immobile, almost frozen. As if no boy had ever kissed the side of her temple before and she had no idea how to react. God. Couldn't she at least make an *effort*?

"Anyway," he forced himself to say easily to Mr. Yeung. "I'd love to race you back. But can I ask that Dolly come with us to be Pinky's co-navigator? We could definitely use the help paddling." He laughed and looked down at Pinky, feeling an evil sparkle in his eye. "You don't mind, do you, sugarplum?"

Smiling too, she put one hand on his knee and squeezed hard enough to nearly crush it to knee-shaped pulp. He forced himself not to yelp. "Not at all, *honeybun*."

"Uh . . ." Mr. Yeung looked from Samir to Pinky and then at Dolly. "I don't mind if you don't mind, Dolly."

Dolly narrowed her eyes at Pinky. "I don't mind at all," she said thoughtfully.

Once they were back home—Mr. Yeung had officially won the paddleboat contest (he'd pounded a Red Bull right before they started, Samir was sure of it) and would probably crow about it for the next century—Dolly went upstairs to take her shower, and Pinky and Samir followed a few minutes later.

"What is your *problem*?" Pinky hissed.

"My problem?" Samir hissed back. "You were the one acting like you hate me!"

She folded her long arms against her torso as they emerged onto the second floor. "Oh. I wonder why." Mockingly, she added, "'Not all of us feel the need to fight with the adults around us all the time, *sweetie.*'"

Samir wondered how one person could be so irritating. "I do not sound like that!"

"'I do not sound like that!'" Pinky said in that same mocking, nasally tone.

"Very mature."

Pinky laughed. "I am so getting under your skin. Seriously? That's all it takes?"

"'Seriously? That's all it takes?'" Samir said in a high-pitched voice, mocking her too. He was vaguely aware that they were in the hallway and could be caught any moment, but she was just too annoying to let it go.

Pinky flicked his chest with her fingers, looking offended. "Stop it!"

"No, you stop it!" He flicked her back on the shoulder, a distant, still-mature part of his brain horrified at the infantile way he was acting, at how quickly she could reduce him to *this*, a toddler version of himself.

But most of his brain was focused on flicking her faster than she could flick him.

They were in the middle of their flicking frenzy when Dolly poked her head out of her bedroom. "Guys? Everything okay?"

Immediately, and by mutual consent, they called a cease-fire and stood close together, smiling at Dolly. "Sure!" Pinky said, her voice not dissimilar to the one Samir had used to mock her. "Totally!"

Samir flashed her a thumbs-up. Giving them a curious look, Dolly disappeared back into her bedroom.

With one last, withering glare, Pinky held her chin high and stomped off to her own room, closing the door with more force than necessary. Blood boiling, Samir stalked off to his room.

Why did he let her get to him like that? He closed the door behind him, taking care not to slam it, unlike some other people. Pinky was clearly an immature, annoying little freak. He'd known this when he'd agreed to her proposition. Okay, so maybe he hadn't realized just how annoying she would be in close quarters. The most frustrating thing was that he needed her. He couldn't back out now.

Fuming, Samir walked to the window and then paced back to his bed. Technically, he supposed he could hop on a plane and head home. But being here with Pinky was still a more appealing prospect than going back to Atherton. He just needed to keep things in perspective, Samir realized, as he made his fourth circuit around the room. He needed to keep his eye on the prize at the end. And in the meantime, maybe he could find ways to express his frustration that wouldn't cast suspicion on their fictitious relationship.

His eye fell on the planner and pen on his nightstand (he'd had to leave his planner behind for possible-water-damage reasons). Hmm . . .

Most people Samir knew had an amiable relationship with list-making. They knew lists were good at keeping you on track. But no one Samir knew loved, needed, *breathed* lists the way he did.

When his mom was going through all of her chemo treatments and could barely keep her eyes open, Samir had taken over their family event calendar/whiteboard out of necessity. Even at ten, when he had to use a stepstool to reach the top of the board, he'd used colorful markers to delineate every single thing she might need— painkillers, specific foods she could keep down during chemo, hourly reminders for her to drink fluids, appointments with the oncologist, the nutritionist, the physical therapist, the dentist, the social worker. He'd even taken to planning out his own meals. There had been no adult to take care of stuff like that; it had all fallen to him.

It didn't take a shrink to see that planning every minute detail of his life also helped Samir feel like he was in control. And now . . . now it just made good sense. Lists helped him feel balanced, like drinking a green smoothie in the morning or going on a six-mile run.

Picking up his planner and pen, Samir kicked off his shoes and hopped on the bed. He tapped his pen on the planner, thinking for a moment. Then, flipping past the weekly calendars to the notes section at the back, he wrote:

10 Things I Hate about Pinky

1. She's impulsive. Completely lets her heart dictate what her brain should do.

2. Impetuous.

3. Overly passionate about *everything*.

4. Short fuse: half human, half firecracker.

5. Doesn't want anyone to be nice to her.

6. Hardheaded and bullish.

7. Doesn't know how to relax. Everything's a fight.

8. Completely nonconforming.

9. Magenta/teal/pink/green hair.

10. Habit of snorting derisively. (What is she, a horse?)

Tapping his pen against his chin, he looked at the list, already feeling 200 percent better. Sure, there was a small part of him that felt a little . . . uneasy about the list, a little bad at having written down Pinky's undesirable qualities. But that part was very small. Almost nonexistent.

Samir filled his lungs with the lightly scented air of the room and then slowly let it out. Yes, he could put up with Pinky's volatile weirdness for a few more weeks. Because at the end of it was a Harvard pennant with his name on it, waiting to be tacked up in a dorm room in Cambridge. And that would last the rest of his life.

CHAPTER 8

Pinky

Pinky finished her shower and texted Ashish. On the floor, Drama Queen ran around, sniffing at all of Pinky's belongings.

Pinky: how did I not realize before how annoying samir is

Ash: what happened?

Pinky: nothing he's just . . .

She thought about it and finished.

Pinky: . . . #$DH%SR#$#@#@

Ash: lol well you know what they say

Ash: behind every hateful relationship is a tsunami of passion

Pinky: what who tf says that

Ash: THEY

Pinky: whatever dude just hope I don't kill him by the end of the week

Ash: he's not really that bad is he??

Pinky considered this. The truth was, it wasn't anything Samir had done that she could put her finger on. It was just mostly . . . his do-gooder, smug, *I'm always right* attitude. He thought she was a selfish, immature brat. Well, better that than being some premature forty-year-old like he was. And what the hell was up with that planner? Planning every single minute of his life, even summer break? Didn't that point to some deep-seated crap? Not to mention, he always knew the right thing to say somehow. He'd fit in seamlessly with her family like she never had. Why was it so easy for a stranger to come in and insinuate himself with her parents? Why couldn't Pinky do that after seventeen years of living with them?

She sighed and typed, **gotta go**

There was a knock at her door and, slipping her phone into her pocket, she called, "Come in!"

Dolly walked in, her hair damp from the shower, dressed in a starfish-print sundress. "Hey."

Pinky put her shoe-clad feet up on her bed, even though her mom would go nuts if she saw, and leaned back against the headboard. "What's up?"

Dolly narrowed her eyes and walked in, taking a seat on Pinky's armchair. "What *is* up?"

Pinky frowned. "Huh?"

"You and Samir."

Pinky waited for more, but Dolly was just watching her quietly. "Yeees?"

Dolly took a minute to think. "There's something off about you two."

Pinky's heart began to beat faster. She sat up. "Off?" she said casually, reaching into her nightstand drawer for lip balm so she wouldn't have to look directly at Dolly. "What are you talking about?"

Drama Queen ran up to Dolly and sniffed her toes. Dolly wiggled them and the possum fell over, dead. Dolly gasped. "Oh my gosh. Is she—"

"She's fine. Just, you know. Being dramatic." Pinky smoothed her lip balm over her lips and smacked them together. "So when do you think my dad's going to rope us all into another Boggle tournament?"

Dolly cocked her head. "Pinky. Really?"

"What?"

"What's going on with you and Samir?" Dolly said, leaning forward. "You can tell me; I'm not going to go rat on you or anything."

"There's nothing going on," Pinky said as convincingly as possible, given that her palms were sweaty. She had no problem lying to her parents, but Dolly was another matter. She wanted to tell her, she did, but . . . she needed to keep this thing as "pure" as possible. The fewer people who knew about this, the less chance there'd be of an accidental slip or something else to derail her—and Samir's—plans.

Dolly's phone dinged and she pulled it out of her pocket, making a face at the screen, fully distracted.

"Cash?" Pinky guessed. Awash in a flood of relief, she hopped off the bed and scooped up Drama Queen's limp body. She walked to her closet and put her carefully back into her shoebox.

"Yeah." Dolly sighed. "He wants to come over."

"What? When?"

"Tonight." A faint blush spread over Dolly's cheeks and neck.

"Hookup session." Pinky nodded knowingly. "Don't do it."

"Don't worry, I'm not." Dolly slipped the phone back into her pocket. "Problem is, he doesn't seem to like hearing the word 'no.'"

"After he burned down our barn?" Pinky walked to the window and leaned out to look at the pile of black wreckage. "Jerk."

"It's my fault," Dolly said, "for hanging out with him in the first place. But there's something just . . . really persuasive about him."

Pinky turned around, her hands on the windowsill. "You can't let him bulldoze you. No means no."

"That's the thing, though," Dolly said, looking slightly tortured. "I kind of want him to come over anyway. I *like* who I am with him. And even though I knew he's no good for me and my parents would be super disappointed in me for hanging out with him, I want to anyway."

Pinky blew out a breath, making her bangs jump. "Yeah. Been there, sister."

Samir

The next day, Samir woke up, brushed his teeth, and took a shower before making his way out of his room. In the hallway, he passed Pinky's parents' empty bedroom and Pinky's closed bedroom door (not surprising; it was barely nine o'clock in the morning, and she hadn't woken up until close to ten so far into his stay) before slowing to look at the large gallery wall of pictures. He'd noticed them before but hadn't really taken the time to look.

There were a lot of photographs, most of them black and white, in black frames with white matting. He touched a frame with his fingertip; it looked like wood, but the texture felt different. Weird. Was it made of plastic or something? But then his attention was caught by a photograph in the center, of two little girls, clearly Pinky and Dolly when they were about seven or eight, in identical pigtails, eating ice creams on the front porch of this house. Dolly's pigtails were immaculate, whereas Pinky's were halfway out of their hair elastics. Her face was smeared with chocolate—even her eyebrows were covered—while Dolly looked like she might be in an ice cream ad.

Grinning, Samir looked at another picture, on the right, of a ten- or eleven-year-old Pinky sitting between her parents on a couch, a tiny kitten in her lap. The kitten's foot had been bandaged, and Pinky was petting it gently, not at all focused on the camera. There was another picture right below it, of just Pinky and her mom, in what looked like a garden, surrounded by butterflies. Pinky was very little, only about four or five, her chubby hands outstretched, her eyes crinkled in delight, her mouth open mid-laugh. Her mom was gazing down at her adoringly, oblivious to the cloud of butterflies around them, as if no one and nothing else existed in the world except for her daughter. How did they get from that to where they were now?

"Samir?"

He turned to find the Shark herself studying him from the bottom step. "Everything okay?"

He smiled. "Yes, absolutely. Just checking out your pictures." Ms. Kumar started up the stairs. "You have a really nice family." He meant it too.

Ms. Kumar gave him a tight-lipped smile in return as she joined him in front of the gallery wall. "Thank you. I wish Pinky thought so."

Samir couldn't think of what to say. Another thing for Pinky's list: Doesn't appreciate the fabulous family she has like she should. "Where was this taken?" he asked finally, pointing to the picture of Pinky and her mom in the garden.

The sound of a door opening interrupted Pinky's mom's response. Pinky stood out in the hallway in an old Panic! at the Disco T-shirt and pirate-themed pajama bottoms. Her multicolored hair was in a frizzy halo around her head, and she blinked blearily at Samir and her mom, as if she couldn't quite place them. "Wh-what's happening?"

Samir grinned. "Wow. You look fresh as a daisy."

She managed a sleepy glare but shuffled closer. "What're you guys looking at?"

"Samir was asking me where this picture was taken." Ms. Kumar caressed toddler Pinky's chubby cheek in the picture, a small smile on her face. She glanced past him at real-life Pinky. "Do you remember?"

"Sure," Pinky replied, her voice all sleep-scratchy. "That's the butterfly habitat."

"Mm-hmm. This was the year after it was built. You could never get enough of the butterflies. Or, as you called them, the 'wuh-wuh-whys.'"

Samir laughed, kind of touched by this mental image, and Pinky slapped him on the arm. "I was *little*."

"Do you guys go back every year?" he asked.

Pinky and her mom exchanged a look. Nonchalantly itching her elbow, Pinky said, "We used to. Not so much anymore."

"Not since Pinky got too cool for her parents." Her mother

laughed. Pinky opened her mouth to respond, but then closed it again. After a pause, her mom added softly, "You should take Samir. All the plants and trees are so much more mature now. He would like it."

Pinky looked at him and shrugged. "Do you want to?"

Samir didn't know exactly what was going on, but it was clear the habitat was a lot more than just a place to watch butterflies flit about for both Pinky and her mom. "I'd love to," he said sincerely.

"Great. It's a date." Pinky's eyes lingered on the picture for another moment, and then she turned for her room. "I need coffee, but first I need a shower. See you guys in a few."

Downstairs, Mr. Yeung was in a frenzied state of cooking in the kitchen.

"Samir!" he said heartily. Mr. Yeung, Samir was finding out, was always hearty. "It's build-your-own-omelet day! What would you like on yours?" He was standing at the stove with an array of bowls before him filled with diced onions, diced tomatoes, diced ham, chopped mushrooms and peppers, and three different kinds of cheese.

Dolly's dad, Mr. Montclair (Samir could never get used to calling an adult by his first name), was on the other counter at the pastry "station." He had almond croissants, chocolate croissants, Danishes, and every variety of doughnut possible before him. "Help yourself, Samir," he said, in calmer tones than Mr. Yeung. "We have so much food."

Ms. Kumar smiled, shook her head, and went to sit by her sister, Mrs. Montclair.

"Wow." Samir's stomach rumbled greedily. "I didn't even realize I was hungry, but now . . ."

"Good, good!" Mr. Yeung said. "Want an omelet with everything on it?"

"Yes, please." Samir got a plate to help himself to a couple of the pastries too. "Would you like some help?"

"Nah, you sit!" Mr. Yeung said, gesturing with a spatula. A little bit of egg yolk splattered on the wall, but he didn't notice. Samir, on the other hand, stared at the splatter, hoping Mr. Yeung'd turn around and wipe it off with a dish towel. It would take, like, two seconds.

Reluctantly tearing his eyes away from it and pouring out a glass of milk, Samir took a seat next to Ms. Kumar and her sister in a sun-warmed chair by the French doors. "Thanks," he said, drinking half his milk in one go. "This is awesome. Do you guys always eat like this?"

Ms. Kumar laughed. "No. This is something we do when we're here at the lake house. Lots of food, lots of choices."

Mrs. Montclair smiled and sipped her tea. "Dolly's still asleep, but she's going to love those doughnuts. They're her favorite. So, Samir, are you enjoying your summer so far? Besides the mishap with your internship, I mean."

"Absolutely." Samir quickly swallowed a mouthful of jelly dough-nut. "I really love this place so far. Super relaxing."

"Good." Ms. Kumar tapped her fingernail thoughtfully on the polished wood table. "You said your internship was with Iyer and Whitman, right? So does that mean you're interested in corporate law?"

"Yes," Samir said, surreptitiously wiping the corners of his mouth with a napkin. He didn't want to have a serious conversation with the Shark while he looked like a three-year-old with a feral cat's table manners. "I've been interested in corporate law ever since I read about the Supreme Court's ruling on class actions with AT&T in 2011."

Ms. Kumar assessed him carefully. "Most young people are interested in criminal defense. That's the cool stuff, right? What they show on TV or in novels."

"Yeah, but . . . I don't know. I'm a pretty steady, reliable kind of person and I think I'd do better with a steady, reliable kind of environment. Leave the criminal work to those with more of a dramatic flair."

Ms. Kumar studied him for another second, and Samir was suddenly afraid he'd said something offensive. But then she laughed. "I like that," she said. "It's great that you already know what you want to do." Her smile slipped off her face and Samir knew she was thinking of her own progeny, who, until moments ago was asleep upstairs, sharing a room with a marsupial.

"Pinky will figure out her own way," Mr. Yeung said, walking over with Samir's omelet. "She's a free spirit, that's all." He beamed at Samir. "You must know that already, huh?"

"Yes," Samir said, meaning it. He'd been in Pinky's social circle enough to know *that* was true. Everyone knew that about her. "And I do think she'll figure it out. Some people just take a little bit longer."

"What are you talking about?"

Samir swiveled to see Pinky at the kitchen door, frowning, her hair wet from the shower. That was record speed for a shower. Was she worried what her family might be saying to him about her? It was weird to Samir, how much she simultaneously cared what her parents thought of her and how much she purposely lived her life so they thought the worst.

"Come sit, Pinky," her dad said. "Want an omelet?"

"Or a pastry?" Mr. Montclair said, still at the pastry station, although Samir noticed there were two fewer doughnuts than there had been when he'd walked in.

"Coffee first," Pinky mumbled, walking over to the coffee maker.

Pinky

It was around three thirty in the afternoon. Pinky, Samir, and Dolly were sitting on the front porch playing Uno, a pitcher of homemade watermelon lemonade sweating on the table between them. The occasional car or SUV trundled by on the street and there were a few boats out on the lake, but for the most part, it was quiet besides the singing of chickadees and blue jays.

"Oh, hells to the yes," Pinky sang, raising her hands in victory. She accidentally knocked one of the striped cushions off the wicker rocking chair, but barely noticed in her victorious glee. "One more card and I'm at Uno, suck-ahs!"

Samir, sitting across the table from her on the love seat, raised an eyebrow. He was sweaty and pink-cheeked; the ceiling fan above them didn't seem to be doing much except pushing the hot air around. "Draw four, suck-ah," he sang back to her, playing a Draw Four card.

"Dammit!" Pinky yelled as Dolly cracked up on her right. "How do you keep doing that?"

"Pride goeth before a fall," Samir intoned, mock seriously. "The universe is on my side, clearly."

"I need a Reverse card," Pinky mumbled, cutting her eyes to Dolly. "Then *you* can deal with him."

"No, thank you!" Dolly said sweetly, taking a sip of her lemonade. "I'm happy going after you. You're too distracted to keep track of my cards."

"Pah!" Pinky said, knowing Dolly was right. She narrowed her eyes at Samir. "Next round? You're going down."

"Bring it," he said, though the seriousness of his threat was marred somewhat by the sweat dribbling into his eye.

"If you're not a Samir-shaped raisin by then." Pinky snorted.

"Oh, Uno, nice. I haven't played that since I was, like, twelve."

They all looked up at the drawling male voice to see Cash Miller strolling up the porch steps, his Gucci sunglasses on, the collar of his shirt popped. He must've walked over from his house, but in spite of the sweltering heat, his hair and clothes were immaculate.

"Ugh, *this* guy," Pinky mumbled, just as Dolly said, "Hi, Cash. Would you like to join us? We've got watermelon lemonade, too."

Samir caught Pinky's eye and raised an eyebrow, probably in an attempt to guilt her for her inhospitable response. It didn't work, though. She stuck her tongue out at him quickly before turning back to her cards.

"Maybe just for a minute," Cash replied, sauntering over to Dolly in a cloud of cologne. He sat in the empty chair next to her, throwing his legs over the side. Maybe because the heat was so stifling, his musk-scented cologne permeated the air and seemed to jab itself aggressively up Pinky's nose.

"Hey," Samir said, after a moment of awkward silence, rising and holding his card-free hand out. "I'm Samir. Pinky's . . . boyfriend."

Pinky darted a glance at Cash and Dolly, but neither of them seemed to have noticed the minuscule hesitation.

Still wearing his sunglasses, Cash curled his hand into a fist, probably wanting Samir to do the same. But Samir just stood there with his hand outstretched, earning the tips of his fingers a fist bump.

Samir's smile faded away and he sat back down, a small frown between his eyebrows. *Ha*, Pinky thought. *Bet he didn't think he'd meet someone more mannerless than me this summer.*

"So, this is it, *seriously*? You guys are just sitting here playing Uno?" Cash remarked, grinning around at them. Then, swinging his hairy legs back around and leaning in close, he added in a near whisper, "Come on. You've mixed some rum in there at least, right?" He nodded toward the pitcher of lemonade.

Pinky looked at her reflection in his stupid sunglasses and rolled her eyes. "It's *just* lemonade, and we're *just* playing Uno."

Dolly smiled, but it looked pained. "Yep."

Cash huffed and looked at Samir. "Dude. You're sitting here with two hot girls and you're playing Uno and drinking lemonade? Really?"

Oh man. Pinky felt almost bad for Samir. There was no way someone like him could take on someone like—

"Pinky already answered that question," Samir said, his voice level and calm, his eyes never leaving Cash's (well, the proximity of his eyes . . . it was impossible to see his actual eyes behind those reflective, douchey shades). "And now we'd like to get back to our game. So feel free to leave."

Whoa. Pinky stared at Samir, her mouth dropping open. She had *not* been expecting that. He continued to gaze coolly at Cash.

Something hummed in the air between the two; Pinky was half afraid Cash was going to launch himself at Samir or something. But in the end, he just scoffed, got up, and began to make his way over to the stairs, "accidentally" knocking into Samir's chair with his knee as he walked past. Samir's eyes blazed and a muscle in his jaw twitched, but he didn't respond.

"Text me later," Cash called over his shoulder to Dolly. Then, doing his one-finger salute in the air, he sauntered down the steps without a backward look at any of them.

Dolly cleared her throat, opened her mouth like she wanted to say something, and then closed it again. Instead, she took a deep drink of her lemonade.

"So, I think it was your turn, Pinky," Samir said casually, and she got the feeling he was giving Dolly a way out without having to make excuses for her douchey friend.

She smiled at him and registered his slight shock at the lack of sarcasm in it before drawing four cards from the deck in the center. Pinky had the unshakable feeling this wouldn't be the last time Samir Jha would surprise her this summer.

Samir

About an hour after the visit from Douchey McDouche (if he was Dolly's boyfriend, Samir had seriously misjudged her decision-making capabilities), Mr. Yeung summoned them to the living room.

"Boggle!" he said, holding up the bright orange box when they were all seated on the many scattered couches and armchairs. The other adults were already in the room, sipping on iced teas and Arnold Palmers. "It's tournament time, baby."

"Oh no," Pinky muttered, leaning her head back on the oversize blue-and-white-striped couch. "When Dad starts calling people 'baby,' you know he's in his overexcited, competitive mode."

"I'm not overexcited!" Mr. Yeung said, though the glint in his eye said otherwise. "Come on, baby!"

"It's best to just nod and smile," Mr. Montclair said to Samir. "Easier."

Samir obliged by nodding and smiling, and everyone laughed.

Mrs. Montclair handed out pads of paper and little pencils to everyone.

"Oh, I'm going to need a bigger pad than that!" Mr. Yeung grinned. "For all the words I'm going to write!"

"Daaad . . . ," Pinky said, rolling her eyes.

"Ready?" Ms. Kumar looked around at all of them solemnly. It was obvious she took her husband's hobby very seriously. "I'm going to start the timer, and when it runs out, you have to immediately set your pencils down. Even if you're mid-word."

"And that word doesn't count," Mr. Yeung clarified darkly. "Also, if you make a word that's not actually allowed by the rules of the game, you face an automatic ten-point deduction."

They were starting to freak Samir out a bit. He caught Pinky's eye; she raised an eyebrow and mouthed, "Accept your fate."

Mr. Yeung, still maintaining very uncomfortable eye contact with all of them, shook the Boggle dice in their covered tray; the sound was like an army of galloping robot horses on a tin roof, but Samir didn't dare so much as grimace. When he was done, Ms. Kumar flipped the timer. All was thankfully quiet except for the scratch of pencil on paper.

Samir looked around at everyone, his eyes coming to rest on Pinky. Her head was bowed, so all he could see was the riot of color on her scalp—lime green, electric purple, burn-your-retinas magenta. She was writing furiously, her eyebrows furrowed, intense concentration on her face.

Considering her, Samir couldn't help but smile a little. Impractical and hotheaded as she was, he had to hand it to her: She approached everything she did with a tsunami of passion that he didn't think he'd *ever* felt, let alone for a game of Boggle. Chuckling to himself (quietly, so she wouldn't hear and throw her pencil point-first at him), he peered at the letters. A slightly evil plan began taking root in his mind as he studied the Boggle board, and he smiled to himself as he began to write.

Three minutes later, Mr. Yeung yelled, "Time!!!" into the silence and Samir jumped so hard, his pencil tore a hole in his paper.

Pinky snorted, but she gave him an innocent look when he narrowed his eyes at her.

"Okay!" Mr. Yeung said, grinning a little wildly. "Who wants to go first, baby? Samir, would you like to, as our guest?"

"Oh." He swallowed, feeling suddenly and ludicrously nervous. "Um, sure." Setting his pencil down on the coffee table, he wiped his hands on his shorts and began to read. "Loud, proud, born, stubborn, torn, snort, snorted, snorts." His eyes unwittingly stole to Pinky's. She was staring at him, eyes narrowed.

"Hmm. Interesting words," she said, tapping her pencil at the corner of her mouth, at the same time that Mr. Yeung said, "Great start, Samir! Great start."

Pinky held his eyes across the space between them, a small smile twitching at her mouth. Samir could feel the *challenge accepted* message she was beaming telepathically at him. It was kind of weird, but he was looking forward to her response, childish and immature as he knew it would be. Maybe, in a small way, Pinky Kumar was beginning to grow on him. Kind of like mold grows on bread.

Once everyone read their words out, Ms. Kumar was deemed the winner of the first round (she actually made the word "syzygy," though no one knew what it was. Mr. Yeung had looked it up and then beamed proudly at his wife when he read the definition out loud). After that they went again, and while Mr. Yeung was doing his spiel about setting their pencils down, Pinky mouthed something to him that he could've sworn was "I'm gonna get you." Samir shrugged, making sure to keep his eyes extra wide and innocent. Dolly looked between them, laughing.

When time was called again, Pinky said, "I wanna go first!"

Everyone—except Samir—looked at her in surprise. He crossed his arms and mouthed, "Bring it."

She smirked and began to read. "Goody, two, shoes, show, off, go, get, lost."

Dolly laughed and shook her head. "Oh boy."

"Uh-uh," Mr. Yeung said, wagging his pencil. "There was no *L* on the board."

"Oh, wasn't there?" Pinky asked innocently, looking at Samir. "My bad."

Samir muffled a laugh. "This definitely calls for that ten-point deduction, Mr. Yeung. Wouldn't you say?"

"Much as I hate to do that to my own daughter, I have to agree," Mr. Yeung said, noting something on the scoreboard.

Samir smiled broadly at Pinky. "Rules are rules."

Pinky sat back and cocked her head at Samir. "Totally worth it," she muttered, crossing her arms over her *There Is No Planet B* T-shirt.

Break was called right then and Dolly stood up and shook her head. "Pinky, I thought you were anti–animal cruelty," she said, mock seriously.

Pinky chortled. "Just called Samir Starbucks, because he was *roasted*."

Laughing, Dolly sauntered out after her parents. In fact, everyone except Pinky and Samir left the room to refill their drinks or use the bathroom (or in Mr. Yeung's case, to memorize the dictionary). Samir scooted closer to Pinky on the couch. "Nice one. And nice list, too. Too bad you had to go and ruin it with 'lost.' There's no way you're coming back from that ten-point deduction."

"I'd do it again in a heartbeat," Pinky said, sipping her Coke.

"Impulsive," Samir said, shaking his head. "Let's see if I can make that word next round."

Pinky rolled her eyes. "Yeah, and maybe I can make the word—" She began to snore, as if she'd abruptly fallen asleep from boredom, her thick hair falling over her shoulder.

"Oh, sorry, are you snorting again? You might want to get that checked by a geneticist. Pretty sure they'll find you're only part human."

Pinky opened her eyes and crossed her arms. "At least I'm not a forty-year-old trapped inside a seventeen-year-old body."

"As I recall," Samir said, leaning toward her so their faces were just a few inches apart, "you're very fond of this body. You can't keep your hands off it, in fact."

Something in Pinky's face changed. He could've sworn her eyes drifted down to his lips for just a fraction of a second, her face a mask of confusion and discomfort at said confusion. As if she was used to always being in control, and around him . . . she wasn't always.

"Ho-kay, who's ready to go again, baby?" Mr. Yeung called, clapping his hands as he walked in from the kitchen, and Samir flew back, as if he'd been electrocuted.

Pinky cleared her throat and sipped at her Coke again. "Me," she said in a squeaky voice he'd never heard before. "Definitely me."

Pinky

They played a few more rounds, with Pinky's dad getting more and more feverish with every turn. "Time!" he yelled after the seventh round. "Pinky, you go first."

"Okay." She glanced up at Samir and then back down again, trying to hide her smile. He was paying attention. Good. "Steady, tad, tedious." She set her pencil down and batted her eyelashes.

"Three words, but that 'tedious' was a good play!" her dad said. "Good strategy, Pinky!"

Samir cleared his throat and crossed his legs in that dude way, with his ankle on his knee. There was a sparkle in his eye that made her want to laugh. "Right, right. Good, um, strategy. May I go next?"

"Sure!" her dad said, thrilled that someone was still awake enough to volunteer. Her family at this point was pretty much just sagging off the furniture, waiting for it all to be over. Even Dolly, although Pinky thought that had something to do with the fact that she'd been typing more words into her phone than writing them down. (Probably Cash again. Ugh.)

"I just have one, actually," Samir said, looking right at her. "Mutinous."

Pinky snorted Coke out of her nose. Laughing, Dolly passed her a napkin. "Mutinous?" Pinky said, when she could finally talk. In spite of herself, she was secretly pleased. *Mutinous.* She liked the sound of that.

Samir nodded. "Mutinous. I think it fits, don't you?"

Pinky raised her eyebrows and shrugged. "I have no idea what you're talking about."

Grinning, Samir shook his head and turned to Pinky's dad as he began recounting his words.

"Okay, I'm calling the game," Pinky's mom said, when her dad got so hyped up about winning the round (again) that he attempted to snap his little pencil, and when he couldn't, threw it against the wall and struck a pose like a testosterone-filled bodybuilder showing off his biceps. "That's quite enough excitement."

"We're just getting started!" her dad said, his face shiny from all his happy sweat. "Can we do another ten minutes?"

Pinky wanted to laugh; he sounded like a six-year-old.

"No, Howard, I think we're all finished for now," her mom said, and there were murmurs of assent all around. "Besides, you'll have a chance to compete again next Friday."

"Wasn't much of a competition," her dad muttered sullenly.

"Friday?" Pinky asked. "What's going on Friday?"

"We have a trivia night to go to at the country club," Meera Mausi explained.

"Oh, is that next Friday?" Dolly asked, making a face.

"What?" Meera Mausi said, cuffing her gently on the chin. "You love trivia night—we do it every summer."

"Yeah, no, I do," Dolly said. "It's just . . . I had plans."

Abe and Meera Mausi immediately swiveled toward her, like two satellites picking up a curious signal. "Plans?" Abe said, in a controlled voice. "With whom?"

"Um . . ." Dolly flashed Pinky a panicked look. "With, um . . ."

"Me," Pinky said, shaking her head slightly. Dolly was *so* bad at this. She had to help her out, even if she loathed Cash. In any fight between adults and her peers, she'd always help her peers. "Me and Samir. Yeah, we were gonna go for a drive, do some shopping, just check out how the town's changed, that kind of thing."

"Oh, well, you guys can still do that," Pinky's mom said, draining the last of her Arnold Palmer. "Just do it during the day instead."

"Where is the trivia night?" Samir asked, looking interested.

"At the Country Club," Pinky said, making sure he—and her mom—heard the capital *C*s in her voice.

"It's very nice," Pinky's mom said, as she knew she would. Her mom thought the sun rose and set with the events at the country club. "It's a good crowd too. You'll enjoy it, Samir."

"What's that supposed to mean?" Pinky asked, bristling.

"What?" her mom said, raising her hands, as if she were the most innocent person to ever walk the earth.

"The way you said that. Why the slight emphasis on *you'll*? Because I couldn't possibly enjoy it?" Her neck felt prickly, the way it always did when she and her mom got into it.

"There was no emphasis!" Pinky's mom threw her hands up in the air. "Stop putting words in my mouth."

"I'm not putting them in your mouth," Pinky said. "I'm just bringing the ones already there into the light."

There was a brief pause as Pinky and her mom glared at each other. Samir cleared his throat. "Speaking of mouths, has anyone read the newest report on flossing?"

Ignoring him, Pinky's mom looked at her dad. "See what I mean? I can't win."

Pinky stood up, clenching her fists by her sides. "Don't talk about me like I'm not here."

Her mom looked at her in wonder, as if she couldn't believe they were related. *Yeah, welcome to the club, Mom.* "Stop shouting and making a scene!"

"I'm not shouting and making a scene!" Pinky shouted. "I don't work for you—stop telling me what to do!"

"Pinky—" her dad began.

"No, I'm gonna go. It's obviously what she wants." And without looking back at her silent, aghast family (and Samir), Pinky walked out of the room and ran to the stairs. Her throat felt tight and painful, but she promised herself she wouldn't cry.

There was a knock at her door a minute or two later. She ignored it. A pause, and then more knocking. "Not ready to talk yet," she called, barely looking up from her art journal, in which she was drawing an abstract floral pattern using her gel pens.

"Um, it's me." Samir's voice came floating in. "I promise I won't make you talk. I have your Coke."

She snorted. "Okay, fine. Come in."

He walked in and closed the door behind him, studying her expression. He held up the Coke can. "I come in peace." He paused. "And I'd like to leave in one piece."

Pinky managed a weak smile. "You and my dad share the same joke book, I think." She took the can from him, set it on the table, and went back to her coloring. "Anyway, don't worry. I'm calling a truce between you and me for now."

Samir sat in the chair opposite her. "Are you okay?"

She looked up, surprised to see the gentle concern in his brown eyes. "Yeah. Fine." Realizing she'd bit the words out and didn't really sound fine at all, she amended, "I'm good. Really."

Samir nodded. They sat in silence while the fan overhead whirred, stirring a gentle breeze in the room. Dusk had fallen outside, casting them in a rosy glow. "Where's DQ?" he asked, looking around.

"She died when I stormed in here, so I'm letting her sleep it off."

Samir laughed.

"What?" Pinky asked.

"Just a funny sentence. She died, so you're letting her sleep it off. Kind of like she's a paranormal creature."

Pinky raised an eyebrow. "You've had it in for her from day one."

"No, I haven't! I have a healthy respect for the undead."

Pinky laughed a little at that. They sat in silence for another moment while she colored, her pen nib scratching softly on the paper. Then, glancing up at Samir through her eyelashes, she ripped a blank page out of her art journal and handed it to him. "Here," she said, pushing the box of gel pens to the center of the table. "It's very soothing."

She expected him to refuse, to tell her it wasn't his kind of thing, but he took the paper and helped himself to a hunter green. "Thanks."

She watched him color for a moment, a small bubble of warmth in her chest. This was better than sitting here alone, she had to admit.

They colored together for a few moments, and then he said, "Does that happen a lot?"

"Which part? My mom and I fighting like gladiators or her talking about me like I'm invisible?"

Samir looked up at her, his pen going still. "You think you're invisible to her?"

Pinky made a *duh* face. "Why?"

Samir shook his head. "No, it's just that . . . to me, as an outsider, it seems like all she can see is you. Like, her thoughts are pretty much always on you."

Pinky considered his words. "Well, maybe in a way that you might think about an annoying headache that doesn't respond to medication."

"Do you ever feel like . . . ?"

Pinky swapped out her rose gold for brick red. "Feel like what?"

"That she says all that stuff because she's worried about you?" He looked at her warily, like he was afraid she might get mad.

Pinky huffed a breath. "Well, she doesn't need to be! I mean, don't you think that's kind of insulting, to be worried about your kid so much? Like she thinks I'm so much of a screwup that I can't even handle tying my own shoes or something."

"Maybe," Samir said. "Or maybe she's just doing what every parent on the planet does. I mean, you saw *my* mom, right? She was always so worried about me. Doesn't mean she ever thought I was a screwup."

"Yeah, but that's different," Pinky said, putting her pen back and folding her hands on the table over her drawing. "Your mom has a legit reason. She had *cancer*. What's my mom's excuse?"

Samir frowned. "You're looking at this all wrong. Your mom doesn't need an excuse. She's your *mom*. It's kind of in the job description for her to be worried."

Pinky laughed, even though what he was saying actually kind of hurt. Big surprise: When it came to Veena Kumar v. Pinky Kumar, she always, always automatically had a guilty verdict. "Oh, great. So you're on her side too."

Samir threw his hands in the air. "There are no sides! Everything's so contentious with you!"

"And everything's so even-keeled with you!" Pinky said, gesturing at him. "Don't you ever get mad? At people besides me, I mean? Or do you have to schedule that in your planner too?"

They glared at each other for a long minute. Then Samir said, "There's a lot to be said for being even-keeled, you know. You should try it sometime."

Pinky studied him for a moment. "What would happen? If you stopped scheduling things in your planner?"

Samir looked at her, uncomprehending. "What?"

"What do you think would happen?" She leaned forward, resting her elbows on the table, her Coke off to the side. "If you just threw your planner aside one day and didn't write anything in it?"

He looked like he was choking on something. "Everything would be utter chaos?"

Pinky wanted to laugh at the horror in his voice. "Or maybe you'd be fine. Millions of people go through life with hardly any planning whatsoever."

Samir cocked his head. "Okay, so what would happen if you made a choice to stop being so roller-coaster-y and decided to just get along with your mom? To not challenge her anymore?"

Pinky shook her head. "Roller-coaster-y isn't a word."

"Don't change the subject."

She met his eye. "I wouldn't know how to do that," she said finally, honestly.

Samir studied her for a moment before nodding. "Yeah, me either. With the planner thing."

Pinky took a deep swallow of her Coke, feeling slightly off-kilter. Had she and Samir actually . . . agreed on something? Or *connected* on it, or something? Weird. "Hey, are you ready for trivia night next Friday?"

"If Boggle was any indication, it's going to be intense," Samir said, smiling a half smile. He had good lips, for a boy. They were kind of bow-shaped and looked really soft. Suddenly and for no good reason, she was thinking of sitting on the couch during the Boggle break. The way he'd brought his face so close to hers, it had made her think of breathless first kisses. And then she thought of the paddleboat, how he'd caught her when she fell, how she'd stood there with her arms around his bare waist. And at the lighthouse—

She felt a warmth spreading through her. Oh God. Abort, abort, abort.

Wrangling her mind back to the present, Pinky blinked. "Ah, yeah, you got that right. If you think a whole room of adults acting like my dad did tonight is intense, that is."

Samir blew out a breath. "Well, thanks for preparing me for that. Maybe I'll wear body armor. In case they throw anything besides pencils."

Pinky chuckled. "I think you can handle them, Muscle Boy."

He raised his eyebrows at her and she flushed. *Why* the hell had she said that? She was turning into some kind of perv. Over *Samir*. Quickly, to distract from her perviness, she picked out an amber orange from the pen pack and glanced at him. "You don't have to sit here with me, you know. You can go do something else if you want."

"Oh, I know," he said, studying the pen pack himself. "But if it's okay with you, I'd like to stay here and finish this picture."

Pinky hooked her foot around the leg of her chair and dipped her head so he wouldn't see the ghost of a smile at her lips. "Sure," she said in the most nonchalant way she could manage.

Samir

A couple of days after the Boggle Debacle, as he'd come to think of it in his mind, Samir and Pinky were downstairs, finishing up breakfast. The adults were more subdued than usual, as if the whole thing with Pinky and her mom had put a damper on their summer. Everyone was tiptoeing around Pinky and her mom, as if they were afraid to set off another thermonuclear reaction. Honestly, Samir felt a little bad for Pinky—it probably wasn't fun to feel like everyone saw you as the troublemaker. But then again, she *was* the troublemaker.

"Oh, look," Mr. Montclair said in a hearty voice, as if to try to cut through some of the tension. He turned his phone to show everyone the screen. "The Ellingsworth Point Butterfly Habitat made it onto TripAdvisor as a must-do summer activity!"

Samir expected Pinky to grunt or to say nothing at all, as per her usual morning routine, but she was sitting up straighter, peering at the screen. "That doesn't surprise me," she said, and her eyes darted to meet her mother's across the table. "It's a pretty magical place." Samir remembered the picture in the hallway, of Pinky as a toddler and her mom smiling down at her.

Pinky's mom smiled faintly. "It is," she said, playing with the tag of her tea bag and leaning back against her dining chair. "You always thought so. Do you remember your fairy princess phase?"

Pinky laughed. "Yeah. I used to bring a plastic magic wand every time we went and pretend to change the butterflies' colors." She shook her head. "So stupid."

"I thought it was precious," her mother countered, and Samir saw Pinky's mouth fall open in surprise.

There was a pause, and then Pinky said softly, "You know what I remember most about our trips there?" She was looking right at her mom. All the other adults had gone quiet, even Mr. Yeung, who was usually extremely talkative in the mornings.

Ms. Kumar shook her head.

"We never fought while we were there," Pinky continued. "Not once. It was like an argument-free zone." She snorted. "I mean, that's a pretty big deal for us."

Ms. Kumar smiled a little at that. "Yeah, it is." She added, "We haven't been yet this summer. Maybe we should go."

Pinky took a sip of coffee and shrugged, apparently nonchalant. But Samir could see the way she held herself, so stiff and straight, that this whole conversation meant a lot more to her than she was letting on. "Sure," she said. "That could be good."

"Good," her mom replied, smiling as she sipped her tea.

There was a tangible relaxing of the atmosphere. An olive branch had been extended and accepted. The butterfly habitat was obviously a special place to Pinky and her mom; and Samir, like everyone at the table, was glad Mr. Montclair had brought it up.

"Hey. Where's Dolly?" Pinky said suddenly, clutching her cup of coffee to her and looking around as if she'd just realized her cousin was missing. Which she probably had. Pinky wasn't the speediest thinker in the morning.

"She went for a run," Mrs. Montclair said. "Needed to clear her head, apparently."

Pinky cocked an eyebrow. "I'm sure she did," she muttered, though Samir didn't think any of the adults heard her. He wondered if she was talking about Cash the Rash.

She gulped down half her coffee, wincing (probably at the heat), and set her mug down in the sink. "I'm gonna take Drama Queen for a walk." Before her parents could say anything else, she zombie-walked toward the stairs.

Samir finished up his food and took his plate and glass to the sink too, rinsing them quickly and sticking them in the dishwasher.

"I'll keep her company." He smiled at the adults and walked up the stairs, frowning.

Pinky was putting Drama Queen's halter on her. She'd already changed from her pajamas into a pair of shorts and a Pride T-shirt. She glanced at him. "Oh. Hey."

"Hey." Samir leaned against the doorjamb. "You just got a sudden itch to take Drama Queen on a walk?"

"DQ needs to go." She scooped the marsupial up and walked over to slip on her flip-flops.

"Right." Like he was buying that. Pinky was definitely up to something. And he was curious. "You mind if I keep you company?"

She stopped on her way out the door and looked up at him, her eyes deceptively innocent and wide. "Oh. You? Now?"

He shrugged. "I mean, I think it'll look pretty weird to your parents if I stay here and hang out with them, don't you think?"

She looked torn. Seeming to come to a decision, she nodded once. "Okay, fine. Come on."

Outside, they walked in the nearly oppressive sunshine in complete silence while Drama Queen rushed around sniffing bushes and leaves and grass. Samir brushed his hair back and glanced at Pinky. He could tell she was strolling toward the lake in a way she hoped looked casual, taking a path he hadn't seen her walk DQ on before.

"Where are we going?" he asked lightly.

She shook her head. "Oh, nowhere. I just thought it'd be nice to go this way, you know, let DQ really stretch her legs today."

"Uh-huh."

They hung a right, making their way around the lake to the

houses on the other side. "So what'd you mean when you said, 'I'm sure she did'?"

Pinky snapped her head to look at him. "What?"

"Back there, in the kitchen," Samir said, pointing his thumb behind them. "Your aunt said Dolly went out for a run to clear her head, and you said—"

"I was just agreeing with her," Pinky said, but she wouldn't meet his eye anymore. She had this determined look on her face as they marched onward, closer to the houses on the other side. DQ was practically running to keep up with them.

A cooling breeze off the lake wrapped them both up. Samir nodded. "Right, just agreeing with her. So the sarcasm I thought I detected . . . ?"

"Wasn't there." Pinky straightened, paying more attention now to the group of people on the far side of one of the houses.

Samir squinted; it looked like a group about half a dozen large, all around his and Pinky's age, clustered in a side yard, laughing and talking. "Who are they?" he asked, though he was pretty sure he knew.

"You'll recognize them. Just wait," Pinky said, her lips in a thin line.

As they got closer, Samir saw that one of the people was Dolly. She was leaning against a large horse chestnut tree, dressed in running shorts and a tank top. Her face had a strange expression on it, like she wasn't even sure why she was there. And next to her was Cash the Rash, tall and muscular, his arm slung casually around her shoulders. His hair flopped in his face, he wore Ray-Bans today and a polo shirt with the collar popped again, and he was smirking as he said something. Samir felt the same dislike he'd felt the first time they'd met like a bitter powder in his throat.

"Hey, Dolly," Pinky called when they got closer. "How's your run going?"

Dolly's face registered first shock and then shame as she took in Pinky's and Samir's presence. Sliding Cash's arm off her, she walked down to them. Cash caught Samir's eye, said something to the short, dark-skinned boy next to him, who then also stared at Samir. Samir let his gaze slide right over them and to Dolly.

"Hey," Dolly said, when she was on the sidewalk. DQ came up, sniffed her shins, and then went back to sniffing the grass. "What are you guys doing here?"

Pinky raised an eyebrow. "Really? Sneaking out to hang with Cash and his crew?"

Dolly's cheeks were pink. She tucked a lock of hair behind her ear and looked away. "He texted me and I didn't want to have to explain to my parents."

Pinky's shoulders sagged. "Dude, I'm not here to judge you. Goddess knows I have no right after all the crap I've pulled. But, like, are you even having fun? Because it looked like you were undergoing a painful dental procedure rather than hanging out with friends."

Dolly sighed and massaged her temples. "I don't know. Seriously. What am I doing?" She glanced at Samir, as if expecting an answer.

Startled at being addressed in this fashion (he'd honestly started to zone out a bit), Samir ventured, "Um . . . getting some air?" He didn't like Cash, but he was in no position to give Dolly boyfriend advice. He'd never even been in a relationship himself.

She laughed a little. "Yeah. Getting some air is about right. I just need to do something different, you know?"

Again, she was talking to him. He nodded in what he hoped was an intelligent way. Was she having some kind of crisis? Shouldn't her parents, the therapists, be involved with this? Feeling completely inadequate, he said, "Yeah, totally. Do something different."

"I mean, don't *you* ever get tired of doing the same old stuff every single day?" she asked him earnestly. "Get up, eat breakfast, blah, blah, blah. Conform, conform, conform. Do what they want you to."

"Not really. Doing the same stuff every day is good for you." But something about what she'd said niggled at him. He'd felt that same sense of ennui when he was still under his mom's thumb, not too long ago. Was he still, in some ways, carrying that burden with him? Was that why he was so . . . controlled? He blinked. No, come on. He was so controlled and orderly because he *liked* to be. It was a choice. He could stop anytime he wanted.

"Yo, Dolls," Cash called, interrupting Samir's reverie. "We're going to go hang out at Krab's crib. You coming or what?"

A freckled, shirtless redheaded boy who was sprawled on the grass sat up and flashed them a peace sign.

"His name is Krab?" Pinky asked, her expression unreadable.

"With a *K*," Dolly confirmed, her face regretful. She sighed. "Yeah, I'm coming," she called to Cash, with less enthusiasm than Samir felt for the idea of meditation (it was too unstructured). Then, turning to Pinky and Samir, she said, "Do . . . you guys want to go too?"

Pinky shook her head. "Less than I want to enlist in the army. Look, you don't need to go do this to prove something to someone, okay?"

"Easy for you to say, Ms. Counterculture," Dolly said, crossing her arms. "I need to do this, Pinky. To see who else I'm capable of being besides vanilla, boring, predictable Dolly."

"I've made a *lot* of mistakes I wish I hadn't made," Pinky argued. "Seriously. You're just seeing the rosy, happy side of—"

"Well, then let me make my own mistakes," Dolly replied. "Okay?"

Pinky sighed, and Samir could tell she was biting back her frustration. "Okay, fine. You have fun if you can. But be careful. And text me if you need me to come get you or give you an excuse to leave or anything."

Dolly hugged her. "Thanks, Pinky. Cover for me with the parental units?"

"Of course," Pinky replied.

Waving to her and Samir, Dolly walked off to join the group again.

After a long second, Pinky turned to go, and Samir followed. He glanced at her sidelong, seeing the tightness in her shoulders, the way she kept nibbling at her lower lip. "You're worried about her," he ventured as they walked.

"A little," Pinky allowed. "Mostly I really don't trust that group. They're very rarely up to any good. And I think Dolly's just with Cash to prove something, and that's usually the worst reason to go out with someone. I should know."

Hmm. Samir sort of wanted ask her what she meant by that, but he realized he also kind of *didn't* want to know what other boys she'd dated. Weird.

"Yeah, maybe," he said, pulling his mind away from that train of thought, closing his eyes when another cool breeze came off the lake, lowering his temperature. "All that stuff she said, though? About being tired of the same stuff, day in and day out? I can relate."

"Oh yeah?" Pinky said, glancing at him. Out on the water, someone started up a Jet Ski. "With your mom, you mean?"

"Yep. It got really tiring, you know. Doing what she expected of me all the time, never really being free to do what I wanted." Samir looked at her. "Not that I expect you to know anything about that."

"Right, because being constantly criticized for all your shortcomings is so much easier," she said, adding her trademark snort at the end.

Samir thought about it. Pinky was criticized a lot perhaps. But she was also freer than most other people in a way. He was coming to see that now, bit by bit. "No," he said finally. "I guess it wouldn't be any easier. But at least you're doing what *you* want to do. You're living by your own standards."

Pinky gaped at him. "Oh my God, Samir Jha. Was that a *compliment* about my—what was it you said at the lighthouse? Oh yes, my 'immaturity and my irresponsibility'?"

He smirked. "Don't push it. I'm just a breath away from a litany of insults."

Pinky laughed and shook her head. "I'm not surprised." They let DQ sniff around for another moment, and then Pinky tugged on the leash so the marsupial would leave the pinecone she was nibbling and follow them. "You know, Dolly says stuff like that too, about my rebellious streak. But sometimes I wonder if it's selfish, you know. My mom certainly seems to think so."

"Your mom loves you," Samir said. He turned to her and put his hands on her shoulders, waiting until she met his eye. Something sparked between them. "You're an easy person to . . . to love." Oh crap. Why had he said that? It had just slipped out of him, ridiculous and saccharine. Was that too much? It was definitely too much. She was staring at him, but with Pinky, it was hard to say if she was happy or getting ready to knee you in the nads.

"You really think so?" she said softly. Okay, so his nads were safe for the moment.

He nodded solemnly. "I know so." And because he thought she needed to hear it again, he said it again. "Your mom loves you."

"Yeah. But does she like me?" Pinky asked, looking up at him and then out at the lake to their right. "That's what I ask myself the most."

He didn't really know what to say to that, so he slipped his hands from her shoulders so they could continue on their walk. As they headed closer to home, Samir realized they hadn't fought once on this outing. Maybe he should alert Guinness.

CHAPTER 9

Pinky

Later that night, long after the parents were in bed, Dolly tapped on Pinky's door.

"Hey," she said, walking in wearing a cotton nightshirt and shorts, both of which were splattered with happy, smiling cartoon hearts. "We haven't really had a chance to talk alone yet."

"Mm-hmm," Pinky said, setting her Kindle off to the side. She'd been sprawled diagonally on her bed, reading. "I noticed you sneaking in right before dinner. And then you came downstairs with wet hair."

Dolly made a face and sat at the foot of her bed, the bedsprings creaking softly. "They were smoking, and I knew my parents would be *all* over that if they smelled it."

Pinky bit back the thousand replies she wanted to make. Dolly had already told her to back off, and that's exactly what she'd do. She wasn't a meddler. In fact, she prided herself on how un-meddly she was.

"What?" Dolly said, giving Pinky a look. "I can tell you want to say something. So let's hear it."

"Well, it's less things I want to say and more things I *don't* want to say. I'm an un-meddler."

Dolly continued to stare at her with an arched eyebrow.

"Ugh, fine. I definitely don't want to say that Cash is not the kind of guy you want to 'prove yourself' with. It's definitely not the same as someone wanting to become a snake charmer sticking their hand into a pit full of vipers instead of starting with, say, a corn snake."

Dolly looked at her for a second and then laughed. "Oh, good. I'm glad you definitely didn't say all that."

Pinky sighed. Sitting up, she hugged her knees to her chest. "Dolly . . . he already burned down our barn. He doesn't even make you happy."

Dolly sank back against the footboard and thought about this. "Well, no, *he* doesn't make me happy. But you know what? Doing this kinda does make me happy. I didn't know I had it in me, you know? Even if Cash isn't the love of my life or anything, at least I'm doing something different."

Pinky stifled a remark about how she hoped Dolly wasn't literally *doing* Cash. "Okay. Well, if you're happy then . . . great." It was obvious Dolly wasn't happy, but it was like she said before—she needed to make her own mistakes.

"So, tell me." Dolly pulled a pillow to her and hugged it. "How are things with your mom now?"

A cool breeze blew in the open window, stirring the curtains. "Great. As evidenced by our very civil behavior at dinner."

Dolly raised an eyebrow. "That was civil? You and your mom didn't speak to each other at all. And Samir and your dad were basically carrying the conversation for your half of the family by themselves."

Pinky shut her book. "Believe me, that was better than the alternative."

"Want me to talk to your mom?" Dolly had played peacemaker in previous years. She was not-so-weirdly good at it, being the daughter of two professional peacemakers.

"Nah. I'm over it." Pinky chewed on the corner of one of her nails, knowing Dolly could smell the bullcrap, but thankful she wasn't calling her on it. The truth was, she was tired of having to have other people play intermediary between her and her own mother. She wasn't even blood related to her dad and they got along fine. So what was the deal with this woman with whom she shared half her DNA?

Dolly let out a world-weary sigh and slumped down on Pinky's bed in a ball. "Why are relationships of all shades so complicated? Why can't people be easy? I mean, not Samir, obviously. He's probably the easiest guy to love."

Pinky raised an eyebrow. "You think Samir's easy to love?" Then, catching herself, she added, "I mean, obviously *I* think so, but I was curious about your . . . um, what you thought."

Dolly reached over and pulled Pinky's comforter over her bare legs. "Well, yeah. He's just so mature and focused, you know? He's effortlessly put-together, he dresses well, and he can hold a conversation with adults without using the word 'bro' even once. He even acts like a diplomat when things get hairy."

Pinky furrowed her eyebrows as she listened. Dolly was right, she realized. Samir *was* a calming presence. And the way he'd come into her room with a can of Coke and just sat and colored with her after that argument with her mom . . . She hadn't realized it at the time, but he'd lowered her blood pressure and her stress level. She'd never had a single real boyfriend do that for her. If anything, they just stoked the fire by telling her how controlling her mom was. Samir was . . . kind of a steadying presence when she desperately needed one. "Huh."

"Yeah. You have a good one there, Pinky. And the way he held his own with Cash when he was being annoying out on the porch the other day? Samir's just easy to get on board with."

Before she could tell her brain to stop, Pinky found herself blurting out with a weird little chuckle, "Well, don't get *too* on board with him—you have a boyfriend!"

Dolly frowned, and Pinky stared back at her, frozen. Then Dolly laughed. "What, are you jealous?"

Pinky forced herself to trill a totally fake laugh, even though she realized that, yes, shockingly enough, that's exactly what she'd felt, hearing Dolly sing Samir's praises: a pinprick of jealousy. Ridiculous.

Oblivious to Pinky's turmoil, Dolly lifted her head up and propped it on her hand. "Anyway, I wouldn't really call Cash my 'boyfriend.' He's . . . I don't know what he is, but 'boyfriend' is definitely not the right word."

Pinky nodded. "I get that. Really. I mean, take—" Whoops. She'd been about to say, *I mean, take Samir, for instance. He's definitely* not *my boyfriend.*

"Take what?" Dolly asked.

"Nothing." Pinky shook her head.

"Pinky." Dolly cocked her head. "Come on. What?"

Pinky looked into her cousin's big, trusting eyes. Dolly might have evolved her secret-keeping skills. She was keeping a few of her own now. Besides, she'd confided in Pinky. It was only fair that

Pinky confide in her, too. Otherwise it was just like she was lying to one more person, someone who really didn't deserve it. "Okay, but this is big, okay? Huge. You have to *promise* not to let this slip to any of the adults."

Dolly's eyes went wide. "Wow, okay. What is it?"

"You remember how you asked me if Samir and I . . . what was up with us, basically?"

Dolly frowned. "Yeah?"

"Well, your spidey senses were right. He and I . . ." She swallowed and then spoke quickly. "We're not really dating."

Dolly's face went from avid curiosity to abject confusion in .2 seconds. "*What?*" she yelled.

Pinky clapped a hand to her cousin's mouth. "Shh!"

Dolly raised her hands. "Sorry," she mumbled. Pinky let her hand drop and sat back again. "*What?*" Dolly said again, but much quieter this time. Her hazel eyes were dancing with glee. "Oh. My. God. This is, like, the most epic con you've ever pulled and you've pulled some big ones."

Pinky snorted. "Right?"

"So what's the point?" Dolly asked, leaning forward. "Why are you guys doing it?"

"I just got really freaking tired of my mom thinking I'm incapable of making any decisions she'd approve of," Pinky said, throwing her hands up in the air. "And the lie just came out that night the barn burned down. Remember, when she was really drilling me? After I'd told her I had this great, amazing boyfriend, I couldn't just rescind it and face her contempt again. I had to, you know, follow through." She pushed her hand through the air.

Dolly nodded slowly, digesting everything apparently. "And Samir? What's in it for him? He doesn't seem like the kind of dude who'd go along with something like this."

"Well, not normally, but his law-firm summer internship fell through."

Understanding dawned on Dolly's face. "You promised him an internship with your parents?"

"With my mom. If he can impress her, which he's already doing. It shouldn't be a problem."

Dolly sat back and laughed. "Wow. This is . . . I feel like I'm in a Heath Ledger rom-com or something."

Pinky shook her head. "If it's a movie, it's the most effed-up movie on the planet."

They stared at each other for a long moment, then burst out laughing simultaneously.

"Pinky," Dolly said, when she could speak again. "You really are something else."

CHAPTER 10

Samir

Friday evening, Samir stood in front of the floor-length mirror in his room, getting ready for the fancy dinner/trivia night at the country club, due to start in an hour. The men were required to wear suits, and Samir was glad he still had his from his doomed internship. He adjusted his freshly ironed pale-purple tie and studied himself critically in the mirror. Not bad, but he wished he had a little pomade; he could style his hair so that a bit fell over his forehead. That tennis instructor he'd kissed had told him she liked that. Not that there were any girls he was hoping to impress here or anything.

His attention was snared by movement outside his window, in the side yard. Pinky was down there in a startlingly sexy gold spaghetti-strap dress, gold chains crisscrossing down the back, giving him peekaboo hints of her glowing brown skin inside. Her hair was proud and colorful as ever, like a multihued flag in the gentle breeze. Samir smiled to himself. She was going to be a total sore thumb sticking out at this function. And naturally, the rest of her family would look like they'd all been born in a country club.

Although he needed to finish getting dressed, Samir couldn't help but continue to watch her. She had sparkly ankle boots in one hand, and the other hand held Drama Queen's leash. The opossum sniffed around enthusiastically, scratching at the ground, but when Pinky reached down to adjust her halter, she went limp and fell over in a dead faint. Samir chuckled as Pinky shook her head, heaved a sigh, and scooped up DQ. She glanced up as she walked back to the house, meeting his gaze. They stopped still, both of them staring at each other for a long moment, until Samir raised a hand. After a pause, she smiled a little, nodded, and headed back in.

Samir walked to the mirror, smiling a bit at his reflection. At least they weren't fully at each other's throats anymore. That was good. Maybe he'd even enjoy himself a bit tonight.

"Good goddess, how many more rounds?" Pinky groaned as she hung her head back. Her cheeks, dusted with what looked like soft gold shimmer, glowed classily in the dim lighting. Her hair, on the other hand, looked like iridescent fire atop her head, and it was drawing enough looks from the genteel country-club patrons around them as if it really were.

"Don't be rude," Ms. Kumar said, looking around at the others at their table to see if anyone had heard. Glancing at Samir, she said, "I'm sorry about her." Apparently the olive branch he thought had been extended when they'd reminisced about the butterfly habitat had been snapped in half.

They'd entered the country-club restaurant through a gigantic stone-mansion-esque building, where Pinky's parents were greeted like royalty by the woman at the reservations desk. Now they were seated at one of twelve circular tables in the restaurant of the country club, which was called, pretty uncreatively, Samir thought, the Restaurant. The country club, though, was called Silver Pines, not the Country Club.

All around them were tables filled with glittering, happy, mostly older white people who wore jewels the size of their eyeballs around their throats and fingers. Occasionally a swell of cultured laughter would fill the space, crowding out the steadier rumbling hum of thirty-two different simultaneous conversations about newly acquired Bugattis and golf and second and third homes on the Italian Riviera.

"Don't apologize for me," Pinky snapped at her mom, her eyes glinting under the soft lights.

Her mom gave her a steely look. "Don't say things that lead to me having to apologize for you."

Pinky rolled her eyes and looked at a passing waiter. "I'd love a red wine when you have a moment," she said, and the man smiled at first, then caught Ms. Kumar's murderous glare and hurried away.

Ms. Kumar turned the glare on Pinky, and Samir felt his own insides shrivel in response. The Shark, out in full *Jaws* mode. "That was completely inappropriate. And don't tell me you've been drinking tonight."

"Clearly not, or I'd be having a lot more fun," Pinky retorted.

There was a prickly silence, and Dolly flagged down one of the circulating waiters and asked for another ginger ale, probably as a distraction.

Taking her cue, Samir said, "Hey, Pinky, why don't we go for a walk? I'm really crap at pop culture anyway, so I doubt we'll be much help, and I'd love to see the grounds."

Ms. Kumar nodded—Samir suspected she couldn't speak without totally losing it—and everyone at the table shot him a grateful look. He scraped his chair back, waited for Pinky, and then the two of them headed out of the main room of the restaurant.

Samir took off his suit jacket as they made their way out into the balmy, muggy summer night outside. "Remember when I said you antagonize your parents a lot?"

Pinky huffed a breath. "Has anyone ever told *you* your perception is probably warped from the fact that you're *afraid* to antagonize anyone, probably because she breastfed you too long as a baby?"

Samir raised his eyebrows. "Wow, are your legs tired?"

"What?"

"They must be, because you're jumping to a lot of conclusions there."

Pinky's confusion cleared. "Ha ha, hilarious. You should consider stand-up comedy."

Samir smirked. "See, I can do stand-up because *my* legs aren't tired."

"That's great. You're on a roll—hey, check this out." She pointed to a metal ladder that was screwed on to the back side of the building, near the staff entrance. She gave it a hard tug and it held. Tipping her head back so her multicolored curls brushed her mid-back, she said, "It looks like it leads to a little ledge up there."

"Yeah, looks like it does," Samir said. "Wanna keep walking?"

Pinky turned to him, a mischievous glint in her eye as she smiled. "Don't tell me you're afraid of heights or something."

"You say that like it's a bad thing. May I remind you that heights are actually dangerous? Like, you can actually break something or *die* if you fall off something tall."

"That's what the cowards always say." Pinky kicked off her boots and stepped on the first rung of the ladder. "Come on, wuss," she said over her shoulder. "Let's go look at the stars." And then she clambered up like it was the most natural thing in the world to scurry up a rickety ladder in the darkness without even knowing exactly where it led.

"If that's your idea of a pickup line, I can probably tell you why you have a problem landing good boyfriends," Samir said, but she only laughed scathingly and retorted, "Yeah, like I'm gonna waste the good ones on you!"

"Wow," she called down a minute later. "It's so pretty up here! You can see the lake and the lights. . . ." Her head peeked over the ledge a moment later. "Come on, Sam!"

"Is there a railing up there?" he called, his voice high and squeaky. "Because if there isn't, you shouldn't peek over like that." He felt his palms getting sweaty on her behalf.

"It's not even that high!" she protested. "Come up; you'll see."

Muttering under his breath, Samir pulled on the ladder, a few flecks of rusty paint coming off on his palms. It held steady. Putting his suit jacket back on, he began a slow, methodical climb up, testing each rung, making sure it wasn't going to give way under him. Finally, he reached the roof.

"Ledge" had definitely been a more accurate descriptor, though. It was tiny and rectangular and kind of alarmingly uneven, as if it were intent on tipping its residents off onto the concrete below.

Blithely unaware of all Samir's misgivings, Pinky sat in one of two flimsy little chairs, her legs thrown over one of the arms. In the darkness, he could barely make out the white glow of her teeth as she smiled. "Hey, you made it!"

"You say that like you were doubtful." He walked across the rust-stained concrete in a crouch, the way he always did when he was somewhere really high. Taking a seat in the chair next to Pinky's, Samir looked out over the edge of the roof at the lake beyond. Glimmering lights from the houses clustered around the lake—one of them Pinky's—reflected on the black water.

Samir took a deep breath and listened to the cicadas whir for a moment. If he held *really* still, he thought he could hear the lapping waves of the ocean in the distance.

After a long moment, Pinky said, into the silence, "What do you think these chairs are doing up here?"

Samir tipped his head back to look at the stars. "Must be where the staff hang out when they need a break from all the rich people. The ones with a death wish, anyway." He paused, and a cool breeze rolled across the rooftop. "It *is* kind of nice, though; you were right."

"What?" Pinky asked.

Samir enunciated his words carefully, turning in her direction. "I said this is nice. You were right."

"This is nice in the light?" Pinky asked, sounding confused.

Samir spoke up, slowly and loudly, wondering if she really *had* gotten into the wine. "You. Were. Right."

She snorted. "Yeah, I heard you the whole time. And anyway, of course I was. Always am," she finished, sounding smug.

Samir turned to her. There was something about not being able to fully see her face that made it seem like anything they said under this curtain of silver stars didn't really count. So he decided to be honest and to ask for honesty in return. "Do you really believe that?"

Pinky began to say something swaggery and brash, appeared

to reconsider, and then spoke again, quietly. "Not really. I know I make mistakes. A lot of them. And . . . I do worry about screwing up something that can't be fixed more than I let on." She took a breath and Samir waited, sensing there was more. "In fact, I think I've pretty much used up all my mom's goodwill."

Samir shook his head, even though it was possible Pinky couldn't see that. "I've seen her interacting with you over this last week and a half, and I can tell she still trusts you. She just seems . . . frustrated. Like she wishes she could get through to you, so you guys could see eye to eye more."

Pinky snorted. "Yeah, her and me both. But it's like we're two alien species from galaxies too far away to even begin making sense to each other."

"I like your family," Samir said. "They've been so welcoming to me. And it seems like you guys really love each other, underneath it all."

Pinky glanced at him, rubbing her upper arms like she was cold, her bracelets jangling softly. Maybe she was; the temperature had probably dipped twenty or thirty degrees from the daytime. "You know the big burned-out husk of a barn in the backyard? You commented on it your first day here?"

Samir frowned at the change in topic. "Yeah?"

"Guess who my mom accused of burning it down?"

Samir studied her for a moment. "You?" He paused, remembering how he'd thought she had done it too. A pinprick of guilt poked at his soul. Pinky was many things, but an arsonist she wasn't. He knew that now.

"Bingo!" She clapped, and the black sparkly polish on her nails glimmered in the dim light. "Why not suspect me, right? I'm the screwup of the family. Why not pile that on me too? And you want to know the worst part? Dolly was the one who did it. She confessed, and her mom told my mom, and still my mom didn't apologize. Because apparently it's my fault that I even gave her a reason to suspect me in the first place." She took a shaky breath and kept going. "And so yeah, you're right when you say I antagonize her. Because it's like, even when I don't, she still finds a way to blame me for stuff. So at least, if it's me doing it, I'm in control of it. Or it's justified, right?" Her voice was high and wobbly as she finished, and Samir felt a thump of sympathy for her, at the very raw pain there. "Wow," she said quietly, a moment later. "I want control too." She glanced at him and then away. "Who would've thought you and I have something in common?" She sniffed.

Samir couldn't see very well in the dark, but he thought she might be crying or close to it. Argh. If there was one thing he couldn't just stand by and watch, it was a crying girl. Needing to offer some form of comfort, he reached out in the dimness to find her hand and ended up jabbing her in the arm.

"Ow!" She slapped at his hand. "What are you doing?"

"I'm trying to take your hand," he said, rubbing his hand where she'd hit him. "It's hard to see in the dark."

A quiet snort emanated from her direction. A moment later, her soft hand was in his, fine-boned, her fingers long and graceful. He went still for a moment, his heart thumping for reasons he couldn't really understand, before he squeezed her hand gently. "I'm sorry," he said, meaning it. "That really sucks."

"Yeah. It does." Pinky took her hand from his, and he felt its loss immediately. "Anyway. Maybe my family has been welcoming to you, and I'm glad. But I don't always feel the love myself."

They sat in silence for a minute and then Pinky's words echoed back to Samir. "So, wait. Dolly burned down the barn? *Dolly?*"

"I know. It's hard to believe."

"But why?" Realization dawned. "Does it have to do with that crowd—the Cash Crab crowd?"

Pinky laughed, a carefree, happy, surprised sound that had Samir smiling too. "Oh man, I gotta remember that one for the next time I see those jerks. Yeah, it was Cash. He brought beer, apparently, and they had lanterns going in there that didn't get put out."

"Wow." Samir whistled. "It's hard to believe Dolly's mixed up with someone like him."

Pinky tried to give him a look, but its effect was blunted in the dark. She'd hate that if she knew. Samir smiled to himself. "She's not perfect."

"I know that," he said. "It's just . . . Dolly reminds me of me a little, you know? She seems steady."

Pinky rolled her eyes and turned to drape her long legs over the arm of her chair. Samir couldn't help it; his eyes grazed over them. "I've noticed." Quietly, she muttered, "Nice that you both feel the same way about each other."

"What?" Samir asked, confused.

"Dolly apparently thinks you're the bee's knees too." She smiled, but there was something faltering and vulnerable about it that Samir didn't understand.

"Right. Well, that's nice, I guess. At least our plan is working on someone." There was definitely a pulse of *something* he wasn't getting, but he wasn't sure what it was.

"Oh, um, that's the other thing. I kind of told Dolly that we're not really dating."

Samir sat up. "You *what*?"

"No, she's cool with it. She won't say anything."

Samir made a face even though he knew she couldn't see it; he wasn't thrilled about letting another person in on the secret. Even if that person was steady, calm Dolly. "Are you sure?"

"One hundred percent."

They lapsed into silence again. Samir tried to listen for the soothing sound of the ocean waves; he was trying really hard not to freak out that Pinky had broken the rules *again*. Rules were there for a reason. Why would she do that? What would possess—

Okay, no. Soothing ocean. Ahhh. Nice and calm.

A moment later, the chair creaked as Pinky swung her legs back over and sat up straight. Oblivious to Samir's inner struggle, she wrapped her arms around herself and said, "I wish my mom would open her eyes a little more. Not once did she ask me if there might be an alternative explanation. Not once. It was like it was so easy for her to believe the worst about me."

Samir slipped out of his suit jacket and laid it across her shoulders.

"I'm not cold," Pinky said immediately, her eyes flashing in the glow of the stars. "It's only, like, sixty degrees."

"Really?" Samir raised an eyebrow. "Because you're literally shaking. I can hear the chains of your dress clattering together."

Pinky sighed. "Okay, maybe a little." He saw movement as she pulled the jacket closer around her and settled against the chair.

Into the silence, Samir said gently, "Did you ever try to tell your mom how much she hurt you by accusing you?"

"Why bother?" Samir could tell Pinky was trying to sound like she didn't care, but the skin of hurt hanging on her words belied her. "It's not like she'll ever change."

When Samir was quiet, she turned to look at him. He couldn't make out her expression, but her tone was half-sarcastic, half-amused as she said, "Let me guess. You totally believe people can change."

Samir chuckled. "Of course I do."

"Of course you do."

"But listen, people change all the time. Maybe not in big, profound ways, but in little, incremental ways that end up changing essential parts of them anyway. It's like a Rubik's Cube—you start with one line at a time, and then everything begins to fit together."

Pinky was silent for a moment. "So . . . is that what happened to you? When your mom got sick, you changed in incremental ways that changed the essence of who you were?"

Samir felt his shoulders automatically stiffen. He didn't like talking about this; actually, he'd *never* talked about it with anyone. But he'd asked for honesty from Pinky and she'd given it to him. It felt only fair that he should do the same. "Yeah, I guess so. Being organized and in control was a matter of survival back then. Now it just feels like . . . something I should do."

Pinky turned to him, her chair squeaking. "But why? Why do you feel like you *should*?"

He hadn't actually realized he'd said 'should.' "Maybe 'wanted to' would've been a better fit."

"But you said 'should.'"

He didn't respond. A cool wind rippled over them again, and

Pinky huddled into his jacket. The breeze felt good to Samir, brisk and cleansing.

"Do you feel like something bad will happen if you don't control and organize everything?" Pinky asked softly.

He turned sharply to meet her eye. No one had ever asked him that before. No one had ever . . . guessed that before. It wasn't something he usually thought about consciously, and if he did, he quickly brushed past it. But that, right there, was the kernel of his truth: Samir was afraid that if he slipped up, if he gave up the intense vigilance over his own life, that everything would come crumbling down around him like it had seven years ago. He felt like he'd been given a second chance when his mom kicked cancer in the ass and that he'd somehow contributed by being hypervigilant, by making sure no mistakes were made with any of her routines. And now, irrational as it might be, he felt that he was helping keep cancer at bay by continuing to be so vigilant, so dedicated, so rigid.

But there was no way he was going to say all this to Pinky of all people. Pinky, who saw him as some buttoned-up tax accountant. She wouldn't get it. He stood and walked to the roof's edge, his stomach flipping lightly with anxiety at the height. The lights danced on the water in the distance, and the lake-scented breeze played with his hair. Slipping his hands into his pockets, Samir closed his eyes for a long moment.

He opened them when he felt a brush of soft skin in the dark and realized Pinky was standing beside him, her hand searching for his. Heart thumping again, Samir slipped his hand out of his pocket and let her take it. Her hand felt good in his, small and firm and sure. "Is this okay in the fake-dating rule book?" he asked, trying for a laugh, but it came out all shaky and wrong. She'd knocked him off-balance—with her questions, her strange ability to see inside him, her beauty, her surety—and he wasn't sure how to recover.

Pinky didn't laugh or acknowledge his question; she just pressed closer to him. Samir's heart thumped louder, more insistently. "Have you thought about getting therapy? Both you and her, I mean."

Samir felt his heart sink. He barked out a laugh to cover up the feeling. "Oh, so you think I need professional help?" He tried to pull away, but Pinky's hand tightened on his.

Pinky turned to him, her eyes warm, soft, and open. A magenta curl caressed her glimmering cheek. "That's not a judgment. There's absolutely nothing wrong with therapy."

"You would say that," Samir said. "Your uncle and aunt are therapists."

"That's true," she allowed, "but I also believe it. What would you do if you fell off this ledge right now and broke your back on the ground?"

Samir raised an eyebrow. "Uh . . . Is that a threat?"

"No, seriously. What would you do?"

"I'd hope you'd call an ambulance for me."

"Right. Exactly. You'd get medical help for a medical problem, right? So why is it any different to get help for a life problem that's causing you so much grief? Why will you accept one professional's help but not another's?"

Samir studied her a second and then shrugged. He couldn't argue with the logic. "When you put it like that . . ."

"There's just such a stigma about mental health and asking for help," Pinky said. "And it's really bad in the Indian-American community. But there shouldn't be."

"Yeah. I guess. I just wouldn't even know where to start."

"There are community centers and stuff with low-cost clinics if you don't want to use your mom's insurance. My school website has a bunch of resources."

Samir shrugged again. "Maybe. I'll think about it."

"Okay."

They stood in silence, watching the houses in the distance, crouched down with the darkness wrapped around them like a blanket, as if they were readying themselves for sleep.

Samir glanced sidelong at Pinky, her glowing face in silhouette, his feelings in a tangle. He'd never seen her quite this soft, quite this concerned before (except with DQ). To be honest, he hadn't realized she *could* be so soft and concerned with another human. She was an iceberg—the wild hair and the eyebrow ring and the "don't give a damn" attitude were the tip, and the concern for others and the vulnerability about her own parents and her path in life were the submerged 95 percent. Did that make him the *Titanic*? He opened his mouth to tell her some of this or all of it or maybe something else entirely, but he was interrupted.

"Jeff, you better slow down or I'm gonna fall flat on my face!" Taking her hand from his, Pinky looked at him, her eyebrows raised, as a slurred, Southern-accented female voice floated up to them. A well-dressed couple was making their way to the parking lot, their voices clear in the quiet night. "I had way too many of those gotdang margaritas!"

"Well, maybe you should've been conducting yourself in a more ladylike manner, Annamae," a guy—probably Jeff—said in an equally thick Southern accent.

"I'll tell you what you can do with that attitude, and it won't be ladylike," Annamae said.

Pinky snorted and then clapped a hand over her mouth. Samir was making such a monumental effort at holding in his laughter that his shoulders shook uncontrollably.

Jeff grunted in response. Then he said, "Well, that's some news about that old butterfly habitat down the road. Guess they'll be putting in some luxury condos. About time, too. Think that'll bring in more business? This location's always been an under-performer."

"Maybe," Annamae replied. "People always need insurance, that's what I say." Then her slurred voice turned elated. "Oh my God! Look at these boots! They're cute, cute, cute."

Pinky gasped softly and looked at Samir, her eyes wide. "Those are mine!" she whispered, so outraged she was practically spitting. Her expression had him laughing so hard (but quietly, so as to not draw the ire of Annamae and Jeff), he was afraid he'd choke.

"Leave 'em alone; they aren't yours," Jeff said, and Pinky nodded enthusiastically in agreement.

"But *look* at these! Jimmy Choo, too." A pause. "Dang, they're a size too small or I'd take them."

Pinky clutched his arm and said out loud, "Thief!"

Samir pulled Pinky away from the edge to avoid a drunken brawl just as Annamae said, "Did you hear that?"

"I didn't hear anything," Jeff replied, his voice fading as they got into their car. "You know what tequila does to you. . . ."

Once the car had driven off, its taillights just twin red dots in the night, Pinky turned to Samir slowly, as if something had just occurred to her. "The butterfly habitat. Did that guy say they were putting in condos where the butterfly habitat is?"

Samir wrinkled his brow. "I think so." Then realization dawned. "Oh no. That's *your* butterfly habitat, right? The one in the picture?"

Pinky nodded, shoved his suit jacket at him, and then began to speed walk to the ladder. Samir followed as he slipped back into his jacket. "I can't believe they'd do that! That place has been here forever! Where will all the butterflies go?"

She raced down the ladder at such speed, Samir's head spun. "Slow down!" he called, but she'd hopped off three rungs from the bottom and was shoving her feet back into her recently coveted boots. "I have to go talk to my parents," Pinky said, pacing in tight little circles as Samir made his way down at a much more sedate—and therefore wiser—pace.

"Right," Samir said, on solid ground again. "Are you okay?"

When she turned to him, he saw her eyes were all shiny, like she was trying not to cry. "No, I'm not okay. Nothing about this is okay!" Then she turned on her pointy heel and began to race for the restaurant door.

CHAPTER 11
Pinky

This was ridiculous. They couldn't just come in and do something like this. There were rules, laws about this kind of thing! Her parents were lawyers; Pinky should know. She yanked the restaurant door open and strode in past the surprised woman at the reservation desk, Samir close but silent on her heels. He was probably wondering exactly what he'd gotten himself into this summer. Well, it was too late for that.

The room where the trivia night was being hosted was filled with jovially raised (tipsy) voices, the clink of glasses, and heavy cologne and perfume. People with graying hair, all of whom were buttoned up into their suits and shiny dresses, looked up at Pinky as she came flying in. They didn't say anything to her, but they raised their eyebrows just a touch to show their disdain in a socially acceptable way at her hair and her eyebrow ring and her scowling expression. A couple of people even leaned in to whisper to each other, their eyes following Pinky, but she ignored them. She was used to that reaction in her parents' social circles.

Pinky stalked up to the table her parents were sitting at. *Be calm*, she told herself. *If you're calm and adult about this, people are much more likely to listen to you. Don't let that temper get the best of you again.*

When her parents and Dolly's family registered her presence, Pinky spoke. "They're closing the butterfly habitat? Have they lost *every single one* of their brain cells?"

Her dad made a face that implied she was not just playing with fire but trying to marry it. Her mom hissed, quietly but ominously, "Priyanka. Sit. Down."

Pinky sat. Samir took a seat next to her. "Tell me they're joking," Pinky said, drumming her fingers on the table hard and fast. How were they all so *calm*? "Did you say anything?" She looked around at her family. "Has *any*one said anything?"

"I know it's really sad," Dolly said, playing with her gold seashell-charm bracelet. "But what can we do? It's been here forever and the town's changing."

"Exactly," Pinky said, leaning forward. "The habitat's been here forever. It gets precedence. We have to do something!"

"I'm glad you're so passionate," her mother said, and Pinky could tell it had taken everything within her to part with this compliment. "But maybe you could reserve your passion for something that actually has a future. This is a done deal, Pinky."

"Though your passion is inspiring," Abe said, smiling gently. A pity smile. A pity compliment.

Pinky pushed her chair back. "I don't give a flying fig about being inspiring. If none of you has the ovaries to do anything about this, fine. I'll do it myself."

"Where do you think you're going?" her mother asked. "Sit down. We're about to begin the final round and then we'll head home together."

"I'm going back home right now," Pinky said. "I'll walk." She turned to Samir as she scraped her chair back and stood. "You should stay."

As she turned away, Pinky heard her mother begin to protest, but then her father said something that sounded like, "Let her go. You know we can't reach her when she's like this."

That was probably true. She wished they'd at least try, though. Pinky walked out of the restaurant and tipped her head back to look at the stars as she went. Sometimes it felt like she was free-floating in space, the only human in orbit among the stars, her words completely soundless from the lack of air.

Five minutes into her brisk walk along a narrow, dark paved road lined with enormous trees (getting her heart rate up always helped her calm her anger beast), Pinky heard furtive footsteps behind her. At least two people. Maybe more. She kept walking as if she hadn't noticed until she was able to duck behind an oak tree. There she quickly slipped off her pointy-heeled boots and held one in each hand by the toe, the heel pointed wickedly outward. Breathing hard, Pinky waited.

It was hard to see anything in the near darkness, so Pinky was taken a little by surprise when two figures materialized close to the tree. She'd heard their footsteps approaching but had assumed they were farther away. *So you douche monkeys surprised me*, she thought. *So what? Bring it!*

Pinky jumped out from behind the tree, her boots held out at eye level, ready to impale. "Haaaaah!"

One of the figures screamed and the other yelled, "Holy mother of what the hell!" and then Pinky felt someone grab her wrists with big hands so she couldn't do the impaling part of her plan.

"Pinky?"

"Samir?" She squinted in the faint light of the stars. "Dolly?"

"Yeah," Dolly said, and it sounded like she was on the verge of hyperventilating and dying. "We—we followed you out to make sure you were going to be okay."

Samir let go of her wrists. "What were you doing? Are those your *boots*?"

"They also function as impromptu eye impalers," Pinky said sheepishly, setting them on the ground and slipping them back on her feet. Then she straightened. "You guys didn't need to come after me. I told you not to follow me."

"No, you told me to stay, which is different," Samir said.

"I know how much that butterfly habitat means to you," Dolly added. "And you're right. It's wrong that nobody said anything when they announced it at the country club. I bet a lot of people are sad about it, though, just like you."

"Again, I'm not sad—I'm mad," Pinky clarified as they all began walking again.

"Well, *I'm* sad," Dolly said. Her glittery blue dress gave off winks of light as they walked. "That place is an institution. I have so many happy memories there from when I was a kid too. I don't want them to destroy it either."

"I visit it every year, at least once before I go home," Pinky said, softening a bit. "It gets more and more incredible."

It was dark, but the softness in Samir's eyes shone through as he looked at her. It was like something had shifted between them on the rooftop. They'd been more real with each other in those twenty minutes than they'd been over the last few days combined.

"I'm still excited to see it," Samir said.

"Sure, we can go tomorrow," Pinky said, touched that he hadn't forgotten. And, she realized with a little start of surprise, she *wanted* to show him. He was someone who'd show it the proper respect. Turning to Dolly, she added, "When'd they say the developer's beginning construction?"

"August tenth," Dolly said. "Right before we leave."

"Right before we leave," Pinky mused. She could feel her internal Kali waking up and stretching. Hungry. "That's what they think."

Drama Queen "died" while Pinky was putting on her halter and leash three days later—the same halter and leash she put on and took off her seven times a day to acclimate her and with which she'd had no problems previously—so she stuffed her face-up in her tote bag to prevent suffocation and turned to the mirror. She was wearing a purple tank top that showed a peek of her midriff and black shorts with silver stars on them. She thought she looked pretty cute for someone who had plans to eff up a developer's whole summer.

Smiling at her reflection, Pinky slid her feet into her purple Converse and made her way outside. Samir stood by her parents' rental car in a button-down shirt with his sleeves rolled up, his broad shoulders outlined nicely in the fabric. He had a casual, quiet confidence about him that was almost breathtaking. Other boys she'd dated for real had been brash and swaggery, loud and proud about their originality and stubborn independence. But Samir was different. It was like he knew exactly what made him cool, and he was happy keeping that information to himself. He didn't need to impress anyone besides himself.

Looking up, he smiled at her, a clean-cut, classically handsome, dentist-ad smile. *Really* not her thing. Normally. And yet, for just a moment, her pulse beat a little bit quicker. Before she told her pulse it was being ridiculous and forced it to calm down.

"Hey," he said, his eyes inscrutable through his shades. "You ready?"

Bringing her mind to the task at hand, Pinky nodded. "I think so."

She pulled her parents' rental into the large ad hoc gravel cul-de-sac where all visitors to the butterfly habitat parked. She and Samir were the only people there and for that she was glad.

Speaking of . . . Pinky glanced at Samir as they got out and began to walk in the still summer sunshine. "Um, my mom suggested you come out here with me because we're dating. I mean, you know, she *thinks* we're dating. You didn't really have to come." She adjusted her tote bag, replete with "dead" marsupial on her shoulder, feeling mildly off-kilter. Samir seemed to have that effect lately.

He shrugged, stuffing his sunglasses into his shirt pocket. "I know I didn't have to. I wanted to."

Something fluttered inside her. Weird. She watched her feet sink into the grass as they crossed a small circular field. "Why?"

"Honestly?"

"Yeah, honestly."

"Because it was pretty obvious from the way you got so upset that this means something really special to you. And I'm guessing it's not very often people get to see a softer side of you, so . . ."

Pinky glared at him. "So it was just morbid curiosity?" Of course it was.

He stopped walking and studied her with a strange intensity. A gentle, warm breeze wafted through, pushing a strand of his thick black hair onto his forehead. Pinky stopped walking too, helplessly drawn in by those eyes. "I don't know why you said 'just.' Morbid curiosity isn't a bad thing. I *am* curious about you, and I won't apologize for it." He held her gaze; her irritation melted away and she felt a touch breathless.

"Oh, right, sure," she said, her thoughts all tangled up in a big, messy ball in her brain. He was curious about her? What did that mean? *Why* was he so curious? Because she was some kind of circus freak to him or . . . or for *other* reasons?

Argh. It was too much to deal with.

"Um, it's right through there," she said, apropos of nothing, pointing toward a grove of pine trees. "Let's keep walking."

She could feel Samir's gaze on her back, but thankfully he began walking and caught up to her a second later. "Wow," he said after another moment had gone by. "It's quiet."

"Yeah." Pinky smiled as they passed through the opening in the grove of pines. "It's far enough away from all the houses and development that it feels pretty secluded. It was a team effort," she added, trailing her hand softly against the rhododendron bushes as she and Samir walked together. "So many summer people and people from town pitched in to build this. What you're seeing is the result of, like, fourteen or fifteen years of careful cultivation and preservation."

Samir whistled low just as a red admiral butterfly flitted past him. "Fifteen years. It was worth it, obviously. I mean, this place

194

looks like a beautiful, colorful jungle. How many varieties of butter-flies come through here?"

Pinky cast him an irritated look. "I don't know. A lot? What does it even matter exactly how many varieties of butterflies we have?"

He looked disbelievingly back. "Isn't this one of your favorite places on the island?"

"Oh yes, I'm so sorry, I forgot who I was talking to. I'll be sure to ask them to set up a placard just for you."

Samir chuckled softly. "That would be nice."

Shaking her head and smiling a little in spite of herself, Pinky turned around to survey the habitat as though through Samir's fresh eyes. The frilly Japanese holly, the sprawling witch hazel, the soft trumpet vines waving in the breeze, the brilliant purple hydrangeas that Pinky had advertently or inadvertently matched her outfit to. The way the monarchs dipped and canted, flitting from one deli-cious treat to the next, blissfully happy in this paradise humans had created for them.

A path meandered through the thicket of vegetation, and Pinky began to walk. "I have so many memories here. So many. My mom and dad brought me here as a toddler, when this was all just first get-ting started. Apparently I helped plant that cluster of summer-sweet bushes over there. Well, I also ripped out what they were planting, but at least I didn't completely destroy it all."

Samir laughed and walked over to her, his arm brushing lightly against hers. Pinky felt herself tense, hyperaware of every single one of their movements. "I bet you were adorable."

"I bet I was a hellion." They walked around an oak tree, watching the question mark butterflies—Pinky's favorite when she was little, owing to their weird name—spin and pirouette through the air, like they were showing off. "I remember having picnics here, on that patch of grassy field. Dolly and I would play tag, and we'd tag each other but also the butterflies. And the butterflies would sometimes tag us, too, on our shoulders or our cheeks with their soft wings, and that was the best thing ever." She smiled at the memory.

"That sounds really nice." Looking around, listening to the warbling, calling, cooing birds, Samir added, "I can't believe they want to raze this."

There was a pang in Pinky's heart. "Raze." It was such a violent word. She couldn't imagine this simply not being here; she couldn't imagine sterile condo buildings where so much life buzzed and hummed and fluttered and grew, defiant in brilliant color.

To distract herself, Pinky got DQ out of the tote bag and set her on the ground, in the shade of the tree. She wouldn't be awake for a while. That done, Pinky ran off to the right.

"Where are you going?" Samir called from behind her.

"Race you to the top of this tree!" she called back, grabbing the lowest limb of the oak tree, which had spread its branches out like it owned the place. "This used to be one of my favorite places in the habitat when I was a kid."

Samir jogged over to her and put his hands on his hips, looking worried. "What is it with you and high places? If I didn't know better, I'd think you wanted to find an easy way to murder me."

Pinky laughed, already a quarter of the way up the tree. "I promise the view's gonna be worth it!"

Samir sighed. "Do you know how long it took me to starch and iron these clothes today? Do you think these crisp lines happen without effort?" But then he grabbed the lowest limb and hoisted himself up anyway.

Samir was a much slower, more careful climber than her, so Pinky waited patiently while he tested each branch with some of his weight before fully committing to climbing on it. At times she wanted to prod him on with her toe, but she knew she'd just freak him out, and then he'd probably refuse to go any farther and he'd miss out on the best part.

Once they were both at the top, Pinky pointed. "Look."

Samir's eyes were shut. "No, thank you. I'm good."

"Sam." He didn't open his eyes. "Are you seriously going to climb all the way up here and not even enjoy the view?"

Sighing dramatically, he opened his eyes. And then gasped. "Whoa."

Pinky grinned, satisfied. "Nice, right?"

"'Nice' is not even the word."

The butterfly habitat sprawled on every side around them, a riot of color and movement. From up here, you could see the scope of everything, how hard the people of the town had worked, how much time and effort and money had gone into it. In the far distance, Lake Spear stretched out like a diamond shard, all the big houses crouched possessively around it.

"I used to bring books up here and just sit on a limb and read. I don't think there's anything more peaceful than that."

"We should do that this summer," Samir said, turning to her. His hands, Pinky noticed, were still clamped really, really tightly on the branch behind him. "Read together in this tree, I mean."

She laughed, leaned a hip against the tree, and pushed him lightly on the chest. "How are you going to read when your hands are practically making indentations in that branch?"

He gazed at her for a long moment, long enough to make her smile fade and her heart start to thrum, her stomach start to dip and twirl in excitement. Then, looking away, he said, "You know what I've been thinking?"

"What?" she asked, still feeling a little breathless from the intensity in his eyes. A wind rustled the leaves all around them, shrouding them in symphony.

"We're still pretty awkward with each other, you and me. Physically, I mean." He met her eye then, and her breath caught. "Remember when I leaned in close to you when we were playing Boggle?"

"Y-yeah, I remember," Pinky said, barely able to speak. She pressed herself back against the tree trunk. Why was he bringing this up? What was he getting at?

"You jumped back. That's not good, you know? What if your parents saw? What if they . . . suspected?" He'd moved closer to her as he spoke, his broad body eclipsing hers, his voice a low murmur. Their hands were brushing on the tree branch behind them, sparkles of electricity dancing between his skin and hers.

"Right," Pinky said, nodding, still staring into his hypnotic eyes. Her breath came faster against her will, and her heart pounded a furious rhythm. "They might've suspected. That could ruin everything. So . . . what are you suggesting?"

Samir grinned slowly, looking every bit an evil J.Crew model. "Practice."

"P-practice?" Pinky heard herself squeak. She wondered if he'd noticed her gaze flickering down to his lips.

Samir

Samir took a step closer to her on the thick branch so they were nearly toe-to-toe, his sneakered feet giant next to hers. He put one hand on the tree trunk by her head, the smell of her fresh, clean shampoo driving him a little bit crazy. "Practice," he said, his gaze caressing her face. "Just so we can feel . . . more comfortable with each other."

"Ph-physically." A pulse flickered at the base of Pinky's throat. He was extremely aware of her midriff right next to his hand, bare and brown and taut. "So we can be more convincing."

"That's right." Samir was aware of how husky his voice sounded. And he was *really* aware of Pinky's hitching breath, the way she batted her eyelashes and swallowed compulsively. She looked completely thrown, for a change, and Samir was enjoying being the one doing the throwing. "Just to be more convincing. What do you think, Pinky?" He caught an emerald-green curl as it blew across her face with the warm breeze and tucked it behind her ear. "Do you want to kiss me?"

Her lips parted and she nodded, her eyes burning with a flame he found incredibly sexy. Samir caressed her jaw, her cheekbone, the bridge of her nose with a fingertip. When her eyes fluttered shut, he brought his hand to her waist, his fingers resting gently against her sun-warmed bare skin, and his lips to hers, only just brushing against her velvet mouth. Pinky gasped softly against his mouth, her arms going around his waist and pulling him in. And then he was kissing her for real, his lips molding to hers, his tongue brushing against her parted mouth, tasting the sweet honey of her tongue.

Pinky

This was Samir she was practice kissing. *Samir.*

The thought should've made her double over in maniacal laughter, but somehow, it didn't. Somehow, Pinky found herself deepening the kiss, inhaling the masculine, clean smell of him, reveling in those broad shoulders, those muscular arms encircling her waist. The thing was, Samir Jha was taking control, and she was letting him. And not just that, but she was *enjoying* this very strange new dynamic to their non-relationship.

Dear sweet goddess, what the hell was happening to her?

Samir

Even in this intense, hormone-high state, Samir was surprised at Pinky's response. He'd hoped to catch her off guard by proposing this practice kiss, but he hadn't expected the depth of her reaction.

She responded to him like she'd been starving and he'd handed

200

her a delicious morsel of chocolate. Her hands roved his back and she pressed tight against his body, her gentle curves doing interesting things to his anatomy. Her tongue ran across his, tasting, *testing*, as if to gauge his reaction. Pinky, normally so confident and take-charge, was suddenly both breathless for more and somewhat insecure. To show her her lustfulness was more than okay with him, Samir put his hands in her hair, cinching her body against his. Her smooth cheek against his, the way she was on her tiptoes, her frenzied hands, that soft gasping—everything about her was driving him intensely, rabidly crazy.

They pulled apart after a few seconds, both of them breathing hard, regarding each other with bright eyes and flushed cheeks. Pinky's bun was a mess, half her hair tumbling down her back. A loose leaf from the branch above them had deposited itself at the crown of her head. Samir got rid of it, pulled her hair tie out gently, and arranged her multicolored curls around her shoulders. Smiling a half smile, he asked, "And how was that for you?"

Still breathing hard, still clinging to him, she said, "G-good. Um, that was, yeah. Good." He smiled and stepped a half step away, his torso pressing into the knobby branch behind him. He was still on enough of a hormone high that the actual height of the tree didn't bother him so much.

After a pause, Pinky said, over-casually, "I think I may need steady practice, though. I'm a really slow learner, so, you know. Just to make sure I really have it."

Samir felt a small smile flicker at his lips. Facing forward, he said, "Mm, yeah. Probably a good idea. We can do it again tonight, if you want." He didn't really know where all this was coming from—the confidence, the suave dialogue, the feeling of surety, especially in the face of Pinky's unsteadiness. But there was something about seeing her wanting him, about seeing her so thrown and so un-Pinky-like, that made it easy for him to step into this role.

Which was ridiculous. If he were to think about it—and he wasn't doing much thinking right then, to be honest—this was a bad idea. What had come over him? Why had he told Pinky he wanted to practice, just so he could kiss her? As if it wasn't enough that she took every opportunity she could to tease him and bait him and drive him mad. As if it wasn't enough that she was so much the mayor of la-la land that she didn't even know what varieties of butterfly inhabited her own beloved butterfly sanctuary. As if he needed her chaotic, turbulent, unpredictable energy in his life.

But be all that as it was, he couldn't deny the truth. He'd been noticing little moments between them here and there for a while now, sparks of . . . something, and up here in the tree, he'd been able to practically *see* the desire radiating off her. And he'd realized he felt the same way. They had a chemistry between them, something strong, that had just taken over the moment. And the crazy thing was, she had felt it too. She had *responded* to it.

Pinky interrupted his reverie by answering his question in this breathy voice that drove him mad, though, naturally, he couldn't show it. He was the one in control here. "Yeah. I want to. I mean, we have to be convincing, after all."

"Guys? I see DQ dead on the grass, but I don't see you. Hello?"

"Crap, it's Dolly," Pinky said, automatically putting distance between herself and him.

"Guys?"

"Yeah," Pinky called. "We're up in the big oak tree! Be right down!"

They clambered down—well, Pinky clambered; Samir went at a pace that respected the height of the tree and the potential lethality of said height—and stood on the ground. Samir noticed Pinky picking at her shorts, putting her hair back in its bun, looking vaguely guilty.

"What were you guys doing up there?" Dolly asked. She wore a summer dress and sandals and, at her feet, DQ still lay dead, near Pinky's discarded tote bag.

"Just showing him the view," Pinky said, her voice a notch higher than usual. She rubbed the back of her neck, and Samir forced his eyes away from the soft skin there. "You know, so he could really appreciate the place."

"Yep." Samir pursed his lips and looked around, hooking his thumbs into his shorts pockets. A rivulet of sweat ran down his back. "I really appreciate the place."

Dolly looked between them, slightly amused. "Oh . . . kay." She spun in a slow circle. "Wow. I forgot how meditative it is out here." She turned back to Pinky. "Remember that time we celebrated your sixth birthday in that meadow? I just remember you burst into tears when your mom brought in those cupcakes."

"Oh, right," Pinky said, laughing. "I'd imagined the butterflies bringing them to me, like in a fairy tale or something."

Dolly chuckled. "Yeah. I didn't know that until I was older and you told me." She sighed and gave Pinky a quick hug. "This place has always meant so much to you."

"Not just to me, to a lot of people," Pinky said, her eyes sparking. "We have to do something."

They heard voices then and turned to see five people, a middle-aged white woman in a business suit, two white men, about the same age, in rumpled T-shirts and pants, and two older women, one black and one white, in shorts and T-shirts, walking through the grove of pines toward them.

"All of this," the woman in the business suit was saying in authoritative tones. In spite of the heat and humidity, her short blond hair was perfectly straight and silky. She sliced her arm through the air, her index finger pointed. Her nails were done in an understated plum-gray color. "I need it flat." The two men nodded.

"If you could reconsider, that's all we're asking," the older black woman said. "This habitat is an important piece of town history."

The woman in the business suit smirked. "History is best left in the past. I'm talking about bringing in *millions* of dollars in revenue to Ellingsworth Point. Besides which, there's no point talking about all of this now. The contract's already been signed; the paperwork's done." She turned dismissively away, not giving the other two women a chance to respond.

"What the hell?" Pinky muttered, looking from the woman in the suit to the other two women. And then she began to stride forward.

Dolly looked at Samir and shrugged. "All we can do now is follow."

Pinky

Pinky strode toward the group, the last lingering effects of the extremely serviceable practice kiss with Samir burning off in the heat of her outrage. (Okay, so the kiss had been more than serviceable. It might, in fact, have been the best kiss she'd ever had, real boyfriends included. And somewhere along the way, she'd . . . stopped practicing. But that was an issue for another day.) (Seriously, though. Where had Samir learned to kiss like that?? As far as Pinky knew, he'd never even had a girlfriend before. Where was the buttoned-up, boring, Harvard lawyer–wannabe mama's boy she'd loved to make fun of?)

The woman in the crisp business suit was briskly giving orders, and the men were nodding but not saying much themselves. The woman was obviously in charge. The two older women who'd tried to talk to her were standing off to the side, deep in conversation. Pinky walked up to them, and Samir and Dolly joined her on either side.

The black woman was the first to notice them. "Hi," she said, a small wrinkle between her eyebrows. The white woman just looked at them, her eyes slightly narrowed.

"Hi." Pinky stuck out her hand, and the two women took turns shaking it, looking slightly confused. "Pinky Kumar. These are my, um, people, Samir and Dolly."

"I'm Gloria," the black woman said, "and this is my wife, Dolores." Dolores gave the three of them a suspicious glare.

Pinky glanced over at the businesswoman and her two lackeys. "I couldn't help but overhear your conversation with that woman, and I want to volunteer my time."

"Volunteer your time for what, honey?" Gloria asked.

"Anything at all," Pinky said. "Whatever your plan is to stop the razing of the habitat." Gloria and Dolores looked at her blankly. "You . . . do have a plan, right?"

"Nothing concrete yet," Dolores said, slightly cagily, Pinky thought. "Why? Why are you so interested?"

"This habitat was built when I was, like, three years old," Pinky explained. "And every summer I come back to—"

"So you're a summer person," Dolores said, folding her arms.

Pinky blinked. "Yeah. My parents have a house out by Ellingsworth Lake."

Gloria looked over at the woman in the business suit, who was now tromping back around toward the parking lot with the two men. Looking back at Pinky, she said, "Whatever we do, it's going to take some serious commitment and some serious work. It's not just a side project for when you get bored."

Pinky shook her head. "I won't get bored. I *love* this habitat. Some of the best memories in my life happened here."

"You don't know Pinky, so you can't know this," Dolly explained, smiling, "but she's the *last* person who'd ever get bored of a project like this." She held open the tote bag containing DQ's seemingly lifeless body. Dolores and Gloria peeked in and their eyes got wide, as if they were suddenly realizing they may be dealing with a group of seriously unhinged teenagers. "That's Drama Queen. Pinky rescued her and plans to rehome her at a wildlife refuge. She's also established raccoon hospitals, pigeon recovery centers. . . . You get the idea. She never gets bored."

Pinky tossed her cousin a grateful smile.

Dolores leaned back from the bag and eyed the three of them carefully. "Well, dears, I hate to be the one to tell you this, but your pet rat is dead."

"She's not a rat," Pinky explained. "DQ's a possum, and she's just pretending to be dead. She'll wake up in a bit."

"Pinky's also ridiculously stubborn," Samir put in, his hands in his pockets. "Seriously. When I first got here, I wanted to drown her in the lake." Pinky snapped her head to look at him. What the hell was he doing? "But now . . . ," he continued, "I don't know. I'm beginning to see how stubbornness can be a really good quality. She can help you with whatever you might need help with. She's really convincing and she doesn't take no for an answer."

Pinky's anger melted away into something softer as she caught Samir's eye. Was that how he saw her? She had no idea any of his thoughts about her hardheadedness were remotely positive.

Dolores didn't look convinced by their soliloquies, but Pinky could see Gloria softening. "Look," she said. "We're thinking about canvassing the area downtown with some flyers, talking to other residents, maybe setting up a town hall meeting to figure out what the best approach to all this is. Would you be interested in helping out with the canvassing and word-of-mouth?"

Pinky nodded eagerly. "Yes, very much."

Dolores shook her head and sighed, and Gloria said quietly, "Let's give her a chance." Turning to Pinky, she said, "Okay. Here's my card." She pulled out a business card from her pocket that said: G+D LANDSCAPING. There was a phone number on it. "Give me a call later today and we'll go from there. No texting. Call me."

Pinky took the card and stuck out her hand again. "Done. Thanks for giving me a chance. I won't let you or the butterflies down."

Gloria smiled a little and shook her head, as if she couldn't figure out if Pinky was being serious or not. "All right, then." And she and Dolores walked off in the direction of the parking lot.

Pinky turned to Dolly and Samir, grinning. "Guys. Thank you

for backing me up like that." Then she noticed what Samir was doing. "Are you taking *notes*?"

He looked up from his planner. "What? It's just so I won't forget the details."

Pinky rolled her eyes and looked at Dolly. "Can you believe this guy?"

"Hey," she said, "he's *your* fake boyfriend."

Pinky snorted. Then, getting more serious, she said, "So I guess I'm going to call Gloria tomorrow."

Samir looked up at her as he put his planner away. "Right. And you're sure you want to get involved? I mean, those two women are strangers."

"It has to be better than sitting around doing *nothing*," Pinky countered. When she saw the hesitation on both their faces, she added, "Guys, come on. Do you really want this gorgeous beauty to be completely decimated just so they can put up luxury apartments here? Do you want some snobbish, snide woman in a business suit to destroy the beating heart of this place, where so many hundreds of people have shared so many hundreds of happy memories, just to put up some boxy, soulless, uncreative cubicles? Just so she can add piles of money to the money piles she already has? What's the point of that? Shouldn't we stand up and say how we feel about it rather than just sitting back and letting this happen to us?"

She could sense it, the shift in their thinking, as she continued to speak. When she finished, Samir spoke first. His eyes shining, he said, "You know what? What the heck. I'm in."

"Really?" Pinky asked, grinning.

"Hell yeah," he said. "This is *completely* against the rules and completely crazy. I mean, *completely*." He paused. "But it's for the greater good, right?" Samir's eyes were a tad feverish, and he really looked like he was asking for confirmation, so Pinky nodded.

"I'm in too," Dolly said, giving her another hug. "Let's do this together. Let's help the town save its butterfly habitat!"

Smiling, Pinky linked her arms with the both of theirs, her blood pumping fast and furiously, the way it did when she knew she was going to help with a cause and *win*. Behind them, DQ, finally awake, chirped happily.

CHAPTER 12

Pinky

The next night, after dinner, Pinky sat out on the deck with the lights out, looking up at the stars. The cicadas chirped and sang in the cool air, which held the tang of lake water. Sitting here felt as comfortable to her as sitting in her room back home in Atherton. Pinky couldn't remember a summer when she *hadn't* felt the warm wooden floorboards under her bare feet, when she hadn't lain back in a deck chair and gazed up at the crystal-clear Cape Cod sky, knowing that sometimes home is more than one solitary place.

Everyone else was indoors or otherwise occupied—the adults were playing a game of poker, Dolly was at Cash's (though her cover was that she was walking DQ, who was with her), and Samir was . . . well, Pinky didn't know where he was. She was kind of avoiding him. That was the whole reason she was out on the porch right now under the cover of darkness.

She leaned back in the chaise lounge and closed her eyes, feeling the stillness of the night pressing down like a warm hand on her skin. Practice kissing Samir . . . Why had she responded the way she had? The wave of desire that had overtaken her had been incredible;

she'd never felt a tsunami like that before. It was as if her body had been a dam, filled to bursting with wanting and lust. All it had taken was one touch from him and she'd opened the gates, letting it all out.

Cringing, she remembered how she'd told him she needed more practice sessions. Arrrgh. If she were him, she'd be totally turned off by the sheer desperation.

Except . . .

Pinky opened her eyes again, her thoughts churning, going over details she'd already gone over thousands of times in her mind. She remembered how he'd gazed at her for a long moment before asking her to practice kiss him. And it wasn't like he hadn't been into it too. Something about his kiss hadn't felt very practice-like. In fact, it had felt pretty . . . genuine. It had felt like the real thing for him, too.

And the way he'd extolled her virtues to Gloria and Dolores and then volunteered to help her with the butterfly habitat, even though she knew going against authority must be anathema for him. It would be like Pinky wearing a T-shirt advertising a credit card company or something—totally out of character. And the heartfelt appreciation he'd shown for the one place that meant so much to her. That wasn't something you did for someone you barely liked or considered a business acquaintance.

Pinky stared off into the darkness at the tree line, her pulse thumping at her throat. And what if Samir was developing feelings for her? What did that mean for her, for them?

Nothing, she told herself firmly. It meant nothing. It could never mean anything because they were completely different. What was she *doing*, fantasizing about a guy like Samir? They were too different.

She'd spent her entire life thinking about who she wanted to be, and she'd very carefully realized *this* is exactly who she was, whether her mother liked it or approved of it or not: Pinky Kumar was, to her core, a wild and free spirit, a puff of dandelion seed on the wind, someone who would never, ever, ever be with a guy whose big dream was to become a corporate lawyer. A guy who made detailed notes in his planner, whose life was scheduled and organized down to the last minute. Because if she went out with someone like that, she may as well call herself Veena Kumar and begin wearing cardigans with pearl buttons.

She heard the sound of the French doors opening and called out, "Yeah, I'm out here, Dad." He always got worried when he couldn't see her for more than twenty minutes. She'd once overheard him telling someone that Pinky was like a toddler; the longer she was silent, the more worried you got about what she was up to.

"Hey."

A wave of feeling rippled through her at the honeyed male voice. She turned to see Samir walking over to her in that casually confident way he had. "Oh." She adjusted the hem of her shorts, which had ridden way up high on her thighs. "Hi."

"You mind if I sit out here with you for a bit?" he asked, gesturing to the empty chaise lounge next to hers.

"Not at all." Pinky found herself sitting very stiffly and artificially as he kicked off his sandals and made himself comfortable next to her.

Folding his hands behind his head, he said, after a moment, "This is nice. Really peaceful. The burned-out husk of a barn in the corner really adds to the ambience."

"Oh, um, yes. I think so too." Her mind was whirring again,

wondering if he'd try to take her hand here in the darkness, or if he'd come out here to talk about *them* or—

"Are you okay?"

"Huh? Yeah, why?" She turned to him. His face glowed in the softly filtered light coming from the house through the curtains at the French doors.

"You look . . ." He frowned. "Like you're in pain or something."

"Oh. I was just thinking."

He laughed. "And it's that agonizing, huh?"

She whacked him on his chest with the back of her hand. His really nicely muscled chest. "Shut up." After a pause, she asked, "Did you really mean it? You want to help me with whatever Gloria has planned for the habitat?"

Samir nodded. "I do. I really want to help you."

"But . . . why?" she forced herself to ask. It was important to her that he tell her. She felt like she'd been going back and forth in her head all day, thinking about the kiss, the things he'd said to Gloria about her, how he'd wanted to visit the habitat in the first place and how he'd volunteered to help with it. She needed to know what Samir's agenda was. Did he really like her? It didn't make any sense; the two of them together made zero sense. So, really, she was hoping he'd tell her what she wanted to hear, something that would make all of this less complicated. She was hoping he'd tell her she was full of herself like he had before. She was hoping he'd give her an out.

Samir looked a little confused. "Do you not want me to?"

"No, I do. I just . . . This is really out of character for you, right?" He nodded his assent. "So why are you doing it? It wasn't part of our original deal."

213

In the dim lights of the deck, Samir's face was frozen and shadowed for a moment, unreadable. And then he smiled.

Samir

It was funny; she was asking him the same question he'd spent all day asking himself. *Why* had he agreed to help her with the habitat in a city he had absolutely no ties to? They were bound to lose; of this Samir had no doubt. So then . . . why?

He gazed into her softly shining brown eyes and ran a hand through his hair, feeling discombobulated. "Why? I don't know. You're loud and obnoxious and pigheaded and sometimes you make absolutely no sense. Most times, actually."

Her eyes turned flinty. "Oh, really."

"Yeah, really. You yell at me and needle me and you make fun of just about every single thing I do. You're a walking ball of chaos; you're practically my biggest fear."

Pinky made a move to gather her flip-flops and go. "Got it. Thanks."

"And you're funny and beautiful and brilliant and probably the most interesting person I've ever met."

She paused, her flip-flops in her hands, and stared at him. "What?"

Samir continued, his heart thudding, his mouth going dry. He was really doing this now, on a semi-dark deck with her family in the house behind them? Yep, he was really doing this now, on a semi-dark deck with her family in the house behind them. Samir knew he should've scheduled this outpouring of feelings in his planner for a better time, but that's what you got when you decided to live life on the edge. All he could do now was plunder forward and hope for the best.

"I've never met anyone like you," he continued, wanting, needing her to see how much he meant it. "I never wanted to, to be honest. Even back in Atherton, I was always intrigued by you, but usually just the way someone might be intrigued by a tarantula in their yard. You want to see it, but you want to keep your distance too, in case it spits face-melting venom or something." Pinky narrowed her eyes, setting her flip-flops on the deck as if to put them on, and he rushed to continue. "But over the past two weeks, I've come to realize something: You say the most astute things and you say them so casually, like everyone should know them. It's like you don't even realize how insightful you are. And you care about everything so—so brazenly and so deeply. You're incredibly brave in the way you live your life. And, somehow, I wanted to be part of that."

She continued to look at him, her lips slightly parted. A flurry of emotions crossed her face, too quick and fleeting for Samir to hold on to and examine a single one. He moved in closer to her, inch by inch, giving her the space to say no, to turn away. She didn't.

Samir pressed his lips to hers and felt her sigh as his hands tangled in her hair, as if she were relieved to be giving in to this feeling, giving in to him. Her hands pressed up against his chest as they fell deeper into their kiss, the night melting away like taffy. As he tasted her on his lips yet again, Samir marveled at the fact that he'd kissed her twice now, and this time there was no pretense of "practice." This time it was all real. He'd laid himself bare to a girl for the very first time. This was him, real, raw, and it seemed like she liked what she saw.

Finally, Pinky pulled back, breathing just as hard as he was. He smiled down at her, tracing her lips with one finger.

"I'm . . . Thank you for telling me that," she said, pulling back and adjusting her hair without looking at him.

He frowned at the sudden coolness in her voice, in her body language. "You're . . . welcome."

She smiled brightly at him and tagged his shoulder with her fist. "Another good practice kiss. Well done, us!"

Samir studied her expression. "Pinky . . . what—are you okay?"

"Fine!" she said, standing and walking down the deck to the railing.

He stood and followed her, coming to stand beside her but keeping his distance. "You're not fine," he said quietly. "I think that's pretty clear. Did I misread . . . ?"

There was a pause. "No," she said, turning to him, her hip pressed against the railing. "You didn't misread anything. I wanted you to kiss me."

He nodded slowly, still lost. "Okay. Then what happened?"

"I don't want us to lose sight of our goal, our transaction," she said, and he didn't miss the light emphasis on the words "goal" and "transaction."

His face cleared. She was letting him down easy. She'd heard what he hadn't said, what was hiding behind his words—that he was beginning to like her. That this was becoming more than just a "transaction" to him. She was letting him know she didn't feel the same way.

Samir took another step back, hurt and rejection like a fine mist around his face. "Oh, okay." He nodded once, looking over her head out at the lake beyond. Lights from the houses surrounding it glimmered on its black surface. "Gotcha."

"Samir, I—"

"No, that's totally fine. I get it." He smiled a little to show he meant it; it wasn't her fault she didn't like him the way he liked her. That had never been their deal. Now he was just going to have to be a big boy and get past it. Had he thought he saw more in her reactions? Had he felt like her feelings for him matched his for her? Yes. But that was immaterial now. Whatever he'd thought, however he'd misunderstood, he heard her "no" loud and clear. "It's for the best, you know? We wouldn't want to cloud up our end goals here."

Something like disappointment flashed across her face. But that was ridiculous, wishful thinking. What would she be disappointed for? He was giving her what she wanted.

"Yep," Pinky said finally, turning back around to look out at the tastefully lit backyard. "Speaking of, I spoke to Gloria on the phone earlier. She said the big issue for them right now is pushback from the mayor. He says the papers have already been signed, the contract's been inked, that there's no way to put this all off. . . ."

Samir struggled for a moment to find his bearings. To let the sting of rejection recede into the background, to force his head back into logical mode. "Right," he said finally. "That's what the developer woman said too."

"Yeah. But Gloria isn't convinced. She thinks that might be just something he's saying so people won't bother him. So Gloria wants people to just keep making appointments to see the mayor, you know, see if we can wear him down by showing him how much support there is from the locals."

Samir shrugged. "Yeah, I guess that could work. So are we going to try to get an appointment with him?"

"Well, I already did. For Thursday morning."

"You did?" Samir raised his eyebrows. "That was quick."

"I think they're really slow in the summertime or something. You'll go with me, right? I'm asking Dolly, too."

"Sure."

"Because I was thinking . . . I mean, it'll be good to go show our support and stuff, but what if we took it one step further?"

Samir frowned, not understanding. "What do you mean?"

"I mean, say the mayor's actually right. Say the big problem really is that the contract's been inked, so they can't *stop* the condo development from happening. But what if we were able to find a different, equally feasible location? And somehow convince the developer to move to *that* location instead? That way the mayor won't have to break the contract and the town can still get the revenue."

Samir smiled. "That would be a really good solution. I can help you look for alternative locations before Tuesday. The plan is to present the mayor with it then, right?"

Pinky grinned. "Exactly."

They looked at each other for a moment, their smiles fading as the reality of her rejection settled back in like a heavy lead cloud. "Right . . . so . . ." Samir patted the top of the railing with an open palm, his mood dampening again as he remembered that she didn't want him like he wanted her. "I'll help you with that. But right now I'm gonna go take a shower and read for a bit, okay?"

Pinky looked at him, a long, lingering thing that held hints of sadness. Like she knew he needed time alone to lick his wounds, to get over what had just happened. "Yeah," she said. "Sure. I'll see you in the morning."

Samir nodded at her and walked back toward the house, forcing his gait to be lighter and quicker than it wanted to be. She'd rejected him. The first girl he'd ever had any real feelings for had rejected him out of hand. Everything he'd thought he'd seen in her eyes, all the hidden, secret messages he thought he'd gotten when they'd kissed, when she'd been in his arms—it was all self-delusion on his part. He was just some naive, ridiculous, hearts-in-his-eyes cartoon character mooning after the worldly, sophisticated girl. He knew it and she knew it. Time and space, that's what he needed now.

He could feel her gaze on his back as he went, but he forced himself not to look.

Pinky

Pinky closed her eyes when she heard the firm, final *thunk* of the French doors closing behind him. All the things Samir had said . . . they were perfect. It was like he'd really seen her, *all* of her, even the parts that he thought of as her worst qualities, and he'd appreciated all of what he'd seen. He wanted to be a part of it. No boy before him had ever come close to appreciating her so well-roundedly. No boyfriend she'd ever had had openly admitted that there were things about her that they simultaneously were aggravated by and loved. No one had ever been that honest, that funny, that . . . that *Samir*. And she'd turned him down.

A part of her felt relieved that he'd gotten the message so quickly; she'd made the decision to keep him at bay for a reason. Someone like him belonged in a different sphere from someone like her. It would never work. They'd be fighting all the time.

But another part of her was scared—terrified, actually—that she always sabotaged herself because somewhere deep down she didn't believe she deserved happiness with a guy like Samir.

Gripping the railing with her hands, Pinky listened to the crickets chirp in the darkened corners of the backyard. She'd never heard such a lonely sound.

It was the next evening, which was also the night before the meeting with the mayor, and Samir and Pinky were sprawled on the floor in her room, a giant paper map of Ellingsworth Point Island spread out between them. They had the windows open, and a lake breeze blew in, trying to make off with the map. Pinky set her box of markers on the corner to weigh it down.

"I still don't see why we're doing it like this," Samir grumbled. "We could just pull it up on my laptop."

"Yes, but it's so much more satisfying to be able to circle things physically," Pinky said, using a fat purple marker to circle the word "Ellingsworth" at the top. "See?"

Samir scoffed. "If you say so."

It had only been a day since she'd turned him down on the deck (Pinky hated to think of it as "rejected"—that felt way too harsh), and she had to admit, Samir was doing a pretty good job of pretending like it had never happened. Pinky had known boys in her life who went from saccharine sweet when they were pursuing her to flat-out mean and bullying when she said no, but that wasn't Samir. She found it both a relief and secretly irritating. Had his feelings for her been worth so little that he could just brush them off and act like they had never even existed? She knew it made no sense for her to feel that way; *she* had turned *him* down. She should be glad he was taking it so well.

"So this is where they're currently planning to put in those awful condos," Pinky said, marking the area with the butterfly habitat with a big red star. "But we'd like them to move it . . . somewhere else." She peered at the map, frowning. They'd been staring at it for so long and were still nowhere close to an answer. "There's nowhere in the town that fits. Nowhere at all. How can that be? How can the *only* location be the butterfly habitat?"

"You're just going to say no again, but I think over here would be a fine proposition," Samir said, pointing with his green marker to an area just outside of town proper.

Pinky sighed. "It's not as pretty or as convenient as the habitat. I just know he's going to use that against us. And that fire-breathing demon of a developer is going to say that too. The people in the condos need the best views and the shortest commute to downtown so they can ask for the most money. But I guess if that's all we have, that's all we have. I'll run it by Dolly later, whenever she gets back from Cash's." She raised her arms above her head and stretched, not missing how Samir's eye was automatically drawn to her exposed tummy—or how he quickly looked away and busied himself with putting the markers back into the box. Pinky annoyed herself by feeling a thud of disappointment.

"So, that's it, right?" Samir asked, standing. "That's our plan?"

"Yeah, I think so." Pinky stood too. "Get some sleep. We're going to be out of here early tomorrow. The appointment's at nine."

Samir raised an eyebrow. "That won't be a problem for me, but I'm a morning person. What are *you* going to do?"

"Don't worry about me," Pinky said, stepping closer to him. "I can be as much of a hellion during the day as I am at night." Samir's eyes widened just a fraction, and Pinky realized the double entendre of her words. "I mean—not just, like, in *bed* at night. I'm a hellion everywhere." Oh God. She was making this so much worse. She felt her cheeks heat and looked away.

There was an awkward pause, and then Samir cleared his throat. "Right. Well, I'm going to bed, then. Um, good night."

Wincing as he walked away, Pinky waited until he'd closed the door behind him to jump on her bed and stick her face into the pillows, hoping for a swift, sweet suffocation.

"Remind me again why we didn't just take the BMW?" Dolly asked, shifting uncomfortably on her bus seat. The upholstery was ripped and, according to her, kept jabbing her in the thigh. *Try being wedged between your aggravated cousin and the boy you just turned down*, Pinky thought grumpily.

"This bus drops us off right at city hall," Pinky explained for the twelfth time, making sure to keep her tone patient. They were here to support her cause, after all.

"Yes, but the bus stop was, like, two miles away from your house,"

Samir said from her other side, waving his hand at his sweaty, pink face in an attempt to cool himself down.

They were all scrunched uncomfortably in an optimistically named three-seater that was really just made for two people. All around them sat people who worked for the "summer people" like Pinky—maids, cooks, groundskeepers. They kept glancing curiously at the teenagers among them.

Samir turned to the window and tried to jiggle it open, but it held fast. The inside of the bus was quickly becoming a stinky steamer, everyone's sweaty BO mixing together in the airless space.

Pinky wiped her brow surreptitiously. "We're doing a good deed for the planet!" she said brightly. "Think about that. We can't try to save the habitat and then drive everywhere. It's unconscionable."

"We drove to the butterfly habitat," Samir countered, his eyebrow raised.

"There was no bus route there," Pinky said thoughtfully. "Although . . . maybe next time we should ride our bikes. I'll have to Google to see at what temperature you're at risk for heatstroke."

Dolly groaned. "How much longer?"

Pinky checked her cell. "Twenty more minutes."

This time it was Samir who groaned.

"We're here to see Mayor Thomas," Pinky explained to the receptionist at city hall.

She was a black woman with the coolest weave, and she looked them all over skeptically. Pinky could imagine why—they were dripping sweat, hair plastered to their skulls and necks, and they probably smelled like a gym locker room.

"We have an appointment," Pinky clarified when the pause went on too long.

"I see. Name?"

"Kumar. Pinky Kumar."

The receptionist checked her computer and then nodded. "All right, please have a seat and the mayor will be with you shortly." Her tone was a little regretful, Pinky thought.

Only a minute later, Mayor Michael Thomas, whom Pinky recognized from the city hall website, came out to greet them. He was an older white man, dressed in a charcoal-gray suit with a blue-and-gray striped tie and slightly scuffed shoes. "Hi," he said, smiling at the three of them. "Which one of you is Pinky Kumar?"

Pinky stood and extended a hand. "That would be me. But these are my colleagues, Dolly and Samir. Can they come into our meeting as well?"

Mayor Thomas beamed at them all. "Of course, of course."

They followed him to his office, which was a mess of papers and books and bookcases. "Have a seat," he said, pulling a stool from a corner of the room so there were three seats facing his.

He went around the desk and sat, steepling his fingers. "So. Tell me what brings you in today. It's not often I get to meet with the bright young minds of the next generation."

A smooth-talking politician—big surprise. It was like they had a handbook or something. Pinky nodded seriously. "Well, we're on a mission, Mayor. A mission to stop the immoral, appalling destruction of a prized relic of our city."

"Say again?" the mayor said. "What relic?"

"The butterfly habitat." Pinky reached into her tote bag and pulled out a photo album she'd curated over the past few days. Flipping the cover open, she said, "This is me, at three years old, helping to plant it. That was about fifteen years ago, Mayor." She flipped another page. "What you're looking at is a team of people from this very city that you love and have sworn to serve, coming together to make this magical place a reality." She flipped yet another page. "For a decade and a half, people from this city have been taking their families there to make happy memories. There have been engagements, weddings, birthday parties . . . even an unexpected birth. The point is, this place is a monument to the lives people in your city are living. This place is a memento of hope, of simpler times, of the importance of taking time to relax, to recharge, to—"

"This is all very touching," the mayor said, tapping the corner of one of the photographs, of a guy on his knee, proposing to a girl. Pinky had printed it off the Internet. She'd found a dozen such stories on social media, all tagged #ellingsworthbutterflyhabitat. "And you're not the first people to come in here about the habitat." Pinky had expected that; Gloria had said she'd been sending waves of people in. The mayor continued. "But I'm going to have to tell you exactly what I've told all the others—I'm sorry. That deal is done."

Pinky stared at him. "Then you have to *undo* it," she said in the calmest way she could manage, though she could hear the anger spitting and sparking at the edge of her words.

She could feel Samir looking at her in her peripheral vision. "There has to be a loophole," he said, much more calmly. "Something you can do to at least buy us time to garner resident support for our petition."

"Sorry." The mayor folded his hands together. "I really admire your passion and gumption, kids. I do. But the truth is, this deal's going to bring the city a lot of money, and we could use it. We're not Martha's Vineyard or Nantucket, but maybe this could help us be. These could be vacation rentals, second homes, primary residences. . . . There are no limits. Besides, DR Developments is not a company the city can afford to antagonize, especially not on the whim of a few kids on summer break."

Pinky leaned forward. "I totally hear that. I understand that you might not be able to stop the condo development completely. That's why we have a proposition. What would you—and DR Developments—think of moving the condos to a different location? They'll still be on Ellingsworth Point Island, and the town could still get all the benefits, without the butterfly habitat having to be razed."

Dolly pulled out her iPad and turned it on to the maps application. She propped it up and set it on the desk so the mayor could see it.

"We're just suggesting DR Developments consider moving the condos to right here." Pinky tapped the screen in the area she and Samir had discussed the night before.

But the mayor was already shaking his head. "That's fifteen miles away from the current location," he said. "I'm sorry, but I know Diana Ria would never agree."

Pinky looked at him. "Diana Ria? That's her name? So . . . Di Ria?"

The mayor gazed back blankly. The guy had zero sense of humor.

Dolly cleared her throat at almost the exact same time Samir made a discreet chopping motion with his hand. *Oh right, focus, Pinky.* "Well, that's very disappointing," she continued. "But I feel it's only fair to tell you that this isn't the end. I'm joining forces with a very industrious, well-organized group of full-time residents of this town who won't let the habitat go without a fight." She wasn't totally sure about all those claims since she and Gloria had only spoken once, but Pinky had faith.

The mayor nodded. "Point taken. In the meantime, my suggestion, if you want it, is to enjoy the habitat before it's gone. You have all summer."

The three of them trudged back into the heat, toward the bus stop.

"Well, that sucked," Pinky said. "He didn't even pretend to listen to us."

Samir looked at her. "I'm sorry."

She held his gaze, realizing what she *really* wanted from him in that moment was a hug. But a hug wasn't just a hug with a guy you'd turned down just a few days ago. A hug was also definitely not just a hug when her stomach still flipped with longing anytime he took her hand when her parents were nearby, her brain playing constant what-ifs. *No Sam hugs for you, Pinky*, she told herself sternly.

". . . okay? Pinky?"

She blinked and came to, to see Dolly peering at her in concern. "Are you okay?"

"I'm fine," she said, sitting on the hot plastic seat in the little bus depot. "Just thinking. You know what? We don't need that dude to save the habitat."

"How do you figure?" Samir asked, wiping his forehead with his shirt.

"I'm not sure yet," Pinky said as the bus came rumbling up. "But I'm going to call Gloria as soon as we get home."

CHAPTER 13

Samir

Samir glanced at Pinky as they sat in the cool interior of the kitchen, both of them on their phones, tall glasses of ice water in front of them on the table after their dehydrating excursion out to city hall.

It had sucked when she'd rejected him the other night, but he was over it. Totally, 100 percent over it. The thing was, he was letting the sun bake his brain a little too much. He was ascribing deeper meanings to the things he felt for Pinky because of this new situation, the lake house, the summer . . . It was all external. None of it had to do with him or how he really, truly felt. Once he'd convinced himself of that, it had been easy to go back to looking at this whole thing as a business transaction he was conducting with an acquaintance. Easy-peasy.

Seeing her morose face as she researched successful environmental protests, though, Samir felt a pinprick of sympathy. "Hey." He waited till she looked up, a tiny crease between her eyebrows. "Want me to teach you how to make gazpacho?"

"Gazpacho?"

"Mm-hmm. It's a great summertime meal, and it's super easy.

Your parents and aunt and uncle will be home soon from their yacht party, right? We could surprise them." Dolly had already escaped to Cash's. For not really liking that guy, she spent a lot of time with him and his friends.

"Um . . . okay," Pinky said, getting up and slipping the phone into her shorts pocket. "I guess. There's nothing better to do."

"That's the lukewarm spirit I like to see!" Samir went to the sink and washed his hands, and Pinky followed, snorting. "Okay, so now we need tomatoes, cucumbers, bell peppers, onions, and garlic."

They walked to the fridge and pantry and got out the vegetables. "How do you know how to cook so well anyway?" Pinky asked, carrying a few heirloom tomatoes to the cutting board on the counter.

Samir shrugged. "It's kind of my hobby." Pointing to the tomatoes, he added, "Can you begin slicing those?" He sniffed at a red bell pepper from the vegetable bin to make sure it was still fresh. "I mean, I used to spend a lot of time cooped up at home, so . . . you know. You have to find ways to make it interesting. Food's just something my mom and I have always been able to bond over."

"Hmm."

"Maybe you can try it with your mom," Samir said, though he honestly couldn't picture the Shark in an apron. Speaking of . . . he grabbed two aprons from the hook on the door of the pantry and held one out to Pinky, who'd begun dicing the tomatoes.

She held up her hands. "Too messy. Could you just tie it around my waist for me?"

Samir paused. "Um, sure." He set his own apron down on the counter and then walked closer to Pinky, holding the one meant for her.

She held still as he slipped his arms around her from behind, pulling the strings of the apron against her stomach and waist, knotting them in the back. His fingers grazed her back through her thin cotton shirt. She'd taken a shower—as he had—after they got home, and he could smell her shampoo, something sweet and herbal mixed with her own soft scent.

"There," he said, his voice just a touch husky. "All done."

She looked at him over her shoulder, her gaze briefly catching on his lips. "Thanks."

"You're welcome." This was the moment when he should step back and away from her. When he should pick up a knife of his own and begin chopping something.

Instead, he stood where he was. And Pinky continued to gaze at him.

There was a moment of hesitance, of resistance, of "this is a bad idea" on his part, but it was crumbling too quickly for him to hold on to.

And then his mouth was on hers and he wasn't sure who had started it or what was happening except that she'd set the knife down and turned to him, her messy hands tangling in his shirt, and they were kissing, falling, deeper and deeper. He studied her expression, looking for hesitation or confusion or regret, but he saw nothing. Just unbridled passion that mirrored his. Her eyes were closed and she was pushing into him, as if she couldn't get close enough. Samir knew he should be questioning this in light of what had happened out on the deck, but he wasn't. He was just accepting it, wanting it, needing it to happen.

Her phone beeped in her pocket between them, startling them both. She jumped back and they stared at each other, Samir's heart pounding so furiously he could practically see it through his shirt.

"I should, um, see who this is." Pinky turned away to wash her hands, though they were mostly clean now anyway.

"Yeah, and I'm gonna go change my shirt," Samir said, holding the tomato juice–soaked shirt away from his skin to make his point. Really, he just needed to put some distance between them.

He ran up the stairs, shaking his head. What the hell was that? Calling it a practice kiss would be completely disingenuous. That had been the real thing. And he wasn't 100 percent sure he'd initiated it . . . which meant what? Did it mean *any*thing to Pinky beyond that she wanted to hook up with him? And was he capable of *just* hooking up with her, without letting it consume his feelings?

Samir groaned as he stepped into his room, peeling off his dirty shirt and grabbing a new one from the drawer. Pinky Kumar was, quite possibly, the most confusing person he'd ever met in his life.

They finished making the gazpacho. Samir made sure to keep at least four feet of distance between them at all times, and it worked out fine. By mutual, unspoken agreement, neither of them spoke of the impromptu kiss. Samir had already said what he wanted to say; the ball was in her court now. If she wanted to take it further, she could. From the looks of it, though, she was pretending the ball didn't even exist.

"Pretty good," she said now, tasting a bit of the gazpacho in her bowl. "My parents are going to be seriously impressed that I had anything to do with this at all."

Samir smiled. "Well, you made it. I just gave you instructions. I'll vouch for you."

"Thanks."

231

He blinked and looked away when she held eye contact. "So, um, who was that? On the phone earlier?"

"Gloria. She wants us to help her canvass the neighborhood later on in July. Oh, and I also got a text from Dolly. She wanted to know if we wanted to go swimming with Cash and her."

Samir made a face.

"Yeah, I know. But she really wanted us to, so I'm thinking we should. I mean, if you don't mind too much."

"I don't mind," Samir said reluctantly. "Besides, we gotta keep up appearances, right? It'll be weird if this is a double date and I don't go."

Pinky smiled. "Thanks."

They walked out to the pier—Pinky dressed in her glittery black Kali bikini, Samir in his much more sensible plain blue swim trunks—after both sets of parents had had two bowls of the gazpacho each. Both of Pinky's parents had looked like they might pop from pride when she told them she'd made it. Samir had flashed her a surreptitious thumbs-up; their plan was working. At least one thing wasn't a total disaster this summer.

Now, Pinky held on to DQ's leash. As they got closer to the lake, she tied it around a skinny tree trunk close by. Samir glanced at her occasionally, but she made no move to talk about their latest kiss. The girl was like a closed book—with some of the pages ripped out. He blew out a silent, frustrated breath, and she looked at him, one eyebrow raised, eyebrow ring glinting. "You okay?"

Okay, so maybe it hadn't been so silent. "Yeah, fine." He ran a hand through his hair. "Where are we supposed to be meeting them anyway?"

Pinky pointed to the water. Cash and Dolly were already in the lake; they came swimming up when they saw Pinky and Samir.

"Hey," Dolly said. "Glad you guys could come. I just thought it'd be nice, you know, if the four of us could hang out a bit more. Make this summer a little more fun." She smiled kind of desperately.

"Sure." Pinky smiled stiffly at Cash. "Hey, Cash."

Too cool to be verbal, he just tipped his head at her.

"Hey," Samir said, slipping into the water.

"So, you staying the whole summer?" Cash asked, doing a lazy backstroke.

"I think so," Samir replied, treading water.

Pinky splashed into the water and emerged beside him just as Dolly said, "Oh yeah. Everyone loves Samir. I think both our parents are going to be really sad when he leaves to go back home. They've kind of adopted him."

Samir laughed. "I don't know about that."

"Really?" Cash said, his blue eyes steady on Samir. "That's cool, man. Do you go to Pinky's school?"

"No, I'm homeschooled," Samir said, feeling that familiar warmth in his cheeks. People made all kinds of assumptions, none of them nice, when you told them that.

Cash was no different. He smirked. "Seriously?"

Samir met his eye coolly. "Yeah. Seriously."

Cash shook his head. "Dude."

Samir knew it shouldn't affect him—Cash was irrelevant—but he felt his pulse kick up at the judgment in his voice. "'Dude' what?" he asked, his voice hard.

Pinky and Dolly exchanged a glance. "Why don't we get our inner tubes—" Dolly began, but Cash cut her off.

"I don't know, bro," Cash said, a lazy, insolent smile on his face. "Being homeschooled is kind of . . . weird. Are you in some kind of cult or something? Like, do you have to impregnate your mom when you turn eighteen?" He chuckled at his own wit.

"*Cash*," Dolly said, her face livid.

When Samir spoke, he made sure his voice was quiet and controlled, but firm. "Don't ever talk to me like that."

Cash swam closer to him, so they were almost nose to nose. "Oh yeah?" he asked, still smirking, though Samir could see the anger twitching just under the surface. "That supposed to scare me?"

Samir just stared at him, willing himself to not resort to anything physical, telling himself he wouldn't be the first to lay a hand on this asshole. But he also wouldn't be the first to look away.

And then Dolly was yanking Cash back, her face red.

"Stop it!" she said, looking up at Cash as she treaded water. Her breaths came in short, sharp pants. "I told you to let it go!"

Cash's jaw was set, a defensive thrust to it. "I wasn't the only one in this conversation."

"No, but you're the one continuing to poke and prod," Dolly said. "Can't you just be nice? For once?"

He glared at Dolly. "I thought you *liked* not nice. I thought it turned you on. I guess it only works for you when your friends aren't around." And then he pivoted, swam quickly to the pier, and got out. He shook out a towel, draped it around his broad shoulders, and stalked off without looking back at any of them.

Dolly turned to Pinky and Samir, her cheeks pink. "I'm sorry," she mumbled.

Pinky shook her head. "It's fine." She glanced at Samir, questioning.

After a pause, he nodded too. "Yeah. Fine."

"No, it's not." Dolly's voice wavered. "He said some nasty things to you, Samir, and I'm really sorry."

"It's not your fault," he said, and he meant it. "Seriously. It's not the first time some jerk's made a joke about my being homeschooled, and it won't be the last."

"It's not just that." Dolly sniffed, her eyes pink around the edges. Was she about to start crying? Samir looked on in concern and vague discomfort. "It's that . . . I'm putting him in your periphery and bad stuff keeps happening. Like first with the barn and then the Uno game, and now with those comments he made . . ."

"You feel guilty," Pinky said.

"Yeah." Dolly blinked fast. "Wouldn't you?"

"Probably," Pinky replied. "I mean, I *have*. I've been in your situation many times, Dolly. It's not like you have the corner on making stupid mistakes with stupid boys, you know."

Was it Samir's imagination or did Pinky look at him when she said that last thing? So now he was a stupid mistake and a stupid boy?

Samir felt himself bristling. "I'm just going to, ah, do a few laps," he called over his shoulder as he launched himself into the water, into exercise, into a few good minutes of lung-burning, brain-quieting activity.

"Are you okay?" Pinky asked later, in Samir's room.

They were back home, and they'd all showered and changed and were basically killing time before dinner. The sun was setting and Samir had the windows in his bedroom open. He loved what dusk did to the world, like a soft, rose-gold paintbrush had swept over it.

He looked up from his bed, where he was reading a law magazine, his wet hair dripping droplets of cold water down his neck, cooling him. "Fine."

"Yeah . . ." Pinky walked in and perched on his windowsill. Her legs looked extra long in that tiny skirt, but Samir forced his eyes to his magazine. "I don't think so. You've been acting weird since that whole thing with Cash. He get under your skin?"

"Nope," Samir replied, trying hard to control the flash of temper he felt, so alien to him. He turned a page and kept up the appearance of reading. "I'm just reading."

There was a beat of silence, two. Pinky sighed. "Sam . . ."

He looked up at her tone, part gentle, part frustrated. It was the "gentle" that always got him. Pinky being gentle, being soft, was almost impossible to resist.

"It's okay if he did," she continued. "I mean, he kind of got under my skin and he wasn't even talking to—"

Samir tossed his magazine aside and got off his bed, striding to where she stood, her back to the window. When they were toe-to-toe, he said, quietly but firmly, "No. *Cash* didn't get under my skin."

Pinky swallowed. She could smell the citrusy soap he'd used in the shower; she could see a single drop of water rolling down the side of the smooth skin on his neck. She could feel the heat of his skin, wafting to her, wrapping her up and holding tight. "Oh," she said, her voice scratchy. "Then . . . what?"

They continued staring at each other, not talking. Her heart was hammering so hard, she was suddenly afraid Samir could hear it. She should tell him to back off, but . . . she didn't want him to. She wanted him to continue standing exactly this close. She wanted to continue to be lost in those brown eyes. And she was fully aware that how she was feeling was completely and utterly at odds with her "let's just focus on our *goals*, Samir" speech out on the deck the night she'd turned him down.

"You," he said, almost angrily. "*You're* the one getting under my skin."

Holy hell. If she'd ever thought Samir was soft, or weak, or too much of a goody-goody, if she'd ever judged him as not being attractive enough for those qualities, dear goddess, she'd been so, so wrong. Her knees were actually *weak*. The boy was projecting some serious alpha male energy, and she was panting for more.

"Why?" she asked him in a challenging tone meant to get even more under his skin. Come on. She was only human. She wanted more of this Samir. She could easily see *this* one striding around a courtroom, controlling it. Dominating it.

"Why?" he asked, his voice deep. "Because I can't figure you out. You tell me you don't have feelings for me one night, and then you kiss me two days later. Sometimes you look at me like—"

"Like what?" Pinky asked, breathless, when he didn't continue.

"Like you want me to take you in my arms, pin you against the wall, and kiss you senseless."

She stared at him.

He stared at her.

"Oh my God!" Dolly burst into Samir's room, her head bent and her eyes glued to her phone. "You guys aren't going to believe this."

Samir seamlessly stepped sideways and took a seat in a chair beside Pinky. She blinked, not really able to see anything because her head was swimming so much. What had happened? What had just happened?

Dolly looked up at them. "He's mad at me because I haven't invited him to the house."

"Who?" Pinky asked, in a voice that was little more than a croak. She cleared her throat. "I mean, who?"

Dolly held up her phone. "Cash! Can you believe that?"

Pinky read the text and shook her head. "Ugh. He's a petulant mess."

"He's just jealous of you, Samir," Dolly said. "I shouldn't have told him our parents like you so much. Now it's become some kind of ridiculous macho competition for him."

Samir crossed his outstretched legs at the ankles, looking completely unruffled. How could he do that? Weren't all his internal organs in tangles like hers were? "Doesn't surprise me. Cash is somewhat of a douche, if you don't mind my saying so."

Dolly sighed and sat on his bed, her cell phone dangling from her hands between her knees. "I don't mind at all. I've decided to call it quits with him."

"Seriously?" Pinky went over to sit by her. "Are you okay?"

Dolly groaned. "I don't really know. I mean, the first 'bad boy' I date and I can't even date him for all of the summer. Am I just *that* boring? What does that say about me?"

"You have good taste?" Samir said with a shrug.

Pinky slung an arm around Dolly. "You're not boring. You're just . . . set in your ways."

Dolly punched her lightly on her thigh and then they all laughed, Pinky locking eyes with Samir for a moment. An invisible electric charge seemed to arc across the room, sparking and spitting between them.

Forget Dolly's boy problems. What was she going to do about *hers*?

A few days later (during which Samir didn't bring up anything else about her getting under his skin, much to Pinky's disappointment), they were all sitting down to dinner on the deck when the French doors opened.

Pinky frowned at her parents in the dim light of the flickering table lanterns. "Are we expecting someone?"

"No." Her mom was frowning too.

Pinky's dad got up to check who it was—they couldn't see from the far corner of the deck—and then she heard her dad's "fake friendly" voice. "Oh, hello!" he said. "You're one of our neighbors, aren't you?"

"Yes, sir," came the reply. "I'm Cash—Cash Miller. I live right across the lake."

CHAPTER 14

Pinky

Pinky darted a glance at Dolly, only to see her cousin just as wide-eyed and horrified as she looked. Her dad's and Cash's voices got closer.

"Dr. Miller's boy, of course! What a nice surprise."

"I just came by to see Dolly," Cash was saying as they rounded the corner. Pinky could now see that he was wearing a white button-down shirt with little blue anchors on it. His usually shaggy hair was neatly combed to the side. He was wearing boat shoes. *Boat. shoes.*

"Oh my God," Dolly mouthed at her, and Pinky grimaced at Samir, who was watching the proceedings with avid curiosity.

"I see," Pinky's dad said, his eyebrows rising in surprise. "Well, we're all sitting down to dinner. . . ."

"But why don't you join us?" Meera Mausi added. "We have an extra seat and plenty of food."

Abe smiled and gestured to the empty seat beside him, which Cash took. "Thank you," he said. "I don't mean to intrude. . . ."

"Not at all," Abe said genially. Naturally, he wouldn't be quite so friendly if he knew Cash was the reason Dolly had burned down the barn earlier this summer. "The more the merrier."

"Thank you, sir." Cash smiled, his straight, white, dentist's-kid teeth all perfect and happy.

Pinky had to hand it to Cash. When he put on his human face, he was pretty charming. Almost Samir-level charming, except something in those flinty blue eyes told you he wasn't nearly as trustworthy.

Cash smiled winningly over at Dolly, who was seated across from him. "Hey. What's up?"

Pinky could tell her cousin was trying not to glare at him, but she didn't quite succeed. "Hi, Cash," Dolly said carefully. "What are you doing here?"

"I came to ask you if you wanted to do some fireworks with me and the crew." He smiled as sweetly as if he were a kid in a lemonade ad. "We have some left over from the Fourth of July, so we're going to set them off, just for fun."

"*Really?*" Pinky interjected pointedly. "Is that even legal?"

Her mother gave her a withering look. "It's *fine*, Pinky. A couple of small fireworks aren't going to hurt anything." She turned to Cash. "I assume there will be adult supervision?"

"Oh, of course." His baby blues were all wide, his face earnest. "We wouldn't dream of doing it without."

Pinky snorted, ignoring her mom's evil eye.

"I'm sorry." Dolly speared a piece of conchiglie pasta with her fork. "I'm busy."

Her parents exchanged a glance, probably wondering what the heck was going on. For Dolly, that response was really high up there on the rudeness scale. It'd be like a regular teenager spitting in someone's eye.

"Oh, come on." Cash leaned back and crossed his arms. He was slowly shedding his human skin and morphing back into Petulant Blond Demigod. "You can't spare, like, thirty minutes?"

"No." Dolly looked up at him, unsmiling. "I can't."

Abe frowned at Cash and then at Dolly. "I'm sorry. Am I missing something here?"

Cash opened his mouth to respond, but Dolly cut in. "*No*," she said, chewing a piece of pasta so furiously, Pinky was afraid her teeth would crack. "We're *fine*."

Cash helped himself to a plate of salad and then sat there, smiling grandly around at everyone. "So. Are you all going to be at the silent auction night at the country club next month? My dad's donating a free dental cleaning. And I've heard the Robertsons are donating a genuine Klimt."

Pinky could practically hear the eye rolls around the table. Her parents were rich, but they weren't pretentious. Cash was what they called a Boston Brahmin, and not a subtle one at that.

"We will be at the silent auction," Meera Mausi said politely. "But we aren't sure yet what we'll be bidding on. It sounds like we'll have plenty of options!"

Abe was playing with his butter knife and eyeing Cash up, as if wondering whether he could take him. Pinky bit the inside of her cheek to keep from grinning. This was actually kind of entertaining. Then she glanced at Dolly, at the abject horror on her face, and felt bad.

There was an awkward silence as everyone ate.

"So, Cash, have you and Dolly been friends for a while?" Pinky's dad said, asking the very specific question that everyone was hoping he wouldn't ask. It was like a special gift he had.

"No," Dolly said, at the same time that Cash answered, "Yes."

There was a beat. Pinky caught Samir's eye; he looked aghast on Dolly's behalf, which warmed Pinky's heart. Until she remembered they still had a lot of unfinished business between them.

"I've known *of* him," Dolly said carefully. "But I haven't—"

"Oh, come *on.*" Cash grinned, completely insouciant. One of his arms was bent and resting on the back of his chair. "Just tell them we've been dating the past three weeks, will you?"

There was a collective intake of breath from Dolly and her parents, as if there wasn't enough air in the room and they were all competing for it. Then the words flew, all tangled up together like a ball of yarn.

"Dolly! You and he have been—"

"Dating? Why didn't you tell us that the—"

"—barn burned down and now—"

"He's exaggerating! I can explain—"

Pinky sat there as the words were flung like arrows across the table, thankful for one, tiny, shameful moment that this time the upset wasn't about her. This time the upset was about Dolly. And judging from her parents' and her aunt's and uncle's faces, they had *no* idea she was even capable of something like this.

For just one small moment, Pinky wanted to stand up on the table and yell, "You see? You see? There's no such thing as a perfect teenager!" but she stifled the urge. Her cousin, her *sister*, was in pain. That was all that mattered.

"Can we all just calm down?" Pinky shouted, and to her immense surprise, they all stopped talking and turned to her. She cleared her throat when they kept staring. "Well, I hadn't really decided what to say after that. . . ."

Cash grinned, his teeth orange in the lantern light. "There's nothing to say, Pinx."

She turned her most withering glare on him. "*Don't* call me that."

Samir spoke into the prickling, sparking quiet. "We've all made mistakes." He looked around at everyone. "I know I've been there a lot. And maybe Dolly made a mistake with Cash, I don't know." He turned to Dolly. "If you're feeling ashamed or embarrassed, don't be." Smiling a little, he added, "I mean, I know that's easier said than done, believe me. But . . . I don't blame you for going out with Cash. For trying something different than you have before."

Dolly smiled back at him. "Thanks."

Pinky felt her heart hiccup unpleasantly in her chest.

"Well, isn't this nice?" Cash's smile was a nasty thing. He turned to Pinky. "My girlfriend and your boyfriend are having a moment."

"I am *not* your girlfriend." Dolly pushed her chair back and stood. "I told you that on text already. This is over. And you need to leave. Now."

Cash glared at her for a long moment. Pinky could see Meera Mausi and Abe restraining themselves from interfering, wanting to give Dolly the space to take care of her own problems. And her own mom was watching everything with a considering stare, as if she were making detailed mental notes.

Finally, Cash scraped his chair back and stood, throwing his napkin down on the table. "Fine." He practically snarled the word. "I'm gone. But you know what? It's your loss. Have fun dating future social workers and elementary school teachers like you usually do." He turned and walked away, his stupid boat shoes flapping against the wood of the deck.

Dolly sat back down and took a sip of water, her hand trembling. Pinky leaned over and gave her a one-armed hug. "I'm proud of you," she whispered.

Dolly clamped her icy-cold hand around Pinky's under the table.

"Well, young lady." Meera Mausi's voice was a tad shaky. "I think we have a lot to talk about. So if you're done with dinner, will you please come up to our room in about ten minutes?" She looked at Abe, who nodded slightly. Then they both excused themselves, got up from the table, and walked away, their heads bent as they spoke quietly together.

"I'm so dead," Dolly said, watching them go. Samir flashed her a sympathetic look.

"I don't think so." Pinky's mom shook her head. "I think your parents have just realized they have a normal teenager on their hands. And that's not the worst thing in the world."

She met Pinky's eye, and just for a moment Pinky thought she saw a spark of understanding, of warmth, of camaraderie there.

Pinky took a swig from her ginger beer bottle. "So, did they tear you a new one or what?"

"No." Dolly sighed. "I mean, they wanted to, I could tell. But their professional training took over and they held back."

They were sitting in the gazebo later that night—much later; it was about two a.m.—and getting caught up. Dolly had been in her parents' room until almost midnight, and then her parents had been in Pinky's parents' room until almost one thirty.

Pinky and Dolly had sneaked out as soon as they could. Samir had gone to bed about an hour ago.

"So, what's your punishment?" Pinky asked. She was most curious about this part. How *did* two therapists punish a daughter who'd been perfect for sixteen years?

Dolly sighed and took a dejected swig of her root beer. "They signed us up for a three-week-long therapeutic family retreat that begins two weeks from today."

Pinky snorted some ginger beer through her nose and grimaced at the intense pain. "Um, what?" she asked, when she could speak again. "What even is that?"

"Exactly what it sounds like. Some weirdo, new-agey retreat where we all sit around in floaty clothes on some mountaintop in Vermont talking about what went wrong and how we can *reassimilate on a shared pathway that honors each of our journeys.*"

"Ew." Pinky shook her head. "Right now I'm kind of glad my parents are lawyers."

Dolly huffed a laugh. "Yeah. You have no idea."

"So they're just going to whisk you away in the middle of our summer vacation?"

"That's the plan. And when we return, I'll be the new, improved me!" Dolly clinked her bottle with Pinky's, but the clink was definitely sarcastic.

Pinky quirked her lips. "For what it's worth? I don't think you need to be improved. You're pretty amazing the way you are. And you know what Cash said when he left? About you dating future social workers and teachers or whatever? He meant that as an insult, but . . . I think it's really kind of great that you gravitate toward people like that. *You're* really kind of great, and you deserve to be with someone who'll recognize that."

Dolly smiled at her in the glow of the backyard lighting. "Thanks, sis. By the way, your fake boyfriend was pretty amazing up there on the deck."

"Oh, right." Pinky took another swig of her ginger beer to hide just how discomfited she felt. "He, uh, kind of sympathized with you, right?"

Dolly nodded. "Yeah. He basically made me feel like not a total douche, and I really appreciated it, you know? He's kind of a rock."

"Yeah," Pinky mused, realizing just how true that was. Samir hadn't just integrated with her family. He was like a soothing balm, smoothed all over their sunburned skin. Or something less weird. She was tired and metaphors were hard.

"You know, I've been thinking." Dolly set her root beer down with a clink. "I'm not the 'bad boy' type after all."

"Oh yeah?" Pinky's heart thumped for reasons she couldn't quite figure out.

"Yeah." Dolly looked out into the yard, at the burned shell of the barn. Soon their parents would have someone come cart it away and it'd be like it never happened. "It's like you said. I think I'm okay dating people who feel right to me. Who are more like me. I don't know if that makes me boring, but . . . I think I'm okay with it even if it does. I need to be true to me, you know?"

Pinky nodded, though her head felt heavy. "Yeah, totally."

Dolly smiled slowly, glancing sideways at Pinky. "So . . . um. I kind of have a question?"

"Okay."

"If you're not using that boyfriend, can I have him?"

Pinky set her own drink down and wiped her suddenly damp palms on her shorts. "What?"

Dolly laughed. "You and Samir are just fake dating, right? Well, once you're all done with that and everything . . . do you mind if I text him? Just get to know him a bit better? I think he and I might have a lot in common, actually."

Pinky was sure a sonic boom had gone off in her chest. She'd seen it coming; of course she had—any moron could have. Dolly and Samir. Samir and Dolly. They made perfect sense, didn't they? Way more sense than Pinky and Samir. They were perfectly suited for each other. In fact, hadn't that been the entire reason Pinky had even chosen him for this whole fake-dating farce, because he was exactly the kind of person her cousin would date? So this was no surprise. Not at all. And, in fact, it was good news. If she could keep in mind that Dolly wanted Samir, then she would be able to curb any inappropriate, ridiculous desire she felt for him, the boring baby lawyer. It was all easy. Simple. Dolly was doing her a *favor*, in fact.

And yet . . .

And yet Pinky's tongue was stuck to the roof of her mouth, as if she'd accidentally glued it there. She tried to speak, but no words came.

"Hey." Dolly had a concerned furrow between her eyebrows. She put a hand on Pinky's shoulder. "Are you okay?"

"Yeah!" Pinky squeaked, finally prying her tongue loose. "Totally!" She smiled and reached for her ginger beer with a shaky hand, almost knocking it over in the process. Taking a deep swig, she said, "You know, this is a great idea. You and Samir. Because, um, he's just too . . . he's too nice, you know? He's really sweet and focused and he really cares about people. And you might *think* he's a total goody-two-shoes mama's boy, but he's not. He has this core of confidence, this security in himself that's completely unexpected." She took another deep drink. "And, um, all those things might be attractive to some people, but to me—"

"Pinky."

"—to me, that kind of thing is . . . I mean, so yes. He makes the world a better place by being in it, but really—"

"Pinky."

She turned to her cousin, her brain pinwheeling. "What?"

Dolly was shaking her head slowly. "Oh. My. God. You like him. Don't you? You really, really like him."

"What?" Pinky said, leaning back a bit. The crickets chirped their own questions. "No, I don't!"

Dolly laughed. "Uh-huh. Okay."

Pinky closed her eyes. "Dolly. I *can't* like him."

"Why not?" she heard Dolly say. "Why the hell not?"

Pinky opened her eyes. "Because! What would it say about me if I did? I'm the free spirit of the family. I'm the one who does the thing everyone else is scared to do. I'm the one who thinks outside the box. I'm the creative, rebellious one! If I date someone as staid and steady and even-keeled as him, someone my *parents* approve of, for God's sake, what would that say about me?"

Dolly studied her for a long moment. "Who cares?"

Pinky stared at her, feeling kind of hurt. "What?"

Dolly shook her head. "Who cares? Who cares what it says about you? Who cares if he's the kind of guy your parents would pick for you? Who cares if you like staid and steady and even-keeled?" Dolly leaned forward. "What do *you* want, Pinky? Forget what everyone else would think or what it might say about your identity. What does your heart say? What does your *soul* say about Samir?"

For one tempting moment, Pinky wanted to say the first thing that flew into her mind: *My soul says it was waiting for him.* But in the next moment, she had swallowed the thought. That was foolish, impractical, ridiculous, two a.m. talk. Pinky had been in enough relationships to know what kind of boy her soul needed. Her soul must be broken or something at the moment. "It's not that easy," she whispered.

"But it could be," Dolly pressed gently. "It could be if you wanted it to be."

Pinky didn't know what to say, so she said nothing. She wanted to have Dolly's easy belief in love and dating, but she didn't. She and Samir were not meant to be together. That was it. What else was there to say?

Dolly studied her for another moment and then sighed. Scooting over on the wooden bench, she put her arms around Pinky. "I get it," she said softly. "I totally get it. Sometimes we have to find our own path forward. It doesn't matter what anyone else says."

Pinky closed her eyes, relieved that, at least for this moment, she didn't have to explain herself to anyone.

Samir

Pinky sat with her legs crossed on the striped couch in a *Rashida & Alexandria & Ayanna & Ilhan* T-shirt. "I've been talking to Gloria." Almost two weeks had passed since the Cash fiasco, and the adults were out at some Saturday morning farmers' market in town. She, Dolly, and Samir had commandeered the living room. "And it looks like the people we have the best chance of reaching with this petition are south of Hennickport Street. She said we should start there with our canvassing efforts."

"Okay. When are we doing this?" Samir was trying really hard not to look at her too often. He found that when he did, his gaze lingered, and then *she* looked at *him*, her eyes going wide and soft. It just seemed like she was sending him all these mixed signals. And so, ever since their conversation in his room, when he'd told her she was getting under his skin and then been interrupted by Dolly, he'd decided he'd let Pinky come to him. He'd decided that before and then wavered, but now he was holding strong. This was it. He was done reaching out. A man had to have some self-respect.

Pinky tucked a lock of pink hair behind one ear. "Tuesday. Gloria said the people south of Hennickport Street are kind of the old-timers. You know, people who're likelier to be resistant to Ellingsworth becoming the new Nantucket, that kind of thing. She said we should start there with our petition. I figured it'd be good if we could dig up some old photographs of our family hanging out at the habitat. They might be a little wary of the summer people, but I figure if we can show them our commitment to this place, how much it means to us and all that stuff, they'd have to come around, right?"

"That's a really good idea." Dolly nibbled on her lower lip. "Okay, how about this? I'll go scope out that area, just kind of get an idea of how many houses per block, what we can hope to do in an evening, that kind of thing."

"Yep. And Pinky and I'll hunt down the pictures of your family at the habitat," Samir added.

"Great." Dolly smiled. "We should be able to get that stuff done today, right?"

"Right," Pinky agreed. Then she made a face. "But you're leaving Monday. You won't be here when we're going door to door."

Dolly looked just as dejected. "I know. But I'll be there in spirit. And as soon as I get home, I'll dive into the deep end with you guys."

"Okay," Pinky grumbled. "But I don't know why the retreat needs to be three weeks."

"Because my parents are freaked out that I'm going rogue, and this is the only way they know how to do something about it," Dolly said, rolling her eyes. She got up and grabbed her keys and purse. "Anyway. I'll see you guys later?"

Pinky nodded, and Samir lifted his hand in a wave. A few moments later, they heard the front door open and then close.

They were alone. The house settled around them.

He looked at Pinky, hoping his nervousness didn't show. "Shall we?"

She took a deep breath and stood. "To the attic."

• • •

It was dusty in the attic, and any notions he had of romantic possibilities were swiftly banished when he saw the bat droppings.

"Bats?" He stared wide-eyed and panicked at Pinky. *"Bats?"*

"Relax," she said, pulling a string. An anemic light bulb shone down on them from the rafters. "They're all dead. That's from a long time ago. And anyway, they hardly ever have rabies."

"Great. Yep." Samir felt a shudder ripple through him. "Ancient bat feces. That's just perfect."

Pinky shook her head and took off for a corner, where a big trunk sat. There were a bunch of boxes on top of it, and when he saw her struggling to move them off, Samir shook off his own fear and revulsion and walked over to help.

Once the boxes were out of the way, Pinky slid the latch on the trunk and opened it. It was filled with dusty picture albums and even loose pictures, the kind that came out of Polaroid and old film cameras. Samir whistled. "There must be a couple hundred pictures here."

"Yeah." Pinky squatted next to the open trunk and looked up at him. "So I guess we better start digging."

"Dude." A laugh burbled up from deep inside Samir's chest. He had a silver photo album open, which he'd been idly flipping through. Most of the pictures were of Pinky's and Dolly's families doing mundane family things like grilling salmon or going for a boat ride or picking apples at the orchard in town. About a dozen so far had been at the butterfly habitat, and those he and Pinky had carefully set aside. But *this* one . . . He held it up to Pinky, laughing harder at her expression as she took it in.

It was a picture of a twelve- or thirteen-year-old Pinky on the pier, fresh after a swim. Her hair was in a giant halo around her head, and she had been mid-blink when the picture taker had snapped the picture. The effect was that she looked like a hybrid between a hedgehog and a blobfish.

She snatched it out of his hand. "Hey! The humidity does strange things to my hair! And that expression on my face was obviously just unfortunate timing!"

Samir chuckled and wiped the sweat from his brow on his shirt. "A likely excuse."

"Next time, I want to see old pictures *your* mom has," Pinky said, narrowing her eyes. They both realized the implications of that statement at the same time—it would never happen, because Pinky didn't want to date Samir. His mom wouldn't be showing her anything.

Samir cleared his throat and looked away, back into the trunk. "Hey," he said, reaching into the bottom. "What's this one?" It was a loose photograph of someone who looked amazingly like Pinky, except her hair was longer (though still a riot of various tropical-bird colors) and her clothes were more dated. Her arm was in the air, fist raised proudly, and she was surrounded by people, all of whom looked like they were marching at a protest.

Pinky took the picture from him, studying it for a moment before flipping it over. "Harvard, 2002," she read. "Oh my God." She flipped the photograph back over and studied it again. "This is . . . This woman is my mom."

Samir leaned over to see the picture more clearly. "Holy crap. That's your *mom*?"

CHAPTER 15

Pinky

That could *not* be her mom. No way. Nuh-uh. Just . . . no.

The woman in the picture was young, probably no more than twenty-one or twenty-two. Her hair was an exuberant mix of colors—neon green and silver and blond and teal. She wore a tank top with a crisscrossed back, a lot like the one Pinky had in her closet, in fact, and a denim miniskirt that came up to midthigh.

The signs around her said things like, WOMEN'S RIGHTS ARE HUMAN RIGHTS and I'M A FEMINIST. WHAT'S YOUR SUPERPOWER? Pinky's cardigan-wearing, corporate-lawyer mom had been a *protester* at Harvard? How had this never come to light? How had Pinky never heard this story?

"That's wild." Samir scooted over so he could look at the picture again. "Your mom. The Shark."

"Yeah . . ." Pinky shook her head, studying the passionate, intense expression on her mom's face. She looked like she held the whole world in her fist. She never looked like that anymore.

"You know what's funny?" Samir said, and Pinky glanced up at him.

"What?"

He smiled a little and tapped the picture with a finger. "You get that exact same look on your face when you're fired up about something."

Pinky looked down at the picture. "No, I don't."

"Yep. Identical. I guess I see now where you get it."

"This doesn't make sense." Pinky shook her head. "This . . . My mom isn't . . . She *hates* protests. And rebels. And people who challenge authority in any way. She thinks swapping out a pastel-blue cardigan for a pastel-yellow one is out there."

"Well . . . does she have a twin?" Samir asked. It was obvious even to him, Pinky guessed, that this wasn't Meera Mausi.

"No. It . . . I guess it has to be her." Pinky sat back, all the way on her butt, and set the picture on her lap. "Wow. I feel weird."

Samir frowned at her in concern. "Is it the heat? Do you want to go downstairs?"

"No, I don't . . . I think I'm just thrown. Like, I don't get it. How is this possible?"

Samir watched her for a moment, his face softening. Then he went and sat beside her, also on his butt. "Have you guys ever talked about her Harvard days?"

"Yeah, but the only things I've heard are how she knew she wanted to go to Harvard from when she was, like, twelve and how I need to get my act together so I don't end up at some scam university." Pinky met his eye. "And she *really* doesn't like it when I tell her all universities are scam universities."

Samir chuckled. "Yeah, I can see how she might not."

"But why would she hide this from me?" Pinky asked. "It doesn't make any sense. This means we're . . . I mean, we're not two completely different species like I thought."

Samir shrugged. "I don't know. Maybe you could ask her."

Pinky raised an eyebrow. "Really? You think I could just take this to her and ask her?"

"Why not?"

"Because she's obviously kept this from me for a reason. She doesn't want me to know." She looked back down at the picture. Why was her mom hiding this? Didn't she *want* to bond with Pinky? Didn't she want to find common ground? A hard lump of hurt lodged in her throat.

"Hey." Samir's voice was soft. When she looked up at him, he put an arm around her shoulder and squeezed. "She probably has a good reason for not telling you. Don't make it worse in your head."

"I'm *not*," Pinky protested, although that's exactly what she'd been doing. After a pause, she smiled a little, conceding.

"Yeah. I thought so." He smiled back.

There was a beat of silence, then two. Samir took his arm away, and she instantly felt its loss. She studied him. "What are you doing here, Samir?"

He looked back at her, confused. "Here, at Ellingsworth?"

"No." Pinky shook her head. "Here, in the attic, with me. Talking with me about my mom."

"Well, we were looking for butterfly habitat pictures." He fiddled with the corner of the photo album.

"Samir." Pinky waited until he looked back at her.

He looked at her frankly then, his brown eyes clear. "I like you," he said simply. "Still."

Pinky's mouth was suddenly very, very dry. So he was just going to say it like that, then. Just out in the open, no guile, no game. "Oh." She swallowed, hearing her throat click in the silence.

"I know you don't want to go out with me. I know you don't feel the same way." He held her gaze. She wanted to protest; that second statement was utterly, completely wrong. But she didn't say anything. "And I respect that. But sometimes I get the feeling that . . ." Samir shook his head and cleared his throat. "Doesn't matter. The thing is, I'm working on it. Okay? I'm working on not liking you anymore. It might just take me a while. So in the meantime, I'm probably gonna do more stuff like this." He waved his hand toward the photograph and looked at her again. "Because I care about you."

Pinky felt like her heart would burst. What he was offering her— it was unconditional caring, unconditional acceptance. He didn't give a crap if his feelings weren't returned. He just wanted to be there for her. No boyfriend she'd ever had had ever done anything close to this.

Suddenly Pinky felt very unsure. Dolly's words echoed in her head: *Who cares?* Why *was* it so important to her that her identity be that of the free-spirited rebel? She looked down at the picture in her hand. It was pretty obvious that identities could end up changing and morphing. Her mom's definitely had.

She looked back up at Samir. "I like that you . . . that you care. About me. So." She wiped the sweat off her upper lip. Gross. "But, um . . . that's all I have right now. I'm just—I'm . . ." She shrugged, feeling helpless. Why wasn't that enough to say yes to dating him, to jumping into this thing with both feet? Because Pinky was a confused, swirling tempest of emotion, that's why.

Samir smiled a little, as if he was thinking the same thing. "Okay. Do you want to look for some more butterfly habitat pictures?"

"Yeah." Pinky got back on her knees and put her mom's picture off to the side. "Yeah, let's. I'll think about all this later."

The adults got back from the farmers' market just as Samir and Pinky had finished trawling through the pictures and carried the best ones down to the living room to spread out on the coffee table. The one of Pinky's mom was tucked into the back pocket of Pinky's shorts, for later review. Dolly was still out; she'd texted that she'd be back in a half hour or so.

"Oh!" Pinky's dad smiled down at the pictures. "What's all this?" Her mom came up behind him, her canvas tote bag full of fresh produce. Pinky stared at her, trying to picture *this* mom in a denim miniskirt, with a protest sign clamped in her hands, and she just couldn't do it. How was it even possible that the two were the same woman?

Her mom frowned lightly. "What? Why are you looking at me like that?"

"Um, nothing," Pinky said, tucking a strand of hair behind her ear. To her dad, she said, "Oh, these are pictures of the butterfly habitat. We're going to try to drum up support from the year-round residents to stop the developer from razing it," Pinky explained.

"I thought we'd agreed that you were done with all that." Her mom's lips were set in a thin line.

"I didn't agree to anything. As I remember, you told me to drop it and assumed I would fall into line like one of your peons at work. Well, news flash, Mom, I'm not a peon you pay. I'm your kid."

Her mom glared at her. "Yes. I'm well aware of that."

What did that mean? That she was *regretful* of that? Pinky rallied. "If you just listen to our plan, you'll see that—"

Her mom sighed. "Pinky, I don't have time for this. I have to dial in to a conference call in less than thirty minutes and I have a lot of research to do before that." And with that, she clip-clopped away into the kitchen.

Pinky watched her go. Research. Her mom was always doing research. "Great."

Her dad rubbed his face. "You know how she feels about protests and upsetting the balance of things, honey. She's just worried about you, that's all."

"Worried for what?" Pinky asked, throwing her hands up in the air. "That I actually care about stuff? That I have principles?"

Her dad leaned over the coffee table and kissed her on the forehead, just as Meera Mausi and Abe came in, also carting bags of fruit and flowers. "Sorry. I'll try to talk to her, okay?"

"Fine," Pinky mumbled. She turned to Samir, who'd been sitting on the couch, watching. He mouthed "Sorry," but that didn't really help.

"My goodness, it's hot out there." Meera Mausi's face was red, her hair stuck to her forehead. "I'm going to make some strawberry lemonade. Would you two like some?"

Pinky's mental wheels began to turn. "Um, actually," she said. "I'll help you make it." She took Abe's bag from him. "Why don't you and my dad watch the game in the den, Abe? We can bring you some juice."

He looked surprised and pleased. "Well, that'll be a treat! Thanks, Pinky."

Pinky made sure to smile extra sweetly. "Sure."

Samir gave her an *I know what you're up to* look, but then he flashed her a thumbs-up and walked with Abe to the den.

"Do you want to rinse these strawberries for me, Pinky?" Meera Mausi handed her a bag of the fruit. She inhaled deeply. "Mm, they smell good, don't they?"

Pinky smelled them too. "Yeah." Her mom had already left the kitchen and sequestered herself in her bedroom for her conference call. Pinky stuck the strawberries in a colander and turned on the faucet. "Um, so, Meera Mausi . . . Samir and I were in the attic today, looking for pictures of the butterfly habitat."

"Oh yeah?" Meera Mausi smiled as she picked out a few lemons. "Find anything good?"

"Yeah, a lot, actually. And, um . . . I also found a picture I wasn't expecting to find. A picture of Mom." Pinky reached into her pocket and pulled out the old photograph, setting it on the counter between them. She rinsed the strawberries and let Meera Mausi digest the picture for a moment. Shutting off the faucet, Pinky said, "That *is* Mom, right?"

Meera Mausi set the lemons on the cutting board and turned to Pinky, her hip resting against the counter. "Yes. That's your mom."

Pinky couldn't quite make out the expression on her aunt's face. Loud sounds of cheering came from the den, but she didn't even glance that way. "But she's got multicolored hair. And she's wearing a miniskirt. And she's at a protest. A *protest*."

Meera Mausi smiled a little sadly. "Believe it or not, Pinky, that wasn't uncommon for your mom back then."

"But I don't get it." Pinky picked up a strawberry and tossed it into the air, catching it again. It made her feel less thrown to have something to do with her hands. "I thought she was this super-serious Harvard Law student. That's what she always says."

"Well, she was," Meera Mausi allowed. "But this was undergrad. And your mom was a very different person during her undergrad years. In fact . . ." She smiled. "She was a lot like you. They even had a name for her back then—Hurricane Veena."

Pinky dropped her strawberry on the floor with a splat. "Crap. Sorry." She grabbed a paper towel and bent to pick it up. "Are you serious? *Hurricane* Veena?" It didn't escape her that hurricanes were tempestuous and wild and hard to predict. Whereas her mom's current name—the Shark—spoke of a cold, calculating predator.

Meera Mausi chuckled and began to peel a lemon. "I know. It's hard to believe, right?"

"So, then, what changed?" Pinky asked. What could turn a person from a hurricane to a shark?

Meera Mausi looked at Pinky. "You know, your mom hasn't shared this with you, so I'm not sure I should. It's her story to tell."

Pinky put down the strawberry and walked closer. "*Please*, Meera Mausi. You know how my mom and I are. If you tell me, it might help me understand her better."

"Hello!" Dolly sauntered into the kitchen. "What are you guys up to?"

"Hey, sweetie," her mom said, kissing the side of her head. "Just making some strawberry lemonade. Want some?"

"Ooh, yes, please. I've been craving your SL; it's like you read my mind or something."

Pinky watched them, their easy camaraderie even after Dolly had gotten into trouble, how easily her mom had forgiven her and vice versa. Something in her heart squeezed. It felt like her mom had been holding a seventeen-year grudge against Pinky for reasons she didn't even understand. Meera Mausi caught her eye and her face softened, as if she knew exactly what Pinky was thinking.

"Dolly, would you mind keeping your dad company?" Meera Mausi asked. "He's in the den with Howard and Samir."

Dolly looked between her mom and Pinky. Her expression changed when she caught sight of the picture on the counter between them. "Um, yeah. Sure. No problem." Smiling tentatively at them both, she turned and left.

Meera Mausi looked at Pinky. "Okay. I'll tell you because it's obvious you're desperate to know. I still think you should ask her, though."

"She won't tell me. I just know she won't." She never told Pinky anything of substance about herself. Why would this be any different?

Meera Mausi sighed and began peeling her second lemon. Then, setting down the peeler, she turned to Pinky. "In that picture, your mom was a senior at Harvard. Her major was mass media and communications."

Pinky nodded.

"She wanted to become a radio personality," Meera Mausi said, smiling. "I remember that. She was really into it for all four years there. She even had a show on the Harvard radio station."

"Mom wanted to be a *DJ*?" Pinky couldn't believe it. Had her mom been taken over by aliens or shape-shifters or something?

Meera Mausi laughed. "Yeah. But shortly after that picture was taken," she continued, more seriously, "she found out she was pregnant. With you."

Pinky felt her stomach contract. "I thought she said she had me after law school. That she graduated early or something." In fact, the story had always been vague but boring enough to keep Pinky from asking more. By design, she realized now. Her mom had said that she'd dated a guy through law school, gotten pregnant with Pinky right after she graduated, and the boyfriend had gotten spooked by the idea of commitment and bolted. Her mom had insinuated that it hadn't been any big loss, and Pinky had accepted that. Howard Yeung was her dad; she hadn't ever needed or wanted another.

Meera Mausi shook her head. "It was right after she graduated college. She was eight months pregnant when she walked that stage."

"Holy crap," Pinky whispered. "And my biological dad . . . ?"

Meera Mausi sighed. "It had been a one-night stand. As I remember, your mom had reached out to him to let him know she was pregnant, that she was keeping the baby, and he could choose to be as involved as he wanted to. He never returned her phone call."

Pinky felt a shot of anger at her sperm donor. "Asshole." And on the heels of that, a thought: Why hadn't her mom just told her this? Because the knowledge of being the product of a one-night stand might mess Pinky up? Or because she was hiding the fact that she'd been *exactly* like Pinky not that long ago?

"Pretty much. But your mom . . ." Meera Mausi looked off into the distance for a moment. "She went through this transformation, almost overnight. Our parents were livid, you know. They accused her of being selfish, of never doing the right thing, of only looking out for herself, of derailing her future—"

"Gee," Pinky said sarcastically. "Sounds familiar."

Meera Mausi gave her a look. "Take your mom and multiply it by about a thousand. They harangued her day and night. I tried to talk to them, but they refused to listen."

Pinky knew her mom's parents were not nice people, which was why they didn't really have a relationship with Pinky. But she'd never been told it had anything to do with her. "You said Mom underwent a transformation?"

Meera Mausi went around and sat on a barstool, and Pinky sat next to her. "Your mother changed her personality overnight. It was radical. I mean, she cut off all her hair and dyed it back to its natural color, she began dressing much more conservatively, she began this super-nutritious diet when she'd been known to eat Doritos for breakfast. But more than that, she decided she was going to go to law school. I'd never heard about her ambitions to become a lawyer before, but when I asked her about it, you know what she said?"

Pinky shook her head.

"She said, 'I want to give this kid the best start in life I possibly can, Meera. And if that means doing something I'd never considered before, then so be it.' I'd never seen her so focused, so . . . committed. It was like she aged ten years the minute she took that pregnancy test."

"Wow." Pinky sat back, thinking. "She went to law school for *me*?"

"Yes. I think just about everything your mom's done since then has been for you. It took poor Howard ages to convince her that he was good enough to spend time with you." Meera Mausi chuckled, but Pinky found she couldn't laugh along with her. Suddenly, her heart felt very, very heavy.

"So . . . I was responsible," she said, the truth weighing her down like a ton of cement blocks. "I was the reason Mom changed. That she became . . . the way she is."

Meera Mausi leaned forward. "Oh, sweetie, no," she said, putting a hand on Pinky's back. "It's not a bad thing. I don't think she's regretted a single moment—"

"Of course she has!" Pinky's voice was harsher than she'd meant it to be. She looked at Meera Mausi through a veil of tears. "No wonder she hates me! I'm the reason she had to give up all her goals. I'm the reason she had to strip all the color, all the personality from her life. Don't you see? She's never forgiven me for it."

"Pinky—"

Pinky held up a hand and took a deep breath. "Meera Mausi, thank you for telling me this," she said, forcing her voice to be calm. "And please don't tell Mom you told me. Okay?"

Meera Mausi looked anguished. "I don't think I should keep this from her. She'll want to know how you're feeling."

"*Please*, Meera Mausi," Pinky said, trying to convey with her eyes just how important this was to her. "Please. Just . . . give me some time to process this, okay?"

Meera Mausi nodded, as Pinky had known she would. She was using her language. "All right, honey." She squeezed Pinky's hand. "All right."

"Okay, it's time." Samir was standing in her doorway, carrying two chair cushions and a book.

Pinky looked up from her art journal, in which she'd been doodling a volcano spewing giant butterflies. She was still in her pajamas, though it was noon the next day. "Huh?"

"It's time." Samir raised his eyebrows meaningfully.

Did they have an appointment she didn't remember? "Time for what?" she asked.

"Time to get you out of this funk." He walked in and stood by her desk. "I'm kidnapping you."

"What makes you think I'm in a funk?"

"Well, I've been in here for almost a full minute and you haven't said anything salty to me yet."

Pinky felt a smile touch the corner of her lips. "Can't argue with that. Where are we going?"

"It's a surprise. Do kidnappers ever tell you where they're taking you?" Samir said, in a tone that implied it should've been obvious. "But first you have to get dressed."

Pinky groaned. "Do I have to?"

"Yes," Samir replied immediately. "You do." A pause. "Come on." He bumped her lightly with one of the cushions. "It'll be fun. And bring a book."

Shaking her head, curious in spite of herself, Pinky got up to get dressed.

He insisted on driving her parents' rented BMW, which Pinky didn't think they'd mind; Samir was as careful a driver as you'd expect. When he pulled up to the butterfly habitat, she turned to him. "What are we doing here?"

He put the car in park and grinned. "Come on."

They walked to the big oak tree they'd climbed on their previous trip here. "We're going up there"—Samir pointed up into the branches—"to read."

Pinky smiled and shook her head. "Because I told you I liked to read up there. But what about your acrophobia?"

"Well, maybe this time we don't go *quite* so high. Also, I brought these." Samir held up the chair cushions. "We can sit on them. I'm hoping to trick my brain into thinking I'm sitting on a chair on solid ground."

Pinky laughed. "That's actually not a bad idea."

He gestured to the tree trunk. "After you."

CHAPTER 16

Pinky

Once they'd tied Drama Queen around the tree trunk at the bottom and were situated on a branch that was both thick enough and low enough to appease Samir, he leaned back and opened his book.

"We're just reading?" Pinky asked, touched and surprised. "You're not going to ask me what happened?"

Samir looked at her over the top of his book. "I figure when you're ready to talk about it, you'll talk about it."

She nodded and, after a pause, opened her book.

She closed it again after a couple of minutes. "I want to talk," Pinky said softly. Maybe it was being up here, above the whole world, hidden by leaves and twigs and branches, that made her feel braver. Maybe it was Samir's steady, open friendship. Maybe it was the fact that she'd found out her mom had been lying to her her entire life, that things she'd taken to be formative truths had turned out to be complete lies. Whatever the reason, Pinky felt she needed to be completely truthful in this moment, and she needed to be completely truthful to someone who was strong enough to hold the truth without judgment.

Samir set his book aside and held her gaze. A gentle breeze blew a strand of his black hair against his forehead. "Okay."

Pinky took a deep breath. And then she told him exactly what Meera Mausi had told her.

Samir stared at her for a long moment after she was done. "So the Shark used to be the Hurricane?" He shook his head, as if he were having just as hard a time believing it as she was.

"Yeah. Apparently."

"Wow." He blew out a breath. "Wow."

"Yeah."

He studied her, a crease appearing between his eyebrows. "Why . . . ? Why do you seem bummed out? It's good news, right? Your mom used to be just like you. You guys have more in common than—"

"Sam." Pinky pinched the bridge of her nose. Why was no one seeing the truth? "She had to give it all up because of me. Every day that she wakes up and sees me is a reminder of what she had and what she lost."

Samir frowned. "Are you sure? Because it seems to me like she changed her life for the better. She's more independent and successful—"

"No, look. She and I are alike, somewhere, deep down, right?"

Samir nodded.

"I can imagine what I'd feel if I had to give my life up for some kid. If I had to go get a corporate job to be able to support her. If my parents basically disowned me. I'd hold a giant grudge against my kid, Samir. I know *exactly* what my mom is feeling."

He was quiet, as if he couldn't think of what else to say. Well, that made two of them. Finally, he leaned forward. "Do you wanna go take a walk or something?"

"Yeah, okay. That sounds good."

Pinky hopped down from the lowest tree branch. Drama Queen took one look at her, keeled over, and died. Sighing, Pinky stuffed her into her tote bag and turned to Samir. "I think we can just leave our cushions and books here, at the base of the tree. We won't be far, and I don't think anyone's going to take them."

They sauntered off through the habitat, their feet sinking into the grass as they went.

"So what do you plan to do?" Samir asked. "With this new info you have about your mom?"

Pinky shrugged, letting the warm sunshine seep in through the top of her head and into her bones. "I don't know. I guess nothing. It gives me a clearer picture of why she hates me. And please don't tell me she doesn't."

"Hey," Samir said, after a moment. "Thank you. For sharing that with me."

Pinky studied him over her shoulder. "Thanks for listening." Her heart beat a little bit faster as she blurted out, "Thanks for always listening. For always being there." She wasn't sure why she was saying it now, except that suddenly the idea of untruths or half-truths made her want to scream. And it was obvious to her now that things she'd thought were true were obviously blatant lies. So what else in her life might she be wrong about? What other "unassailable truths" were actually complete fabrications? For instance, the idea that someone like her couldn't be with someone like Samir. How true was that when people were so utterly malleable and changeable?

They wound their way through a maze of rhododendron bushes, deeper into the habitat, past a cluster of chestnut trees. There were a few different varieties of butterflies flitting around them now, mourning cloaks and monarchs and Eastern black swallowtails. Pinky added, "I know that wasn't in the job description when I asked you to come out here."

"I don't mind," Samir replied, as a question mark landed lightly on his shoulder before taking off.

They went deeper into the habitat still, until they came to a little spot with a bench and a fountain. Pinky remembered, vaguely, "helping" her dad set the bench up when she was four years old. As she remembered, she'd sat on it and bossed him around in her four-year-old drawl. She turned to Samir by the fountain, now dry, thanks to the heat wave, and set the tote bag with DQ in it down. "What you said before, in the attic. About me not feeling the same way about you?"

He was suddenly still, sunshine glinting red in his dark hair. "Yeah."

Pinky took a deep breath. She opened her mouth and closed it again, looking around them at the bench, the silent fountain, the piercing blue sky. Then she forced herself to say, "That's not entirely true."

A muscle in Samir's jaw twitched. "No?" he said carefully.

"Actually, that's not true at all." Pinky took a step closer to him. Two blue butterflies perched on them, one on Samir's arm, one on hers. "Samir . . . I like you too."

The effect of her words was immediate—his eyes brightened, and his mouth curved into a small smile. "Really?"

"But—"

He hung his head. "But."

She waited until he looked back at her. "But I'm scared," she said, her voice barely a whisper. A big monarch butterfly landed in her hair and then flitted away. "I've always been the one who doesn't give a damn, the one who has a litany of no-good boyfriends, the black sheep of the family. Frankly, I've *liked* being the black sheep. It's easy and there aren't any expectations to fulfill. And if I date someone like you . . ." She trailed off for a moment and then said, "That's not even saying how different we are. How can we hope to make something of these feelings that won't end up in total disaster?"

A bright blue butterfly hovered between them, as if listening in on their conversation. Samir put a hand to her cheek. She laid her head against his palm and closed her eyes for a moment, reveling in the strength of him, in the warmth of him. "Pinky, I don't know the answer to that. No one can. People who seem perfect for each other on paper end up being total disasters. People who are completely opposite end up being happy. I don't think there's really a way to tell which relationship is going to work out and which one isn't." He paused. "As for your other question . . . I don't know that either. I don't know what it would say about you if you were to date someone like me. And I don't know what it'd say about me if I were to invite your beautiful, mind-spinning chaos into my life." He chuckled, a thick strand of his hair lifting in a warm, gentle breeze. "The only thing I know is that I'm happier with you than without. Maybe you should ask yourself that question. Are you happier with me or without?" He was trying to say it neutrally, Pinky could tell, but his voice shook at the end. Her answer really mattered to him, she realized.

Pinky thrilled. "Really?" she whispered. "Do you really mean that? You're happier with me than without?"

"So much happier," he said, gazing right into her eyes.

Pinky knew it was completely awkward to ask him what she was about to ask him next, but she found the words coming out in spite of herself. She had to know. Before she made any big decisions, she needed to know once and for all. "Samir . . . What do you think of Dolly? She's . . . pretty perfect for you, right?"

After a brief, confused pause, he smiled at her as if he knew exactly what she was thinking. His hands slipped from her cheeks to her waist as he pulled her close. "Pinky Kumar," he said softly, his gaze slowly sliding down over her face to her lips. "There is no one like you. And there is no one who makes me feel the way you do."

"I like you," she whispered, against his mouth. "I like you, Samir Jha."

And then they were kissing, and she felt a dozen soft wings all over her arms, her legs, brushing against her hair, as if the butterflies too were celebrating in this astonishing and exhilarating fact.

Samir

"I can't believe you're leaving for three whole weeks," Pinky said.

She and Samir were standing hand in hand in the driveway the next day, watching Dolly's family pack up their rental Jetta. Pinky's parents were talking to Dolly's parents by the car.

"I know." Dolly reached over and hugged Pinky, her eyes shut tight. "I'm gonna miss you guys." Pulling back, she looked at them both with a sly smile. "But be honest—it's not like you two lovebirds will even know I'm gone."

Pinky flushed. Samir knew she'd told Dolly what had happened at the habitat—how she and Samir had confessed their feelings for each other and began officially going out (for real)—and apparently Dolly had been completely ecstatic for Pinky and Samir.

"That's not true!" Pinky said in mock outrage.

"Yeah, yeah." Dolly smirked. Then, getting serious, she said, "You've got the streets I laid out for you to canvass, right? Damn, I wish I could stay."

"Yep, we've got them," Samir replied, feeling bad for her. She'd obviously much rather be here, doing stuff for the butterflies, than off in Vermont on some kids-who've-screwed-up retreat. "And we're gonna get started on that tomorrow."

Pinky sighed. "Have a good time—as good as you can anyway. I really don't feel like you even need to go, though. I mean, you learned your lesson, right?"

On cue, an orange Jeep Wrangler drove by, and a dude yelled out an expletive. An empty beer can landed on the driveway.

Mr. Montclair looked livid. "I might just put in a call to Dr. Miller. Tell him what his son is up to."

Mrs. Montclair put a hand on his arm. "Let's just go." She called over to Dolly, "Ready, honey?"

Dolly sighed. "Hopefully in three weeks, Cash will be over himself."

Pinky and Dolly hugged again, and then Dolly trudged over to her parents' car and climbed in. Mrs. Montclair walked over to Pinky, pulled her to the side, and gave her a hug. She whispered something to her, but Pinky shook her head. Sighing, Meera cupped Pinky's chin and walked away. Samir could imagine what had been said; Meera wanted Pinky to talk to her mom, and Pinky had demurred.

Pinky's parents, Pinky, and Samir waved to them as they drove off.

"Well." Samir turned to Pinky as her parents walked back into the house. "It's just us now."

She smiled up at him. "Just us."

The next morning, Pinky loaded a box of paper into her parents' car. Gloria had emailed Pinky a PDF, and she'd printed out fifty flyers.

"Okay, so what's the plan again?" Samir asked her. "We just walk up to people and hand them these flyers?"

"Pretty much," Pinky said. "Give them the flyer, give them the little Gloria-approved spiel, and then hurry back home for personal-pizza night."

"You don't have to say it with that sarcastic curling-sneer thing you have going on," Samir said, bumping her gently with his shoulder. "It'll be fun."

Pinky gave him a withering glare. "My dad puts pineapple on his pizza."

Samir blinked.

"*Oh* my goddess." Pinky turned to him and put her hands on her hips. "You like pineapples on your pizza, don't you?"

Samir gave her a *what?* look. "It balances out the jalapeños!"

Pinky shook her head and laughed. "I don't think we could be more opposite if we were custom-designed to be."

Samir snorted. "Like maybe Kali made you the north-pole magnet to my south-pole magnet?" He appeared to think. "You know what? That actually makes sense."

Pinky frowned, confused. "What?"

Samir grinned and wrapped his arms around her waist, bringing his mouth down to hers. "I just feel so . . . *attracted* . . . to you. Magnets would explain it."

She laughed again, and the true, genuine joy there lifted his heart. "Samir Jha." Pinky looked into his eyes. "You make me happy." She planted the softest, sweetest kiss on his lips. Samir closed his eyes, reveling in it. Pulling back, Pinky added, "But you'll also make us late. So let's get going." Winking, she let him go, got into the driver's seat, and buckled in.

Smiling, Samir got in too. This summer was turning out to be about a 1,000 percent better than he'd expected. He could just imagine the look on Ash's face when he and Pinky sauntered back to Atherton, holding hands. His first ever girlfriend, and it turned out to be Pinky Kumar. Feisty, swirling-tornado Pinky Kumar. Still smiling, he shook his head a little. Life was weird.

Pinky glanced at the box of flyers wedged on the floor of the car next to Samir's feet. "I really hope these work. Gloria put so much effort into them."

Samir looked down at the flyers and pretended to study them, even though he'd seen them already. "They will. They're bright and concise and powerful."

There was an Eastern tiger swallowtail butterfly in the center, its black and yellow wings taking up most of the width of the page. The top of the page said, STOP! in bold red letters at a diagonal. And on the bottom, OUR BUTTERFLIES, OUR HABITAT, OUR TOWN. SAY NO TO DEVELOPMENT! TOWN HALL MEETING ON SATURDAY, AUGUST 1ST, AT 2 P.M.!

"I wish the meeting were this Saturday instead of next. I feel like speed is of the essence," Pinky said, chewing on her lower lip. "But Gloria said with this Saturday being the Ellingsworth Lantern Festival and everything . . ."

"No, next Saturday's definitely better." Samir reached over to smooth a strand of hair off her face. "Besides, aren't we doing that whole campout, grill-out thing with your family to celebrate the Lantern Festival anyway?"

"Don't remind me," Pinky said, but she was smiling. She put the car in drive and backed out of the driveway. "We do that every year. It's pretty fun, actually. A whole bunch of people from the town do it too."

"So we're going to be camping in a tent on the bank of the lake?" Samir couldn't help it; his mind immediately flashed a picture of him and Pinky wedged into their sleeping bags, pressed up against each other in a warm, balmy tent under a starlit sky.

She quirked her lips and glanced at him like she could hear his thoughts. "My parents will be sharing the tent with us."

Samir cleared his throat and ran a hand along the back of his neck. Her words were like a bucket of cool water. The Shark, sharing a tent with him. Probably judging the quality of his snores. "Oh, uh, yeah. I knew that."

Pinky snorted. "It's pretty cool. We release biodegradable floating lanterns and stuff. We'll have to leave DQ at home, of course. They call it the Ellingsworth Lantern Festival, but it's really just an excuse for everyone to shoot off whatever fireworks they have left over from the Fourth of July. DQ really won't like that." She paused. "I hope she's okay at home right now."

"She's got her fruit and her litter box. Besides, your parents said they'd keep an eye on her."

"That's what I'm afraid of," Pinky muttered as she signaled left and turned onto the main highway.

Pinky knocked on the door of the small yellow cottage. The gravel driveway beside it was barely large enough to hold the decrepit pickup truck in it, let alone Pinky's parents' rental, but she'd managed it somehow. When they heard the doorknob turning, she took a deep breath and readied her version of a friendly smile.

"Hello!" she said brightly to the seventy-something-year-old white man who answered his front door but left the screen door closed. He had a puff of hair around either ear but was otherwise bald as a cue ball. "Have you heard about the luxury condos that are going in where the butterfly habitat currently is?"

"Eh?" the man said, a ferocious frown on his grizzled face. "What's that?"

Pinky darted Samir a nervous glance. Leaning in slightly, she said, louder, "Have you heard about the dev—"

"I don't need a house cleaner," the man said, about to shut his door.

Pinky glared at him. "We're not house cleaners."

The man harrumphed as if he belonged in a cartoon. Samir

was starting to get kind of annoyed. "Then what are you doing on my property?" He looked from her to Samir and then back again. "You're not from around these parts, are you?"

Samir raised an eyebrow. "And why would you say that?"

The man squinted at him. "You just don't look like you belong here."

"Let me guess," Pinky said, and Samir could see her making a monumental effort not to crumple the flyer. "You're going to ask us where we're from next. And when we say California, you'll say, 'No, where are you *from* from?' We're done here." She thumped the screen door with the heel of her hand and turned to walk back to the car.

Samir nodded at the man. "Good day."

"All right, then." The man stood watching them as they walked off his property.

"Jerk," Pinky whispered as they got back in the car.

"You know, this might not be the safest thing to be doing right now," Samir said, looking around. A few of the cars in the neighborhood had stickers like, KEEP HONKING I'M RELOADING or I PLEAD THE 2ND. He could feel his good sense warring with his need to support Pinky in her mission.

"He was just a run-of-the-mill racist," Pinky said, pulling out of the driveway and heading back down the street. "Not like we haven't seen a million of them."

Samir held tightly to the dashboard as Pinky sped away. "Okay, but are racists even going to listen to us, then? Plus, I don't know . . . this whole area looks like it's populated by those survivalist people who have, like, twenty-two guns per family member. Maybe we should just abandon ship."

Pinky looked at him seriously. "I don't want to walk away right now. Not when we're doing something so important. But if you feel unsafe, I can take you home."

Samir shook his head immediately. "I'm not leaving you."

Pinky squeezed his arm and then put her hand back on the wheel as she drove. "Okay. But I promise, if it gets even slightly more scary than that, we'll leave. Deal?"

"Deal." Samir shook his head. "You're a pretty cool person. You know that, Pinky Kumar?"

She glanced at him, smiling, before returning her gaze to the road. "A time or two, Samir Jha." Her small smile morphed into a beaming grin. "Aha! Now, here's a person who'll probably appreciate our efforts."

Samir glanced out the window to see a house painted a bright turquoise with neat white shutters. The windows all had window boxes full of bright flowers, and an old brown van in the driveway was plastered with bumper stickers that passionately espoused a number of pro-environment slogans (Samir's favorite was MAY THE FOREST BE WITH YOU).

Pinky pulled into the driveway behind the van, and Samir handed her a flyer as they walked up to the house. Before they could knock, a white woman in her fifties with salt-and-pepper cropped hair opened the door and smiled. "Hello!"

"Hi." Pinky thrust the flyer at her. "Can I tell you about our butterfly habitat?"

"You mean the one down the road?" the woman asked, glancing down at the flyer. "It's such a shame they're building those condos down there. Of all the places they could've chosen."

"Exactly!" Pinky looked like someone had told her they were about to populate the earth with bees and plants and do away with humans completely. "It's a total tragedy, right?"

"Angie, who are you talking to?" The white woman, Angie, was joined by a white man in his early sixties. He leaned against the doorjamb and regarded Pinky and Samir closely with clear blue eyes. His thin arms were folded against his chest, and his silver wedding band caught the light. "Hello," he said, his greeting much more guarded than Angie's.

"Good morning." Samir held out a hand. He had the feeling *this* man would respond better to a more polite, professional demeanor. "I'm Samir, and this is Pinky. We're spreading the word about the butterfly habitat and how it's about to be razed. A local resident named Gloria Washington is organizing a town hall meeting a week from Saturday so residents can brainstorm options to save it."

Pinky shot him a look that was half-amused, half-impressed. Turning back to Angie, she said, "Um, yeah, that's right. So if you two would consider coming . . ."

"We try not to get too involved with stuff that isn't directly our problem," the guy said, his lips thinning.

"Oh, come now, Charles." Angie's smile was gentle. "It's just a town hall meeting. These kids put in so much effort getting these printed and driving all the way out here." She turned to Pinky. "I haven't seen you around, so I'm guessing you live out by the lake?"

Pinky nodded. "My parents have a house there." Charles's eyes narrowed, and Samir could see the thought bubble above his head: *I'm not putting my neck out for some entitled rich kid who's just gonna fly out and forget about this in another month.* Pinky rushed on. "But

I'm not the one spearheading this; like I said, it's all Gloria Washington, and she and her wife are year-round residents. We're just supporting her and the other residents who don't want this to happen. You say this isn't directly your problem, but I think it is. I mean, how's it going to be when that habitat's gone? What else are they going to bulldoze and raze? Do you want this to become the new Nantucket, ridiculously clogged with traffic each summer?" She paused, then said softly, "That butterfly habitat is one of my most favorite places in the entire world, and I know other people here on Ellingsworth feel the same way. It would mean so much to me—and to your neighbors—if you and your wife would come."

Angie and Charles glanced at each other. Then turning back to Pinky, Angie said, "I'll be there, honey."

Pinky smiled. "Thank you. Thank you so much."

Samir shook both their hands. "We really appreciate it."

As they walked back to the car, Pinky pumped her fist. "One down, only nineteen more to go."

Samir knew she wasn't being sarcastic. She was genuinely happy about the slow-as-molasses progress they were making. For the first time, Samir realized Pinky Kumar might just be an optimist who spent her time masquerading as a cynic. And somehow, that made him like her even more.

CHAPTER 17

Pinky

By the end of the day, they'd handed out flyers to all the houses on the block and gotten twenty-three of those homeowners to sign the petition as well.

She paced the length of Samir's room, bubbling with energy. She'd just gotten off the phone with Gloria, who had been genuinely impressed with their progress. "Okay, so that was a good start, but I really think we should aim to do two blocks a day for the rest of the week and next week, you know? Think of how many people we could reach. And think of what a show that would be, right, if, like, sixty people showed up to the town hall meeting and everyone was in an uproar about it. The local paper would do a story. . . ." She felt so energized, she was sure she could hop on the ceiling if she really wanted to. "Right?"

Samir laughed. He was leaning against the window, his arms crossed, watching her fondly. Now he walked up to her and wrapped his arms around her waist. Her heart beat furiously; she still wasn't used to this, to them.

They were a *them*. The thought made her laugh a little.

Samir bent down and placed the softest kiss on her lips, and her knees legit went weak. "Have I told you before how beautiful you are when you're impassioned?"

She gazed into his eyes, her breath coming short and fast. "Yeah, only like thirteen times a day," she said, but the breathless quality of her voice took the sarcastic edge off her words.

Samir bent down again, so they were just a millimeter apart. "Good. That's very good." And then his mouth was on hers again and they were kissing, wrapped up in each other like nothing else existed.

When they finally came up for air, Pinky smiled at him. "So? Was that listed in your planner too or did I catch you by surprise?"

His smile slipped off his face around the same time that his arms slipped off her waist. "Yeah, you've made jokes like that before, and it was about as funny then as it is now."

Ouch. Pinky frowned. "It *was* just a joke. Why're you being so sensitive about it?"

Samir looked up at her. A muscle in his jaw twitched. "Maybe it's just not as funny as you think. I told you, being this organized was sort of a survival skill for me."

"But it's not anymore," Pinky said, trying to remain calm, though she was feeling pinpricks of irritation at his tone. Why was he being so defensive when he'd confronted her quirks and foibles with no tact at all? "Don't you think the fact that you're so sensitive about it might indicate that you're using it as a crutch? It's not healthy!"

"Oh, so you want to talk about things that aren't healthy?" Samir said, his eyes flashing. "Fine. Let's talk about the fact that you constantly complain about how your mom treats your poorly and yet you jump at the chance to do everything you can to piss her off. Have you told her about the town hall meeting yet?"

Pinky threw up her hands. "Don't change the subject just because you don't want to talk about your stuff! You have a problem! Ever since you were little and your mom almost died and the only thing you could control was what you were going to fill your days with!"

Samir's cheeks went pink; his voice rose. "You don't get it, Pinky. You don't know what it means when a parent almost dies and that parent happens to be the only person you have in the world. Okay? So please, forgive me if I don't want to take your advice on this."

They stared at each other for a full minute, and then all at once, Pinky felt the fight go out of her. She had a tendency to coopt other people's fights as her own, she knew that, but this—this wasn't her fight. Not even a little bit. Samir didn't want her help, and that meant she needed to back down.

"Fine," she said quietly. "You're right, and I'm sorry. I think I should go to bed. Good night."

"Thanks for the apology. Good night," Samir said, rubbing his jaw, not meeting her eye.

Pinky turned and walked out of the room, her heart cold and heavy. Maybe some things were just too difficult to reconcile. Maybe some people were just too different to fully understand each other after all.

"Last one." Pinky hammered the stake into the ground with her rubber mallet a few days later. It was Saturday, the day of the Ellingsworth Lantern Festival. "We're all set up."

"Excellent!" her dad said from the other side of the tent. It was supposed to fit six people, but it had been just her and her parents in there for the last few years. They liked the extra room but didn't mind giving a bit of it up for Samir. "Now let's get that campfire going."

"On it," Samir said, carrying the firewood to the little ring of stones a few yards away. Pinky's mom was tying DQ's leash to a tree.

All around them, other summer people were laughing and talking while they set up their own tents, getting ready for the lantern releasing in an hour or so, at sunset. The lanterns had been delivered that morning by a store in town and were sitting in a little wooden shed farther up the bank. A few families were already lining up to get their lanterns out.

"Don't forget the fire starters," Pinky said, grabbing them from her dad's bag and walking to Samir to hand them over. He smiled at her, and she smiled hesitantly back.

Although they hadn't talked any more about their spat, he'd withdrawn just a little into himself. Pinky hated seeing it—he'd blossomed this summer; he'd thrown himself into everything with an enthusiasm she'd never seen before. But she didn't know what to do about it, so she pushed the thought from her mind.

"Hey," she said, watching Samir start the fire. "I thought we could go grab our lanterns. My parents and I usually decorate ours a bit, make them a little more special. I brought markers and stuff. You want to?"

Samir shrugged. "Yeah, sure. Let me just finish up here."

As he did his thing, Pinky's mom walked by. She studied her mom, marveling at the fact that she used to be someone completely different seventeen years ago. Someone Pinky might even have been *friends* with, if she'd been alive back then. "You know, your possum's getting rather large," her mom said, frowning slightly. "Maybe we should think about taking her to that rescue organization a little bit sooner than we'd talked about."

"She's fine," Pinky countered immediately. "She's not *that* big." She didn't know why she felt so defensive about it, except . . . it wasn't DQ's fault how big she was. She hadn't asked to be her size. And she hadn't asked to be abandoned by her mom and nearly die of heatstroke. Maybe Pinky felt a sense of camaraderie with her.

Sighing, Pinky's mom began to walk away. "It was just a suggestion."

"All right." Samir stood, brushing off his hands. Behind him, the little fire crackled, growing bigger with every second. "Ready?"

They stood in line, waiting for their turn to grab their lanterns, in near silence, making occasional small talk. Pinky wanted to say more, to talk about the planner-size elephant in the room, but every time she glanced at Samir and saw his preoccupied gaze, the set of his jaw, she swallowed her words. It wasn't worth it to fight. She needed to know when to let things go.

When it was their turn, they walked to the little shed that smelled like heat and wood and mildew and pulled out four lanterns. Feeling their papery texture, the slight heft of them resting in her palm, Pinky was hit with a wave of nostalgia so strong, she almost keeled over.

Blinking, she shook her head as she and Samir walked back down to their campsite. "It's crazy how little moments weave together and become this, like, heavy tapestry of life, isn't it?"

Samir gave her an amused look. "Yeah, I guess so."

"I mean, really, it's just mundane moments. Setting up the tent. Grabbing lanterns from a shed. Putting on sunscreen. But in the larger framework of life, it's all so vital to who we are." She glanced at Samir, at the way he was effortlessly carrying two large lanterns in one hand. "Hey. What do you want your legacy to be when you're gone?"

"My legacy?" Samir said, raising an eyebrow. A breeze off the lake ruffled his hair. "I'm not sure I'm important enough to leave a legacy."

"We all leave legacies," Pinky said as a group of ten-year-olds ran past, screeching. "I mean, maybe Oprah's legacy is one the world will remember, but less famous people leave legacies their immediate family members and friends, if they have any left alive, remember. Our legacies are just the way we've lived our lives, what we leave behind when we go."

"Hmm." They were at the tent now, and Samir set his two lanterns inside. Pinky followed him in and did the same. The tent was large enough that they could both stand up straight inside it. "My legacy would be . . . being the youngest graduate of Harvard Law. Or the youngest partner in a really good law firm."

Pinky felt a beat of disappointment at his answer. He was so much more than those goals. She opened her mouth to say so, then closed it again. "*Or* maybe your legacy could be making the best gazpacho."

He looked up at that and laughed. It lifted her spirits to see his eyes crinkle up in mirth. "Yeah, maybe. And maybe you'll be remembered for being the best opossum wrangler this side of the Mississippi."

Laughing, Pinky slipped her hand into his, feeling relieved when his fingers tightened around hers. "Yeah. Maybe."

They headed back out of the tent, to sit by the fire. Pinky's parents, sitting on little logs around the fire, were busting out the marshmallows, chocolate squares, and graham crackers.

"On second thought," Pinky said, "I think my legacy will be the one who saved the Ellingsworth butterfly habitat."

Her mom looked up from the plastic container of Hershey's chocolate bars she held. "You're still doing that?"

"Yep." Pinky took a breath and a seat beside her mom. "You know, Mom, you could help us. I mean, you're, like, the most badass lawyer in the world practically—"

"That could be a PR disaster for the firm." Her mother's brown eyes held hers. "I told you, Pinky. This is not our fight."

"But there are local residents who want to fight this too. Don't you want to help them? Don't you want to stand for something again?" Pinky cleared her throat. "'If you don't stand for something, you'll fall for anything'—Alexander Hamilton. Or maybe it was Peter Marshall. Reports disagree."

"I believe it's also a catchy country tune by that fellow in the cowboy hat!" Pinky's dad put in helpfully.

Her mother looked less than impressed. There was a furrow between her brow Pinky didn't much care for. "What do you mean 'again'? I've never done anything so foolhardy."

Pinky regarded her mom quietly for a half a second, feeling torn. She hadn't wanted to say anything about her mom's sordid past without careful planning. But she could feel the words pushing on the backs of her lips, eager to come out. She couldn't take her mom's lofty judgment anymore, not when she *knew* for a fact that it was completely uncalled for and hypocritical.

"That's not completely true," she found herself blurting out, even though her mom's complete denial was making her doubt herself just a tad. Maybe that picture had been of her mom's twin, whom her mom had then murdered and buried in the basement. In this moment, that was kind of easier to believe. "Meera Mausi told me about your undergrad days at Harvard."

Her mom's frown smoothed over. She blinked rapidly and looked away. She was thrown, Pinky realized, looking at her in wonder. She'd never once in her entire life seen her mom thrown. "Meera shouldn't have told you that," she said quietly. "That was a time in my life that I'm not proud of. Nothing good can come of talking about it."

"But why not?" Pinky leaned forward. "Mom, you and I are alike—"

Her mother turned to her. "We are *not* alike! Don't say that."

"Veena," Pinky's dad said in a warning tone from across the fire, shaking his head. "Pinky, she didn't mean it like that. Why don't you explain what you mean?" he continued, turning to her mom again.

"There's no point," her mom said, looking away. "I said what I said for a reason."

Pinky pulled back, hurt locking its jaws around her torso and clamping down. For a full two seconds, she couldn't say anything. She could feel Samir's warm gaze on her from across the fire, but she couldn't bring herself to look at him. Was that the worst thing her mother could possibly imagine—being compared to Pinky? Was she just that desperate to not be lumped into whatever loser category she thought Pinky was in that she'd deny her entire past? Pinky swallowed. Of course it was and of course she was. Pinky was a symbol of everything that was wrong in her life. She'd been a fool for thinking bringing Samir here as her fake boyfriend would change anything. Her mom would never respect her.

"Right," Pinky said curtly, her eyes on the fire. She could feel tears just behind her stony facade and willed them away. "I'm not like you, so I guess I must be like my asshole, one-night-stand sperm-donor dad, huh?"

Her parents and Samir all stared at her in horrified silence. Pinky felt her heart shrinking even smaller, into a little hardened pit in her chest.

They sat in silence for a moment.

"Well, if it isn't the Kumars!"

They all looked up to see Cash walking toward them, smiling an indolent, annoying little smile.

Pinky scowled at him. "What do *you* want?" He was the whole reason Dolly wasn't here to draw the attention away from this train wreck of a conversation she'd just had with her mother.

"There's no reason to be rude," her mother said. Turning to Cash, she added politely, "Hello, Cash. Would you like a s'more?"

Cash grinned. "Nah, thanks. Haven't had one of those since I was ten."

Ooh, you're so cool, Cash, Pinky wanted to snap. *Go pickle your liver in beer instead.*

"What can we do for you, Cash?" Pinky's dad's usually exuberantly happy voice was strained with annoyance. Pinky smiled to herself as she reached over and grabbed a Hershey bar. Across the fire, Samir rolled his eyes at her and she grinned, feeling even better.

"Well, I actually came over to talk to Pinky." Scratching his stomach through his shirt, he said, "My mom says our cleaning lady said you turned up at her house? With a flyer or something? And the woman at the seafood market said the same thing."

Pinky stiffened. Crap. This was not how she'd wanted her mom to find out about the town hall meeting she was helping with. "Um, right." She adjusted her ponytail and ignored the skewering looks her mom was tossing her way.

"Priyanka," her mom said in a voice that was just two notches higher than her usual one. "Would you mind sharing with me what the flyer's for?"

Standing, Pinky glared at Cash. "You can go now." Shrugging, he sauntered off.

Reaching into the pocket of her shorts, Pinky got out her cell phone and pulled up a picture of the flyer she'd been handing out all week.

Her mom took her phone and looked at the flyer, her expression hard. "You can't get people all agitated about this." She looked up at Pinky. "We don't live here. This isn't our problem."

"I already told you, I'm just joining a cause that the town residents have already organized. Besides, this is everyone's problem!" Pinky said, sitting back down.

"I told you to leave it alone," her mom said. "This—" She squeezed her hand around Pinky's phone, as if she wanted to crush it. "This is . . ."

"Something *you* would've done twenty years ago?" Pinky couldn't help but ask.

"Pinky," Samir said, shaking his head. "Just . . . maybe let it go for now?"

She stared at him, not really able to believe he'd just said that. He'd been with her when she'd found the photo. He'd heard what her mom had just said to her. And he was taking her mom's side? "Are you serious?" she said, huffing a laugh. "You're on her side?"

"I'm not taking sides. I just . . . I don't think anything productive's coming out of this, that's all," he said, sticking his hands into his pockets.

"I agree," Pinky's mom said. Because of course she did. Of course she agreed with Samir.

Pinky dug her toe into the sand and forced herself to say nothing.

They stood at the bank of the lake with all the other families, dozens and dozens of people all holding their lit lanterns, their faces glowing in the gathering dark. Samir and Pinky stood close together, each of them holding their shining lanterns like magical orbs meant to grant secret wishes. Pinky had decorated hers with a drawing of butterflies emerging from a cocoon of stars, and Samir's had an abstract design that looked like swirling smoke enveloping people. It seemed kind of sad, but when she'd asked him about it, he'd just laughed and brushed her off. There was a palpable excitement in the air, and Pinky pushed the fight she and her mom had just had—and the comment Samir had made, taking her mom's side—to the back corners of her mind.

"At the count of ten," Mr. Parker said into his megaphone. He beamed around at them all, winking when he caught Pinky's eye. "We will let our lanterns float into the air. Remember to whisper your wish into it first!"

The Parkers were black and one of only three other families of color who also owned a lake house on Ellingsworth. Pinky's and Dolly's parents had had them over for dinner many times over the past few summers. Mr. Parker was always the one who led the lantern-lighting ceremony. As the mayor of his city back home, he was kind of used to taking charge, Pinky supposed. And no one else wanted to do it anyway.

There were murmurs of excitement all around. Pinky smiled at Samir, and he gazed back, his smile somehow muted. "Better wish for something good," he said.

Pinky laughed. "Oh, I am."

His eyes crinkled a little at that. "I guess it's no surprise what you're going to be wishing for. Does it rhyme with 'utterfly crabitat'?"

Pinky shrugged. "I can't tell you, Mr. Jha, or it won't come true."

"All right," Mr. Parker said, his voice reverberating in her ears. "Ten . . . nine . . . eight . . ."

Pinky took a breath and looked over at her mom and dad. They were standing a few dozen feet away, giving Samir and Pinky their privacy. She studied her mom's face but couldn't decipher her expression. What would she wish for this year? For her daughter to become more like her? For a different daughter altogether? The thought made Pinky's throat hurt, and she swallowed away the threatening tears.

"Three . . . two . . . one! And release!"

Pinky released her lantern at the same time as Samir released his, watching her butterflies rise higher and higher, disappearing off into the night sky. She tipped her head back to watch all the lanterns float into the indigo velvet sky, lighting the night up like a thousand fairies watching over their town. The still, black lake reflected their light, and it was like dual universes, both lit up, both starry, both floating and dreamy.

Pinky felt a brief sense of vertigo, of fear, of not knowing which universe she belonged in. She laid her head on Samir's firm shoulder, sighing as she felt his arm wrap around her, anchoring her to this place, reminding her where she was.

CHAPTER 18

Pinky

It was the following Saturday, officially August, and the town hall meeting to organize the big protest against the developer had just concluded. Pinky didn't know if her parents had forgotten about the significance of the date (unlikely) or had purposely made plans at the country club that morning, but either way, she was glad she'd been able to attend without having to get into a giant fight about it. Now she turned to Samir, Gloria, and Dolores in the otherwise empty hall, grinning. "Oh. My. God."

"Thirty-three people." Gloria shook her head, smiling, as she gathered up her notes and papers. "That's really not a bad showing."

"Not bad at all," Dolores agreed.

"I know!" Pinky laughed, catching Samir's eye. He smiled back. "And we were afraid we might not even have *ten*." Pinky squealed. "Gloria, Dolores, I think we're going to save the habitat. This protest is going to kick major developer butt."

Gloria laughed. "You might be right."

Once Pinky and Samir were on the bus, Pinky turned to him, still floating on a cloud. "Wasn't that amazing? Do you think the plan we all came up with in the meeting might work? That it could actually, really work, I mean?"

Samir smiled. "I think everyone was feeling pretty optimistic."

Pinky frowned a little as the bus drove right into a pothole, jostling them. "That's not really an answer."

Samir sighed. "Pinky, I think it's great that you have all this support. But will it be enough to save the habitat?" He shrugged. "I'm not sure."

She studied him. "I thought you were all gung ho about helping me. What happened?"

"I *do* want to help you," he insisted, running a hand along the back of his neck. "It's just that . . . I don't know. This feels kind of unrealistic. I'm glad you're passionate and all, but stopping the entire thing? Going against this big-shot developer?"

Pinky faced forward, feeling cold. She'd told herself Samir's comment siding with her mom the night of the lanterns had been a one-off. He'd been acting weird since their argument about his planner, and maybe he'd just been tired. Maybe he'd made an off-the-cuff remark without realizing how it sounded. But now . . . now she wasn't so sure. "Wow, that's good to know," Pinky found herself saying. "So you think this is just me being my irresponsible, immature self, huh?"

Samir sighed. "That's not what I said at all."

What had happened to him? When had he begun to sound like her mother? And then, in the next instant, it came to her: This was how he always was. He'd never tried to pretend to be anyone else.

This was their fundamentally different nature, showing itself in the real world. This was what she'd been worried about all along.

Samir

As they rode the sweltering bus back to the lake house, Samir gazed out the window. He could feel Pinky glancing at him, but he just couldn't bring himself to look at her. It had been encroaching on him since his fight with Pinky about the planner, about how she just didn't understand his life, his world. And now he couldn't really ignore it anymore. Everything in his world seemed washed out, faded somehow as he came to terms with the truth that had been staring him in the face the entire time.

He'd thought he and Pinky could overcome their differences, that they could be together in spite of them. But maybe that had just been the magic, the madness of summer. Real life was very different from Ellingsworth Point Island, with its butterflies and sunshine and sparkling lake. He'd deluded himself into thinking otherwise. Pinky, with her passion and fire and boundless enthusiasm, had seemed like an impossible dream, but one within reach.

But there were some dreams even glittering, floating lanterns couldn't make come true. It was time he accepted that before he got in too deep.

Pinky

"Do I have to go?" Pinky asked her mom the next weekend as she sat on the bed in her room, painting her toenails. Samir and her dad were out shopping for a tux for Samir. The silent auction at the country club was a much fancier event than trivia night had been, and his suit just wouldn't do. "I mean, what am I going to do there? Samir and I could just chill here. It's not too late; we can just text Dad and tell him."

"I don't want you and Samir here by yourself," her mom said, and Pinky blushed in spite of herself.

"Come on, Mom—"

"No, Pinky. That's it. End of discussion." She walked out, leaving Pinky looking after her.

It was the Thursday after the town hall meeting, and she and Samir were hobbling along, not really talking about anything at all, even though there was so much to say. Although their arguments—it seemed there were more and more of them these days—kept resounding in Pinky's head, she kept pushing them aside, not sure what to do with them. What she'd told Samir before was still true: She *was* happier with him than without. But she knew, too, that there were some stark differences between them. So what was she supposed to do about that?

Shaking her head, she brought her mind to easier-to-handle matters. The Yeung-Kumars—and one Jha—were due at the silent auction night at the country club soon. It was annoying, because all Pinky wanted to do, all she *had* done all week, was plan the protest that had been decided at the town hall meeting. With Gloria's permission, she'd gotten all their numbers and set up a group in WhatsApp. It was pretty cool how hyped they all were. It wasn't just her, for once.

Pinky's mind flashed back to the argument she and her mom had had at the lake. How her mom had told her she was nothing like Pinky and Pinky was nothing like her. There was an acid pain in her stomach at the memory. The truth was, no matter how her mom felt about Pinky, Pinky couldn't help but wish her mom could go back to being the person she'd been before she got pregnant with Pinky. What might their relationship look like then? There was no point to these thoughts, other than to torture herself, but Pinky couldn't help feeling a pang for the mother she'd never had.

She walked to her closet and opened it. Because the Yeung-Kumars seemed to be invited to these kinds of "fancy" events often during their summers at the lake house, she'd packed a few glitzy dresses. She pulled one out of the closet that matched the teal streak in her hair exactly and held it in front of her as she studied herself in the full-length mirror.

It was like she lived two lives, one as Pinky the Protester and the other as Pinky the Privileged. With her multicolored hair and eyebrow ring visible above the long, glittering teal dress, it was like Pinky had been cleaved in two, simultaneously both people while fitting neither persona completely. Sighing, she tossed the dress on her bed.

"Whoa." Samir watched as she walked out into the driveway where he stood with her parents. Pinky's hairstyle—a crown braid—had taken longer than she'd expected. "You look . . . like a mermaid. A punk thrasher mermaid."

Pinky laughed and looked down at herself. "Yeah, I guess so." She took him in, all handsome in his tux. "And you look . . . like my dad."

"Hey now," her dad said, all pouty-faced. "What's wrong with that?"

Samir laughed and pulled at his bow tie, looking uncomfortable. Too late, Pinky realized her comment had probably reminded him of exactly what she herself wanted to forget: that they both walked in very different worlds.

Once they got to the country club and showed the woman at the desk their invite, they were ushered into a grand hall with a domed ceiling and hardwood floors. The entire space was buzzing with conversation and muted laughter. On one side of the hall, an auction table had been laid out. On the other end was a giant bar. Stiff-backed waiters were walking around, offering people drinks and appetizers off silver trays.

Pinky leaned into Samir as they followed her parents to the auction area. "Think my mom will go ballistic if I take off my shoes?"

He snorted. "Do you really need to ask that question?"

"My shoes are killing me." She looked down at them. They were beautiful, but her feet were already screaming at her.

"We could always sneak off and hide out on the rooftop," Samir suggested, and they looked at each other, smiling at the memory of their shared secret, when things seemed a lot simpler.

"Here's that dental cleaning from Cash's dad," her mother said, swishing over to the table in her long mauve gown like a regal queen.

"Something I get for free through my insurance," her dad said, quirking his eyebrow at Pinky and Samir.

Pinky laughed and walked down the table hand in hand with Samir, both of them browsing the collection of photographs and paintings and trips for sale. "Ugh." Pinky pointed to a card. "Look. It's from Di Ria. A chance to bid on one of those awful condos." She looked over her shoulder to make sure no one was watching and then slid the card under a nearby painting. "There. That's better."

"You can't do that!" Samir hissed, looking mortified.

Pinky laughed. "Relax."

Samir made a show of mopping his brow. "You're going to get us kicked out of here."

"Would that be such a tragedy?" Pinky asked, laughing and leading him away.

There was dancing. Of course there was dancing.

Samir turned to her, one hand outstretched, as the music began to thump. "Do me the honor?"

"Great idea!" Pinky's dad said, and he and her mom sailed off to the dance floor.

"Come on." Samir smiled. "If your parents can do this . . ."

"Oh, all right," Pinky grumbled, though she was secretly pleased to see at least a small twinkle of Samir's formerly playful personality. "If we must."

An enormous chandelier hung above the dance floor, casting pin-pricks of colorful light on their skin and clothes. As they dipped and twirled in the sea of other rich people, Pinky couldn't help but feel just a little bit like a movie star, on the arm of a very handsome co-celebrity.

She smiled up at Samir. "I'm really happy you decided to come out here, you know," she said softly, near his ear. "I'm glad you decided to be my fake boyfriend this summer."

He laughed. "Yeah, me too." There was something about his eyes, though, the way they were looking through her just a bit. He was distracted.

"Do you really mean that?" Pinky asked, feeling her heart thump in her chest.

Samir studied her expression for a long moment as their feet moved in synchrony. His hands tightened just slightly around her waist. "Yes. I am." A pause. "But . . ."

Pinky's heart thumped harder. "But what?"

Her parents spun by them, dancing like they were that old guy and that old woman who used to dance together all the time—Fred or Ted or something and Ginger.

Samir continued. "I mean, this has been nice, but Atherton's my real life, you know?"

"Sure, but you can take parts of this summer with you," Pinky pointed out. "You're going to get an internship with my mom. And I'm your girlfriend."

He paused, opening his mouth and then closing it again. ". . . Yeah."

Pinky frowned, her heart pounding. "Well, don't sound enthusiastic." She waited, but Samir didn't rush to reassure her. Something sick wriggled in the pit of her stomach. "What?" she asked. "What is it?"

But before Samir could respond, someone tapped Pinky's shoulder. She turned to see Chrissy Paige, one of her lake house neighbors, regarding her with a mask of disapproval. "Young lady," Chrissy, who was in her midseventies, said. She wore a stiff gold brocade jacket that encased her like a shiny box. "Are you the one who's part of all this brouhaha?"

The last notes of the song came to an end, and Pinky took her arms off Samir's shoulders reluctantly. She really wanted to finish their conversation. "Um, I'm not sure. It depends on what you mean by 'brouhaha.'" Pinky flashed an ostentatious smile that showed all her teeth. "But most likely, yeah."

Chrissy Paige didn't look too impressed by Pinky's confidence. "I see. And you think it's responsible, do you, to humor the locals the way you have, and not just humor them, but *join* them in their madness?"

As far as Pinky knew, Chrissy wasn't British. But she still spoke as if she were, maybe because she thought it made her sound fancier.

"Excuse me, but what's going on here?"

Crap. It was her mom, who'd come sweeping up to them in that mauve gown that frankly should've come with a giant crown. Pinky smiled. "Nothing," she said automatically, never one to involve her parents in things that they didn't strictly need to know about.

"Your daughter, I'm afraid," Chrissy Paige said, ignoring Pinky entirely now that there was a real live adult in the mix, "has turned into something of an insurrectionary. Have you heard about the town hall meeting she attended?"

Her mom frowned and looked at Pinky. "I thought we agreed you weren't going to be involved in all that."

Chrissy Paige's face spread into a victorious grin. "Ah. So you didn't know."

Samir cleared his throat. "Why don't we all sit down?"

Her mom looked at him and then around the hall, seeming to realize they were still in the middle of the dance floor and couples were all coming together for a sickeningly sweet rendition of "Heaven" by Bryan Adams. "Yes, let's."

They walked back to their table, where Pinky's dad was sitting, sipping at his mai tai. He beamed around at them all. "Everything okay?" But his expression fell as he took in the murderous expression on Pinky's mom's face, along with Pinky's defensive chin jutting out. Samir, as always, looked cool and collected, and Chrissy Paige still looked victorious.

Everyone took a seat, Pinky's mom sandwiched between Pinky and Chrissy and Samir on Pinky's other side.

Pinky's dad frowned. "What's going on?"

"Good question," her mom said, turning to Chrissy.

Chrissy was only too happy to oblige. "Your daughter has managed to pair up with a few local residents who are in quite a frenzy over the old butterfly habitat being replaced by luxury condos. Condos that will provide more people better living options, might I add." She looked pointedly at Pinky as she said the last bit.

Pinky leaned forward. "But the condos can go in a different location. You can have both—the good stuff for the town *and* keep the habitat intact."

Chrissy Paige huffed a laugh. "Oh, really? And has the mayor been receptive to this idea?"

"Well, not exactly," Pinky said, "but—"

"Hold on." Pinky's mom held up a hand. "What, exactly, was discussed at the town hall meeting? As I understand it, the habitat razing's a done deal."

"It's supposed to be," Chrissy said archly. "But the town hall meeting was where a few local residents and your daughter organized some kind of *protest for tomorrow,* on the day they're supposed to break ground. Now, let me tell you, Diana Ria is a *very* dear friend, and I will not have her disrespected this way."

Pinky's mom turned to Pinky slowly, her eyes glinting in a dangerous way. "Priyanka," she said carefully, her voice perfectly modulated. "Is this true? You've agreed to take part in a protest tomorrow?"

Pinky thrust out her chin. "Yeah. And a lot of people—most of whom aren't represented in the country-club bracket, by the way—are really excited about it. They feel purposeful. They feel like they can finally take control of what's happening to their town and—"

"That's enough." Her mother's voice cut across her own. "It is absolutely *ridiculous* that you think you can come here for two months out of the year and cause havoc like you do back home!"

Pinky felt such a sharp sting of hurt, she couldn't speak for a moment. Was that all her mom saw this as? Some ridiculous flighty whim? So the connection Pinky thought they'd had when they were reminiscing about the habitat at breakfast was all what? Another one of her mom's misinterpretations? "I am not *causing* havoc. I'm participating in the havoc," she said, instead of the million and one other things she wanted to say, like, "Oh, I cause havoc in your life, do I? Is that why you hate me?" or "Yeah, I guess I've been wreaking havoc on you since seventeen years ago; so sorry about being born!" or even "Do you seriously not remember what that place used to mean to us? How can you be this cold?" She cleared her throat and spoke as calmly as she could, trying to take a page from Samir's book. "I'm merely lending my hand to protect those less fortunate than I am."

"Are you talking about the butterflies? Or the residents?" Chrissy Paige asked, looking dubious. She took a martini from a passing waiter and ate the olive. Pinky wanted to take the toothpick and prick her on the nose.

"Both!" Pinky said, beginning to lose her patience. "Does it really matter?"

"Oh, yes it does!" her mother said, turning to her, eyes flashing. "Are you seriously going to sit there and ask me if it matters?"

"You know what matters?" Pinky asked, in a last-ditch attempt to have *some*thing good come from all this. "Our *habitat*. Our butterfly habitat, the one we helped build. Don't you remember?" She paused, and then said in a rush, "You should come to the protest with me tomorrow, Mom. We can do it together. We can save that place together."

But her mom just looked at her like Pinky had asked her to go to a rave with her. "I most certainly will not, and neither will you!"

"Let's all take a deep breath." Pinky's dad looked extremely nervous. He flashed a *help me* look at Samir.

"Yes, let's," Samir said, sitting up straighter. "Perhaps we should table this discussion for now."

"That might be a good idea," her mom said in a dignified tone.

Dignified. She was being *dignified* and *reasonable* and *calm* and all of those things that made Pinky want to scream. How could she keep her emotions out of all of this? Was she a total robot?

"It makes me so mad that what you care about is that I'm going to cause a disruption to some millionaire developer!" Pinky erupted. "Instead of being mad about the developer razing all our memories!"

Her mother frowned. "What are you talking about?"

"The butterfly habitat!" Pinky shouted. A few people at nearby tables turned to look in her direction, but she didn't care. "Don't you even remember? Don't you even *care* that we had some of our happiest times there? Were you just bullshitting me at the breakfast table when you said you wanted to go with me this summer?"

Her mother stared at her for a long time. "What?"

"You know what?" Pinky said, standing and scraping her chair back. She was vaguely aware that hot tears were spilling down her cheeks. "Whatever. I'm done with this. I'm going home."

"Wait!" her mother called to her retreating back. "Let's talk about this!"

Pinky laughed and turned around. "Don't pretend like you give a crap," she told her mom. "Just give it up already. We all know the truth anyway." And then she pushed her way past all the swankily dressed people and raced outside into the night.

"So this is your new thing now, huh?" Samir called.

Sniffling, Pinky turned around to see him chasing her to the parking lot. "What?"

"Running out of country-club soirees," he explained as he took off his tux jacket. "And I guess mine is chasing you out. Are we going to climb onto the roof again or what?"

"No," Pinky said, turning back around. "I'm going home."

"Pinky." He caught up with her and took her upper arm. She turned to look at him. "Hey." Samir's face softened when he saw the mascara running down her face. Gently wiping her tears, he said, "It'll be okay."

"No, it won't." Pinky's voice wobbled as fresh tears coursed down her cheeks. "No matter what I do, Samir, she's always going to find a reason to criticize me. When it's me against the world, she's always going to side with the world."

He didn't say anything; just held her while she cried, his hand rubbing soothing circles on her bare back where the dress didn't cover her. "Let me take you home," he said finally. "Your parents gave me the key to their car."

"Okay." Her voice come out all muffled since her face was pressed into his chest. "How are they going to get home, though?"

"They said they'd find a ride with someone. Come on." Samir took her hand and they began to walk together through the empty parking lot, toward the rental car.

Samir

"Here you go," Samir said, handing her a mug of steaming peppermint tea. "I sweetened it with just a touch of honey."

Pinky smiled as she rested her back against his headboard, her knees drawn up. "Thanks."

They were still dressed in their party attire, though Samir had taken off his bow tie, and they'd both kicked off their shoes. Samir's heart hurt at just how beautiful she looked.

Pinky took a sip of the tea and closed her eyes. He sat at the foot of the bed, watching her, wanting to take away her pain but knowing he was powerless to do that. When she opened them again, he asked, "Feel a bit better?"

She nodded. "I've stopped crying, so that's a plus, right?"

He smiled a little.

Pinky took a breath, and he could tell she was trying to ramp up her courage for something. He could guess what that "something" was—he'd been thinking about it since she'd brought it up at the club. Part of him didn't want her to ask him the question, not when she was already so raw, not when she'd already cried a river of tears. He didn't want to add to her pain. But the other part knew it was time to be honest. It was time to have this conversation.

"Samir . . . what happened back there? At the club? I was talking about still being your girlfriend and you still having the internship, and . . . you had this look on your face." Her hands tightened around her mug.

Samir closed his eyes for just a fraction of a second before opening them and holding her gaze. "I . . . Pinky, I really like you. Okay?"

She was barely breathing. "But?"

He shook his head. When he spoke, his voice was barely audible. "Don't you feel it? Something seismic, just below the surface, wanting to pull us apart?"

She bit her trembling lip. "I know. I've felt it, Samir. I've had doubts too. But we could fight against it. We could figure it out. We can't just let this go. You said it yourself; people who are completely different have relationships all the time that work out."

His heart was breaking at the tenor of her words, because he could tell her heart was breaking too. But wasn't this the kindest thing? What was the point of limping along like they'd been doing this past week, not pointing out the glaring red flags that hung between them, ignoring the warning signs? Pinky deserved someone like her—someone bright and bigger than life. Someone who'd take risks, whose life wasn't governed by the rules and neat lines his was. Samir waited until he could speak without his voice giving way.

"Pinky," he said finally. "My life . . . My life is very different from all this." He gestured around her colorful room. "I have a strict regimen I stick to, with everything. My studies, my activities, my—"

She sat up straighter. "What are you saying? That I don't fit into your schedule?"

He shook his head. "Don't put it like that. That's not what I'm saying."

"Then what are you saying, Samir?" Her voice rose. "Don't you see you're making a choice here? You're choosing that closely regimented, granulated life over me! Over us! If you're going to do that, at least have the decency to face it!"

"I don't have a choice!" he said, his voice rising to match hers, his anger overcoming his sadness. Why couldn't she see what was so glaringly obvious to him? Why couldn't she accept that he was nothing like her, that he'd *never* be anything like her? "You keep making it sound like I do, but not all of us have wishy-washy, happy, sparkly, rainbow-hued lives, Pinky! We had this summer, and it was great, okay? But maybe it's time to wake up!"

"Don't tell me to wake up when *you're* the one who's sleepwalking through life!" Pinky snapped, setting her tea down with a crash. "At least be honest with yourself!" She thrust her hand in the air and slammed into the mug of tea by accident. It spilled all over Samir's nightstand, dripping down in a sticky puddle into the slightly open nightstand drawer.

"Damn it!" Pinky grabbed a few tissues out of the tissue box and yanked open the nightstand drawer to dab at the mess.

And then she stopped short, staring.

CHAPTER 19

Pinky

As she was wiping the wet planner pages in his drawer, her eye caught on a word.

Pinky.

It was her name. In Samir's planner. Frowning, Pinky set the wad of wet Kleenex aside and pulled the paper out.

10 Things I Hate about Pinky, it said at the top. She looked at Samir. "What is this?"

He leaned over to see, and his face went white. "That . . ." He reached over to take it from her, but she held it away from him and turned her attention back to it.

"Number one, she's impulsive," Pinky read, her voice wooden. "Completely lets her heart dictate what her brain should do. Number two, impetuous." Her heart squeezed and squeezed in her chest; the pain was indescribable. She didn't know what else to do, so she kept reading. Her eyes ran down the list, taking in each thing Samir had meticulously numbered and written, each thing that he hated about her. "Hardheaded. Bullish. Nonconforming."

"Pinky." Samir knelt beside her, his voice breaking. "Pinky, no. I wrote that a long time ago. Please, it's not . . . I'm not even sure why I kept it—"

"Everything's a fight," she read, her voice now barely more than a whisper. When she looked up at Samir, he shimmered through the veil of her tears. They stared at each other.

"Please," he said again, sounding stricken. "You have to believe me. I didn't mean to . . . This isn't even true anymore."

She shook her head, smiling just a little bit. "No, that's the thing," Pinky said as fat, hot tears rolled down her cheeks. She didn't think she'd cried in her entire life as much as she'd cried tonight. "None of this is wrong. Every single thing is precisely true." She swallowed. "It's all the things that make me *me*. And you hate them all."

"I don't!" Samir said, taking her cold hands in his. "I really—"

"It's right there at the top of the page in your handwriting," she said, almost wanting to laugh at his ludicrous denial. "Of course you do. It's okay, it's fine. You're not the only one. I'm sure my mom has a very similar list." Pinky stood, ripping her hands from his, and went around him. Still facing the door, she added, "I just want to know one thing, though. If you really hate all these things about me, why the hell did you even go out with me? Why the hell did you tell me you liked me?"

"Because I *do* like you!" Samir said, his voice rising. "Don't you get it? Pinky, I don't feel like that anymore!"

She looked at him over her shoulder, smirking. "Right. Is that why it was so easy for you to make the decision to give me up?"

And finally, to that, Samir had no response. Pinky turned around and walked out of his room, leaving him behind.

The pain exploded in her chest, in her bones, in her every cell, once she'd closed and locked her door behind her. She flung herself on her bed, buried her face in her pillow, and wept, her chest heaving, feeling as if her entire world were raining down on her, piece by piece.

The crazy thing was, she'd expected this of her mom. Pinky'd figured her mom wouldn't understand why she felt the need to save the habitat, and although she'd hoped that her mom might come around once she remembered the good times they'd had there, it hadn't been a total surprise that she hadn't. That was her *mom*. They'd never seen eye to eye. It was the whole reason Pinky had hidden the big protest from her in the first place.

But Samir . . . he'd stuck by her side; he'd been her unlikely ally from the beginning. He was like no one else she'd ever dated. He was sweeter than she'd expected and more confident. She'd understood him and he'd understood her.

She had thought.

But now she saw that whatever this was between them had never been to him what it had been to her. Pinky had opened her heart to him fully, completely aware that he had the power to hurt her, never believing for one moment that he would. And the entire time, the entire time, he'd been thinking, *Well, this is fun, but there's no way it's going to last. I'll get what I can here and go home. My real life will resume and Pinky will be just a distant memory.* Or maybe he'd envisioned a friends-with-benefits type of situation. She clenched her pillow with angry fists, wanting to scream into it.

How dare he. How *dare* he treat her like some kind of throwaway doll. The entire time she'd thought Cash was the douche, and she'd had no idea she had one of those under her own roof. That she'd invited one to the lake house for the summer and then fallen in love with him.

She turned her red, hot, wet face to the side, breathing hard, staring out the window at the darkness. Fallen in love with him? Yes, she realized. She was in love with Samir. And the tears began again, in earnest.

Samir

Samir sat in the armchair in his room, his hand covering his mouth. This was what he'd wanted, right? This was where their relationship had been headed all along. That was what he'd been trying to get her to see. Not that he didn't have feelings for her—of course he did—but that, no matter what, no matter how they tried, they were doomed to fail. Because of how different they were.

This, breaking up, was inevitable. He was just being honest with her when she asked. He'd never intentionally misled her into thinking something obviously false. The Samir Jhas and Pinky Kumars of the world weren't meant to be together. That was a logical, incontrovertible fact.

So . . . why did he feel sick to his stomach? He was experiencing none of the satisfaction that he usually got from making a rational, mature decision. Instead, he felt like he was making the biggest, most moronic mistake of his life. Every fiber of his being was drenched in regret and remorse.

The truth was, what he wanted most in that moment was to get up and rush to her room, to take her into his arms, to kiss her until her head spun, until she realized exactly how much she meant to him. To take back everything he'd said, to apologize, to tell her he wanted to be with her anyway, logic and good sense be damned. He closed his eyes, feeling like someone with an iron fist had just punched him in the stomach. He bent over, his body, his soul, crying out for hers. He wanted to soothe her, to undo the hurt he'd done, but where was the sense in that? Why did his brain know one thing but his heart insist on another?

Moving to put his head in his hands, Samir caught sight of the loose planner pages Pinky had found in his nightstand. On impulse, he strode across the room to his messenger bag, which was hanging neatly from a hook in his closet, and withdrew his planner. Opening it up, he began scanning the weekly calendar going back to the beginning of the year. Pages and pages of notes in his neat, blocky handwriting that soothed him just to see. Each part of his day planned out, so he could see everything coming. Breakfast. Tennis. Schoolwork. Listening to music. Basketball with Ashish. Shopping. Cooking with his mom. It was all scheduled in there, nothing at all left to chance. This was his life the way he liked it, here in black and white, predictable, manageable, *controllable*. No surprises.

And yet . . . Samir paced to the table in his room and set the planner down, pausing to look out the window at the dark, subdued lake. A silver moon glimmered on its surface, watchful and quiet. And yet . . . the best thing in his life so far, the most inspiring, amazing, scintillating thing—falling for Pinky—had happened unplanned. She'd texted him out of the blue, and he'd accepted her offer to be her fake boyfriend on impulse. There was nothing in his planner about that. One of the biggest disappointments of his life—losing that internship in DC—had *also* happened unplanned. He'd done everything he was supposed to; he'd been diligent and watchful, and the rug had still been pulled out from under him. So what did that say about life?

"Life's what happens when you're busy scribbling in your planner," he said into his empty room, then wanted to laugh because he sounded like one of those inspirational quote posters you might find at the gym.

What if he'd been living some thin facsimile of life until Pinky had come along and thrown it all into turmoil? What if her chaotic energy wasn't what would throw his life off course—what if it was her chaotic energy that had given his life *a* course? He'd done things here he never would have dreamed of doing if he hadn't answered her text: He'd pretended to be a fake boyfriend to land an internship; he'd kissed a girl who'd scared him at first; he'd then fallen for said girl; he'd made friends with the Shark—and a strange opossum; he'd climbed rooftops and treetops when he much preferred standing on solid ground.

Samir turned and walked to the bed, where she'd left the stupid list he'd made. He snatched it up, fully intending to tear it into pieces, to feel the paper disintegrate between his fingers. Instead, he found himself reading the list, top to bottom, over and over again.

He'd written this. He'd written all these hateful, mean words because back then he hadn't understood Pinky at all. He hadn't seen the fragile, beautiful light she carried inside herself, like an entire universe of stars and suns and moons held in one person's body. He hadn't realized that her veins, her arteries, were just a road map to lead him to her. He hadn't realized that everything she did, he'd begin to treasure. He hadn't realized that, for the first time in his life, he would know what all those poems and novels and songs were about. He hadn't known, couldn't know, back then that when Pinky Kumar had invited him to be her fake boyfriend for the summer, what she'd really done was create a perfect storm for him to fall in love with her.

He was in love with her.

Samir stared down at his own handwriting, the words he'd scrawled going blurry as his eyes filled with tears.

"I love you," he whispered into the empty room. "I love you, Pinky."

But it was too late. She was gone.

Pinky wiped her eyes and watched the sun come up. It had been a restless night, and her entire body felt soggy with the tears she'd spilled. But today was the day of the protest. She had a responsibility to those she'd promised to support. Pinky had to be there, breakup or no breakup. Mom's disapproval or not.

She was washing her face when someone tapped at her door.

She opened it to find Samir on the other side, one hand up on her doorjamb. He was still wearing the same clothes from the night before, and there were dark bags under his eyes.

"I'm sorry," he said, looking like someone who was being torn apart on the inside. "I'm so sorry. Please, Pinky, talk to me about this."

She forced herself to keep her face neutral, even though she wanted to slap him and kiss him at the same time. "There's nothing to talk about, Samir."

"Yes, yes, there is." He tried to take her hand, and she jerked it away. "I've been a total fool. I just realized—I realized we're perfect for each other. Well, maybe not 'perfect' if we tabulated the pros and cons, but—but we belong together. And I know—I know I can't take back the words I wrote, or said, but I can't just let you go like this. This can't be it. Look, why don't you make a list about me? It'll make you feel better."

She stepped back, out of his reach. "I'm not going to make a list about you."

"You should," he said, his eyes earnest. "You should. I know there are things about me that drive you crazy. So just lay them on me. Come on."

Pinky turned and strode into her room, and he followed. "Samir, this is stupid. Okay? I'm not going to just make a list—"

"You know you want to. Come on. Just say whatever you're thinking. I made a list about you. It's only fair that you make one about me, too."

"Fine." She turned around, her temper flaring as she heard the words "I made a list about you." He had. He had, and it was bullshit. "Numbers one through ten on my list: You're a boring coward." His eyes blazed with pain, but she kept going. "You say it's because it was a survival skill and you had no choice but to become who you

321

are, but I have to wonder. I mean, no almost-eighteen-year-old boy wants to have his entire life planned out, second by second, minute by minute, day by day. So you can deny it all you want, but all of this planning, all of this organizing, has nothing to do with surviving anymore. It has to do with you being afraid to just live life." She spat the words at him, not censoring herself, inciting herself to be as cruel, as mean as possible because she wanted him to feel one-tenth of the hurt she'd felt last night. If Samir Jha had thought of her as a plaything, a way to pass the time this summer, she could play at that game too. "And so I guess I should thank you," she continued, not paying any attention to the way his face had gone pale, a muscle in his jaw jumping as each word she hurled hit him head-on. "I'm *glad* we're not going out together anymore. Fake dating, real dating—I'm done with all of it. Because I'm sick of being with a tedious, gutless drudge like you."

They stared at each other, Pinky panting a little, feeling a curious mix of shame and guilt swirling under her skin. She pushed it away, deep inside her. She had no reason to feel ashamed. Samir had used her; he'd been cruel too. Now he was still and subdued, the exact opposite of her. After a long moment, Pinky said, in a calmer voice, "I have a protest to get ready for. So if you'll excuse me . . ."

Samir nodded. "Yes. Okay." He turned to go, but with one hand on the doorknob, he looked at her over his shoulder. "Thanks for being honest with me. Can I . . . ? Can I still come and help?"

Pinky held his gaze. "I'm going by myself. I can't stop you if you show up. But don't expect me to drop everything and listen to you. I'm going to be working, Samir. In that hardheaded, bullish way I have. So leave me alone. Okay?"

He studied her face for a long moment. Maybe he was looking for some give, some hint that she didn't mean what she was saying. He must not have seen any, because he nodded once and pulled the door open. "Got it," he said, his voice quiet.

Much as it hurt her heart, much as the tears threatened to come again, Pinky strode to the door and closed it, firmly, after him.

Samir

She'd been gone an hour. Samir paced his room, back and forth, back and forth, pushing his hands through his hair. She wouldn't even talk to him. She wouldn't accept his apology. She'd barely *looked* at him. He'd screwed this up so badly. Samir didn't think he'd ever, ever screwed anything up so horribly in his life.

And all the things she'd said about him . . . She'd called him a boring coward. She'd said he was flat and colorless, tedious and gutless. He'd felt little pieces of his heart break off as she spoke, until it was just a splintered, ragged thing in his chest. And after he left, he'd felt a blaze of fury at her words, even though he'd asked her, goaded her, into saying them.

But now . . . as he paced, he forced himself to face up to a tiny, incessant question in the deepest, darkest recesses of his mind. It glimmered there like a piece of metal catching the light.

Was she right?

Samir stared out the window at the lake, his hands pressed to the tabletop under the window. A large water bird, probably a heron, lifted off the water in a graceful arc. Was the entire reason he'd been so controlling, so rigid, simply because he was deathly afraid? Terrified to take a risk? This entire time, he'd thought his life was safe and protected; he'd thought it just made good sense to live the way he did. But maybe, maybe he'd just been too scared to face the truth the entire time.

Pinky had called him gutless, and maybe . . . maybe that wasn't so far off. Maybe he *had* been living his life like a coward, like someone too afraid to fully engage with it. But could he really base his entire life, all of his decisions—big and small—on the desire to avoid something that might never even happen? What if nothing bad ever happened in his life, but nothing great ever did either? What would he think when he looked back and realized he'd never truly *lived*?

Pinky, on the other hand, lived for herself. She knew what it was she needed to do in this world, she knew her purpose, and she charged into the fire willingly, over and over, if it meant she could help someone else. It didn't matter if she was afraid or sad or hurt, or if some giant douche had made a list about her that he had no right making. All that mattered was that she lived bravely, that she lived passionately, that she *lived*.

Samir felt a fizzing, tingling feeling on his limbs as he realized he had purpose now too. He knew exactly what he needed to do.

He walked out of his room and down the hall toward Pinky's parents' closed door. It was just past seven. He knew they'd had a late night last night, but he couldn't wait any longer. Taking a deep breath, mustering all his courage, he raised his hand and knocked hard on their door.

Pinky's mom answered the door, dressed in her pajamas and a robe. Weird to see the Shark in pajamas covered with roses. Okay, focus. She frowned at him. "Samir? Is everything okay? Where's Pinky?"

"Pinky's at the protest," he said, and her face hardened. "And we need to talk. May I come in?"

CHAPTER 20

Pinky

She was the only one there, but that was okay. The official meeting time was eight o'clock, and she still had about twenty minutes to go. Pinky parked her bike and took the backpack off her shoulders. She'd packed all the basics that you need for a protest: granola bars, bottles of water, sunscreen, markers and poster board, even bathroom wipes in case anyone needed some. She had no idea how long they'd be here, or what was going to happen, but that was okay. It was okay because Pinky knew they could do this; they could stop the developer together.

From the little carrier she'd rigged onto the back of her bike, she pulled out DQ and placed her on the grass. DQ went into a sniffing frenzy immediately, scattering butterflies in her wake. Her mom was right; she *was* getting really big. Soon it'd be time to say goodbye. The thought brought a wave of gloom with it, and Pinky blinked rapidly. Saying goodbye was becoming a thing in her life, and she didn't like it.

To distract herself, she looked around at the habitat, in the slowly dawning morning, her chest full of feelings. She remembered feeling loved here, feeling like she belonged. With her parents and Dolly's family when she was little, and with Samir, so recently. This was where they'd confessed their feelings for each other. This was where she'd finally admitted how she felt, when she'd finally been brave enough to take that step, to let go of her fears.

Remembering all the things she'd said to him earlier that morning, she felt a wave of guilt wash over her. It had been cruel. It had been unkind. And the truth was, while she felt there was a kernel of truth in everything she'd said, she'd lashed out at him like a wild animal in pain. She'd felt the agonizing pinch of knowing that she'd loved him that much and she hadn't been loved in return, and so she'd flung her words in his face, wanting them to sting like acid. She'd felt—and even now was feeling—all the old and familiar insecurities, like wild coyotes slobbering and grinning, circling her in a pack. She wasn't good enough, and he'd seen that. All those things her mom hated about her—her temper, her passion—Samir hated them too. Pinky had never thought she needed to change, but for the first time she wondered if she really had been wrong about that the whole time. Was she just . . . too much . . . as a person?

But in the next moment, she straightened her shoulders and smoothed out her hair. She wasn't about to start doubting herself for some boy. If she was too much, it was Samir's fault that he couldn't handle her. She'd apologize to him for being needlessly cruel, to clear her own conscience. But she wasn't going to apologize for being who she was.

Pinky turned in a slow circle, listening to the birds tweeting sweetly. A butterfly brushed against her cheek, as if it were saying hello. Being unable to handle her may be Samir's fault, she realized, but there was something else she had to acknowledge: By being her authentic self, by *choosing* to not censor her personality, Pinky was also resigning herself to a life alone. Maybe someone like her was just meant to go through life in solitude, with no one except herself in her corner. Samir, she realized, had joined her long list of boyfriends past. She was wrong to have thought he might be different.

Pinky blinked and brushed away a tear. She could do that. There were worse things than being alone.

"We're the first ones here, huh?"

Pinky looked up at the voice to see Gloria walking toward her, dressed in bright coral capri pants, a white shirt, and sensible sneakers. She was accompanied by her wife, Dolores, who was talking on her cell phone. Gloria smiled. "We are."

"Well," Gloria said, setting down her own backpack. "it's only just eight o'clock now. I bet some others will show."

"I hope some others will show," Pinky said. There had been a lot of excitement on the WhatsApp group, but being excited over text and actually showing up were two different things. If very few people showed up . . . well, that would be it. The habitat would be finished, and she'd just have to accept it. Heck, even if everyone on the group showed up, so what? That didn't mean it would make an iota of difference. A protest was just a protest. The mayor might still be unmoved. The developer might not listen to the suggestion for a new location. This might all be for nothing.

Stop it, she told herself. *You're starting to sound like Samir. And your mom. Stay positive.*

Movement by the parking lot caught Pinky's eye, and she looked up to see Angie, one of the people whose houses she'd canvassed, walking up, dressed in a short-sleeved button-down shirt and shorts. And behind her was her husband, Charles. Her *curmudgeonly* husband, Charles.

"Oh, hi." Pinky tried, and failed, not to let her surprise show. "Hi, Angie. Hi, Charles."

Charles looked at her with those sharp blue eyes like he knew precisely what Pinky was thinking. "Shocked to see me?"

"Not shocked exactly . . . ," Pinky began.

Angie swatted Charles on the arm. "Oh, leave her alone. Don't mind him, honey," she said to Pinky. "He's grumpy without his cup of coffee in the morning."

"Oh! Well, I can take care of that," Pinky said, removing a thermos from her backpack.

The smile Charles gave her was 100 percent genuine. Pinky tried not to stagger back in shock.

"Thank you." Charles poured out a little bit into a recycled paper cup Pinky had brought.

"Bringing coffee to a protest is a genius idea," Gloria said, smiling at Pinky and then at Angie and Charles. "Hi. I'm Gloria Washington. This is my wife, Dolores."

All the adults shook hands, and Angie said, "Thank you for organizing this, Gloria. Pinky came by our house to tell us about it and . . . well, someone needs to do something about it." She glanced at Pinky. "It's nice to see the younger people taking an interest too."

Gloria gave Pinky a little smile. "Pinky's been a big help. Did you hear about her idea for a new location? Not that Mayor Thomas has bought into it yet . . ."

Pinky tuned out a little as they rehashed the location saga and looked around. The recycled coffee cups sat on a little wooden bench that also held Pinky's and Gloria's other supplies, including a few signs they'd made over the past couple of weeks. She'd been worried then that they hadn't made enough, but now, looking around at the vast expanse of green and realizing that she, Gloria, Dolores, Angie, and Charles were the only ones here, Pinky felt a little foolish. Like maybe they'd been too optimistic about the chances of winning this thing. Again she thought of Samir urging her to be cautious after the town hall meeting and felt a fresh wave of pain engulf her.

"Why the long face, honey?" Gloria asked. The adults were frowning at her in concern.

Pinky forced a smile. "Oh, nothing." A question mark butterfly settled on her hair and then on Gloria's before flitting away. "I just . . . um, I guess I'm a little disappointed that no one's here yet. That doesn't bode well for the protest."

"Well . . ." Gloria glanced at her watch. "It's only eight, and the developer's crew won't be here till nine. So we've still got time. Maybe there'll be a few stragglers."

"Or maybe not," Charles said, his clear blue eyes holding Pinky's and then Gloria's. He straightened the collar of his button-down shirt and took a sip of his coffee. "I think it's important to be realistic about these things. I'm here because Angie wanted to support you." He smiled fondly at his wife. "But the truth is, many of us locals are probably feeling the same trepidation I was. For a lot of us who live and work here . . . getting tangled up with those who run the city—and, in a lot of cases, those who employ us—might not be the wisest course of action."

Gloria nodded. "I hear that, Charles. I really do. Dolores and I have our own landscaping company, and honestly, a job like the condo developments would probably set us up for the whole year. But we have a solution, like I said, one that Pinky came up with. A relocation, not a complete shutdown. They just need to get on board with that. And with the amount of energy and support I felt at the town hall meeting, I really thought we could turn things around." She looked out at the mostly empty parking lot in the distance. "But maybe I was wrong."

Pinky felt her heart sink. "I really want people to show up," she found herself saying. "I really want to save this place."

"I know you do, sweetie," Angie said, patting her shoulder. "It's a good cause. Listen, even if other people don't come, all of us here can give this developer's crew a piece of our minds. Show them they can't just come in here and do whatever they want and no one's going to fight them."

Pinky gave her a watery smile. "Yeah, that's true." Even though a whopping five protesters might send the exact opposite message of the one they were hoping to send. Pinky sighed and turned to get a bottle of water from her pack.

There was a faint rumble in the distance, like a big vehicle approaching. Pinky spun around, frowning. Was the crew here early? But then, out on the main road, she saw a long line of cars speeding along.

"Is that . . . ?" Pinky said faintly. "Are all those cars headed *here*?"

Gloria, Dolores, Angie, and Charles turned to look, and she heard Charles swear under his breath in disbelief.

Gloria took Pinky's hand on one side and Dolores's on the other, squeezing them just as the first in the line of cars turned onto the gravel road leading to the habitat entrance. She looked first at Dolores and then at Pinky with shining eyes. "I think they are."

"But . . . but there must be at least fifty cars!" Pinky said, her eyes going wide. "Where did they all come from?" A part of her thought they must be the developer's cronies, that Di Ria wanted to put a lid on this protest before it even began.

But then people were piling out of the cars and Pinky saw that they held bright signs, with environmental slogans, and that they were wearing T-shirts with butterflies on them. The same Eastern swallowtail butterfly that had been on the flyers. Under the butterfly, the caption read: *Save Our Habitat!*

"Hi!" one of the women called. She was dark-skinned, with her hair up in a bun. "Gloria! Dolores! And Pinky! It's Gabriella from the WhatsApp group!"

Pinky waved, laughing, as a wave of people started across the habitat toward where they stood.

The woman in the bun walked up to Pinky, Gloria, and Dolores and handed them all neon green T-shirts. "Here," she said. "This is for you guys. My dad's company made these for us based on your design, Gloria. Hope you don't mind; we just ran with it. There was no time to ask if it was okay."

"Hey, I'm all for people running with things." Gloria grinned, slipping her T-shirt on over her clothes. "The habitat belongs to all of us."

Pinky slipped her T-shirt on too. "Wow, thank you. But who's your dad? I mean, you brought so many people, too. . . ."

The woman laughed. "My dad's Hector Fernandez; he runs

Hector's Ellingsworth Print Shop in town. See?" She pointed to an older Hispanic man Pinky remembered from the town hall meeting. "After the town hall meeting, he began to reach out to all our family and friends and, well . . . The older generations of my family have lived in this town for over sixty years. We know a lot of people."

Pinky looked around at the people swarming around her, adding their own supplies to the supplies already on the bench so they were spilling off and onto the ground. Crates of water and signs and poster boards and markers and fruit.

Gloria laughed. "I'd say so."

"So." Gabriella rubbed her hands together just as a little girl came running up, her hair in pigtails. Gabriella put her hands on the girl's shoulders. "This is my daughter, Paloma. How can we help you all set up?"

Paloma squealed and pointed at DQ, who was lounging near Pinky, watching all the people. "Oh my gosh! Is that your pet rat?"

Pinky laughed. "She's a possum. Actually, Paloma, it would be such a great help if you could be in charge of her this morning. What do you think? Does that sound good to you?"

Paloma looked as if all her dreams were coming true. Taking DQ's leash from Pinky, she said solemnly, "It would be my pleasure to be your possum assistant."

Pinky, Gloria, and Gabriella grinned at one another over Paloma's head.

Pinky was running around between the various groups, spreading instructions or advice from Gloria, giving the little kids who'd come (there were at least a dozen) markers and positive feedback, when she felt a hand on her shoulder. She turned to see Dolly grinning at her in a *Save Our Habitat!* T-shirt.

"Ho-ly crap!" she said, her hazel eyes wide.

"You're back!" Pinky wrapped her cousin in a hug and closed her eyes, a lump in her throat. She hadn't realized until now how alone she felt in this crowd of people. They were nice and funny and kind, but they weren't *her* people. None of her people had shown up. Until now.

Pinky pulled back and smiled at Dolly. "How was the retreat?"

Dolly appeared to think about it. "Actually, not horrible. I think my parents and I did some really important, powerful work."

Pinky rolled her eyes. "You are *such* a therapist's kid."

Dolly laughed. "Yeah, I don't think there's any escaping it. But seriously, *what* is going on here?" She looked around at the bustling crowd, a big smile on her face.

"I see you got the T-shirt," Pinky said, gesturing to what Dolly wore over her leggings.

"It was foisted on me by a little girl with the cutest pigtails the minute I stepped out of the car. Oh, and she had DQ on her leash too."

Pinky chuckled, though she could feel somewhere that it wasn't her usual, full-hearted chuckle. Everything felt a little bit . . . flat right now. She was ridiculously happy that Gloria's campaign had been a success—there must be more than a hundred people here—but still. Some big part of her felt empty. "Yeah, that's Paloma. She's sort of become my unofficial right-hand woman like I've become Gloria's. To answer your question, I think what you're seeing is the power of networking and a whole bunch of people who really, really care what happens to their town and their habitat. Thankfully. It was looking really rough for a while there; I think even Gloria was beginning to lose hope."

"Right . . . well, that's great!" Dolly studied Pinky's expression hesitantly. "It *is* great, right?"

Pinky nodded and forced a smile. "Yeah. It's great."

Dolly obviously wasn't buying it. "Something happen?"

Pinky looked at her, her smile fading. "Have you been to the house?"

Dolly shook her head. "Well, I mean, kind of? I dropped my parents off, but I came straight here without going inside." She looked around. "Where's Samir? And your parents?"

"They're not coming," Pinky said, fiddling with the pen she was holding. A swarm of monarchs flew by them and she watched them swoop and glide for a moment. "We had a big fight last night."

"You and your mom?" Dolly asked in concern.

Pinky wanted to laugh. "Um, yeah. That's how it started. But then we got home and . . ."

"And?" Dolly asked, leaning in.

"Samir and I broke up." Pinky said it in a rush.

Dolly's mouth popped open. "What happened?"

"It's a long story." Pinky sighed and looked at her watch. "And we have only about twenty minutes until the crew gets here."

"Twenty minutes is enough." Dolly grabbed her wrist and led her to a spot under a chestnut tree, away from the chaos. "Tell me what happened."

And so, looking into her cousin's worried eyes, Pinky did just that.

Dolly shook her head when Pinky was finished. The sounds of a few protesters laughing washed over them, but she didn't turn away. "He made a *list*?" she asked finally. "I can't believe he made a list. What a jerk thing to do. When did he make it?"

Pinky swallowed, feeling the hurt like a fresh wound again. "He said it was a while ago, before he began to like me. But I don't know. It just felt so . . . personal. You know? All the things I'm most insecure about, all the things I know my mom wishes were different about me, he just put those down on a sheet of paper and went to town. It was awful."

Dolly scooped her up in a hug. "Oh, Pinky, I'm so sorry."

"It's okay." Pinky pulled back. "Actually, I said some pretty horrible things about him too. I called him a boring coward and a tedious drudge."

Dolly's eyes widened. "Wow."

"Yeah. And my mom . . . she just doesn't give a damn about this habitat. I thought it would be just as important to her, you know. We have so many memories here. . . ." To Pinky's horror, her eyes were beginning to fill with tears again. She blinked them away. "These past thirteen hours or so have been pretty crappy, to be honest."

Dolly slung her arm around Pinky's shoulders. "I'm so sorry," she said again, as if she couldn't think of what else to say. Her voice was high and wobbly, as if she were trying not to cry too. "You know, maybe later we could—"

"Hey," a familiar voice said, and Pinky and Dolly both spun around.

CHAPTER 21

Pinky blinked. Was this a weird mirage her broken heart had come up with? What she was seeing was Samir, standing tall in front of her, heartbreakingly handsome in a rumpled shirt and a pair of shorts. His hair was mussed, still damp from the shower.

Dolly turned to Pinky, her eyes wide. So Dolly could see him too. This really *was* happening. All Pinky could do was shake her head slowly. "I have to go."

She began to brush past him, and he kept pace with her. "I won't take up more than five minutes of your time," he said quietly. "I just have something I need to read to you." Pinky looked up at him, confused, then stilled at the expression in his brown eyes. "Please."

She glanced at Dolly, who shrugged, like, *I'll do whatever you want.* Pinky took a breath. "Okay," she said, folding her arms over her chest. "But just five minutes." She nodded slightly at Dolly, who gave Samir a hard look and then melted away.

She and Samir stared at each other for a long moment, Pinky trying very hard not to cry. She'd missed him, she realized. She'd missed him even though they'd barely been separated at all. *Well, get used to it*, a voice inside her head said.

The leaves above them rustled in the wind, a hushed song. "I'd like to read you a poem I wrote," Samir said, pulling out a piece of paper from his pocket. His eyes met hers again and held them. "It's called '10 Things I Love about Pinky.'"

Pinky felt frozen in place, her feet rooted to the ground.

"Number one, she's impulsive," Samir said, still looking at her. "She completely lets her heart dictate what her brain should do."

She shook her head. What was he—what was this? For a moment, she felt her heart harden in her chest. Was he making fun of her? Was this some kind of weird joke, a way to hurt her? But when she searched his face for any hint of meanness, of payback, Pinky found none.

Was this real?

"Number two," Samir continued, still not looking down at the paper he held in his hand. He'd memorized all of these, Pinky realized. "She's impetuous, like an ocean in a storm. Number three, she's so passionate about everything." A few protesters walked past, turning to look curiously at them, but still, all Pinky could look at, all she could hear, all she could see, was Samir in front of her, reading his poem. "Number four, her short fuse, like she's half human, half firecracker." He smiled gently at her, and she found herself returning his smile. "Number five, she doesn't want anyone to be nice to her." He paused. "Because she's so independent. She's so very true to herself." Blinking, he continued. "Number six, she's hardheaded and bullish . . ."

Pinky found herself stiffening. This was one of the ones that had hurt so much yesterday.

". . . in the best possible way. In a way that tells you she won't let the problem go because she cares so much about who the problem's affecting." Samir looked at her again, and it was as if he could see only her and no one else. "I think the world could use some of her bullishness, to be honest. Maybe it wouldn't be such a wreck."

Pinky felt something in her heart give, just a little. He sounded like he meant it, 100 percent.

"Number seven, she doesn't know how to relax. Everything's a fight. It's because she's so fervent. But maybe she just needs someone supportive to be there for her, to have her back, to show her that she's accepted."

A tear rolled out on Pinky's cheek, and she swiped it away.

"Number eight, she's completely nonconforming. She keeps things fresh. She has a mind of her own. Number nine, her multicolored hair, which needs no explanation." Pinky huffed a laugh at that. "And the tenth reason I love Pinky, but certainly not the last reason I love Pinky . . . her habit of snorting derisively. It's amazing. It's a sound I'd miss if it were gone." He put the slip of paper back in his pocket and gazed steadily at her, his brown eyes focused and intent.

Pinky gazed back, her heart thumping.

Quietly, Samir said, "I'm so sorry. I never should've made the list. But now that it's out there, I want you to know, I would never change these things about you. Not for anything."

Pinky shook her head and another tear rolled down her cheek. "I'm sorry too. I should never have said those awful, mean things about you. I was trying to hurt you because I was so mad—" She gave a wrenching sob, and Samir pulled her to him, cradling the back of her head.

"Shh. It's okay. I know you were angry. But you know what?" He pulled back and she looked at him. "You were right," he said, almost wonderingly. "You were right about why I've been so rigid, so controlled, for so long. It was fear. That's all it was. Fear. And another thing? I don't care if we make absolutely no sense on paper. I'm beginning to realize the best things in life rarely do."

Pinky felt her heart begin to race. "So . . . so what does that mean?"

He gave her a gentle smile. "That means that I told my mom I want to be mainstream schooled this year, and she agreed. And she also agreed to the both of us getting some counseling."

Pinky clapped her hands to her mouth. "I'm so happy for you," she said, infusing her words with the love she felt. "Samir, you're easily the bravest person I know."

He smiled at her, his eyes twinkling. "Really?" he asked, his voice just a breath.

"Really," she whispered back.

He took a deep, steadying breath and looked her right in the eye. "So here's something I want to know, then. I'm hoping to introduce my friends back in Atherton to my new girlfriend, Pinky Kumar. If she'll still have me."

Pinky felt a smile spreading on her face, slow and warm and steady. Two swallowtail butterflies circled them, as if listening in. "She'll have you," Pinky said, bringing her mouth to his. They kissed like they'd never stopped kissing, like the fight had never happened. With each touching and parting of their lips, Pinky showed Samir how sorry she was for all the things she'd said that she hadn't meant, how truly, deeply glad she was that they were working things out, how joyful he made her, how full her world was when he was in it. When they pulled apart, Pinky added breathlessly, "I'm so happy for you."

Samir cupped her cheek in one hand. "I'm happy for me too. And I'm happy for you." He looked around at the crowd. "I mean, just look at this."

They took in the happy, energetic crowd until someone yelled, "The crew's coming! Everyone lock arms!"

And then she and Samir were racing forward, determined to stop the inevitable.

Samir

They made a human chain of protesters, all of them arm in arm, so the guy in the excavator couldn't get past them. Dolly met Samir's eye and grinned, and he grinned back, knowing he'd been forgiven.

"Save our habitat!" they chanted, their voices rising in a cloud. The guy in the excavator looked confused for a moment and then alarmed. Samir saw him pull a cell phone from his pocket and dial.

Samir looked over at Pinky. Her rainbow-hued ponytail was blowing in the breeze; her eyes were scintillating and fiery. She was always a part of something bigger than herself, a selfless force. He wondered how he could ever have seen anything different when he looked at her.

A tidal wave of gratitude crashed over him when he thought of how she'd agreed to be his again, wholeheartedly. Samir knew how his life needed to change, and now he could do it with Pinky at his side. Not leading him, not making his decisions for him, but simply there to support him. And he would support her, in every way he knew how.

Speaking of . . . Samir scanned the main road past the habitat, looking for a familiar car. He hadn't said anything to Pinky, just in case it didn't pan out, but he hoped it would.

He really, really hoped it would.

Pinky

"Oh, great," Pinky muttered, seeing the shiny Range Rover with the DR Developments logo on the side come screaming up the road and into the gravel parking lot. Even with Dolly on her left and Samir on her right, she felt a surge of nerves at the thought of the oncoming unpleasantness.

Di Ria got out of her car and stamped over the gravel and the grass, past the excavator, to where the line of protesters began. "Just what do you people think you're doing?" she said, in what Pinky knew she hoped was an imperious voice. Really, it just came across angry and petulant.

The protesters all looked at Gloria, so she spoke. "We don't want you to raze the butterfly habitat." As if it were supporting her, a monarch alighted on her shoulder and sat there, spreading its wings.

"All these people with me are Ellingsworth residents, and they don't want this either."

"Save our habitat! Our town, our say!" the townspeople shouted in response.

Di Ria narrowed her eyes. "This is *ridiculous*," she spat. "I already have a contract." She looked back at the guy in the excavator. "I'm calling the police. You're all trespassing," she said, loud enough for all the protesters to hear. "Don't worry, Rick. We'll get this mess taken care of immediately." Sniffing, she pulled her cell out of her pocket.

There was a murmur through the crowd.

"Don't worry." Gloria spoke again, calmly. "We're peacefully protesting. Just don't escalate it when the police arrive."

Another car crunched onto the gravel as she spoke. Pinky narrowed her eyes. It was a silver BMW. "Is that . . . ?"

Dolly gasped softly. "Is that your . . . ?"

"Mom," Samir said, smiling at her. "That's your mom. And a special guest."

Pinky couldn't quite believe it as her mom got out of the car in an Armani pantsuit with creases sharp enough to draw blood: full-on Shark attire. Then the passenger door opened and out stepped Mayor Thomas.

"The mayor?" she said, looking at Samir in utter shock. "What's my mom doing with *him*?" Holy crap. Pinky's palms began to sweat. Were they here to stop the protest? Was her mom going to drag Pinky away? To slap everyone with a restraining order, telling them not to get close to her minor daughter?

"I think we—and Gloria—should be a part of that conversation."

343

Samir inclined his head toward them as her mom and Mayor Thomas walked over to Di Ria, who was lowering her cell phone.

Pinky turned to Dolly, shaking her head. Her entire body trembled, and she stiffened her back in an effort to look marginally braver. "I'm going to go do this, I guess."

"Go." Dolly nodded seriously. "Good luck."

Heart hammering, Pinky grabbed Gloria, and she, Gloria, and Samir walked through the field, past the excavator, and joined the small group of adults.

"But I have a *contract*," Di Ria was saying. "This is completely ludicrous."

"Look at the support of the townspeople, Diana." Mayor Thomas waved a hand toward the group. "I mean, just look at that. I never thought we'd see support of this magnitude."

Wait, what? What was he saying? Pinky looked from him to Di Ria to her mom, hoping for some clarity.

"Be that as it may," Diana said, glaring around at them all. "As I said, we have a contract. A legal right to continue with this."

"Actually, Ms. Kumar and I read the contract together this morning." Samir stepped forward. From his pocket, he pulled out his phone and consulted the screen. "And according to page eight, there was a feasibility clause built in. Here's what it says: 'Seller shall have a period to determine the feasibility of proceeding with this transaction. In the event that Seller is not satisfied, in its sole and unreviewable judgment and discretion, with the feasibility of Purchaser's acquisition, financing, and ownership of the Property, this Agreement shall automatically terminate.' Which, in non-legalese, means that if the city residents are angry about this development, the project isn't feasible and can be terminated before closing. And as I understand it, the feasibility period doesn't end until you break ground." Pinky stared at him, her mouth open. Ho-ly crap. Who even *was* her boyfriend??

Samir paused and looked at Pinky's mom, who was smiling. "Am I correct in the way I read that?"

"Absolutely," she said, nodding. "Well done." She turned to Diana. "So, in essence, you could get nothing and be forced to abandon this plan altogether." Diana's face got very, very pale. Pinky wanted to leap into the air and click her heels together, but she refrained. Just. "However, I don't think that'll be necessary. Samir and I had an emergency meeting with the mayor this morning, and it does seem like your condos could bring in more revenue to the town, which certainly isn't a bad thing. It's the *location* that the residents object to."

"Exactly," Gloria said, her eyes dancing with the excitement Pinky was feeling.

Pinky's mom continued. "So, we have a proposal based on some excellent research Pinky and Samir did. There's a patch of land, just past the highway, that's currently unoccupied. It's hard to build on, but you have the resources. You can have it for a fraction of the price that this would cost you. And we think it would be much more beneficial to you and your target buyer. It's right off the interstate, for one, which is incredibly convenient. And it would have a view of the ocean from the very top floors."

Diana Rea appeared to consider this. "I'll have to have my lawyers look this over, of course," she said, tapping one long fingernail on her phone screen. "But I don't think I have any objections at this time. Although this is very unorthodox."

Pinky's mother nodded and extended her hand for a firm handshake. Diana Ria shook, then walked off to speak with the excavator driver. The mayor cleared his throat. "Excuse me," he said to them. "I should go speak with the residents."

Gloria nodded. "Actually, I'll come with you. I'd like to break the news to them, if that's okay."

"But of course," the mayor replied, smiling.

They trudged back toward the protesters just as the excavator began to back out. Everyone looked at Gloria with expectant faces. A few scowled at the mayor.

"Good news!" Gloria said. "Thanks to some excellent legwork by Pinky Kumar and Samir Jha"—she pointed at them and Pinky flushed, while Samir put his arm around her shoulders and squeezed—"and this esteemed attorney from San Francisco"—here, Gloria pointed at Pinky's mom—"and of course your powerful enthusiasm"—gesturing at the crowd—"the butterfly habitat will not be razed!"

The crowd cheered so loudly, Pinky's ears rang. Gloria continued. "And the mayor was so blown away by your support in this matter, he was more than willing to offer Diana Ria a different spot for her condos. One far away from your neighborhoods." Not strictly true, but it was nice of Gloria to toss him a bone. He'd come around.

Mayor Thomas raised his hands to quiet the cheering and then began to give a little humble-braggy speech. Pinky supposed he couldn't help it. He *was* a politician, after all.

She turned to her mom, with Samir at her side. "Thanks for the assist," she said carefully, still not sure exactly what had transpired. "You . . . you didn't have to do that."

"Yes, I did." Pinky's mom stepped forward and put her hands on Pinky's shoulders. "You needed my support and . . . I should've given it to you a long time ago, Pinky. A *long*, long time ago."

"I'm going to go find Dolly." Samir squeezed Pinky's hand briefly and began walking away.

"What do you mean?" Pinky asked her mom, her heart thumping in disbelief. "Are you saying . . . ?"

"I'm saying I'm sorry," her mom said, looking her right in the eye. "For all the times I told you to change who you are. For all the times I didn't support you like I should have. For all the times you felt so alone." She blinked rapidly, her eyes pink around the edges. "I love you. You're my only daughter, and I don't know what I'd do without you."

Pinky licked her dry lips. "Then why?" she asked. "Why have you always seemed so disappointed in me?"

Her mom smiled a little. "It wasn't disappointment, Pinky. It was fear."

"Fear?" Pinky frowned a little.

"I was so afraid you were turning into me. I was so afraid you were just like me."

"But I thought you said we weren't anything alike," Pinky pointed out, remembering that conversation, the horrible sting of hurt and rejection.

"That's what I wanted to believe." Her mom shook her head. "I *desperately* wanted to believe that. Because who I used to be . . ." She stopped and looked away, as if gathering herself. "When I found out I was pregnant with you, my parents told me I was selfish. That I could never look after a child."

Pinky was silent as she listened, not wanting to break the spell of her mom's uncharacteristic candidness.

"They were being mean, but they were also honest. And they were right. I'd spent my life just flitting from one passion to the other, fighting for those less fortunate than me. A lot like you." She caressed Pinky's cheek. "And that was good for then. But when I got pregnant, I realized I had a little child to take care of. I realized how ill prepared I was for that. I'd lacked focus, and that would affect not just me, but you as well. It was the lowest point of my life. I was terrified; I sank into a depression for a while. I didn't want that happening to you. I didn't want you to ever feel like you didn't know how to handle something life threw your way. I wanted you to be secure in this world, to be well set up. But you seemed hell-bent on following the same path I took."

Wow. This was a whole different perspective from the one Pinky had had all along. Her mom had been motivated by fear? In a way, she hadn't wanted to change who Pinky was. . . . She wanted to change who *she'd* been. "So, then, why are you here?"

"Two reasons. One, because I didn't realize just how much the habitat meant to you. I thought . . . I thought you'd forgotten all the good times, Pinky."

Pinky stared at her mom. "What? How could you think that?"

Her mom blinked and looked away, just for a moment. "We fight so much. It just seemed like . . . like you didn't really care anymore."

"Of course I care!" Pinky said, the lump in her throat reemerging.

"After you left the club last night, I knew I had to be involved. I was planning to come anyway. Then . . . Samir spoke with us this morning. He'd been reading the contract—apparently he'd emailed the mayor for a copy—and he thought he'd found a loophole. He asked me to do some research on other places DR Developments could build, and well . . . You know me. Research is what I do best."

"Right." Pinky's eyes sought out Samir in the crowd. He stood by Dolly, laughing at something she'd said. Pinky's heart squeezed with happiness and love.

"But more than anything," her mom said, drawing her attention back. She held Pinky's eye. "I want you to know that I'm so sorry for ever making you feel that I didn't care or that I don't love you exactly how you are. I'm sorry I doubted you and didn't appreciate all the beautiful fire you hold inside you. I promise, I'm going to stop parenting from fear now."

Pinky hugged her mom. "I'm sorry too, Mom. I'm sorry I've always been so hostile, pushing you and prodding you into fighting with me." She tucked a lock of hair behind her ear. "I'm not proud to say this, but . . . I guess I felt, at least if we were fighting, we were connecting. I just wanted you to see me, in some way, even if it wasn't in the best way." She took a deep breath. "But from now on, I promise, I'm not going to get under your skin anymore."

Her mom raised an eyebrow, and Pinky laughed. "Stranger things have happened!" And somehow, instinctively, she knew they were going to be okay.

They were walking back to her mom's car when a woman in a *Save our Habitat* T-shirt came up to them. "Hi," she said, smiling down at DQ, who was walking nicely on her leash. "This must be Drama Queen."

Pinky nodded. "It is! I think she's been our official mascot for this protest."

The woman laughed. "Yes, I think so. But I was talking to Gabriella, and she said you're looking to find a permanent home for her?"

Pinky glanced down at DQ and then back at the woman. "Yes, I am, actually."

The woman extended a hand. "I'm Marie Trent. I volunteer at the Cape Cod Nature Preserve over on Nantucket. We specialize in rehabbing wounded native animals. I could take her off your hands if you'd like."

Pinky glanced at Samir and Dolly, who gave her a small smile. Her mom patted her shoulder. Pinky scooped up DQ, who, of course, immediately died. She handed her prone body to the woman. "She does that a lot," she said, hearing the wobble in her voice. "But she's a really good possum. I have some money saved up, and I'd love to donate it in her name to your habitat. Since you're going to be giving her such a good home and everything."

"That would be lovely, thank you. I'll be in touch about that via Gabriella soon." Marie took DQ with the utmost care and gentleness, as if hauling fake-dead marsupials was something she did all the time for fun. "And I can send you pictures of DQ to keep you updated on her progress, if you like?"

Pinky smiled. "Yeah. I would really like that."

They watched Marie walk away with DQ. After a moment, in unspoken agreement, they all climbed in her mom's car and headed home. Summer break was officially winding down.

CHAPTER 22

Samir

"I was very impressed by the feasibility clause you found," Pinky's mom said to Samir a few days later. "Truly."

"Yes, Veena told me about it, and I have to agree," her dad added.

They were having dinner out on the patio for the last time before they flew home the next afternoon. Samir had been able to get a seat on their flight.

"Thank you," he said, not able to help the little bit of pride seeping into his words.

Pinky's parents exchanged a glance, and then her mom spoke. "We'd like to offer you an internship at our law offices, if you'd be interested."

Pinky squeezed his knee under the table and grinned. Samir tried to chew his shrimp in as dignified a manner as possible and swallowed it before saying, "Wow. That would be . . . I mean, that would be amazing. Thank you."

Her mom nodded once. "Sure. Just call me once you're back in school and we'll figure out the details."

"I will," Samir said as a grin lit up his face. "I definitely will."

"And, Pinky," Ms. Kumar said, turning to her. "I know you're busy with things, but I was hoping we could go visit the butterfly habitat early tomorrow morning before we leave for the airport. Just the two of us."

The two Kumar women held each other's gazes for a long moment before Pinky smiled and said, "I'd love that, Mom."

"Ugh, I can't believe this is all over," Dolly said, leaning back in her chair. Pinky was sandwiched between Dolly and Samir, all three of them on chaise lounges. Dinner was done, and the adults were cleaning up. They'd insisted the three of them—Samir, Pinky, and Dolly—go hang out on the deck and not bother with the dishes. "Another Cape Cod summer behind us." She turned to Pinky and Samir. "Hey. Do you think you guys'll come next summer? Even though you'll be, like, getting ready for college and everything?"

Pinky took Samir's hand on one side and Dolly's hand on the other. "Of course we will," she said, and Samir squeezed her hand gently. "It wouldn't be summer without the madness and magic of Ellingsworth." She smiled at Samir, and he smiled back.

Later, Samir and Pinky sat on the pier, dangling their bare feet into the warm, dark water of the lake. There was no one else around for once.

"Hey," Samir said. "You want to send Ash a picture?"

"Of the two of us?" Pinky asked, laughing. "We might give him a heart attack, but yeah. Let's do it."

They kissed, and Samir held his arm out and took a selfie with flash. He sent it to Ashish with a text that said, **Guess who's dating? Your two faves!**

The response came not even a minute later.

What the hell are you guys joking omgggggggg wtf wtf this is the best thing to ever happen to our friend group since Oliver and Elijah ommmmgggggggg

Pinky laughed as Samir fired off a response. **Yeah dude I'm kind of in shock myself. But like a really good shock**

His phone beeped again.

I mean Pinky is pretty shocking just don't let her electrocute you

Pinky snatched Samir's phone away and typed, **This is Pinky and you're gonna pay for that**

Oh shot, the response came, **sorry dude I'm just like WHAT THE HELL IS GOING ON**

Pinky cackled and typed, **Yeah same. We'll try to explain when we get home.**

Samir added a few exploding head emojis and then put his phone away.

"I don't think he's going to get over that one for a while," Pinky said, shaking her head and watching the ripples from her feet in the lake.

Samir snorted. "No kidding. I have a feeling he's going to be video chatting me tonight to get all the details. No way he's going to be able to wait till tomorrow like a normal person."

"No one ever accused Ashish of being normal," Pinky agreed.

Samir put an arm around her shoulders, and they sat, looking out across the lake at the inky violet of the encroaching night.

"You know," Samir said, taking a deep breath. "I'm going to miss this place."

"Me too." Pinky looked at him solemnly. "But I meant what I told Dolly earlier. You can come back again next summer. If you want to, that is, Mr. Jha."

"I'd love to, Pinky Kumar," he said, and then chuckled.

"What?" she asked, frowning.

He shook his head. "Isn't it weird? Fake dating somehow turned into all this." He gestured between them. "It turned into true love."

Pinky smiled a little and looked down at her feet in the water. "I can't help notice, you've used that word before. 'Love'?" She glanced shyly at him. "Do you . . . ? Do you really mean it the way I think you do?"

Cupping her cheek, Samir leaned over and planted the softest kiss on her lips. His heart thrummed in his chest as he looked into her brown eyes. "I love you," he whispered.

Her face lit up like a thousand fireworks. "I love you too," she whispered back.

And they sat together, heads touching, watching as the stars began to peek out, one by one. The night was theirs.

Acknowledgments

And then there were three. I can't believe I got to spend three entire books in the Dimple and Rishi universe! This could never have happened without my amazing, wonderful readers. I'm so thankful to all of you for your support and enthusiasm for these characters and this happy, fun universe where everything always works out in the end.

Thanks also to my lovely editor, Jennifer Ung; my scrappy agent, Thao Le; and Simon Pulse for letting me publish this, my fifth novel with them! Somehow, they keep letting me write words without snatching away my laptop, and for that I'm eternally grateful.

Lastly but definitely not leastly (I have the horrifying feeling I've made that joke in a previous acknowledgments section), thank you to my steadfast, loving, patient family for putting up with a wife and mom who also doubles as a writer. They say having a weird mom builds character, and I really, really hope that's true.

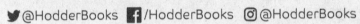